MW01194729

13 MONTHS HAUNTED

Also by Jimmy Juliano

Dead Eleven

13 MONTHS

HAUNTED

\ a novel \

JIMMY JULIANO

DUTTON

DUTTON

An imprint of Penguin Random House LLC
1745 Broadway, New York, NY 10019
penguinrandomhouse.com

Book design by Laura K. Corless

Interior art: Visual effects background © The7Dew/
Shutterstock.com

LIBRARY OF CONGRESS CATALOGING-IN-PUBLICATION DATA
Names: Juliano, Jimmy, author.
Title: 13 months haunted : a novel / Jimmy Juliano.
Other titles: Thirteen months haunted
Description: [New York] : Dutton, PRH, 2025.
Identifiers: LCCN 2024046375 | ISBN 9780593475898 (hardcover) |
  ISBN 9780593475904 (ebook)
Subjects: LCGFT: Thrillers (Fiction) | Novels.
Classification: LCC PS3610.U5348 A616 2025 |
  DDC 813/.6—dc23/eng/20241004
LC record available at https://lccn.loc.gov/2024046375

Printed in the United States of America
1st Printing

The authorized representative in the EU for product
safety and compliance is Penguin Random House Ireland,
Morrison Chambers, 32 Nassau Street, Dublin D02 YH68,
Ireland, https://eu-contact.penguin.ie.

For my family, always

I live on the corner of a dead-end street and the end of the world.

—Grey_Street_Summer_2000_Polaris_Amphitheatre.mp3 (3:02–3:10)
   Artist: Dave Matthews Band
   Album: Unknown Album
   Location: C:\Downloads\Napster

13 MONTHS HAUNTED

PROLOGUE

September 2024

Piper Lowery-Palmer was the most notorious member of the family, although Anders had scarcely heard of her before the wedding. She was his third cousin, and he could remember her name coming up at previous family gatherings. According to an aunt at a Christmas party one year, she was also a bit of a recluse, "living somewhere in Iowa with the cows." Of course, Piper wasn't there to clarify.

It wasn't until his first cousin Margot got married that Anders learned more of Piper's story, and even then, he had his doubts about the facts, since the person telling him the story was a bit drunk.

"Way out there in Iowa," his uncle Al said, waving his hand in the air for emphasis. He smelled of a freshly smoked cigar. "She lives with her husband, I think. Can't remember his name. She had that thing a while back with the ghost business."

"Ghost business?" Anders asked.

"Best of my knowledge. Why were we talking about her again?"

"You brought her up."

"I did?"

"Yeah."

"Why did I do that?"

"We were talking about my thesis."

"Ah! That's right. You're writing a college thesis? You don't look a day over fifteen." Uncle Al laughed heartily, turning toward the bartender. It wasn't the first time Anders had heard a similar comment about his looks, and being seated at the kids' table didn't help his case, either. He looked over at his primarily preteen nieces and nephews, dressed impeccably in junior-sized suits and Etsy-bought dresses, each child glued to their phone. Anders had attempted to engage his tablemates earlier, to see what types of things they were doing on their devices—none of them were interested in talking much.

Gin and tonic in hand, Uncle Al turned back toward Anders.

"Now, what's this thesis all about again?" he asked.

Anders had already told him, but he told him again.

"It's about the viral phenomenon," Anders said. "You know, why things go viral online. I'm exploring the history of it, mainly from the nineties and early two thousands."

"What's your angle?"

"I don't know. I guess I don't have one yet."

Anders had been researching for a few weeks, looking for the perfect throughline for his project. Most of the famous viral events from that time were videos or GIFs: Dancing Baby, the Hampster Dance, Star Wars Kid, the *Boom Goes the Dynamite* sports reporter. Much of what he discovered was new to him, and he found the media entertaining, if a bit dated and quaint. Some of them he'd seen before, like the short, security-camera-style video of a disgruntled cubicle worker whacking his computer monitor with a keyboard—the clip was called badday.mpg, and Anders had been disheartened to learn that it was staged.

Still, despite his growing collection of early-Internet artifacts, he wasn't any closer to solving his primary problem, which was that he didn't have an argument. He was merely gathering research, and he didn't know what he was trying to prove, if anything. His faculty advisor in the history department expected an update soon, and Anders didn't really have one.

"You said something about a ghost?" Anders asked Uncle Al, cling-ing to the most interesting thing the intoxicated relative had men-tioned. In his research, he had come across a few famous email chain letters that revolved around the paranormal, as well as a handful of jump-scare videos that had made the rounds. Maybe this was in that ballpark.

"Well, sure, yeah," his uncle replied. "You don't know the story?"

Anders shook his head. "And it went viral?"

"Sure did. That's what made Piper so famous. That was up in . . . now, what's the name of that town up north where all that stuff happened . . . Clover Creek, that's the one. Bunch of crazies descended on the town. It was chaos."

"A ghost?"

"There an echo in this place? Go on now, look it up."

Anders retreated to his table in the corner of the banquet room, excited by the fresh possibilities. He took a seat in his chair, and soon his face was aglow with the light of a screen, just like the kids around him. His giddiness quickly turned to disappointment. He figured search-ing for Piper online would be a slam dunk, but there was nothing. An-ders then searched for Clover Creek, and he had to scroll a bit until he found it. It didn't seem like viral content at all. Just a couple of short blurbs about handfuls of "paranormal enthusiasts" converging on the town in the year 2000, tipped off by blog posts on the Internet. Piper's name was not mentioned, and Anders wondered if this was the incident Uncle Al was referring to. He figured it had to be.

That's when his epiphany struck, as he stared down at his phone, Sister Sledge's "We Are Family" blaring from the speakers that flanked the DJ booth.

Active viral content, Anders thought.

Most viral media seemed to be passively shared, and that was that. But what about something viral that triggers a form of behavior other than resharing online? Like ghost hunters assembling in a town after reading blog posts?

Anders still didn't know what this was. The articles were short on details, and they didn't even contain the blog posts they mentioned. He wasn't sure of Piper's involvement, and he didn't know how to get in touch with her, if what had happened up in Clover Creek was the result of anything even approximating the word *viral*.

But he smiled, satisfied.

He might have something.

. . .

Anders had been on the road for hours and seen plenty of cows. Cornfields, too, as expected. He passed through the town of Clear Lake, the site of the plane crash that killed Buddy Holly, and music, too, apparently, if the Don McLean song "American Pie" was to be taken literally. Not much longer until he'd arrive in Meservey, the home of the mysterious Piper Lowery-Palmer.

She'd been gracious enough to invite Anders to her home to speak. Days earlier, Anders had texted with her husband, Robbie—Piper didn't have a phone, Anders learned—and he'd arranged everything. Anders was surprised she'd agreed to the interview request. It was sometimes challenging to read between the lines of text messages, and Anders initially got the distinct impression that Piper wasn't interested in talking. But he tried his best to convince her, texting that he would be forever grateful and playing up his familial connection. Whatever he did, it worked, although he was surprised that she didn't want to just do the interview over the phone—well, her husband's phone. Anders was happy to make the drive, though. He felt it added legitimacy to his thesis investigation, and the history department had agreed to cover his travel expenses. Those expenses did not include the six-pack of beer Anders purchased at a gas station after filling up his Hyundai, but when it didn't show up as a line item on his receipt, he planned to submit it to the university anyway. He figured it was well-earned.

Anders arrived at Piper's black-and-white farmhouse in the late afternoon. There was a silo and a couple of barns. A stream meandered off to the east, and Anders had to slow to allow a handful of chickens to cross in front of his car as he headed up the long gravel driveway. It was a sizable plot of land, and Anders could spot only three other homes in the distance from all directions across the flat Iowa landscape. Reclusive, indeed.

He parked, then sat for a bit with the engine off. He'd thought he was prepared. The questions he'd planned on asking were written in a notebook on the passenger seat. He even had an old-school tape recorder, not certain that his phone contained enough memory to properly store a long voice memo. Still, he was nervous. He just didn't know what to expect. At the wedding, he'd asked a few more relatives about Piper. There was a caginess when people spoke about her. Either they didn't know her story or they wouldn't say. But whatever had transpired in Clover Creek had resulted in multiple deaths—although the exact events were still a mystery. Anders didn't know how many people had died or why—it wasn't clear from the fragment of an article he'd dug up online. "After a few deaths in the area" was all he got on that front. That was it. As such, Anders didn't really know what he was walking into, but he got out of his car and decided to walk into it anyway.

He was greeted at the front door by Piper and Robbie. Anders's nervousness quickly fizzled away. The pair were affable, chatty. Both were in their late forties but looked considerably younger. Piper was dressed in white, billowy linen pants and a loose-fitting patterned top, which gave off a free-spirited vibe. Two golden retrievers nuzzled at her hands. She nodded at Robbie, who then went to the kitchen to grind some coffee beans.

Anders sat across from Piper in the living room, and his eyes scanned the space. A small patio lay beyond open French doors, and the cool September breeze filled the room. An easel sat in one corner, surrounded by a variety of paints and brushes. The dogs sprawled out at Piper's feet, and Anders hit Record on the tape recorder, placing it on the coffee table between them.

"Thank you so much for doing this," he said.

"We're family," Piper said. "Can I make a request?"

"Yeah, of course."

"My primary ask is to not publish this."

Anders nodded. "That's fine. It's only for my course. No one's going to see it except my professors."

"Would you mind changing my name in your project as well? I'm sorry. We just value our privacy, is all."

"No, no, I get it. That's not a problem. I really appreciate you doing this."

"So, where do you want to begin? I'm assuming you want to know about the girl?"

Anders hesitated. "I didn't know there was a girl. This is the Clover Creek story, right?"

Piper's eyes twinkled.

"Oh, I promise you, it's quite the story."

\part one\

DIALING . . .

CHAPTER 1

I'm going to need a Catholic priest to fix this mess."

The irritated voice came from Piper Lowery's left, from a technology staff member hunched over a laptop at the teacher's desk. Piper didn't know if he was talking to her or talking to himself, and she didn't know how to respond. She turned her head toward him and smiled politely.

"I don't know what he did to this thing," the tech guy said, meeting Piper's eyes and speaking quietly. "It looks like it's got every virus in the book, and others I've never seen before. Son of a gun really did a number on this machine."

He motioned toward Mr. Fisher, currently at the chalkboard, diagramming a sentence in front of a classroom of about twenty eighth graders. Above that sentence and to the right, in impeccable cursive, was *October 12, 2000,* and under that, a list of homework for the week. Piper and the tech guy—she never did catch his name; he'd already been in the classroom when Piper had arrived ten minutes prior—were sitting off to the side while Mr. Fisher taught the finer points of grammar to America's youth. Piper was due to present to the students on behalf of the Clover Creek Public Library any minute, but Mr. Fisher was on a roll and didn't appear to be stopping anytime soon.

Piper wished the man jabbing away at the computer keyboard would stop talking. She didn't know the first thing about computer viruses and felt it was extremely rude to carry on a conversation while class was in session. She'd sensed a few heads from the first row of students turn in their direction when the guy said *son of a gun,* and she didn't want to encourage him to keep going. For a moment, she considered shushing him. But she wasn't a teacher—only a guest from the library—and the man wasn't even a colleague. So, she just smiled again, with a bit of an *Okay, are we done here?* look added for good measure.

The tech guy closed the laptop dramatically and sighed. He scratched his unshaven face and adjusted his glasses.

"Tell Glen it might be a while before he sees this thing again, though I don't suspect he'll miss it. In fact, tell him to never touch another computer again. He's got the kiss of death." He ran his finger across his neck, simulating a throat slash. He laughed and winked at Piper before snatching the laptop and walking toward the classroom door. He about ran into Mr. Fisher on his way out, dodging the teacher at the last possible moment with an exaggerated skip of his feet.

Why are tech people always so weird? Piper thought.

She didn't think he was hitting on her with the wink, although being a fresh-faced twenty-two-year-old woman in a small town, she wouldn't have been surprised if he was. It had happened before.

But this time? Nah.

The guy was just odd.

She thought back to the tech staff from her college days, and there was also something just a bit off about them. Not *bad,* just a tad askew. Lacking in the social skills department, mainly. The most normal tech guy she'd ever known was her older brother, Sam, who was a programmer at some software development company in Des Moines—she never could remember the name. Sam could watch an entire extra-innings baseball game with strangers at a sports bar, and no one found him unusual. Piper always thought he'd dodged a bullet.

She realized she was being judgy and tried to cool it.

Like I'm the master of charm all of a sudden? Who am I, Bob Barker?

"Ms. Lowery?"

The teacher's voice shook Piper from her thoughts. She quickly rose from her cracked plastic chair and smoothed out any creases in her long black skirt. Piper strode to the center of the classroom, her heels clacking on the tiled floor—she'd picked them up at a thrift store in Madison, and they still felt a little funny to her. Mr. Fisher crossed behind Piper, positioning himself behind his desk.

"You all remember Ms. Lowery from the public library?" Fisher announced to the class. The silver-haired, ponytailed instructor had the perfect teacher voice. Bassy and booming without trying too hard. This was Piper's third time visiting Fisher's class, and she was impressed every time he spoke. The man was a total pro.

"Please give her your undivided attention," he said, taking his seat.

Piper cleared her throat.

"Hi, everyone, it's so nice to see you all again," she said, really laying on the pleasantries. Her voice cracked on the word *again*, and she coughed into her closed fist. She wasn't used to public speaking. When she took the job at the public library, she hadn't expected to ever be in front of a large collection of people, doing the *Goooooooood morning, Vietnam!* thing. She thought she'd be doing peon tasks. Shelving books, inventory. Real wallflower stuff. But Piper quickly learned that being a peon—at least, at the Clover Creek Public Library in northern Wisconsin—meant public school outreach. Library card sign-ups, book donation drives, and, on this particular visit, the Spooktacular Scary Story Contest. It was an annual event, Piper had learned, and the library clerk who'd run it in past years had joined the Peace Corps and gone to Africa. Now it was Piper's gig.

"You might remember the last time I was here," she continued, finding her groove, "I let you all know about the scary story contest that the library is hosting this Halloween season. I'm hoping that some of you budding horror authors decided you're up for the challenge. Let's see those hands! Who decided to write a story for the contest?"

A few hands raised. Two. Five. Six.

Not bad, Piper thought.

Another hand slowly went up, from a girl tucked in the back-left corner of the classroom. Piper didn't remember her from her previous visit, and she immediately decided that she *would* have remembered her. For starters, in a sea of brown- and fair-haired children, the girl's short and curly red locks really stuck out. Piper's hair was reddish, too, of course. But she was more of a strawberry blonde. This kid's hair was *very* red, like a ripe tomato.

But it was more than just the mop that gave Piper pause.

It was the look on the girl's face. Her eyes. There was something about them. Corkscrew bangs nearly reached the girl's glasses, and behind those glasses, Piper detected fear.

The kid looks scared, Piper thought.

It made Piper glance over her shoulder, thinking a spider had dropped from the ceiling or a wasp had crashed the party.

But no, nothing.

Piper turned back to the class, and she quickly recovered from her momentary loss of composure. She scanned the room. None of the other students had odd looks on their faces. No fear in their eyes. Whatever the red-haired kid had seen, the others hadn't. Or maybe the kid had just imagined something.

"Okay, great," Piper said haltingly. "I'll come around and collect them, and if any of you still want to participate, then *yes*, there is still time. Drop them off at the library by Monday, and you'll be entered to win some amazing prizes!"

God, I really am Bob Barker, she thought.

Piper walked up and down the rows, collecting the stories from the eager handful of writers. She caught snippets of conversations as she moved through the classroom, overhearing two boys enthusiastically sharing their AOL usernames with those around them—so loudly that most heads turned in their direction and Mr. Fisher had to tell the boys to quiet down. When Piper reached the girl with the red hair, she took a closer look into her eyes. They seemed calmer now, less fearful, albeit meek and timid. Piper was struck by an immediate urge to help the kid, like she'd stumbled across an injured puppy on the side of the road. *How* she would help this kid, she hadn't the first clue, but the feeling stuck.

The girl handed over three handwritten and stapled looseleaf papers to Piper. "Mr. Fisher told me about the contest yesterday," she said shyly. "I wanted to enter."

Piper took the papers and thanked her. The girl said no more, merely looking to her right, at a woman in jeans and a gray, baggy sweater, sitting perpendicular to the front-facing student desks, nose buried in a novel. She looked to be in her late forties, with slightly unkempt, frizzy hair. Piper guessed she was a classroom learning aide.

The woman did not look up from her book.

. . .

Piper stuck around for a bit and chatted with Fisher, returning to the cracked blue chair near the teacher's desk. A classical playlist drifted from a boom box on a bookshelf—Piper thought it was Beethoven, but she wasn't sure. She remembered a few of her old teachers playing music in class, and she'd always dug the vibe. Fisher's students were busy working on a language arts assignment—Piper didn't catch what it was exactly. Some worked in pairs; others worked solo. She heard the words *verb* and *conjunction* thrown around, so she figured it was an extension activity from Fisher's sentence-diagramming lesson. The students appeared focused, and the hum of learning permeated the space along with the classical tunes. The red-haired kid worked alone, sometimes turning to the woman in the gray sweater and softly asking questions.

"She moved here last week," Fisher said from the seat at his desk, his voice not rising above the music and chatter in the classroom. "Interesting kid."

Piper felt embarrassed. "I didn't mean to watch her. I'm sorry."

"Don't be. It's our job to watch the students. Well, not *your* job, but you know what I mean."

Piper smiled. She enjoyed hearing Fisher speak. While she had a tendency to sputter when she talked, Fisher's words always seemed deliberately chosen, delivered at a pace that both kids and adults could process. Never too fast, never too slow.

"Her name is Avery Wallace," he continued, "but she never introduced herself. The kid's barely spoken a word since she got here. I know her name because it showed up on my attendance report, oh, last Thursday, and because I had a nice, long conversation with the principal about her this past Monday."

Piper felt a bit unprofessional getting into personal details in front of the students and scanned the room. The students worked and conversed. Fisher's voice remained low, and no one seemed to be paying attention to them. Still, Piper stood and turned her back to the class, subtly blocking Fisher from view, just in case.

"Is everything okay?" she asked.

"That remains to be seen. You've probably noticed she's a little quiet and withdrawn, but that's certainly no cause for alarm. I've had plenty of shy students over the years. They're often my most thoughtful students, some of my best achievers. But Avery—I'm concerned because . . . well, there are a few reasons, actually."

"What's that?"

Fisher leaned forward and nodded over Piper's shoulder toward Avery and the woman. "For starters, her classroom learning aide is her mother."

"Is that normal?"

"Haven't seen it in my thirty years of teaching, to be frank. The mother insisted. Demanded, actually. That's what I spoke with the principal about on Monday. The school wasn't looking for trouble and just rolled over. She's not even on the payroll. Still processing, is what they told me, but I'm not even sure she's going to be an official hire."

"She's volunteering?"

Fisher chuckled. "That's one way of putting it. Don't let that little secret get out, otherwise I might have a few more parents itching to shadow their kids all day long, and they might use—oh, what's her name again—Susan as their example." He pointed his index finger down toward the desk and twirled it around a few times, making circles in the air. "Helicopter parents. But this one takes the cake. I haven't seen her leave the poor kid's side once. She even escorts her to the restroom."

"Seriously?"

"Every time."

Fisher turned to grab a stack of papers, and Piper returned to the cracked blue chair, her gaze drifting in the direction of the pair. Avery worked silently, eyes downcast at a worksheet on her desk, pencil moving quickly over the page. Susan had returned to her novel. To their left, two boys joked and giggled, sometimes looking toward Avery. One of the boys—a scraggly-looking kid in a Green Bay Packers pullover sweatshirt, the one who had been loudly sharing his AOL username earlier—dramatically inched his chair farther away from Avery, putting his hands on his cheeks and making an exaggerated scared face, like he was a villager encountering a monster in an old black-and-white horror movie. The incident was over almost as quickly as it had begun, and the boys turned back to their worksheets.

But Piper had seen everything, picking up on the behavior immediately.

Bullying.

Piper had been bullied herself as a child—when she was nine, an incident occurred where she was running toward an ice cream truck and she fell on the pavement, badly scraping her knee. The driver stopped and got out of the truck to check on her, and that's when other kids arrived at the scene. To their eyes, Piper had been *hit* by the slow-moving ice cream truck, and the rumors swirled from there. The truth made no difference. For the next five years—though the nickname occasionally resurfaced in high school—Piper was known as "the ice cream girl." On paper, the nickname didn't seem so bad. But when other students called her by that phrase, there was a casual menace that really stung. Sly smiles, mischievous eyes. If a teacher overheard it and didn't know the story, it might have sounded like nothing, but Piper was being mocked for allegedly being bumped by a vehicle that moved at the speed of a glacier. The nickname stuck, and Piper simply tried to ignore it, hoping it would go away—but it persisted. Middle school was the worst, though. She was especially tormented by a pack of popular girls— whispers and giggles behind her back, cruel notes slipped into her locker. Piper kept her head down and moved on. The bullying wasn't a turning point in her life, but it was no picnic, either, and it wasn't until a few weeks into her first semester at college in a new town that Piper realized she'd finally shaken the moniker. The "ice cream girl" memories emerged from time to time, and as Piper watched the two boys in Fisher's classroom crack jokes and continue their light abuse of Avery, Piper could almost hear the laughter of her own bullies, could unfold the old notes written on loose-leaf saying things like *There's a sale on Fudgsicles in the cafeteria today, better hurry!*

The boys' behavior was certainly less discreet than writing an anonymous note. Piper turned her head to inform Fisher of what she'd seen, but the instructor put his hand up toward her, stopping her from speaking.

"I saw it," he said. He brought his hand down, and Piper noticed the chalk-stained cuffs of his dress shirt. "It's been a problem all week. I've talked to him a few times, and it looks like I'll have to do it again."

This guy is a good teacher, she decided.

Fisher stood, and he glanced at his desk, a confused look crossing his face. "Have you seen my . . ."

"Oh, right," Piper said. "I forgot to tell you. The tech guy said it has a virus. Or, many viruses, he thinks. He said you may not be seeing it for a while. Might be kaput."

Fisher laughed heartily. "He can keep it. I never wanted it in the first place. I'm part of the technology committee, even though I'd prefer not to be. A handful of teachers are piloting the new laptops."

"Looks like it's not going so well for you," Piper joked.

"Went online once and the whole thing went to hell. I even put my email address on the syllabus, but only one parent has ever emailed me. So I'm not sure why I'm even bothering with the thing at all." Fisher turned to walk away, but Piper stopped him.

"Mr. Fisher, I—" She glanced around at the students—the boys from earlier were focused on their worksheets, their joking and antics forgotten. Satisfied the situation wasn't escalating, Piper gestured toward the door. "Can we step into the hallway for a second?" Piper knew Fisher had to deal with the bullying situation, but something was nagging at her. She promised herself she'd be quick.

Fisher hesitated, then nodded. He followed her out, the chatter and maybe-Beethoven fading as the door closed behind them.

"Mr. Fisher," Piper began.

"Glen, please, when we're not in front of the kids."

"Sorry. *Glen,* I don't want to seem like I'm prying or being nosy, but—"

"No, no, go ahead. What is it?"

"You said, a moment ago, you said 'a few reasons.'"

Fisher furrowed his brow. "A few reasons?"

"You said you were worried about Avery for a few reasons, the first being her mother."

"Oh," Fisher said. Even though they were alone, Fisher leaned in, his voice dropping to a whisper.

Piper smelled stale coffee on his breath.

"It seems that, before she and her mother moved to town, she lost two members of her family. Her father and sister. They both died suddenly, is my understanding."

"Oh my God," Piper said.

Fisher's words echoed in Piper's head, and that's all she heard. *They both died.* Piper wondered if Avery suspected they had stepped into the hallway to discuss *her*, to whisper about her dead family members. Piper felt terrible, yet she wanted to know more.

"And you should hear what the other kids are saying about her," Fisher said softly. "The rumors."

"What are they saying?"

"Awful, dreadful things. Not that I believe a word of it, but . . . they're saying that her old house, where Avery used to live before she moved here, was haunted. And that her sister and father were killed by what lived inside."

CHAPTER 2

8:39 P.M.—A Whole New World   THURSDAY, OCTOBER 12, 2000

Hey! I don't really know what this is, or who's reading. I guess I'll find out.

I'm still settling into my new digs in the Northwoods. I graduated college in May, moved back home for the summer, and worked a seasonal job as a ropes course instructor at an adventure park. You know, one of those places where you zipline from platform to platform, moving through obstacles—I helped people do things like that. It was fun.

But the season ended, and now I'm here. It's my first time living completely on my own, and even though it's been over a month, I'm still getting used to the change. My little apartment bumps up against the forest, which is exactly what I was looking for. It's just me and my dog, Ripley, making our own way. I took a job as a librarian (well, library clerk), which is never what I expected to be right out of college. I majored in outdoor recreation, but one of my professors hooked me up with the library gig. She had a connection in town, and here I am. The job pays the bills, but all I really want to do is canoe and explore and all that jazz. Kind of put my degree to work, right? The town is small, less than fifteen hundred people. Smaller than I'm used to, that's for sure. But there are plenty of trails, a nice community center, a *really* yummy bakery, and a pretty decent pizza place. I also counted eight churches, which is a pretty crazy number per capita.

Anyway, there's no better time in my life to have this kind of an adventure, starting fresh in a new place. Is this technically called a gap year? Maybe if I'm planning on attending graduate school. Who knows?

Rip and I have hit a few trails and even done some overnights already. There's some really nice first-come, first-served campsites about thirty-five minutes from here (and then a thirty-minute paddle). Last Saturday we found ourselves a private little island and set up shop there. Very clean, some nice stumps around the fire grate. The east side of that particular flowage is the "quiet" zone, and it was definitely as advertised. It was just us and the loons. They should be headed south soon, so I'll enjoy their company while I can. No bear sightings yet, and I'm determined to spot an elusive moose. They're about as rare as Bigfoot up here, but people have seen them.

What else? This will sound dumb, but I'm still reeling from this scary story I read like a half hour ago. Horror isn't my thing—I'm a bit of a baby with all that stuff. Always have been. But I'm running this student Halloween contest at the library, so I have to suck it up. This one girl's story got to me. She's new in town, and the rumor around here is that she used to live in a haunted house. Like, a *legit* haunted house, where something killed her dad and sister. And then she wrote this, and, well . . . just read the story. I'll put it below, if anyone wants to check it out:

The Thing in the Closet

My sister Rose had nightmares. At least, I thought they were nightmares. She told me she heard noises from her closet. Scratching and loud breathing. One night the door even jiggled. Rose jammed her desk chair under the handle and slept in Mom and Dad's bed that night.

But the noises didn't stop. Then came the whispering from the closet, things Rose couldn't understand but that made her so scared she couldn't move. And that's when she saw her breath in the air, she told me, when the whispering started. Her room was cold, like a frozen winter morning, and wisps of air floated out from under her closet door. Rose knew the thing was inside.

I didn't believe her. We looked in the closet during the day, and of course there was nothing there but clothes and toys. But bad things don't come during the day. The bogeyman comes at night.

When the noises started coming from my own closet, I began to believe. It was dark and late, and I was alone. And then there was no more scratching or breathing or jiggling, only the squeak of my closet door and a low growl. I guessed whatever had been in Rose's closet had also been in my own, and it had grown stronger from tormenting my sister. It can open doors now, I remember thinking, and even though I knew the thing was nearing my bed, I didn't run or scream. Instead, I closed my eyes and lay still. If I pretended the bogeyman wasn't real, maybe it would slither away. But if I'd opened my eyes, I would have seen my breath in the air. It was even colder than Rose had described.

It came for me then. It reached under my blanket, and I felt its hands on me. My feet first. Its fingers felt like icicles. I wouldn't look, though. I hoped it would go away if I didn't look.

Its hands moved up my body and found my neck and squeezed. Not enough to choke me, and I don't know why it didn't choke me. Maybe it just wanted to know what it would be like to squeeze a child's neck without killing it. I knew its face was inches from mine because I could feel its breath on my cheek. But I wouldn't open my eyes. I just wouldn't.

I lay still, and maybe the thing grew bored, because it left. Maybe that's all it wanted to do that night. Just frighten a little girl. The temperature in my bedroom grew warmer, and I knew then that it was gone. I thought maybe it was all a nightmare, but I couldn't think about that for very long because I heard a scream from down the hall. It sounded like Rose.

I jumped from my bed and ran into the hallway, slamming into my mother. She grabbed my shoulders and looked down at me.

"What's wrong with your nightgown?" she asked me.

I peered downward. My nightgown was completely stiff, like it had been inside a freezer overnight. It was starting to defrost, and beads of water fell to the carpet. It was in that moment that I knew, for sure: I had not had a nightmare.

The bogeyman was real.

My mom stared, but she didn't look scared. Her eyes were more curious.

"Was that you screaming?" she asked me.

I shook my head, and I heard another scream.

Rose.

I ran to her room, my mother not far behind me. My sister was not in her bed, but I had an idea where she might be. I threw open Rose's closet door and was hit with a blast of arctic air. My mom noticed, too, because she immediately wrapped her arms around her body. But she didn't seem scared like me. Her eyes were knowing.

I heard Rose's desperate cries for help. They came from somewhere in the closet, but each time she screamed she seemed farther away. I broke my mother's hold and tore through the closet, yanking clothes from hangers, desperately searching. I looked to my mom for help, but she just stood there, kneading her fingers into her arms. It was like she already knew.

Rose was not inside.

My sister's screams faded away to nothing.

Creepy stuff, right?

<u>Vibes</u>: Uncomfortable
<u>Current Jam</u>: "Uninvited" by Alanis Morissette

[comment on this | comments]

CHAPTER 3

She'd hoped that typing out her first journal post might purge any unsettling thoughts that lingered after reading Avery's story. Piper had created the account on the platform weeks ago, but she'd done nothing with it. Her page had sat there, vacant. She'd decided to change that, and her intention was to write about canoeing and camping, maybe hiking with Ripley. Real banal stuff. And she *had* done that, but then Piper had found herself writing about the very thing she was trying to forget, even typing out Avery's story wholesale, as if she couldn't stop her fingers from doing it.

Now it was there, online.

Living and breathing on her computer screen.

She decided it might be a good thing, that if the story's existence was shared it wouldn't be as macabre, because she wouldn't be alone with it anymore. *Horrible things usually come when you're alone,* Piper thought, *especially in the movies.* But no, even after clicking Post and sending the story into the abyss of the World Wide Web, Piper still felt that funny quiver in her stomach.

In fact, she was officially spooked.

And she wondered why.

Piper slumped into her desk chair, Avery's story—handwritten on stapled loose-leaf paper—resting beside the keyboard. Ripley, her yellow

Lab, lifted his head, studying Piper from his curled-up position on the floor. At around fifty-five pounds, he was smaller than other yellow Labs, made up of a mix of breeds—there was definitely some beagle in there. Some people called him a mutt, but Piper didn't mind; in fact, she found it endearing. The shift in her demeanor hadn't gone unnoticed by Ripley. Piper gently reached down and placed her left hand on the animal's neck, running her fingers through his golden fur, some of it now flecked with gray. Ripley dropped his head, relaxing.

Piper, however, was not relaxed.

Am I overreacting? she thought.

She knew that she was. It was just a scary story, she tried to tell herself, one of many she'd been reading in front of the television in her above-garage apartment in Clover Creek. Piper hadn't been reading the kids' stories very closely. Her attention was divided between the tales of horror and Must See TV on NBC. She'd saved Avery's story until the end, and it had been a purposeful choice. It was almost like Piper knew it would alarm her and she wanted to give the other stories a fair shake first. Piper had skimmed through many encounters with werewolves and vampires—and even a humorous story about a cursed microwave—before she'd eventually arrived at Avery's. Not even Noah Wyle and the season premiere of *ER* could distract Piper from its contents.

This story can't be real, can it?

She recognized how stupid the thought was the moment it arrived, and she dismissed it outright. *How could something like this be real?* A monster in a bedroom, a frozen nightgown, a child vanishing inside a closet—the story was clearly fiction, yet Piper couldn't shake her disturbed feeling all the same. She remembered what Fisher had told her the kids were saying about Avery: haunted house, dead sister, dead father. The story she'd written contained two of the three.

And that stuff about the mom . . . how sinister was that?

Piper picked up the story and skimmed the pages, homing in on a few passages.

Her eyes were more curious. . . .

Her eyes were knowing. . . .

It was like she already knew. . . .

Piper dropped the papers to her lap. Avery's words seemed to imply the mother was involved with the character's disappearance—at the very least, her behavior was suspicious. Piper thought of Avery's real mother, whom Fisher had said never left the girl's side. Something seemed off there, for sure. Not in a *complicit in a supernatural death* sort of way, but certainly concerning.

Piper's hand found Ripley's head again, and she scratched behind his left ear. The dog softly whined his approval. She reread the entire story, more slowly this time.

This is not a good look for this kid, she thought.

Does she not know she'd be feeding ammunition to the rumors if anyone got hold of this?

She sat there for so long just thinking that the screen saver on her Windows 98 computer activated. It was the code from *The Matrix,* a film that that had been released the previous year. Green symbols and numbers rained from the top of a black screen, vanishing and reappearing in rhythmic patterns. It was hypnotic, mesmerizing—orderly yet chaotic at the same time. Piper's brother, Sam, had installed the screen saver on the computer months before, and even though Piper wasn't a huge fan of the movie, she'd left it there. Partially because she liked it, but also because she wasn't quite sure how to change it.

The distraction helped clear her mind. Piper rose to her feet and paced the small living room, feeling a little better knowing she'd identified the reason she was upset by the story—she was simply concerned for Avery's well-being. Piper had already witnessed the bullying, and it would get much worse if the other students knew that "the kid with the dead sister from the haunted house" had written a first-person-POV story about a monster in a haunted house that kills the narrator's sister.

So why did she write this thing?

Piper returned to her computer, and Ripley switched positions, collapsing with a sigh at Piper's feet under the desk. Piper put her hand on the computer mouse and wiggled it, the *Matrix* screen saver disappearing. She noticed a black smudge on the tower next to the monitor—a splash of coffee, no doubt; Piper had gotten hooked on it in college during late-night cram sessions—and rubbed it off with her thumb, before smoothing out the yellow and black Best Buy sticker proclaiming: *Remember: Turn your computer off before midnight on 12/31/99.* Piper hadn't heeded the sticker's advice, and her computer was fine. Society, too. All that remained of the Y2K scare was this sticker on her machine.

Piper refreshed her online journal page, wondering if any comments would appear. None did, which didn't really surprise her. In the infinite void of the Internet, how would anyone know her page existed? Piper hadn't even told her brother or mother that she'd created an account. Her friends were in the dark, too. Truth be told, she'd just thought the blogging thing would be kind of fun. She'd stumbled across a few online and had an urge to join the party. So she did. The anonymous aspect made it weirdly thrilling and empowering—other users didn't know her, and she didn't know them. She planned to keep it that way.

Piper refreshed her page again. Still no comments. She closed out of her journal, returning to the America Online welcome screen. Staring at the gaggle of icons—the purple mailbox, the printer, the file cabinet, the happy group of faceless digital people encouraging her to click on them to chat with friends—Piper did the math in her head for how much complimentary Internet access she had remaining of the promised seven hundred hours from the install disc.

Five hundred hours?

Five hundred fifty hours?

She'd gone online every day the past four weeks, often to read emails and connect with college friends. She still wasn't sure if AOL rounded her time online.

If I check my email for ten minutes and then log off, does that count as one hour?

She didn't know, and every time she thought to look it up, she decided it didn't matter. Piper was simply satisfied that she was able to get online *at all* in her small place. When she'd learned the apartment was above the owner's detached garage, she'd half expected to be without electricity and heat, surrounded by moldy rafters and pink insulation. Her expectations couldn't have been more off. For starters, the garage wasn't used to store a vehicle. The landlord, a friendly and soft-spoken elderly woman named Ms. Hermann, kept her Buick outside, and the garage itself was stuffed to the gills with decades of the woman's accumulated belongings. A real pack rat, that one. But the kicker—to Piper's extreme delight, because the only piece of furniture she owned was a squeaky futon—was that the studio apartment came surprisingly well furnished. Queen-size bed, kitchen table, entertainment unit, plush couch, maple desk—all used, no doubt about that, but more estate sale quality than garage sale. Piper found the lived-in nature of the furnishings to be rather cozy, and she never even reassembled the futon. Her bed was tucked near the front of the apartment, by the window overlooking the driveway, Ms. Hermann's house, and the edge of the forest. Each morning, Piper loved waking up, lifting her head to see sunlight slicing through the trees and hearing the rustling of the woods. She doubted that would ever get old. The place even had cable *and* its own phone line, allowing Piper to access the Internet without having to share the line with Ms. Hermann. To Piper, that was an absolute coup.

She thought about how lucky she was every time she went online, and thought it again that night, hand on the gray computer mouse, eyes on the screen. Satisfied with her journal for the time being, Piper now had a fresh goal in mind:

Avery Wallace, what happened to you and your family?

Curiosity gnawed at her, but it was also more than that.

The bullying incident in Fisher's classroom had been playing on a loop in her head since she'd left the school. Piper felt bad for the girl, saw a little bit of herself in her, remembering the "ice cream girl" taunts from her own childhood. Honestly, she just wanted to help.

Piper launched AskJeeves.com—her search engine of choice when writing research papers in school—and waited. Slow to load, as usual. Irritated, she clicked over to Napster, which she always kept open. She'd discovered the music-sharing program during her senior year of college, and her friends with personal computers had had a field day downloading songs. It was a total trip—Piper hadn't paid for a CD in over a year. Any song, anytime, with the click of a button. Piper couldn't imagine a more novel concept. Her MP3 collection was slowly growing, and she took a look at the music files she'd downloaded the previous day:

Lou Bega—Mambo No 5.mp3
Phish—Gin and Juice.mp3
OAR—That Was a Crazy Game of Poker.mp3
Rusted Root—Ecstasy.mp3
Guster—What You Wish For.mp3

She resumed the "Ecstasy" download—it had stalled out—and checked back on Ask Jeeves. It had loaded.

Finally.

Piper typed "Avery Wallace" into the search bar but found nothing. She tried every search combination she could think of, including the name of the girl's mother, but she couldn't locate any obituaries or information. This didn't really surprise her—she didn't know the city or state where Avery used to live prior to moving to Clover Creek. That knowledge would certainly have helped.

She tried a few more search engines. AltaVista. Lycos. Yahoo!.

Nothing.

Piper remembered her friend telling her she'd had good experiences using a website called Google, and Piper gave it a go.

No dice.

Frustrated, Piper closed out of the web browser, opting to catch up on emails. She learned that her own mother was heading to Maryland to take care of Piper's grandmother for a few weeks. Piper responded that it was fine, and she'd be sure to call her if she needed something. She answered a few Instant Messenger pings, checked the weather for the upcoming weekend.

But her thoughts stayed with Avery.

She distracted herself with more Napster, searching for a few songs and restarting the download process. She hoped it would work. Napster was great, but the files were sometimes fraught with errors. Some songs had skips and pops; others were mislabeled completely. Piper was certain the particular bluegrass cover of "Gin and Juice" she'd downloaded was not performed by Phish, but the file was certainly identified as such. This sort of thing worried her—*How do I know I'm not downloading some gnarly virus or something,* she thought, *or some weirdo saying God knows what and labeling it as a Britney Spears song?*—but she wasn't about to stop using Napster. Really, what was the worst that could happen?

She caught her own reflection in the computer monitor, which made her think of Avery's eyes.

That look of *fear.*

It prompted Piper to search for "In Your Eyes" by Peter Gabriel; she clicked Get Selected File. The blue progress bar for the MP3 file slowly crept forward, and any thought of a computer virus vanished from Piper's mind. She clicked back to the Internet browser with no real intention in mind, just the endless possibilities of the World Wide Web tempting her to return.

It was nearly two thirty A.M. when Piper finally called it quits, exhausted. The dog had retired to bed hours ago. Still, Piper had the energy to check the closet before she lay down, the idea of a bogeyman still fresh in her mind.

She couldn't help it.

CHAPTER 4

December 14, 1999

From the Diary of Avery Wallace

I had another visit with Dr. . . . . *Something* today. I feel bad not remembering her name, but there have just been so many of them. She asked me specifically about scary things—movies and books and stuff like that. I know what she was trying to do. She was trying to see if I'm making everything up, if some horror film is stuck in my head. The doctor is friendly, but sometimes I feel like I'm being interrogated. But I'm not lying about anything—something was in Charlotte's bedroom, and it killed her.

The doctor and I talked for a long time anyway about my love of spooky things. Like how Charlotte and I would have backyard sleepovers in a tent, and Charlotte and I would snuggle together, reading horror stories and doing creepy voices. I miss that. It bums me out that we will never go trick-or-treating together again. The doctor and I talked a little bit about Halloween, and I told her it's usually my favorite day of the year. This last Halloween was . . . different. I don't know, it was a weird day. I didn't dress up or go trick-or-treating. I didn't even watch any horror movies. I wasn't in the mood, for obvious reasons. But still, the day felt important somehow. I couldn't explain it.

Then we talked about scary movies for a while—Charlotte showed me my first scary movie when I was eight, I told her. It was *Carrie,* and I had trouble sleeping for a week (Carrie's arm coming out of the rubble at the end gave me nightmares). The doctor asked me about the last horror movie I saw, and I had to think about it a little bit—I finally remembered that it was *The Blair Witch Project,* and that Charlotte and I saw it together last summer. We bought tickets for *The Iron Giant* but snuck in to see *Blair Witch,* and the movie really freaked us out, even though we knew it was fake. In the lobby afterward, a bunch of people thought it was actually real. The doctor hadn't seen it and didn't know what I was talking about, so I had to explain the whole thing. The movie is about three college students filming a documentary about the Blair Witch, a creepy legend in Maryland. They go missing in the woods, and a year later their "footage" is found—and that's the movie. It shows them being stalked and killed by something in the woods. And like, a year before the movie was released, a super-legit-looking website came out called BlairWitch.com that had all this information about the missing filmmakers, news articles, interviews, lore about the witch, and fake police reports. Charlotte and I became OBSESSED with the witch mythology and the clues about the missing students. We had SO MUCH fun pretending it was real, going down the rabbit hole and finding really weird and freaky websites, pranking our friends, sending them creepy links and videos. "Did you hear three people died making a documentary about a witch? This is crazy!"

The doctor scribbled a bunch of things about the Blair Witch stuff, said just before our session ended that she would go to the video store and rent it. I left not feeling any different, and I wondered if I was supposed to. Mom drove me home, and everything was the same. My house was still ground zero. That's where it all happened. That's where Charlotte was killed, and that's where the evil thing is, right now. I'm in the living room writing this diary entry.

And it's here.

CHAPTER 5

Fisher's eyes flickered as they moved across and down the page. A half-drunk brandy old-fashioned sat before him on the bar, near where the teacher's elbows rested. Piper tapped her mug of beer with her fingers, anxious for the man to finish reading. She'd only taken two small sips. She wasn't in the mood to drink—at least, not until Fisher had given his thoughts on the story.

He turned to the next page, finished, and flipped back to the first page, starting anew.

Thorough, Piper thought.

This was her third time visiting Thompson's Pizza and Pub, and she liked it, determining early on that the emphasis was on *pub*. She and Fisher were two of about seventy patrons that night, an impressive number, considering the size of Clover Creek. She did the math and worked out that about 5 percent of the town's population was currently within the pub's rustic wooden walls. The town's unofficial numbers swelled with tourists during the summer months, Piper had learned, but the carousers who surrounded her that Friday night were undoubtedly local. Deer and moose heads adorned the space, along with an assortment of other stuffed critters. Antlers hung from the ceiling, decorated with lights, and a stone fireplace rested in the center of the space, rising through the exposed rafters, a fire blazing at its core. A healthy chatter surrounded Piper and Fisher, drowning out the Red Hot Chili Peppers song that carried from the speakers mounted in the corners.

Fisher finished reading and placed the papers on the bar, taking a sip from his spirit, smacking his lips together when he was through.

"And?" Piper asked him.

He set the drink down on a stained coaster. "She's a gifted writer."

"There's nothing there that concerns you?" Piper surprised herself with her own directness. This was her first time seeing Fisher outside the walls of the middle school, but she found her rapport with him to be rather comfortable.

"I wouldn't say there's necessarily anything *concerning* here," Fisher said.

Piper was a bit taken aback at the instructor's more subdued reaction, but she knew she shouldn't have been. She'd visited Fisher's class multiple times and seen him with the students, pegging his philosophy. Maybe it was the ponytail, but he seemed to be a very liberal guy, one of those "nurture the creativity of students" type of teachers. Piper'd had a few of them growing up. In the system long enough, they played by their own rules. Kids loved them; they gave the administration nothing but headaches. Fisher seemed like the kind of teacher who would read banned books aloud in class, because, well, rules be damned. Power to the people, to the *kids*.

Still, this situation seemed unique.

"Glen," Piper said, formulating her words carefully. "Isn't it just strange? People are saying her sister and father were killed in a haunted house, and now Avery writes a story about a similar scenario?" She worried about how that sounded to Fisher—unhinged, she feared, as if she were professing some belief in the supernatural. But that wasn't it. The real concern was that Avery was potentially exposing herself to more bullying, especially if her story ended up winning the contest and became public for everyone to see. This would be like Piper giving class presentations in middle school about how much she loved ice cream. She'd have been asking for more ridicule.

"Just so we're on the same page," Fisher began slowly, "you don't think Avery is recounting an actual incident from her life?"

"Like her sister was killed by a closet monster?"

Fisher's eyes narrowed, studying her.

"God, no," Piper said. "I don't believe in bogeymen. I'm just worried about Avery's well-being."

The teacher exhaled dramatically. "You had me worried there for a moment."

Piper still couldn't fully articulate exactly what she was feeling, why she had been so insistent on meeting with Fisher at the bar to discuss Avery. It wasn't solely the story that unsettled her—although that was certainly part of it. Something just felt *wrong* with Avery, something she couldn't quite put her finger on, and she couldn't ignore the urge to find out why. The story was a tangible piece of the puzzle, sitting right there in front of them—a thread they could both pull, hoping it might unravel some answers. Again, Piper couldn't quite explain it. It was a gut feeling. An uneasiness. Sort of like an intuition, but not quite.

"How did she die?" Piper asked. "Avery's real sister. Sorry, that sounded *really* crass."

Fisher shook his head. "I honestly don't know. A colleague told me the father died in a car accident, but I'm not sure about Avery's sister."

"So where did the haunted-house stuff come from? The rumors, I mean."

"Not sure. Maybe someone knew someone who knew someone. You know how these things spin out of control."

Piper placed her hand on Avery's story, running her index finger up and down the page. A splash of alcohol had settled on the second paragraph, smudging Avery's words. "I'm sorry if I sound like a broken record right now, but if people are whispering about her, making fun of her—why would she write this?"

"I haven't the first clue. Maybe this is her way of thumbing her nose at the rumors. Taking them head-on."

Piper very much doubted this. She had seen the girl in class. Avery seemed more troubled than anything, not some headstrong kid willing to fight for herself. Piper simply shook her head, looking down at the loose-leaf pages.

"It's a *damn good* scary story, though, wouldn't you say?" Fisher continued. "Without reading the competition, I assume she stands a pretty good chance of winning."

"She does."

"Then I'm quite happy for her."

"Well, that's *something,*" Piper said, taking another drink of beer, thinking it tasted somewhat flat.

The teacher sighed. "Ms. Lowery, I hope I'm not coming across as unsympathetic. I *am* concerned for the child. The mother's behavior is certainly unorthodox, and Avery often seems a bit . . . how do I put this . . . *disturbed,* at times. I just don't want to jump to any conclusions here." He gathered his thoughts for a moment. "I suppose, independent of any rumors of *haunted houses* and things of that nature, it's possible Avery is working through some things on the page. Processing her emotions."

"Like how she feels about her mother?" Piper asked.

"How do you figure?"

"I don't really know. It's just interesting how the mother in the story was so suspect. Like, she already knew about the bogeyman, knew what happened to Rose before she even saw the empty closet. Maybe I'm reading into it too much. I probably am."

Fisher scratched his chin, thinking. "I'm just wildly speculating here—and I know next to nothing of Avery's family history, mind you—but maybe Avery's mother knew about the sister's death before Avery did, and then waited to break the news to her? And now Avery holds it against her? Again, that is on-the-spot conjecture that I don't want attributed to me, but if something like that *did* happen, Avery could be channeling her emotions in a short story. She wouldn't be the first writer to do that, and she certainly wouldn't be the last. If that's what she's doing, I applaud her for it. Writing can be therapeutic."

"What's her deal, anyway?"

"Avery's mother?"

Piper nodded.

"I wish I knew. But losing your husband and your daughter? That can't be easy. Maybe that's why she won't let Avery out of her sight. Maybe she refuses to lose her, too."

Fisher's remark seemed to summon a heaviness into the air above them, and with that, the Avery portion of their conversation ended. Piper felt that Fisher's measured response should have made her feel better about everything, yet she remained unsettled.

Her curiosity from the previous night still festered, as well as a renewed urge she'd felt the first time she met Avery in the classroom.

She wanted to help this girl.

. . .

The sun had nearly gone down. Piper had been walking for ten minutes, and she'd be back at her apartment in ten more. She stuck to the bike path that ran parallel to the highway, which she'd heard was used by snowmobilers in the winter months. Across the highway was a forest of pine trees that seemed to extend forever.

She passed a powersports store and then a food market, walked another quarter mile, and crossed the empty highway into her neighborhood. She wouldn't have called her neck of the woods in Clover Creek a "subdivision" in the traditional sense, but it was similar. It consisted of about forty homes on three roads, each street extending straight north before dead-ending at the forest. Piper had grown up a typical suburban kid, but this was different. These yards were bigger; the homes were close enough to spot your neighbors but far enough away to maintain a comfortable privacy. Fences didn't seem necessary, and not one home in the neighborhood had one. Piper's above-garage apartment was part of the last house on Turner Lane, and from there, the street just kind of sputtered out. No dead-end sign, just pavement turning to dirt, which meandered a bit before stopping at the tree line. And that was it. No more town.

Piper was close now, about eight houses away. After passing a home where jack-o'-lanterns grinned from the porch, she detected a blur to her right—a couple of boys running through a yard. Although it was near dark, she still recognized one as Shane from Fisher's class, the one who had bullied Avery the day before. He was still wearing that gray Packers sweatshirt. She continued walking, watching as the boys ran around the side of the house and into the backyard toward a fire pit, laughing and giggling. There was no fire burning, but Piper thought she spotted the handle of an ax pointing skyward, the blade embedded in a log. Three red gas cans rested nearby, one of them tipped on its side. The boys were a bit farther away now, but Piper found herself stopping to watch them, and she wasn't quite sure why.

Shane shook an object and placed it in the center of the pit—*A can of some kind?*—and then disappeared behind the house. He reemerged moments later, now brandishing a rifle. The boys took cover behind an upturned picnic table on the side of the house, about thirty yards from the pit. Piper watched Shane lean out from one side of the table, lying on his stomach, steadying the rifle. *An air rifle? A BB gun?* Piper didn't know her firearms, nor did she care to. Shane took aim at the pit and fired one, two, three times.

Pop.

Pop.

BOOM.

The third shot did the trick. The bullet made contact with the can in the pit, and the can exploded. It made Piper jump back. A small fireball accompanied the explosion, and the boys erupted in laughter.

A man came charging in the pair's direction. Piper wasn't sure where he had emerged from, but his hostile gait certainly made his presence known. She recognized him instantly—Piper had seen him before on a riding mower. Midforties, barrel-chested, bushy beard. Shane's dad, she assumed. He was an absolute bear of man, but he moved swiftly toward the boys. As he passed the ax buried in the ring of the fire pit, Piper thought she detected a slight hesitation.

Is he going to grab it?

Thankfully, he did not. He bypassed the ax and the smoking can, reaching the boys and seizing the hood of Shane's sweatshirt, yanking him to his feet. The rifle dropped from Shane's hands. The man dragged the child along the side of the house, smacking him four times across the face with his free hand, as Shane put up his arms in self-defense. The man barked obscenities, and Piper heard the boy cry out before they disappeared into the garage. The other boy stood near the upturned picnic table, looking not quite sure what to do.

Piper felt the same. She scanned the neighborhood, and a few people had come out of their houses. No one ran over; they just watched from their front stoops before returning indoors.

A wave of emotions swept through Piper. Shock first, then pity. But then she remembered how Shane had bullied Avery in class, and she felt satisfied that he'd received some comeuppance for his unruly behavior. *A big ol' dose of karma,* she thought. She shook off that last feeling, upset with herself.

No kid deserves to be hit like that.

Even the worst of them.

She didn't know if Shane was one of the worst of them. But if he was, she understood where that behavior came from now.

Daddio.

Father beats son; son bullies kids.

Tale as old as time.

Piper realized she'd been standing outside the boy's house for far too long, and she started moving again, a little faster this time, anxious to be home. When she'd walked about one hundred feet, she looked back over her shoulder and saw Shane's father, now out on the front lawn, hands on his hips, watching her. She stuck her hands in her pockets and turned her head straight, pretending she didn't see him.

Her legs moved faster now. Piper hustled to her apartment without looking back again, wondering if he was still watching.

CHAPTER 6

The library was beginning to feel familiar.

It took some time, as adjusting to all new places does, even if the library wasn't very big. Piper estimated the Clover Creek Public Library was about one-third the size of her library growing up. One story, with a sizable basement. Main floor for checking out books, below deck for quiet study and research. *The stacks,* people called the basement.

It was Monday evening, and the library had just gotten online. Two banks of computers on the main floor, one computer in the stacks. Part of a state grant, Piper had been told. All dial-up modem connections, like Piper's connection at her apartment—broadband Internet still hadn't made its way to their rural location. Eleven different computers, eleven unique phone lines sending users to the World Wide Web. There was no dedicated tech person at the library, and a few men had come from out of town to handle the setup. They'd left when the computers were up and running, and that was it. The library would need to figure out how to handle sign-in and sign-out, create accounts, and so on. For now, the computer accounts would be shared. The log-in information was printed on sheets of paper and displayed in a tabletop sign holder next to each machine. The patrons didn't seem to mind. They were simply excited to be connected, personal privacy be damned.

A handful of eager kids took the computers on their maiden voyages. Piper wondered how many of the students had the Internet at home—the school didn't have computer labs. She'd assumed that many homes had AOL, like hers, but judging by the enthusiasm of those at the library, Piper guessed these were the children without home access. And boy, were these kids primed to be online. She watched them navigate excitedly to Yahoo! Games; a pair of girls spent considerable time on Barbie.com. One boy found his way to a first-person shooter game but was quickly redirected to math games after his mother sauntered over. ESPN.com saw a fair amount of library traffic that day, and three high school boys surfed professional wrestling websites for at least two hours—the "dirt sheets," one of the boys called them, and Piper had no idea what that meant but nodded like she did.

It was probably her favorite day working so far. She wouldn't say she had a passion for library science—it was just a gig to pay the bills—but this, she liked. The energy, the joy on the kids' faces. Piper wouldn't have minded if every day were like this.

Then Avery and her mother arrived.

Piper hadn't thought about them much the past couple of days, not since she showed Avery's short story to Fisher—she'd been happily distracted by hiking and canoeing over the weekend. She thought she might have let it go. But when she spotted Avery and her mother browsing the new-releases table, Piper realized she hadn't let it go at all.

Susan hovered over Avery, bending down to whisper in the girl's ear. Avery wore headphones around her neck, the cord connected to a device in the pocket of her forest-green hoodie. They moved to a table marked *Reel Reads,* consisting of a variety of movie-related books—and Susan kept her left hand on Avery's elbow. When Avery pointed at a book, Susan's hand inched down Avery's arm, settling on her wrist. As the pair moved from the table toward the computer stations, Piper stepped back into an aisle of books, wary of being caught spying. Avery paused suddenly, looking around; Susan whispered in her ear again, and Avery shook her head.

Susan's hand stayed on her daughter's elbow, and Piper saw her grip tighten.

This is just so weird, Piper thought. *Avery's too old for this.*

The bullying made more sense.

The kid practically has a bull's-eye on her back.

A computer cubicle opened up, and Avery's mother took a seat at the keyboard. Avery dragged a chair over from a nearby table—keeping her head down, looking at the floor—and parked herself directly behind her mother, facing away from the computer, the backs of their chairs touching. Two more computer stations emptied, but Avery showed no interest in math blasting or building digital Barbie avatars. Piper was surprised. Every single kid the last few hours had behaved like an Internet junkie in need of a fix, but Avery couldn't have cared less. She just sat there, back-to-back with her mother, staring off in the complete opposite direction of the screen. Avery eventually pulled a device from her hoodie—it was a Walkman cassette player. She slipped the headphones over her ears and fiddled with the buttons on the player. An annoyed look crossed her face, and she shook the Walkman, spinning it this way and that, examining it. She removed a covering on the back and switched the batteries around, but her efforts appeared in vain. Defeated, she brought the headphones back to her neck and sank into her chair, staring off, looking extremely bored. Piper wondered why she didn't at least start browsing the aisles of books, but then she remembered what Fisher had told her.

Avery's mother must be with her at all times.

Is wandering the library and looking at books considered "being away" from her mother?

Can she not leave her mother's orbit at all?

Susan appeared focused, hammering away at the keyboard, clicking on different links on the screen. She didn't seem to be keeping an eye on her daughter. If Avery wasn't allowed to wander off alone, there seemed to be a certain amount of trust that she wouldn't.

She's like a trained dog, Piper thought.

Her heart broke a bit. Piper quickly walked to the *Reel Reads* table, grabbing a few of the books she thought Avery had been pointing at earlier. Books in hand, she approached Avery and Susan, pulling over a rolling chair and sitting in front of Avery. On cue, Susan spun around in her chair to face her.

"Susan, right?" Piper asked, sticking out her hand around the child.

The woman did the same, and they shook hands. Still, she gave Piper a curious stare.

She's probably wondering how I know her name, Piper thought.

"I'm Ms. Lowery," Piper said. "I was in your daughter's class the other day. Glen—Mr. Fisher—told me you were new in town. I work here at the library."

"Nice to meet you," the woman said, relaxing. "We just moved here from downstate." She corrected herself. "I mean, we *used* to live downstate, and then we—it's a long story. Anyway, I apologize for not remembering you, it's just that—"

"Oh my gosh, it's fine."

"—we're still getting acclimated."

Her general kindness disarmed Piper. She'd expected Susan to be aloof or standoffish, her social skills as odd as her parenting, but the woman interacted with her surprisingly normally.

"I know what you mean," Piper replied. "I've only lived here six weeks."

"Oh. Do you like it so far?

"Yeah, you know. Living that wilderness life."

Susan smiled politely, and Piper sensed an awkwardness in the air. The woman was itching to turn back to the computer. Piper knew it—she'd interrupted her.

"So," Piper stammered, "I just thought I would recommend a few books to Avery, if that's okay?" She held up the books so Susan could see them.

"Of course." She touched Avery's shoulder. "Would that be okay, sweetie?"

Avery nodded, and Susan waited an extra second, her hand lingering on Avery's shoulder, perhaps seeing if her daughter would change her mind. When Avery didn't, Susan spun back to the computer before quickly turning around again.

"I'm so sorry. I'm being rude. I just have a lot of things to do right now. It's so nice that you got these computers. They're very helpful."

"Oh, no, please. Get back to what you were doing. I'm the one who stopped you from working. I'll just chat books with Avery for a bit, if you don't mind."

Susan smiled again. "Of course, of course. You two talk."

She swiveled back to the computer and immediately started clacking away at the keys. Piper looked at Avery, holding up the two books—one of them was handmade, consisting of laminated pages bound together by three round silver rings.

"Have you heard of these?" Piper asked her. "Or seen the movies? I thought you might be interested in them."

Avery took the books from Piper's hands, examining the laminated one first.

"Is this a real book?" she asked. Her voice was as soft as it had been in Fisher's classroom.

"Kind of," Piper said. "Have you seen *The Matrix*?"

Avery nodded.

"This is a *Matrix* comic series that was published on the Internet," Piper said. "Someone here printed them out and laminated them, so people could check it out. It's not official." She chuckled. "Hopefully we don't get sued."

"Cool," Avery said flatly, placing it on her lap and looking at the second book: a small paperback entitled *The Blair Witch Project: A Dossier*. She studied the cover for a few seconds, her eyes quivering.

"I saw you looking at it earlier," Piper said. "We just got it a few weeks ago. Someone actually complained about it after they saw it on the table, if you can believe that."

"Really? Why?"

"I don't know, exactly. I wasn't working when it happened. Maybe they thought it was real and the library was promoting witchcraft or something." Piper shrugged. "It was just a movie. Did you see it?"

Avery glanced upward, as if trying to remember. "I haven't—wait. Yeah, I did. It was a while ago, though."

"I heard some other kids talking about it, but I haven't read it. I mainly just shelve the books." Piper again glanced over at Mom, worrying she was doing something wrong.

Should I not be talking to Avery?

No, Susan gave me permission.

The mother was hunched over the keyboard now, leaning closer to the computer screen. Piper couldn't see what she was doing.

"So, what do you think of Clover Creek?" she asked Avery.

The girl shrugged, flipping through the pages of the *Blair Witch* book. "It's okay." Her face carried the look of classic teenage indifference— Piper thought she seemed a little older than the other eighth graders. She wondered if Avery had been held back at some point, or maybe she had one of those right-on-the-cutoff birthdays.

"Have you explored the area at all?" Piper asked.

"A little."

"There are lots of cool trails and places to camp around here. You know, if you're into that sort of thing."

"Are you?"

"Yeah, that's why I moved here. Took the cheapest place I could find. My apartment is literally above a garage. Ripley and I like it. He's a good boy."

Avery closed *The Blair Witch Project: A Dossier,* placing it on her lap on top of the laminated collection of *Matrix* comics. She furrowed her brow. "Is Ripley—"

"A dog. Sorry, I forget to clarify sometimes. He took to his new home pretty quickly. I was a little surprised. You know dogs. They can be super sensitive and dramatic. Especially about change."

"We live in a cabin."

"That's pretty neat!"

"Yeah, it's not an Abe Lincoln cabin, though. There's electricity and stuff. We aren't living off the land or anything."

"That's definitely cooler than a garage."

"There's part of an old tree in front that looks like a hand. You can climb inside of it. It's really creepy."

Surprisingly, Piper thought she knew exactly where Avery was talking about. "Near the river? Not far from—gosh, there's a name for it—but a trailhead, right?"

Avery nodded.

"I've taken my dog there before, and I thought the same thing. That *is* a creepy-looking tree."

"Like it's from a scary movie or something."

Avery's voice remained gentle and hushed, but Piper sensed a difference in her demeanor—less withdrawn, she decided. And the fear that had been in her eyes wasn't present. Still, she seemed nervous. Piper noticed her knee bobbing up and down, her fingers fidgeting and drumming the books on her lap. She constantly reached up to mindlessly adjust her thick black glasses or play with the foam ear pads of the headphones. Avery didn't look back toward her mother, but there was an awareness there, like she was constantly mindful of what was happening behind her.

"Is school here pretty different than your old one?" Piper asked, immediately wishing to take the question back. It had just slipped out, and she was worried about triggering the kid with inquiries about her past, thinking it could drum up difficult memories about her sister and father.

Happily, Avery just rolled her eyes. "It's a bit Boonieville up here, I guess."

"'Boonieville'?"

"Yeah, you know. Like, I'm worried in gym they'll teach us how to trap a raccoon or something."

The delivery was so dry, so matter-of-fact, that Piper thought if she'd been drinking something, she would've done a spit take. Her sudden fit of laughter came out as a snort, which caused Susan to peer at them before shifting back toward the computer. As she did, she adjusted her body a bit, like she was trying to block the screen.

"I heard you guys start with making moonshine in home ec," Piper joked.

"Did you hear about that?"

She tilted her head. "Wait, what?"

"I guess mobsters used to come up here during . . . oh, what was that called, when people weren't allowed to drink? Like, the whole country, I mean."

"Prohibition?"

"Yeah, that's it. We learned about it in class. Planes would fly in from Canada with alcohol. This area was a big hideout for mobsters and stuff. I guess there were FBI raids up here. That's what Mr. Fisher told us. I don't know, I thought it was neat."

"That is pretty neat."

"I know, right?"

At that moment, Piper forgot all about Avery's story, the rumors, even her odd behavior that day they'd met in class. The girl sitting in front of her was just a normal eighth grader. A bright, funny, interesting one at that. They talked more, and Avery's knee stopped shaking. Her hand stopped scratching her thigh, and she stopped fixing her glasses. Piper wondered what had changed.

Piper glanced over at Avery's mother's computer. Susan's body was still blocking most of the screen, but a sliver of the monitor's contents peeked through. Piper could tell that the mother was on AskJeeves.com, and although it was difficult to make out, Piper thought she could decipher one of the search terms:

Haunted.

Curiosity seized her.

What is she searching for? Piper thought.

"Ms. Lowery?" Avery asked. Piper snapped back.

"Yes?"

"Have you picked a winner yet?"

Piper's mind was blank, and she didn't respond.

"For the scary story contest?" Avery clarified.

Piper looked at Susan again, trying to figure out whether she was listening.

"I think we're announcing the winner right before Halloween," Piper told Avery.

"Did you read mine yet?"

"I did! And between you and me, it gave me the willies."

Avery blushed a bit, her cheeks turning a similar color to her hair. "Really?"

"Oh, yeah. It gave me nightmares."

"Are you serious?"

"Big-time."

"Are you having more contests?"

Piper was now half listening, trying to home in on Susan's search terms. She could barely make out the screen.

"Ms. Lowery?"

"Oh, s-sorry," Piper stammered. "I'm not sure, but I can ask for you. I wouldn't be surprised if we did a Christmas writing contest or something like that. Would you like me to find out?"

Avery nodded. "That'd be cool. I like to write."

"Well," Piper said, "I'm happy to read your writing anytime." She leaned in closer to Avery, and she dropped her voice. "Between you and me, I gave your scary story the highest score. Don't tell anyone, okay? At least not until the results are out."

Avery smiled sheepishly. "Thanks," she said, opening *The Blair Witch Project: A Dossier.*

Piper tried to gauge if Avery was actually interested in reading the book or not. She wasn't sure.

"I can find you some batteries, if you want. For your Walkman."

"Really?"

"I'm sure we have some somewhere." Piper rose, then stopped. "What are you listening to?"

"I tape songs off of the radio."

Piper remembered doing that as a kid, even as recently as a few years ago, before Napster changed her life. She located fresh batteries rolling around in a drawer behind the checkout counter and delivered them to Avery, who thanked her with a smile. Avery brought the headphones up to her ears, and her eyes gleamed when the music fired up. Piper returned to her cart of books, keeping one eye on the kid and her mother the whole time.

Mom surfed the Net, and Avery stared off into space, lost in the songs spinning from the cassette player.

Neither of them moved from their spot.

. . .

The fear returned ten minutes later, as Piper pushed a cart of books from one aisle to another.

Piper saw it in Avery's eyes, but this time she also felt it herself. The look on the kid's face was so startling, it made Piper glance around the library, wondering what she could be so fixated on. She spotted nothing horrifying, no stranger lurking about.

She sees something, Piper thought. *Just like she did in the classroom.*

Avery slipped the headphones down, wrapping her arms around her body. She stood and tapped her mother on the shoulder, whispering something in her ear, her head turned away from the computer station and toward the exit.

Piper couldn't hear what was said. She was on the other side of the main floor, but she hadn't taken her eyes off the two of them since they'd arrived. She wondered just what it could be that seemed to terrify this poor kid to her very core, and she questioned if it was all in Avery's head. Just the thought of it—this kid imagining something—made Piper's blood run cold. Because now *Piper* was imagining horrible things around her:

A dark figure floating above them, arms outstretched, waiting to strike. Scaly wings, hungry eyes. A demon, come to claim Avery. It circled the patrons, dipping and diving, angling for a bite. Piper didn't actually see this, of course, because it wasn't real, but she felt the goose bumps, could almost *feel* its presence.

Avery and her mother left moments later. Piper thought they were hustling a bit at Avery's urging. It was like Avery wanted to leave something behind, couldn't wait another second to get out of there, almost as if they were making an *escape*. The moment they left, Piper felt like a weight had been lifted. Like whatever terrible thing Avery had imagined had followed them into the night. The computer station that Avery's mother had been using was still vacant. Piper knew it was wrong, but she headed in that direction with a singular intent.

See what Susan had been searching for online.

Piper pulled up a chair. She hoped that because they were so eager to leave, maybe Susan hadn't cleared her browser history. She logged in using the posted credentials—*Thank you very much, shared log-in*—and went directly to the Internet browser history, but it was empty.

Mom had cleared it.

Buoyed by Susan's *haunted* keyword search from earlier—*That was what I saw on the screen before, right?*—Piper was struck by an urge to reread Avery's scary story. The collection of student stories was behind the checkout desk in the library offices, but Piper chose to fire up her online journal instead, where the story also lived, to give it another once-over. When the page loaded, she was met with a surprise. There were two comments on her post. One from a user named candlecatnip, which simply read:

Creepy

The other comment, authored by mooncorpse, read:

Any updates?

Piper had no clue who these candlecatnip or mooncorpse people were or how they had discovered her journal. But she felt a mild thrill run through her body, a strange sense of importance.

Any updates? she thought.

Do I have any updates worth sharing?

Maybe . . .

Piper cranked out a few quick sentences.

About "the kid seeing things."

About the mother searching for the keyword *haunted*.

She added that she was worried about the girl's mental well-being, before closing with:

Vibes: Perplexed
Current Jam: "Don't Fear the Reaper" by Blue Öyster Cult

That song just popped into her head, as it had every so often since the previous spring when the "more cowbell" sketch aired on *Saturday Night Live*. Piper and her college housemates had been watching the program that night, a box of wine passed among them, doubling over in laughter—the "more cowbell" expression had become a stupid running gag among the group, especially when the joke came out of the blue.

How is the pizza?

Not bad, but it really could use a little more cowbell!

She left the library a few minutes later, missing her friends and humming "Don't Fear the Reaper." Feeling the brisk October wind on her face, she wondered what exactly the kid was seeing that no one else could.

CHAPTER 7

February 19, 2000

From the Diary of Avery Wallace

Olivia visited today. I hadn't seen her in a few months. She was edgy when she walked inside—I could immediately tell. The first thing she did was examine the downstairs, the foyer, the living room, the hallway. Her eyes were looking everywhere but at me. She didn't mention it, but it was so obvious that she'd heard the rumors about me living in a haunted house. If she had asked, what would I have said? I really don't know, so I'm glad she didn't.

Once we sat down on the couch, she relaxed a bit. We talked about school, who had a crush on whom, computer club. She asked me for a couple of things, which I didn't have. The first was the original GIF file of the bunny in black glasses, the digital avatar I used to use for projects in club. I told her I didn't have it anymore, and she said it wasn't a big deal, that the other kids in the club could just re-create it. She didn't want to spoil the surprise, but she did anyway: They were making me a "We Miss Avery" website, and they wanted to put the bunny GIF on it. I promised to be surprised if I ever saw it. The second thing she asked me for was the usernames and passwords to some remote servers I used in club. I didn't have them, I told her. Honestly, I didn't know what she was talking about.

I didn't realize how much I missed talking about regular school stuff, how much I missed hanging out with everyone. She told me about some fun things the club did without me, and I was pretty jealous. Like, they went ghost hunting in a cemetery in the middle of the night, and our friend Tyler had secretly brought fireworks and shot them off, which freaked everyone out, and then they had to run away when a police officer showed up. Olivia clammed up, stopping the story, either because the ghost-hunting stuff was in poor taste, or because my mom was in the room. Apparently, the police never found out it was them. I told her that her secret was safe with me, and my mom said it was safe with her, too.

It was nice to feel normal, just for a bit. But then I watched Olivia's eyes as she left—again, looking everywhere but at me. It was like she thought something would jump out the moment she left.

And I remembered my life is anything but normal.

CHAPTER 8

The school day was almost over, and Piper was in the hallway.

It was Thursday afternoon, three days after Piper had spoken with Avery and her mother at the library. She'd just visited a sixth-grade classroom, and now her jacket wouldn't zip. Piper stood there fiddling with it. The final bell was about to ring, and even in a school as small as Clover Creek Middle School, the hallways could get a little crazy. Rambunctious boys, hustling girls. Unprepared, you could accidentally catch an errant elbow, even take a tumble.

She decided later that her zipper was not meant to catch. That she was *supposed* to be there among a sea of rowdy children, supposed to see what happened.

The bell rang, and the hallway filled up quickly. Piper did not wish to navigate the current, so she backed up against the hallway wall, waiting for the rush of students to pass. Lockers clicked open and banged shut. Kids chatted, laughed, yelled to one another. Large backpacks swung around wildly. To her right were Shane Brockway and a couple of other boys at their lockers. Even among the cacophony of middle school noise, she could make out pieces of what they were saying:

"This is going to be so good. . . ."

"She's never been away from her mom, like, ever. . . ."

"Her mom is so weird, dude. . . ."

"Just wait. . . ."

"Here they come. . . ."

Piper felt it.

Something terrible was about to happen.

Avery and her mother emerged from a classroom. The boys spotted them, and Piper saw a mischievous glint in their eyes. They started weaving their way in Avery and Susan's direction.

Do something, Piper thought. *Move your feet, head that way, stop whatever's about to happen.*

But she didn't. It was like she was frozen in place.

Piper watched it all. Two of the boys walked in between Avery and her mother, and one of them dropped his backpack to the ground. The other backed into Avery, separating her from Susan, forcing her into the flood of students cascading in one direction down the hall. Susan was temporarily blocked, and Avery was pushed forward.

Jesus, just do something, Piper thought. *Be the adult.*

Still frozen, she could only watch.

Avery looked terrified. The kid glanced back toward her mother with a pleading expression on her face, and her mouth opened, like she wanted to call out. Nothing came. A desperate, pitiful look crossed her face. One of resignation, like she knew she was caught in a trap and there was no escaping.

Susan was still stuck in the traffic jam. Avery was farther away now, ten feet, fifteen feet.

Shane was waiting.

He grabbed her by both shoulders and steered her quickly and forcefully toward a door. Not a classroom, Piper guessed—there was no window. Perhaps a small office, or a closet. Whatever the case, Piper was certain Shane was going to throw her inside. What he was going to do with her then was anyone's guess. The girl finally cried out.

"Help me! Somebody help me, please!"

The pleas shook Piper from her paralyzed state, and she rushed into action. She darted across the hallway and was pretty sure she knocked a couple of children to the ground as she desperately wormed her way through the torrent of middle schoolers. It was all a haze. She was acting on instinct now, fueled by newfound adrenaline. Avery continued to wail.

"Oh God! Please, help!"

Shane pushed the windowless door open, and Piper spotted shelves of cleaning supplies in the tiny space, a mop and bucket on the floor. A custodian's closet. Shane shoved Avery inside before pulling the door shut and holding on to the exterior handle with two hands. He leaned backward, leveraging himself against Avery's attempts to escape. Piper could hear Avery's shrieks growing shriller and more hysterical with each passing moment, and then she was there—Piper shouldered Shane out of the way, turning the handle and pushing the door open so quickly she nearly fell inside the closet herself. But she stayed on her feet, and Avery rushed forward, falling into Piper's arms in the open doorway. Tears stained her red cheeks, and words choked out of her.

"I felt it!" she said, repeating the phrase over and over again.

Piper gripped her tight. Avery sobbed into Piper's chest, the hallway growing still as students stopped to gawk at the scene. Piper looked down the corridor, and Avery's mother was rushing toward them, a look of absolute panic on her face. Avery suddenly released Piper, and she dashed toward her mother. The girl practically leaped into Susan's arms, who immediately wrapped her daughter in a strong embrace. Susan was sobbing now, too, and even though Avery's face was buried in the crook of her mother's neck, Piper could make out the new words Avery was frantically repeating.

"It was coming."

. . .

Piper beelined to her computer when she returned to her apartment, not stopping to stoop and pet Ripley, which was her usual routine. Piper instead dropped her purse on the floor and flopped into the desk chair, putting her hand on the mouse, the *Matrix* code disappearing, the desktop now fully visible. Piper double-clicked the AOL icon, and the computer modem dialed a phone number—there was a rapid succession of beeps, followed by mechanical whirs and squeals, and then a sustained crackling static as the device connected to the larger world.

Welcome!

You've got mail!

Piper ignored the message and went immediately to her online journal. She had to wait, of course, as the website slowly loaded—*My computer lab at college was so much faster,* she thought, growing impatient—but when it finally did load, she created a new post and just wrote. She remembered what Fisher had told her about writing helping people process their emotions, so she transcribed the scene in the hallway blow by blow, but with each new word that displayed on her computer monitor, instead of growing calmer, she grew more and more worried for Avery's sanity.

What was she talking about?

What was coming?

Piper hadn't the first clue.

She clicked Post, picturing the new entry traveling through underground wires at light speed, emerging on mooncorpse's computer monitor, perhaps in Florida, and then lighting up candlecatnip's laptop screen in Ontario. Of course, Piper had no idea where these anonymous Internet commenters lived—really, they could have been anywhere. But she pictured them refreshing her page and eagerly awaiting her update before she logged off her machine, not having time to wait for their potential comments. She glanced at the taskbar at the bottom of the monitor.

4:12 p.m.

Piper figured she had just enough time to change clothes and let Ripley mark up the neighborhood—one of his favorite activities. She had to be back at the school by five o'clock.

She'd been summoned to the principal's office.

. . .

Even as an adult, Piper was intimidated.

She had never been sent to the principal's office as a kid—not once—and here she was, a grown woman, feeling like she'd done something wrong.

Fisher sat to her left. The door was closed, but through the slim window Piper could see Susan and Avery sitting outside the office, near the secretary's desk. Avery looked despondent, and Susan had her hand on the back of her daughter's neck, slowly kneading her fingers into the child's skin.

"I apologize for not meeting directly after the incident," the principal said, settling into his high-backed executive-style chair. His desk was a mess. Stacks of papers and folders, multiple coffee mugs, a Black-Berry phone sitting precariously near the edge close to Piper. A gold nameplate read *Mr. Christian*—Piper didn't know his first name, and he hadn't offered *any* name when they'd met. She didn't judge him for his lack of courteousness. The guy looked frazzled, tired. His cheeks were dotted with black and gray stubble, and Piper noticed the sweat stains underneath the armpits of his white collared shirt. "I was in a meeting that I couldn't get out of. Tell me what happened in the hallway."

Piper didn't leave out a single detail but also didn't give any backstory. Just the facts of the incident.

"I'm glad you were there," Mr. Christian said, leaning forward, and Piper waited for a *but* . . .

But you shouldn't have shouldered Shane out of the way like that. The boy's family is threatening a lawsuit against the school for your use of physical force.

There was no *but*.

Only a look of gratitude on the principal's face. He turned his head toward Fisher.

"Glen, I asked you here because I know the students in question have a history, especially in your class," he said. "Did you see what happened?"

"I did not."

"What are your thoughts?"

"I've never seen anything like that happen before in this school. What Ms. Lowery described goes beyond horseplay, beyond bullying, beyond what I've seen in my classroom. It was dangerous, aggressive. The type of behavior that needs to be nipped in the bud."

Mr. Christian nodded, thinking to himself, and it took a few seconds for him to respond. "How do you think the boy should be punished?"

Fisher chuckled. "That's not for me to decide, Mike."

Mike, Piper thought.

He looks like a Mike.

She peered out the doorway window again.

Susan and Avery were still there, and Piper saw Susan whispering into Avery's ear, much like she had at the library. Avery gazed off, absently nodding her head. Susan's hand moved around her daughter's shoulder and rested on her arm.

The mother's eyes flicked toward Piper.

Embarrassed, Piper quickly averted her stare, looking up toward the ceiling.

The principal spun in his chair and rose to his feet. He walked to the large window that faced the parking lot and put his hands on his hips, looking outside. It was a bleak, windy day, and Piper saw an empty bag of potato chips skitter across the asphalt like a tumbleweed. The lot was almost completely empty.

"Let me talk to Avery first, and her mother," he said. "Then I'll ring up the Brockway father. Let him know what I'm thinking."

A pregnant pause filled the air.

Piper thought she knew why.

The Brockway father.

She imagined he could be as tough on school administration as he was on Shane. Maybe not *violent,* but no peach, either.

"What are you thinking?" Fisher asked.

Another pause.

"Indefinite suspension," the principal finally replied, not sounding incredibly confident.

"Suspension?" Fisher repeated.

Piper noticed surprise in his voice.

Mr. Christian nodded. "At least to start. Give everyone time away from each other, to cool off. Then I'll reevaluate." He pinched his eyes closed, rubbing the sockets with his thumb and forefinger. "I don't like this, Glen. I really don't. What was that kid *thinking?*"

There was an exasperation in the man's voice that Piper couldn't shake. *That Brockway kid is a special kind of trouble,* she thought, *and so is the old man.* She almost spoke up then, about seeing the boy's father smack him around a few days ago. But she didn't.

How would that information help anything?

Surely, they've dealt with him before, anyway.

The principal sighed deeply. "You two can go. And thank you again, Ms.—gosh, I'm sorry."

"Lowery," Piper replied.

"Right, Ms. Lowery—I've had a day here, you'll have to excuse me. You didn't need to do what you did. We're all very appreciative."

Fisher and Piper passed Susan and Avery as they left, and Susan gave Piper a small smile and nod before they walked into the principal's office, which Piper read as gratitude. It wasn't much, but she appreciated the gesture. Avery didn't look up, merely stared downward, staying directly at her mother's side.

The door clicked closed, and Fisher rubbed the top of his head before saying to Piper, "Want to get a drink?"

"God, do I," Piper responded.

· · ·

They were back at the pizza parlor and pub, sitting at the bar. Fisher nursed another brandy old-fashioned, Piper a beer. She was already finishing her second, even though they'd only been there for forty or so minutes—she was a lightweight, and this was lot of alcohol in a short amount of time by her standards. Surprisingly, they hadn't talked at all about Susan and Avery. Neither wanted to, Piper guessed. With the pub bustling around her and a little bit of a buzz coursing through her veins, she decided, in that moment, that she needed a break from it all. No rumormongering, no online journaling, just enjoying a few drinks.

It was a little odd that her first real friend in town was someone nearly forty years her senior, but Piper leaned into it. And Fisher really seemed to be becoming an actual *friend,* more than simply a professional acquaintance. He did most of the talking, which Piper chalked up to the liquor. She enjoyed hearing him talk, anyway—it reminded her of professors from college she'd admired. Piper learned about his three grown daughters—the youngest a veterinarian, the older two teachers, like him—all living out of state, and Piper could tell he missed them dearly. The few times Piper spoke at length, she thought she saw Fisher's eyes glistening, the way a father looks at his daughter, and she found it rather touching.

And then she spotted Shane's father.

Mr. Brockway.

Piper wasn't sure how long he'd been there, watching them, but she eventually noticed the man side-eyeing them from a booth. She recognized him immediately—that broad face and bushy beard were impossible to miss. Her thoughts quickly returned to the previous week, when Shane had exploded the can with his rifle. She remembered the anger on his father's face, his hand whirring through the air and smacking Shane on the side of the head.

He's a violent child abuser, Piper thought.

And now he's walking this way.

Words caught in her throat. She reached forward and pulled twice on Fisher's button-down sweater, motioning with her head toward Shane's father. The man was striding purposefully toward them, a tallboy can of beer in his hand. He sported perhaps the most shit-eating grin Piper had ever seen.

"Glen Fisher!" he called out, still ten feet away but moving steadily closer. Piper noticed his bloodshot eyes, and his alcohol-laden breath reached Piper before he did. "How we doing this evening?"

The man squeezed himself in between Piper and Fisher—no small feat, considering the guy could have moonlighted as a lumberjack; heck, maybe he *was* a lumberjack—and turned toward the instructor. Piper scooted her stool closer to the bar, craning her head to the right so she could see both their faces.

"Doing okay tonight, Mr. Brockway," Fisher replied.

Mr. Brockway, Piper repeated in her head.

Fisher is being deliberately respectful, more than this man deserves.

Mr. Brockway grunted, and he took a long swig of his beer, running the sleeve of his green and black flannel shirt across his lips when he finished. His beard was dark and wet with booze.

Piper wondered if he knew about Shane's suspension or if he'd been here, drinking, when the principal tried to phone him earlier.

"I was sitting over there," he said, "having a good time, and then I saw you. I thought, wow, a world-class educator in our midst." He paused, perhaps to allow his sarcasm to really sink in. "And then I thought, I really need to take advantage of this situation. So, I figured, hey, let's have a little parent/teacher conference right here, right now. Maybe chat a bit about my boy's suspension from school."

Oh, yes, Piper thought. *He knows all right.*

Fisher merely nodded, turning in his seat so he was facing forward toward the bar and away from Mr. Brockway. He signaled to the bartender that he would like his check, but Piper didn't think the bartender noticed.

"Now, where are you running off to?" Mr. Brockway asked. "Stay right there. Next round is on me, friend." He patted Fisher on the shoulder, a little harder than a friend ever would. He leaned across the bar and shouted to the bartender over the music. "Hey, Pete! I'll have two more of whatever Fisher was— Wait a second." He swung his head around to look at Piper. "You interested in what we're drinking, sweetheart?"

Piper noted his eyes. She'd seen those eyes before, many times in college, in fact. They were the after-midnight eyes, the ones that were painfully obvious when the lights came up at last call. The word *sweetheart* grated on her, and she recoiled inwardly.

She merely shook her head. "No, thank you. I'm fine."

She wished she were back in her apartment. Snuggled in a blanket, Ripley curled up beside her. But she wasn't about to leave Fisher alone with this guy. No way.

"Suit yourself," Mr. Brockway said dismissively. He swung his head back around toward the bartender. "Just two of those, Pete. That'll do fine. You can put them on my tab."

"Mr. Brockway, I—" Fisher started.

"No, no, no, no," Mr. Brockway interrupted. "This is my treat. Just wanted to thank you for all you do. Teaching the kids all day, busting your hump. Those kids can be a handful, you know what I'm saying? Especially my son, so I hear. So much so that they don't even want him at school no more."

Fisher's eyes moved between Mr. Brockway and Piper. "Why don't we schedule something? Something during the school day?"

"You don't think I have a job? Is that what you're saying?" Anger dripped from Mr. Brockway's voice.

"Of course not," Fisher said. "That was my mistake."

"I work my forty a week, same as you. I drag my ass out of bed at six thirty in the A.M. every day, because I gotta take care of my boy's needs. Ain't no mother around to do that dirty work, God rest her soul. No, I'm making breakfast and making sure he's got all his books and papers ready for the school day. Lord knows I'd like that extra hour of sleep, but it ain't happening. I take care of my boy. Did I say that already?"

"You did, yes," Fisher responded.

Mr. Brockway nodded proudly. "So I ain't got no time *before* school, or *during* school, because I'm clocked in, but I guess I could make time after school, but a man needs a little bit of time to himself, you know what I mean? Time to tend to his needs. Speaking of." The bartender set down two old-fashioneds, and Mr. Brockway clinked Fisher's glass, which the teacher hadn't touched. He downed the drink in one gulp, stifling a burp as he set the glass down. "Now, being that we're both here, and I'm a busy man with no time to meet during my boy's school day, I figured, why not have a chat right now?"

Piper noticed a few customers at the bar watching them. But the music was pulsing, the chatter was constant, and no one was coming to break this up. Fisher's face was calm, and now he was looking at Mr. Brockway with understanding in his eyes. Piper knew he was trying to de-escalate.

"You're a busy man," Fisher agreed. "And I know you care about your son a great deal. Why don't we do this over the phone one night? It will be a bit more peaceful; we'd be able to understand each other more clearly. Gets pretty loud in here, wouldn't you say? I would hate to shortchange you. I want to make sure your needs are met."

Mr. Brockway grimaced. "What the hell is that?"

"I'm sorry?" Fisher asked, his expression puzzled.

"Under your sweater. Your shirt." He pointed a shaky finger at Fisher's chest. Piper gawked at the sheer size of the man's hand.

"Oh." Fisher pulled one side of his button-down sweater to the side, revealing part of a tie-dye shirt underneath. Piper could see a grinning skeleton face, although the rest of the shirt remained obscured.

"That some sort of Satanism thing?" Brockway asked. "Devil worship?"

Fisher frowned slightly. "Not at all." He undid the top few buttons and pulled the sweater to the side a bit more, revealing a dancing skeleton. It wore a purple robe with flowing sleeves and a matching jester's hat, smiling as it danced with a bouquet of roses in hand. "It's *Seasons of the Dead* artwork. I picked it up during the '93 tour."

Mr. Brockway still looked perplexed.

"It's a Grateful Dead shirt," Fisher clarified. "The band."

Mr. Brockway chuckled dismissively. "Looks like devil worship to me. You should be the one getting suspended, not my boy. Promoting evil and debauchery in the school, and it's my boy who gets sent home. Was that your idea? Kicking my boy out of school for a few days?"

"I didn't see the incident, no," Fisher replied. "Everything was handled by the administration. Maybe you'd like to speak with them about it. I'd be happy to set that up for you."

"But you got that girl in class, right? The one with that witch for a mother?"

"I'm sorry, you said—"

"You heard me right. She's a damn witch."

The word *witch* brought the conversation to a temporary halt. Piper had absolutely no idea what the man was talking about. There were the haunted house rumors, for sure. But this was the first time she'd heard the word *witch* thrown around.

Wait . . .

Piper remembered something then—recommending *The Blair Witch Project: A Dossier* to Avery, telling her someone had complained about the book.

Was it Mr. Brockway?

Maybe. But then again, this was a small town with a big church presence. She reasoned it could've been just about anybody in Clover Creek.

"Mr. Brockway," Fisher said, breaking the silence, "I don't think it's entirely appropriate to level those accusations against the girl's mother, and as far as the incident in question—"

"I saw it," Piper finally interrupted. "I saw the whole thing. I'm the one who rescued that poor girl from the closet."

Her gall surprised even her. She'd been a bystander so far, but now she was directly involving herself.

I'm in the ring now, she thought.

Ding ding.

Mr. Brockway spun all the way around to face her. Piper looked directly at him, but in her peripheral vision, she noticed the look of pure surprise on Fisher's face. He clearly hadn't expected Piper to interject.

"Do I know you, missy?" He looked her up and down, and Piper wanted to puke.

"No, we haven't met before. I'm Ms. Lowery, and I work at the library."

"Dennis Brockway."

"Mr. Brockway, I—"

"Dennis."

"Mr. Brockway," Piper continued, noticing the sneer on his face when she refused to address him by his first name, "the girl and her mother did nothing to antagonize your son. They were minding their own business."

"That's cute," Mr. Brockway said. *"Minding their own business."* He laughed to himself.

"It's true. Your son shoved her into a closet for no reason at all. It was completely unprovoked. I got her out. She was terrified."

His upper lip curled into a sneer. "You're the woman who—now, how did the principal put this on the telephone—*came to the poor girl's aid?"*

"I did, yes."

"So, you're throwing your lot in with her, I take it?"

"What are you talking about?"

"You're taking her side in this."

"There are no sides," Piper said with a mixture of defiance and confusion. "A person—a *child*—was in peril, and I acted. I would do it again, right now."

"I'm sure you would."

Piper tried to respond, but her mouth just hung open.

What does that even mean?

"World's changin'," Mr. Brockway said. "People ain't the same. Values ain't the same. There's more of a tolerance for wickedness, immorality. And if you're coming to the aid of that kid, then I question what's going on *up there*." He pointed at Piper's head, and then at her heart. "And *in there*. Strange allegiances, I'll tell you that much. Very strange."

Piper was flabbergasted.

There was no way to respond to accusations from so far out of left field, so she didn't.

Mr. Brockway turned away from Piper and put both elbows on the bar, dropping his head. He looked to be thinking, and he smiled to himself. "Just what exactly do you know about the Wallaces?"

Not much, Piper thought.

And what exactly is he getting at anyway?

"My brother, Nathan, he lives down in Grangeville," Mr. Brockway continued, looking straight ahead now. "Told me all about the Wallaces and what happened to that family. It's witchcraft, is what it was. Told me something unspeakable happened to that girl's sister and father. Told me the mother was into the occult, that she was messing around with something in that house. It killed that girl's sister. Killed her father, too."

The rumors.

That's where they came from; that's how they traveled all the way up here.

They came from adults, from people who should know better.

"That mother stumbled across something evil. I'd put good money on something still skulking around their old place down in Grangeville. Nathan told me the church came out to take a look at it. Two men. They just wanted to help, and that mother kicked them out of the house. Can you believe that? Kicking men of faith to the curb? Something not right about that." He shook his head, rubbing his thumb across a coaster on the bar. "I know it sounds like I'm spreading rumors and all that, but sometimes rumors got teeth, know what I'm saying? You go ahead and take a look at that house, you'll see."

"Maybe I will," Piper said. She wasn't actually considering it—not at the moment, at least. She'd never even heard of the town before. It was more of a rebuttal than anything, her way of playing tough. But the name of the town stuck in her head just the same.

Grangeville.

Mr. Brockway scoffed. "Suit yourself. But don't say I didn't warn ya."

"I'll take it under advisement."

The man bit the inside of his cheek, clearly irritated. Piper wondered how many Clover Creek residents had stood up to this guy before.

"Look," he blurted, "all I know is, the mother and that girl are probably up to the same tricks here, doing occult stuff in *my* town. I don't know how it all works, or if that mother is still casting spells, but I do know that she won't leave that girl's side. Watches her like a goddamn hawk. That's what my boy tells me, anyway. Something's not right about that."

Mr. Brockway paused, making deliberate eye contact with Fisher and then Piper.

His eyes made Piper's skin crawl, and she looked away.

He noticed Piper's dismissive look.

"What, you don't believe me?" he said, incredulous. "You don't believe my brother? He is a God-fearing man, a churchgoing man. Just like me. Every Sunday, my whole life, sure as the sun rises. Take my boy, too. He knows right from wrong, good from evil. And he told me that when that young girl looks at him—when the mother looks at him—he feels the presence of something truly monstrous. So, when you tell me she didn't antagonize Shane, that's a load of *grade-A horseshit*. Their very presence in the school, in your classroom"—he spun and jabbed a finger into Fisher's chest—"that's as antagonistic as it comes. That family is carrying something with them, I'd bet my very life on it. Something dark, something Mommy summoned from the darkness. And I don't like it. It's not natural, whatever it is."

Piper sat, stunned. She wondered what it took for someone to truly think this way, to speak this way, to raise a child this way. To beat your son with one hand, then try to protect him with the other.

It's the liquor, she thought.

At least, right now it is.

But this wasn't just because of the numerous rounds he'd already thrown back, with more to come, she imagined. He had a compass. A code. The liquor just brought it to the surface, made him more willing to share what he thought with his son's teacher and a woman he'd just met at a bar.

Plus, he doesn't seem too bright.

For God's sake, he thought a Grateful Dead logo had something to do with devil worship.

Piper kept those thoughts to herself. Frankly, she didn't know how to respond at all. Neither did Fisher, it seemed. They both just let Mr. Brockway's words hang in the air, and the smirk on his face indicated that he'd taken a measure of pride in that, was satisfied he'd gotten the final word. He straightened up, grabbing his tallboy from the bar.

"Now, if you'll excuse me," Mr. Brockway said, "I'm going to get back to my party over there. You keep an eye on that girl, Glen. On that mother of hers. And when my son comes back, I trust you'll treat him fair and square, just like the other kids. He's a damn good boy. You two have a nice night."

He leered at Piper before he walked away, and she again felt abject revulsion course through her body. Fisher still appeared shell-shocked. The two locked eyes.

"You ready for that check now?" Piper quipped.

It was all she could think to say.

. . .

Fisher insisted he give Piper a ride home. She declined, and when he insisted further, she declined again. She didn't feel threatened by Mr. Brockway, more creeped out. Piper didn't feel he would come after her, which is what she assumed Fisher was thinking. Mr. Brockway was just like a million other guys. All bark, no bite. At least when it came to her, she figured.

His own flesh and blood? That was probably a different story.

The last thing she asked Fisher before they parted ways was about

Mr. Brockway's religious beliefs, if they were common in the area. She assumed they might be, based on the number of churches in town, as well as the sheer abundance of billboards she'd passed driving up to Clover Creek, giant signs proclaiming things like *Hell is Real!* and *Jesus is Lord!* Once she was north of Wisconsin Dells, the billboards were almost as regular as the mile markers on the highway. Fisher informed Piper that, yes, people took their religion very seriously around these parts, but Brockway's specific viewpoints—occultism, summoning evil and all that—were more of the outlier variety. "But we probably have a few more outliers up here than most places," he added with a smirk. Piper didn't know if that made her feel better or worse as she headed out the door of the pizza parlor and pub, into the night.

She trekked to her apartment alone, embracing the northern air, thoughts racing. Piper certainly found it interesting—*Is that the right word,* interesting?—that Mr. Brockway's brother's version of events lined up somewhat with the story Avery had submitted for the Halloween contest, regarding the mother's suspicious behavior.

But Avery's story was fiction.

Clearly.

Listening to the rantings of an intoxicated child-beater was not going to sway Piper toward a belief in the supernatural or lend credence to those outlandish rumors, no matter what the guy's idiot brother insisted. And *man,* talk about cut from the same cloth, those Brockway brothers. Piper simply couldn't shake what an unlucky break it was, that guy living in the Wallaces' old town—a coincidence Avery's mother surely had not anticipated. Piper wondered how much longer Susan and Avery would last in Clover Creek and whether they had bought their cabin or just rented it.

Maybe they're already gone, she thought.

After weeks of bullying and the hallway incident, she wouldn't blame them.

Gazing down the long highway, Piper looked as far west as the darkness would allow. She was looking for red taillights, and if she'd spotted them, she would've wondered if they belonged to Avery and her mother, bidding adieu to this town for good. But she didn't see anything, only the highway disappearing into the black night.

Piper turned into her neighborhood. It was chilly, and she saw her breath in the air. She didn't mind. It was refreshing and crisp, the antithesis of the smoky atmosphere of the pub, and it made her anticipate her next overnight camping trip—just her and Ripley. This made her feel better, more hopeful, and she pulled her Discman and headphones out of her purse. Piper slipped on the headphones and pressed Play, the CD inside spinning to life—she'd downloaded a handful of live, unreleased Dave Matthews Band songs and burned them that morning before work. She'd heard the new songs at a concert the previous summer, and she was excited to relive them. The first notes of "Raven" filled her ears, and she bopped to the music as she walked along the road.

But then she heard a different sound.

Screaming.

She stopped in her tracks and ripped off the headphones, unsure if the sound was a part of the recording.

Did I download another jacked-up MP3?

Piper heard it again. A horrible, gut-wrenching howl.

It was not the MP3.

She shoved the headphones into her purse. The shrieking came from her right, from the Brockway residence.

No, was her first thought.

No no no no no no no.

The screaming continued, and Piper wondered if Mr. Brockway had come home and was taking out his drunkenness on his son. The last time Piper had seen the man abuse Shane, she'd stood there, frozen, and now she was doing it again. She didn't know whether it was right to step in, though she'd certainly stepped in when Shane had locked Avery in that closet.

So I'm willing to help one kid but not another?

Does it matter if one of the kids is rotten?

She decided it didn't and began walking briskly toward the Brockway front door. The screaming continued, and Piper pictured Mr. Brockway with a belt or a wooden spoon, smacking the boy over and over again. Or maybe it was worse. Maybe he was using a closed fist or a baseball bat.

You like that, boy? she imagined Mr. Brockway sneering.

That'll teach you to talk back to me.

Get over here and take your punishment like a man.

Could she stop him? Probably not. But maybe her presence would shake him from a drunken stupor, just long enough for her and the boy to escape.

Piper was close now. Ten feet from the door. She heard another scream, and then what sounded like a body tumbling down the stairs.

Then a *crack*.

It sounded like bone.

Another hideous scream, followed by a gargle.

Piper approached the door, her hand trembling. She drew a shaky breath, gripped the golden handle, and pushed it open. She was not prepared for what she saw.

Shane Brockway was lying at the foot of the stairs, his right leg bent in an unnatural direction. His limp left arm was sprawled toward Piper. The boy's face was stark white, his eyes wide open.

And floating above the child, there was something else.

A black mist.

But it had substance, weight. Defined edges, in the shape of a person, though it certainly was no human. The figure seemed to shift and swirl before Piper's eyes, like endless drops of blood dispersing in rushing water. It had arms—*yes, two arms*—and they were wrapped tightly around Shane, and it had a body that seemed to meld with the boy's. The figure hovered over him, their faces touching, its head vibrating unnervingly. It looked to be smothering him. But there was no blood, no gaping flesh wound, and Shane wasn't moving.

Then the figure stopped.

The mist rose a few inches into the air, releasing Shane in a disturbingly fluid motion. It was then that Piper noticed the figure had no legs—its form ended abruptly at the waist, the rest dissolving into a trail of inky darkness, as if the lower half of its body was simply melting away.

And then it spotted her.

Its head snapped to the side, and even though Piper didn't see any eyes, it seemed to look *directly* at her.

And for those few seconds, she felt as though she was staring into an abyss, an endless void that was nothing but utter darkness.

The figure vanished.

All that remained was the Brockway boy in the foyer, the light gone from his eyes.

And it was Piper's turn to scream.

\part two\

CONNECTING...

CHAPTER 9

piedpiper77's webjournal   [entries | friends | userinfo]

6:42 A.M.—The Plot Has Extremely Thickened   FRIDAY, OCTOBER 20, 2000

I'm freaking out.

Something is happening here, and I don't know what. A kid from my town just died, and I saw . . . something. I want to call it a ghost, but I'm not sure. A figure? A black mist? It was there and then it disappeared.

I've never been a "ghosts are real" person. Heck, I've never even been in the "I want to believe" camp. But I know what I saw. I didn't imagine it. Gun to my head, right now, if someone asked me, "Do you believe?"—I'd say yes. Which is absolutely nuts.

I'm struggling to accept the truth, even though it's right here, scratching and clawing away at me. I feel like this *has* to be connected to the new girl in town—yes, the one who wrote the scary story, the girl who allegedly lived in a haunted house that killed her sister and father. The girl had a history with the boy who died, so it's not totally random that I'd make this connection. Did something follow her here? Is that what I saw? I can't believe I just wrote that.

I don't know what to do. I wish none of this ever happened, that I could just throw my gear in the car and go camping and forget about all of this.

Maybe I'll do that anyway, see if it helps.

<u>Vibes</u>: Tired
<u>Current Jam</u>: "Take a Picture" by Filter

[comment on this | comments]

CHAPTER 10

A re you going to call Mom?" Sam asked.

"I don't know," Piper said. "Should I?"

"You probably should. She'd want to know."

"That I found a dead body?"

"She should hear it from you. What if she hears it from someone else? That would be weird."

"I guess."

Piper sank into the couch, the cordless phone at her ear. She'd just told her brother the whole story. The haunted house rumors, the overbearing parenting, the bullying. Every detail about the Avery scenario and Shane's death had been laid bare—*especially* the black mist Piper had seen disappear in the air above the boy's body. She'd described it almost as a haze, similar to a waft of cigarette smoke, but thicker, darker, more defined. Like it had substance, like it was *something*.

But it was more than that.

She felt she'd been in the presence of a hostile form of energy.

Something malevolent.

Pure *evil*.

She didn't tell the police any of that, even though it had been firmly on her mind as she sprinted into the Brockway kitchen looking for a telephone. But when she dialed 911 and spoke with the operator, she didn't mention the black mass. Why would she?

I would've sounded absolutely mad.

And a child needed help—that was the important part.

Even though she was certain the boy was dead.

On that matter, there was no doubt.

She didn't believe that had truly sunk in yet. The only dead bodies she'd ever seen before that night had been lying in caskets, faces caked in ghastly, mortician-applied makeup. This was different. This was someone who had been alive seconds before, then was simply *gone*. She wondered about the lasting effects this would have on her, and she imagined she still hadn't totally processed it yet.

Maybe that black mass is a blessing in disguise, she thought.

Otherwise, I'd be fixated on that poor boy.

His empty stare.

His twisted leg.

The utter stillness.

"Are you okay?" Sam asked. "I know that is a really obvious question, but I just don't know how else to ask."

"I don't know. I think I will be."

"Are you sure that you saw a 'dark mist'?"

Piper couldn't help but notice the skepticism in his voice. It was a skepticism she'd tried to adopt herself but hadn't been successful.

"Yes," Piper said. "It *looked* at me. I wasn't seeing things."

"Maybe it was smoke or something like that. You told me they had a fire pit in the backyard, right?"

"Yes, in the backyard. Not the *foyer*. And there was no fire. I'm positive."

"Was there a candle? Or did the kid have a cigarette?"

"That's stupid."

"I'm just trying to help you, sis. He probably had an aneurysm or something. Then fell down the stairs? I don't know. Maybe he had an asthma attack, tripped and broke his leg. It could have been anything."

She threw her head back, frustrated. What he was doing right now was *the Sam Way*. He'd been like this since they were kids, always correcting Piper, always thinking he knew better. She could remember it being something as trivial as sitting at the kitchen table, telling him about her favorite breakfast cereal, and Sam would say, "Well, actually . . . ," and then explain how *his* cereal was far superior or was healthier. It was an older-brother thing, she'd always thought. Something baked into their sibling dynamic that was supposed to be there. Piper never had the last word. Not ever. She pictured him, holding his telephone, looking out his apartment window at the small skyline of Des Moines, Iowa, rolling his eyes as she described the black mass over Shane's body, and the thought of him making *that look* enraged her a bit.

Sensing her distress, Ripley craned his neck from his position on the other side of the couch, then moved and rested his head on Piper's thigh. She scratched behind his ear, and it calmed her down.

"I know what I saw," she said.

"I'm not doubting that you saw it. But maybe it was a trick of the light. I'm sure it was a really emotional moment, and you can't really trust your eyes in a situation like that. Don't they say eyewitness testimony is notoriously unreliable?"

"Why can't you just support me right now?" Piper was growing progressively irritated. Yes, the supernatural would be a leap for *any* rational person to make, but she was his sister, for God's sake. If that's what she said she saw, he should believe her.

Sam sighed on the other end of the line. "I'm sorry. I'm trying to support you. I just don't think it's healthy to think this kid was killed by a black mist, or whatever you called it. I guess I'm trying to be level-headed and calm you down."

Piper resisted the urge to go off on him.

I don't need to be calmed down, she thought.

Something evil did this.

It was right there.

"Sam," Piper said, focusing on Ripley's gentle demeanor, hoping it would seep into her, "I know it sounds crazy. I'm fully aware of that. But if you'd experienced what I just experienced, you would give me the benefit of the doubt. So can you give me that right now? Just for a bit? Pretend this is connected to the Wallace family. Humor me, I guess."

"You really want me to humor you?"

"Yes, *humor* me."

It was not a suggestion.

There was a slight hesitation before Sam began speaking again. "Okay. Was this girl—what's her name again?"

"Avery."

"Maybe Avery pushed him down the stairs or something. Like, some kind of revenge thing? He hits his head, and now he's dead."

"Sam, there was no one else in the house. The police walked through it, like, five minutes later. And what does that have to do with the mist that was—"

"I'm just exploring all possibilities here. She could've run off, or maybe she hid, and they didn't find her. Kids are good at hiding, you know? I'm just saying. He bullied her, and she got revenge. Maybe she's a murderer."

The word stung a bit.

Murderer.

Piper considered this. "I don't think so. And I *really* think I would have seen her, or the cops would have found her. She's just a kid, not some master criminal."

"Right, right," Sam responded. Again, Piper sensed the skepticism in his voice. It was a little patronizing, but at least he *was* humoring her. That was what she'd asked him to do.

Still, it made her blood boil.

"None of what you're saying explains that dark *thing* floating over the kid's body," Piper said.

"I . . ." He paused again. "I don't think I have any explanations for that. Other than . . ."

Say it, Sam, Piper thought.

Say, "You're delusional."

It's right there on the tip of your tongue.

He cleared his throat. "If no one else was there, and you think the black mist is somehow *connected* to this family . . ."

"Yes, go on."

"You told me that the guy, the brother down in, uh—"

"Grangeville."

"Yeah, the stuff about the mother summoning an evil spirit, or whatever, at their old house in Grangeville, that they brought it with them. I don't know, maybe the family is harboring an evil presence and only the mother can control it. She decides to *summon* that presence to the surface. You know, *wham.* It takes out the bully. To protect her daughter."

Piper considered the idea. She couldn't determine if it was outlandish or sensible, which was a problem.

"Do you really think so?" she asked.

"Look, I'm just trying to make sense of everything. Maybe *Mommie Dearest* unleashed the black mist figure from afar. It tracks, is all I'm saying. Kind of."

He was just about done humoring her—Piper could tell. Yet, she was impressed with how quickly her brother was able to formulate a pretty solid theory, as far as supernatural theories went. She decided it was due to his not being neck-deep in everything, having a cleaner perspective. Still, Piper couldn't believe they'd arrived at this potential conclusion, that *Avery's mother might be controlling a dark spirit,* but here they were. Piper remained skeptical, but it was a possibility.

God, I really believe in this stuff now.

I'm one of those people.

She wondered how crazy she sounded on the phone to Sam but quickly decided it didn't matter.

She'd seen what she'd seen.

And what she'd seen was dangerous.

Could the black mist be used like some sort of attack dog?

It was enough to make Piper's head spin.

"Do you know officially how he died?" Sam asked. "Like, what the doctors said, I mean."

Yes, I know what happened.

A black mist did this.

"No, I don't," Piper said. "I'll probably find out soon, I guess."

And whatever they say, you'll know the truth.

You saw it.

It looked right at you, for God's sake.

"Have you told this stuff to anyone else?" His voice carried a different weight than earlier.

"No." The word rolled off her tongue quickly and defensively. She didn't mention her online journal, although the thought had entered her mind.

Does anonymous web journaling count?

A pause on the other end.

Piper thought she might've dropped the call.

"Sam?" she said.

"I'm still here," he said.

"Look, can you help me with this?"

"What do you want me to do?"

"I don't know. I really suck at searching for things online. You're way better at that than me. Do that thing where you write code, or whatever."

"To search what?"

"Ghost websites, or those weird forums where you submit things about paranormal stuff you've experienced. Maybe someone else has seen what I've seen. I went to a few, but you need to make accounts, and the searching is nonexistent—"

"You want me to scrape websites? Is that you're talking about?"

"I don't know what it's called. Just help me."

"Okay, let me see what I can do."

He sounded annoyed, but at least he'd said he would help. Piper sidestepped into other topics. Clover Creek, camping, Sam's work in software development. It felt good not to discuss the black mist or the dead body, but thoughts of Shane lingered, gnawing at her. And Sam didn't repeat his question—*Have you told this stuff to anyone else?*—again.

But he had been worried.

Piper could tell.

His inquiry had simply drifted away, and Piper was content to let it sink.

. . .

Her computer beckoned.

She logged on directly after her phone call with Sam, the crackling and beeping of the modem a familiar and comfortable escape.

Piper queued up fresh downloads on Napster first, eager to burn a new playlist for a long hike with Ripley. She opted for more poppy, up-beat choices—Janet Jackson, Christina Aguilera, Backstreet Boys, TLC, a few others—and as the downloads began, she wished Napster were the only thing on her mind. Of course, it wasn't. Her journal was waiting right there, and before she could even decide if returning to it was a healthy thing to do, the cursor was moving to the shortcut link, Piper's finger clicking the mouse.

There was fresh activity.

New comments on her last post.

And not just mooncorpse and candlecatnip, although they had re-turned, providing fresh insight. Now there were more users, names she didn't recognize.

Seven of them, in fact: darksphere, verocity, jenna74, northbynorth-best, dreamfinder, mrsoundwolf, and bluegnomegarden.

Piper still had no clue how anyone was finding her online journal.

Are they keyword-searching creepy *or* ghost?

Do they just surf random blogs?

The comments this time around were more involved, more inquisitive, as if these people were participating in a role-play game.

If you know the town where the girl is from, you should go check out the haunted house, read a comment by darksphere.

Verocity chimed in with, *How far is the town? You should really go see if the rumors are true. Then you'll know what you're dealing with. Please write more!*

Multiple users wanted more specifics, like the names of the people involved.

Bluegnomegarden simply responded with *OH MY GOD!!!!!*

Mooncorpse expressed concern, writing, *You said it disappeared, but where did it go? Is it still out there? You better watch out. I wouldn't mess around with this stuff.*

Reading these comments, strangely, calmed her. Even the ones from users who were concerned for her well-being. In a way, the sentiments' existing solely on the Internet made her entire predicament seem fake or made-up—like she hadn't *actually* seen a terrible entity disappear over a boy's broken and dead body—and for a moment, Piper felt as if she were a performer or entertainer of sorts, tap-dancing for these anonymous people. Like it was role-play—even though her situation was far too real. Still, it made her feel better, listened to. *Respected.* She had phoned her brother with mixed emotions, seeking validation for her experience yet still wanting to be talked out of what she'd seen, knowing full well it was impossible to believe. But then she'd realized, *No, I only want the validation,* and Sam had only given her that through gritted teeth, with a dose of condescension thrown in.

He's wrong, Piper thought.

I saw that thing.

She again read the comments on her computer screen—scrolling down, then scrolling up.

They believe me.

These random people on the Internet are treating me with more dignity than my own brother.

She craved more of that validation. And, she decided, the commenters raised some salient points. This *thing* could still be out there. She wasn't positive it had killed Shane Brockway—*Although I very much doubt those dark arms were releasing the kid from a cuddly embrace*—and Piper felt compelled to investigate further. She needed understanding, and at that moment, she had none.

Piper opened a new tab in her browser and searched *Grangeville newspaper office.*

She had to make a call.

CHAPTER 11

SAM'S WEB SCRAPING SESSION

2000-10-20 21:36:32.123 [main] samwise943@hobbitonstation:~$ ./
autoscraper.sh -s "dark mist" "clover creek"

2000-10-20 21:36:32.927 [main] INFO Project Mist Forum Scraper—Starting
web scraping session . . .

2000-10-20 21:36:38.789 [main] INFO Project Mist Forum Scraper—Accessing
URLS: http://paranormalwisconsin.net, http://wisconsinghosthunters.com,
http://submityourghost.com, http://midwestghostencounters.net

2000-10-20 21:36:38.850 [main] INFO Project Mist Forum Scraper—Creating
New Accounts . . .

2000-10-20 21:38:59.223 [main] INFO Project Mist Forum Scraper—Logging
In . . .

2000-10-20 21:39:42.098 [main] INFO Project Mist Forum Scraper—Extracting
forum posts . . .

2000-10-20 22:01:36.401 [main] INFO Project Mist Forum Scraper—Web
scraping session completed successfully.

2000-10-20 22:01:36.502 [main] INFO Project Mist Forum Scraper—0 Results
Found

2000-10-20 22:03:12.874 [main] samwise943@hobbitonstation:~$ ./ autoscraper.sh -s "dark mist" "grangeville"

2000-10-20 22:03:12.935 [main] INFO Project Mist Forum Scraper—Starting web scraping session . . .

2000-10-20 22:03:19.453 [main] INFO Project Mist Forum Scraper—Accessing URLS: http://paranormalwisconsin.net, http://wisconsinghosthunters.com, http://submityourghost.com, http://midwestghostencounters.net

2000-10-20 22:03:19.564 [main] INFO Project Mist Forum Scraper—Creating New Accounts . . .

2000-10-20 22:05:41.756 [main] INFO Project Mist Forum Scraper—Logging In . . .

2000-10-20 22:06:24.319 [main] INFO Project Mist Forum Scraper—Extracting forum posts . . .

2000-10-20 22:30:35.612 [main] INFO Project Mist Forum Scraper—Web scraping session completed successfully.

2000-10-20 22:30:35.723 [main] INFO Project Mist Forum Scraper—0 Results Found

CHAPTER 12

9:22 A.M.—Just the Facts, Ma'am   SATURDAY, OCTOBER 21, 2000

My brother emailed last night. He did some web scraping on a few web-sites for sightings of a "black mist" in my area and the girl's old town. He said he found nothing. Bummer.

BUT I called the newspaper office of the girl's hometown last night and a reporter called me back this morning. I just got off the phone with him. Must be a slow news day around those parts. Anyway.

Here's what I found out:

1. Her sister died of a virus. This happened a little over a year ago. The reporter wasn't sure what it was, but it happened quickly. She wasn't murdered, didn't go missing or anything like that. Nothing spooky, just a tragedy.

2. The family moved away several months later.

3. The father died about six months ago. He was back in the area (the reporter wasn't sure why—he was just going off an article he'd

found), and he got in a single-car accident on the highway a few hours outside of town. The reporter said there were no tire tracks or swerve marks, so the police didn't think he was avoiding an animal. They think maybe he fell asleep or was distracted by his BlackBerry, which was found in the car with him. He went right into a tree, full speed, the police determined.

4. The reporter has not heard any haunted house rumors.

5. He's not sure if anyone lives in the house right now.

That's all I've got. I don't work tomorrow, so I'm thinking about taking a drive down that way. It's not that far, maybe four hours or so. Might check out the house, if I can find it.

I think it could help, right?

Vibes: Indescribable
Current Jam: "I Need to Know" by Marc Anthony

[comment on this | comments]

CHAPTER 13

April 12, 2000

From the Diary of Avery Wallace

It's been weeks since Dad died. The guilt hasn't left me. It's a burning feeling in my chest that won't go away. Mom says it's not my fault, even though we both know that's not true. It was my idea to leave. If we'd never left Grangeville, Dad would never have gone back to the house alone, and he'd still be alive.

My thoughts continue to travel back to the house. I can't help it. There is this flash of a memory that appears from time to time, one I can't seem to grab on to. It's hard to explain, but I just can't shake this feeling that I have about our old house.

Something is still there.

CHAPTER 14

Piper half expected the house to be Gothic. Pointed arches and doorways, a steepled roof, maybe some gargoyles for good measure.

It wasn't.

The house in Grangeville was cookie-cutter, suburban. It reminded Piper of the home she grew up in. It was also easy to find. She'd located the address in a gas station phone book, and it still listed Richard and Susan Wallace as the residents. Curious, she'd also searched the phone book for *Brockway,* and there it was. *Nathan Brockway.* Just like Dennis Brockway had said. This troubled Piper—*The guy wasn't lying about having a brother in Grangeville*—but it also increased her anticipation about what she'd discover inside.

A blue Dodge Neon was parked in the driveway: It appeared the house had a new resident. Piper parked across the street, and she slowly made her way to the front door, questioning again why she was doing any of this, how she'd gotten to the point where she was willing to spend her Sunday investigating a rumored haunted house.

The dark mist flashed in her mind.

It was just for a moment—about the same amount of time she'd seen it hovering in the Brockway foyer—and it made her remember why she was there.

Piper rang the doorbell with no hesitation, but when she heard footsteps and saw the dark silhouette of a person walking to the front door through the frosted glass, she panicked. She hadn't thought of a story as to why she was here, why a complete stranger from up north wanted to see the house. It had been a four-and-a-half-hour drive, and still, she hadn't thought to come up with something.

The door opened, and a man stood in the doorway. He was in his late forties, Piper guessed, with a slight paunch and a combover, dressed casually in sweatpants and a white undershirt. His unshaven face showed a couple of days' worth of stubble. The man looked at her somewhat suspiciously, and Piper wondered if he thought she was a door-to-door salesperson.

"H-Hi," she stammered. "You don't know me. My name is Piper."

He was still caught off guard, not looking to interject, so Piper kept going.

"This might seem really weird, but I was wondering if I could look around your house?"

"You want to—"

"I'm sorry, I just launched right into it. I live up north in Clover Creek, and there's a family that just moved there that used to live in this house."

She considered lying then. Telling the man she was a relative, or that she was a family friend who was looking to locate an item lost in the moving process. But she decided to go a different route.

"I'm writing a blog," she said. "I heard that this house used to be haunted, and I just wanted to take a look. My readers want to know what's inside." She said that last part kind of sheepishly.

At this, the man's eyes lit up. "You heard my house is haunted?" He seemed pleased, excited.

"I know, it's really weird."

He looked her up and down. Nothing sexual, Piper decided—more to see if she was on the level, or maybe a threat. Seemingly satisfied that she was not a potential ax murderer, the man invited her inside.

He shut the door behind her. Piper surveyed her surroundings: a staircase just off the foyer, a nearly empty sitting room on the left, what looked to be an office with closed double doors on the right. She had hoped to sense a malevolent entity the moment she entered, traces of evil that had lingered after the Wallaces had left. *The potential birthplace of whatever it is that I saw,* she thought. But no, it was just a house. A pretty barren one, at that. There was no artwork, no family photos lining the staircase. The man walked down the short hallway toward the back of the first floor, and Piper followed.

"What's the name of your blog?" he asked, turning his head to look at her. "I keep up with a few of them. Sports ones, mainly. Some tech ones."

"Oh, I guess it's more of an online diary than anything."

It was true. She'd often thought of it as a blog, but the website advertised itself as a journaling platform. *Blog* sounded more official, although she felt anything *but* official. Piper became a little embarrassed, thinking she'd misrepresented herself, that the guy thought she had hundreds of thousands of readers or some ultra-official URL.

"Oh, yeah. I've seen those diary websites," he said.

"Do you have one?"

"I'm not that interesting," he said, pulling out a stool for her at a breakfast bar. "You said it's Piper, right? I'm Bill. Bill Oakley."

"God, you think I would've asked you that. I'm so sorry." She took a seat, and Bill settled on the stool next to her. The kitchen was clean, neat. Off the kitchen was the living area. Just a couple of powder-blue couches and a television. There was a fireplace, and the mantel was empty.

"No, no, it's fine," Bill said. "So you're saying my house is *actually* haunted? Or you heard that it was haunted?"

"Heard. Weird, right?"

He looked at her purse. "So, is this an interview? Do you need to record this or take notes or—"

Piper chuckled. "I honestly hadn't thought that far ahead. I just got in my car and came here. You know, a total whim."

Bill smiled. "Well, okay, then. I'm not sure what I could tell you about this place. Everything seems normal. Quiet. No hauntings or ghosts or anything like that."

"When did you move in?"

"About six weeks ago. Sharon, my wife—*ex-wife,* well, soon to be ex-wife—we're getting a divorce. This is my new place, I suppose. Close to her, close to the kids." He looked off, thinking about something, and then Piper noticed a twinkle in his eye. He looked back at her. "Haunted, *really?*"

"You seem intrigued."

"It's not every day someone rings your doorbell and tells you that you live in a haunted house. Honestly, this is the most exciting thing that's happened to me in months."

The near-empty house made sense now. This was a man living alone, probably for the first time in a long time. She felt herself loosen up, happy that she was seemingly making this guy's day. Or month. Or *year.*

"Your neighbors haven't said anything?" Piper asked him. "About this house?"

"Haven't spoken to them much. Outside of a few introductions, a few pleasantries here and there."

"No welcome basket, I take it?"

He chuckled. "Not yet."

"So you don't know anything about this place? About the family that used to live here?"

He shook his head. "Not much. Just that it had been empty for quite a while. The guy across the street . . . God, what's his name? I'm not much of a neighbor. Anyway, he told me that a family lived here, a girl died, and they moved out months later. It kind of sat here for a while, apparently. He thought they might come back, but they never did. And that was it. Kind of ho-hum as far as stories go. He was pretty matter-of-fact about it."

"He didn't mention a couple of pastors or priests coming by, and the mother kicking them out? That she was all, what's the word, *occulty?*"

She felt gross repeating the rumors—even if they might have been true—but did so anyway.

"Are you serious?"

"That's the scuttlebutt."

Bill looked like a kid on Christmas morning. "Oh, come on," he said, a grin crossing his face. "Don't leave me hanging any longer. What's the deal with this place?"

Piper told him the story. Halfway through, she was struck by how *made-up* the whole thing sounded, and she wondered if Bill actually believed a single word. She watched his expression change with each roller-coaster turn of her tale—if he wasn't buying it, he was certainly enjoying it.

When she finished, she asked him, "So, what do you think?"

"I'm thinking I should check out that online diary of yours," he said. "Do you want to look around?"

. . .

They walked the house together. Piper asked him numerous times if he was comfortable doing this, and Bill continually assured her that it was okay. He showed her the primary bedroom, and Piper was a bit saddened to see a king-size mattress on the floor. No bed frame.

"I'm waiting for the Black Friday sale," Bill joked.

Piper wasn't sure what she was looking for, but her eyes examined every inch of every room all the same. White baseboards lined the floors upstairs, with matching silver doorknobs on the doors. They moved to the next bedroom, and Piper felt a mournfulness fill her gut. Not solely because the bedroom was only partially furnished—a stark reminder of Bill's divorce and living arrangements—but because Piper was looking at what had undoubtedly been a child's bedroom.

It could have been Avery's bedroom, she thought.

Or her sister's.

She remembered what the reporter had told her, something about a virus taking the girl quickly. Piper knew it probably wasn't in the twin bed before her—*They wouldn't have left the bed behind, would they?*—but the girl could've fallen ill inside this very room. Maybe even died.

Or . . .

There was the other thing.

Rumors of the mother summoning a dark force, something that killed the girl.

Piper thought of Avery's story then—she couldn't help it. She imagined it being real, a blow-for-blow retelling of actual events, even if they directly contradicted what the newspaper reporter had told her on the telephone.

She got sick.

Died of a virus.

No matter. She'd come all this way, she figured, might as well explore every option.

Piper slowly opened the closet door, but there was nothing inside. Just a couple of stray metal hangers. Piper put both hands on one part of the wall anyway and leaned her forehead against it. She knew she looked silly—like some kind of psychic or medium—and she wondered about the look on Bill's face, standing in the bedroom outside the closet as he watched her, but she didn't care. She just closed her eyes, listening for screaming from realms beyond, treating Avery's short story as fact. She heard nothing.

Just silence.

The same silence she heard in the other closets, the same absence of evil presences she felt in every room upstairs.

Nothing.

Nothing.

Nothing.

They moved downstairs, and Piper asked if there was a basement. There was an unfinished one, Bill told her. Mainly concrete, filled with boxes of Bill's things. They explored that next, and it was more of the same. Piper wouldn't have said she was entirely surprised. If the black mist had followed Avery and her mother to Clover Creek, it made sense that there would be nothing here.

Why did I think there would be? Piper thought.

Because a drunk at a bar and some Internet commenters told me so?

Still, she was disappointed.

She knew her journal readers would be, too.

They finished on the main floor. Living room, kitchen, sitting room. Piper had just about given up hope when Bill opened the double doors of his office next to the foyer. It was the most well-furnished room of the house. There was a workstation with a computer, a comfortable-looking black office chair parked in front. Crystal CD-ROM cases lined a long shelf along the top of the desk. Two large speakers flanked the gray monitor, and a printer rested on another shelf above the computer tower. But it wasn't the computer station that gave her pause. It was what was behind it. That portion of the wall looked brand-new, or like the original wall had been recently touched up. Piper hadn't noticed any other new paint or work done on any other area of the home.

"What happened here?" she asked.

"You know, I'm not sure. When I moved in, this wall right here was in bad shape. It looked like someone got halfway through fixing it and then stopped."

"How bad was it?"

"Honestly, it was all beat up."

"Really?"

"Yup. There were a bunch of holes everywhere. Big ones, at that."

"Why, do you think?"

"Beats me. I didn't really think anything of it and had it patched. Just one of those things, you know? Maybe it was an abandoned home renovation project or something. But now that you're telling me this place might've been haunted, I'm reconsidering." He laughed, and Piper joined him, hers sounding a bit forced.

She gazed at the wall, wondering what could've happened. Again, her mind traveled back to Avery's short story, one of the first things that got her into this mess. Avery had written about a bogeyman in the closet, and Piper wondered how it might connect.

But that was a closet, not a wall in the office, she thought.

And that was just a story, anyway.

Right?

Piper continued to stare at the wall, baffled. Maybe it was something, maybe it wasn't. She knew the online commenters would speculate wildly.

But at the moment, she hadn't the first clue.

CHAPTER 15

[entries | friends | userinfo]

11:01 P.M.—Road Trip Results   SUNDAY, OCTOBER 22, 2000

Hey. I went to the house, like you all wanted. You might be bummed to learn there wasn't anything out of the ordinary. Only a beat-up wall in the den downstairs. Nothing too weird about that. Honestly, my house senior year in college had similar problems, and no one ever accused that place of being haunted.

Sorry to disappoint everyone.

Vibes: Weird
Current Jam: "Absolutely (Story of a Girl)" by Nine Days

[comment on this | comments]

CHAPTER 16

The knocking surprised her.

It was eight on Monday morning, and Piper had just gotten out of the shower. She threw on some fleece pants and a T-shirt, drying her hair with a bath towel as she made her way to answer. She assumed it was the landlady.

Piper felt her heart in her throat when she opened the door.

Standing there, hands jammed in the pockets of a brown Carhartt jacket, was Dennis Brockway.

She'd never felt more vulnerable. This wasn't a crowded bar—this was her home, she wasn't wearing a bra, and her hair was still wet. She felt the damp ends tickle the back of her neck as her mind fumbled for what to say to a man who'd recently lost his son.

"Oh," was all she managed.

Ripley trotted over to the hulking figure in the doorway. The dog sniffed Mr. Brockway's boots and blue jeans, and the man bent down and scratched behind the dog's right ear. Ripley's tail wagged happily. Piper was struck by the man's sheer girth, how he seemed to absolutely dwarf her Labrador.

Mr. Brockway straightened and cleared his throat. "I apologize for barging in on you like this. Is it okay if I come inside?" His voice was hoarse, cracked. He'd been crying, Piper realized. She nodded absently and moved aside.

Mr. Brockway entered and moved aimlessly around the apartment. Ripley followed him, sniffing at his heels. The man ran his hand across the top of Piper's sofa, and he looked around.

"Nice little place you got here," he said. "I helped Linda fix it up a few years ago. Laid down the flooring, worked on the bathroom. Some of it was kinda tricky. I hope it's okay."

He plopped down on the sofa, not bothering to unzip his jacket. Piper gently took a seat in the easy chair a few feet away, thankful she'd moved her basket of laundry from that spot after she'd woken up. She felt safer in the easy chair, not sharing the sofa with him. Still, his demeanor was certainly different than it had been at the bar. The drunken swagger was gone. The man before her looked lost, broken.

"I'm so sorry," she said. "About your son."

Ripley lay at her feet now, and she was grateful for his presence. Mr. Brockway's lips drew together, and he nodded, looking off. His jaw clenched, and Piper knew he was holding back tears. She wondered how comfortable he was showing emotion in front of strangers—she practically was one.

"Can I ask what happened?" Piper asked him.

"That's what I came to ask you about." He rested his elbows on his knees, interlacing his fingers together. He rocked forward and back, meeting Piper's gaze.

"I told the police everything."

"I know you did. But I just want to hear it from you."

Piper grew nervous, and she focused on maintaining her composure as she spoke. "I heard . . . screaming as I was walking past your house." She paused, gathering her words. "It sounded like a person was in trouble. I went to the front door, and I heard someone fall down the stairs. I opened the door, and I found him there. In the foyer. He was . . . already gone."

She realized that she hadn't said his name. It seemed less personal that way, like the incident was a dream or a passing thought that never materialized.

But she knew it wasn't.

The boy's name was Shane, and something killed him.

A black mist.

Mr. Brockway held Piper's gaze. She detected an anger there, below the surface. She was terrified of it emerging, and she looked down at her hands, realizing she was wrapping and unwrapping the towel around her wrist. She wondered what it would take for his rage to break through.

Three drinks?

Five?

He hadn't been drinking this morning, she thought. Or hoped.

His eyes softened. "That's it?"

"I called the police right after I found him."

"There was nothing else?"

Piper shook her head.

"Are you sure? Think, *damn it.*"

His anger flashed, and Piper dug her nails into the towel. She looked to the doorway, hoping that Ms. Hermann would pop in. Or maybe Fisher would stop by, even though he'd never been there.

No, he's teaching right now.

Teaching one fewer student.

You're all alone.

Piper searched for words, not sure how to respond to Mr. Brockway's inquiry. She'd told him what she'd seen, told the police the same. What else was there?

Oh, that's right.

The black mass that was smothering his son.

She hadn't told the cops that, so how could she tell the boy's father? Piper just didn't know how it would look for her, saying she saw one thing and then changing her tune a few days later. She envisioned a police officer's response if she went to the station later that morning.

"You saw what now, ma'am?"

Then she pictured Mr. Brockway's response, and she doubted it would be as polite.

"Dennis," she said, "I wish I knew what to say. I'm so, so sorry. There are no words. I mean it. I wish I could've done something, heard his screams sooner. . . ." She trailed off, not sure where she was going with her explanation.

Mr. Brockway shot off the sofa, and Piper froze. He lumbered toward her—a towering presence—and morbid thoughts flashed through Piper's mind.

He's going to put his hands around my neck. . . .

Squeeze until I'm blue . . .

Bury me in the forest . . .

She tried to say something, to scream, but the sounds caught in her throat. She couldn't even move. She was stiff with panic, her body unable to defend itself. Ripley sprang to his feet, and the dog stood there, tail between his legs, confused. Mr. Brockway moved past them both to the front window, resting his arm on the sill and his forehead on the glass. Piper exhaled, and the dog lay back down. She was shaking now, and she realized that the towel was wrapped around both her wrists, like she was about to use it to choke an attacker. Piper undid the twists, hoping Mr. Brockway didn't notice. The man turned his head, looking at Piper with one eye.

"It just don't make no sense," he said, his voice turning feeble. "Doctors did the autopsy yesterday. And you know what they tell me? They tell me Shane died of a brain aneurysm."

He let the phrase hang there for a moment—*brain aneurysm*—and Piper thought he did so deliberately, to give her time to dwell on it. He wanted to see her reaction. She gave him none. She kept her poker face, even though the autopsy results certainly caught her off guard.

If someone is killed by a black mass, she thought, *is that what medically occurs?*

She obviously had no idea, and then thought back to her brother's first reactions on the phone. He'd predicted it: a brain aneurysm. The Sam Way had won out again, at least according to the coroner.

Piper continued to stare at Mr. Brockway, stone-faced, offering nothing.

The man continued. "I say, *a brain aneurysm?* Really? My boy? Healthy as a goddamn horse. Ain't no problems before that night. Not a one. And you know what else?"

Piper shook her head.

"His computer was broken. Machine was only six months old, and he took damn good care of it. It was a birthday gift. And somehow all them cords were yanked from the wall, electronics all fried up. Police didn't even notice that stuff, but I did. Now, why would that happen on the same night he died? Computer worked fine that morning—he was on some website when I needed to make a damn phone call—and I haven't touched the machine since my boy passed. But I tried to use the computer yesterday, and it won't turn on, and that's when I notice the unplugged cords. I plug 'em back in, and it still won't start. So I open it up and look inside, and you know what I see? Little bulges on the motherboard. Streaks, discoloration. Burn marks. Thing was all fried up, like it had some serious water damage or something. Doesn't work at all. Totally dead. There was an empty bottle of soda on the floor, which is likely where the liquid came from, I imagine.

"I told the doctor and the police about this, and you know what they tell me? That maybe he just unplugged the cords on his own, or maybe he yanked out the cords with his feet in a panic when the aneurysm set in. Knocked over a drink, too—that's how the motherboard and what-have-you might have short-circuited. Or he could've done it by accident, they say, before he died. Just a bad spill, then unplugged it to take a look. But I doubt that. He took *fine care* of that thing. I know my boy; that wouldn't happen. Something doesn't smell right here. You know what I mean?"

Piper sat motionless.

She didn't know what he wanted from her right now.

Just what does he think happened to that computer, and why does it make a lick of difference?

On the night in question, Piper hadn't gone upstairs, never saw the broken computer. Not that she would've noticed it anyway—it was just a computer tower, which sounded like it sat on top of or underneath Shane's desk. She'd simply called 911 and gone back outside, sitting down on the front stoop in a daze, waiting for the authorities to arrive. Investigating the house had never occurred to her. After what she'd seen, she didn't want to be in the house *at all.*

"And what about the rest of his room?" she asked.

"What do you mean?"

"Was there anything weird or—"

"Rest of his room was fine."

"But you think someone might have—"

"Goddamn it, I don't know what to think," he snapped. Mr. Brockway pushed himself off the window, pacing around Piper's small apartment. He stopped by the television. "I'm sorry if it seems like I'm harassing you about this, miss, really, I am. It just makes no sense. My boy is gone, doctors and police say one thing . . ." He stared hard at Piper. "You're positive? No one else was at my house that night?"

His voice was not threatening now. It was pleading, desperate. Piper almost broke. The man clearly thought there was more to his boy's death than a medical tragedy. He was searching for answers, just like her. She was moments away from telling him what she knew, what she saw. But she convinced herself not to.

You can't change your story now.

Brockway will hurt you.

He will hurt other people.

Piper didn't know that for a fact. But she'd seen him be violent before, had heard his drunken ramblings. She'd witnessed how the principal had nearly trembled in fear at the thought of even *speaking* to him over the phone.

She shook her head softly. "I didn't see anyone. I'm sorry, but I didn't."

"Not even . . ."

Piper knew what he was going to say.

The girl.

Or her mother.

He was thinking that—Piper was positive. His son had just gotten suspended for bullying Avery, and he had already decided that the Wallace family was dangerous and into the occult.

Then his son had died.

Piper knew he believed it was more than coincidence.

Mr. Brockway had thought he'd discovered an anomaly with the broken computer, and now he was trying to make a connection. He didn't quite know what the connection was yet, but he was *damn sure* of who was involved. If he'd tied one on that morning, he would've said their names. As it stood, he let the words hang there, and Piper let them. She stared at him, expressionless.

Mr. Brockway gritted his teeth, fighting back tears. He glanced upward now, toward the ceiling. "Okay, okay. Just thought there might be more to this, is all. If you remember something else, anything at all, you let me know. Wake is on Wednesday, funeral is on Thursday. You can disturb me then, or any time of day before that. I mean it. Anytime." He thanked her and left, stopping to scratch underneath Ripley's chin one last time. When the door clicked and the plastic blinds covering the small window had finished rattling, Piper felt an enormous weight lift from her chest. She hadn't realized it when the man was there, but she'd felt like she was being crushed their entire conversation.

When she heard his boots descend the final step, the tears came pouring out of her. Ripley rose to his feet and placed his head on top of Piper's legs, and Piper brought the towel up to her face, wailing into it.

If there were ever a moment to tell Mr. Brockway the truth, that was it. But the moment had passed.

She hoped she would not regret it.

CHAPTER 17

Piper expected a police officer to show up at the library that same day to ask more questions.

She knew it was silly.

Mr. Brockway was grasping at straws with the computer stuff. Piper knew that; he knew that.

So Shane broke his computer.

So what?

It was like that wall in the Wallace den in Grangeville.

Possibly something, but very likely nothing.

On the subject of the wall, Piper had checked her journal comments before heading into work after the confrontation with Brockway. The online reactions were mainly subdued and disappointed, penned by the same commenters as before and a few fresh drop-ins. There was some theorizing about the wall being the origin of the bogeyman from Avery's story—that perhaps Charlotte's room *was* the den—but that didn't make a whole lot of sense.

Piper's frustration over what she'd seen in the Brockway foyer only grew. Every hour that had passed since the swirling black mass vanished, she'd questioned it more. And now, with the news of the brain aneurysm, she wondered how close she was to deciding she had a screw loose and had imagined the whole thing.

God, she thought, *my brother will really do a victory lap over this one.*

She pushed the thought from her mind and instead focused on her rather banal duties at the library. Shelving, scanning, helping folks log in to the computers. Before she knew it, it was nearly four P.M.—the end of her shift, although the library would stay open another four hours—and she couldn't wait to head back to her apartment. She longed for a cool breeze, for a night walk with Ripley. Quite frankly, she just wanted to be *gone* from the library. For the entire day, the atmosphere inside had been stilted, the air heavy. People generally kept their voices down, but today they'd seemed lower, more hushed than usual. It was Shane's death. Piper felt it. In a community as small as Clover Creek, Piper was certain that everyone knew. It was as if the entire library was in mourning, and Piper wondered what the school felt like. She was happy she hadn't been there recently and wasn't due to return for about a week.

Piper looked at the clock. Three forty-five. She had a few more books to shelve and thought with a little luck, she could grab her purse and waltz out a few minutes early. Piper looked around for the library director—in the stacks, she hoped—and spotted new visitors walking through the entrance.

Avery and her mother.

Their presence surprised Piper, and a book she was shelving fell from her hand to the floor. She wondered where the pair had been since Shane died, if Avery had been attending classes.

Why wouldn't she? Piper thought.

It's not like anyone other than Mr. Brockway actually suspects Avery's involvement, right?

She doesn't need to lie low.

Piper picked up the book from the floor and reached up to shelve it on the top row. When she brought her arm down, Avery and Susan were directly next to her. Piper felt herself stiffen in surprise.

"Ms. Lowery?" Susan said, Avery at her side.

"Yes?" Piper managed.

"Is it okay if we talk?"

. . .

The three sat together at a table in a private study room, the door closed. Piper could see all three of their reflections in the glass wall that faced the library's main floor. She felt uneasy—*Is that the right word, uneasy?*—being alone with the two of them, a combination of the rumors that had followed them to Clover Creek, Mr. Brockway's speculations, and even Sam's "humoring" over the telephone a few days prior. Still, she felt safe, and why wouldn't she? Piper was in a public place, and nothing *officially* tied this family to what she had seen in the Brockway foyer. Only stories, conjecture.

Susan cleared her throat.

"I first wanted to properly thank you for what you did for Avery the other day," she said. "The incident in the hallway."

"Oh," Piper said. "It was nothing. Really."

Avery slouched in her seat, not looking at either Piper or her mother. Her headphones were around her neck again, and she was staring off into space.

"There's no need to be modest," Susan said. "We're both just extremely grateful for your kindness. Is there anything you wish to add, honey?" She looked at her daughter, and the girl snapped to attention, blushing.

"Thanks," Avery said quietly, adjusting her glasses.

"You can do a bit better than that," Susan replied a little sharply, flashing Avery an irritated look.

"Come on, Mom," the girl said, squirming in her seat. She sighed dramatically, then looked at Piper. "I just really appreciate it. It was scary, so thank you for getting me out of there. For stopping him." Her gaze floated back toward her mother.

Susan tousled Avery's hair. "That's better," she said, before looking at Piper. "It hasn't been the easiest transition. For Avery, for myself. We don't always feel welcome in certain places."

"Like school?" Piper asked.

Susan nodded. "It's been a challenge. And that's putting it lightly."

"I'm sure you heard about . . ." Piper couldn't help herself. Her eyes met Susan's, and the woman nodded. Piper didn't need to finish the sentence.

Shane's death, Piper thought.

The kid who bullied your daughter is dead.

Piper pondered Susan's true thoughts. She wondered if the woman's gut instinct when she heard the news was to feel relief, happy that her daughter was going to be able to catch a break now.

Or maybe she knew before everyone else did, Piper thought.

If she actually had something to do with it.

That idea just popped into Piper's head, even though she didn't want to think it. She simply couldn't help it. Piper tried to read the woman's eyes then. She looked for guilt or culpability. She saw neither. What she saw was grief, understanding.

She knows what it's like to lose a child.

"Has he been to see you?" Piper asked.

Susan furrowed her brow. "Who?"

"The boy's father."

"Why would he do that?"

Susan's ignorance filled Piper with relief—apparently Mr. Brockway hadn't surprised them at their cabin, the way he had Piper at her apartment.

Thank God.

"I just heard that he's talking to parents about what happened," Piper said. "He's still trying to figure everything out. So, don't be surprised if he talks to you."

There, Piper thought. *I warned her. Just so she knows.*

Susan nodded solemnly, and Piper's gaze moved to Avery. The kid's eyes were unfocused, and she was mumbling something, one hand fidgeting with an ear pad on the headphones. Piper wondered if she was quietly singing along to music but couldn't hear anything drifting from either pad. Looking closely, she realized the cassette player was off, so

Piper listened more intently, trying to make out what Avery was saying. She couldn't. Avery was just whispering to herself. Piper had only met the girl a handful of times, and she didn't know if this was a new behavior or something she was accustomed to doing. Whatever the case, it certainly struck Piper as odd—another thing to add to the list. The whispering continued, and Piper determined that whatever Avery was saying, she seemed to be repeating it over and over again. Susan picked up on the behavior, as well.

"Avery?" she said. "Honey?" She put her hand on her daughter's shoulder, and the child jerked to attention.

"Yes?" Avery said.

"Are you okay?" Susan asked.

"Uh-huh," she replied. Avery seemed oblivious to the fact that she'd been saying anything at all.

"Well," Piper said haltingly, "if there's anything more I can do for Avery, please don't hesitate to reach out. I'm not at the school a whole lot. Just a couple times a month, and my schedule there isn't regular. But I'm more than happy to recommend more books, or work with her here at the library, or—"

"You took the words right out of my mouth," Susan said. "That's kind of why we're here. Avery really enjoys the library, and we were wondering if you'd be interested in doing a little tutoring. Helping Avery with her writing, things like that? She loves writing. Don't you, honey?" Susan reached over and gently caressed her daughter's shoulder.

Avery smiled shyly, and Piper didn't know how to respond. She found herself reeling a bit from Susan's relative normalcy, her decency. At that moment, Piper realized that this was the most she'd ever heard Susan speak. She was affable, kind. A *mom*.

Mr. Brockway's brother actually thinks she's a witch?

Do I think she's a witch?

At that moment, Susan was just a caring mother having a chat, tending to her daughter's needs, responding in a very measured way to the death of a child. She was not the potential controller of a black mist that was summoned from the darkness, as Sam had speculated. Witch or no witch, Piper found herself a bit flattered by the request.

"Sure, wow," Piper said. "I'm happy to study with Avery, make something work whenever you think is best. If that's okay with Avery, of course." She turned her eyes to the kid—she was spacing out again. It reminded Piper of electronic toys she'd played with when she was little, when the batteries were low. They'd groan to life but wouldn't behave normally. They were slower, unreliable, not the same. Then they'd sputter and turn off completely.

She thought she might be looking at Avery a bit funny, so she turned away, pretending not to have noticed anything. Susan rubbed Avery's shoulder a bit more firmly, and Avery perked up, adjusting her glasses.

Fresh batteries.

"That would be fun," Avery said.

Susan beamed. "It's just nice to have *someone.*"

Piper assumed that Susan didn't know that she knew. Dead father, dead sister. They had never spoken about these things. It gave the word *someone* a bit of extra weight, weight Susan didn't know Piper would feel. Piper smiled warmly at Avery.

"I have some time right now," Piper said. "What do you want to do?"

. . .

Avery had quite the smorgasbord of assignments. Math worksheets, a science lab report, an analysis of Guy de Maupassant's short story "The Necklace." Piper remembered the story from her middle school days, and it brought her joy to know that Fisher was using it in his class. Avery pulled one worksheet from a red, beat-up spiral notebook. Piper caught a quick glimpse of the pages within, the lines and white space filled with cursive script and doodling. She spotted a couple of dates and assumed it was Avery's diary or journal, and she felt bad snooping, quickly looking away.

The room was quiet, save for a buzzing light overhead and the scribbling of Avery's pencil. Piper helped when asked, which wasn't very often. She mostly followed along with Avery, interjecting at times to suggest Avery elaborate a bit more in her free-response answers. Susan had cracked into another novel, and she didn't intervene much—only to request Piper's email address and phone number, to arrange future sessions. It was a bit odd—two adults in the room, only one engaged—but Piper reasoned it was fine. Susan's statement from earlier had stuck with her.

It's just nice to have someone.

To Piper, that explained everything.

About forty-five minutes into the session, Susan closed her book and looked at Avery.

"Honey, would it be okay if I used the restroom?"

"Sure," Avery said softly.

Susan stood, and then she hesitated. "Do you have to go?" she said tentatively to Avery.

Avery shook her head.

More hesitation.

"It's okay, Mom," Avery said. "We've talked about doing this."

Susan nodded slowly, and then her eyes moved between Avery and Piper. "You two stay right here, okay?" At that moment, Piper felt like one of Susan's kids, eager to obey a parental command. "I'll be right back," Susan said firmly, and she left the room, the door closing behind her.

Piper felt a peculiar aura in the air. She knew about Susan's demands to the school administration, and she'd never seen the pair more than a couple feet apart—Avery getting shoved inside a custodian's closet notwithstanding.

Is this the first time in . . . how long? Piper thought.

It felt wrong, illegal even. Still, Susan had put her trust in her, and Piper quickly determined that the only thing that would get her out of the room would be the fire alarm. She looked past Avery into the library.

A child and her father checking out a mountain of kid's books, patrons typing at the banks of computers, a group of boys huddled around a television playing Super Smash Bros. on a Nintendo 64. The boys were getting a little too rowdy, and the librarian was marching in their direction. Piper couldn't see Susan anywhere, which meant she and Avery were truly alone.

"Ms. Lowery?" Avery asked.

"Yes?"

"Have you ever played before?"

"Played what?"

"Super Smash Bros."

Piper hadn't realized the girl was looking that way, too.

"No, I haven't," Piper said. "Have you?"

Avery nodded. "My friend Kylie had it. Actually, it was her brother's. But we played a lot."

"Is she from your old town?"

"Yeah. There was even a club at my school. Gamers Club." Piper thought she caught a glint in the kid's eyes behind her thick frames. "We had tournaments and stuff. It was pretty cool."

The girl was coming to life again, yet Piper still found Avery's demeanor a little puzzling. Her words were always spoken softly, but there was often an undertone of enthusiasm or giddiness, as if someone else was trying to break free.

No, it was the *same* person, but different, in a way.

Piper couldn't quite explain it.

"We can play Smash when they're done, if you want," Piper said. "I think the checkout time is only for forty-five minutes, so they should be finishing up soon. I also heard some kids talking about an online tournament thing. Not Smash, but something else. I could find out more about that for you, too."

The look returned. Just a flash. The look Piper had seen in the classroom, and then again the first time she saw Avery and her mother at the library.

Fear.

"No, that's okay," Avery said.

The fear vanished, and Piper was a bit perplexed.

And curious.

"Did you play a lot of video games?" Piper asked. "Before you moved here?"

"I guess. We played a lot of Smash, and a few kids in Gamers Club really liked GoldenEye, but they didn't let us play that a lot because of the guns and stuff. So we had to go to someone's house for that, usually. I was pretty good. But I liked the computer more."

Piper couldn't help but notice the past tense.

Liked.

"What kind of things would you do on the computer?" Piper asked.

Avery shrugged. "I don't know. We had a computer club at school, too, and we did a bunch of stuff. Chat rooms, downloading things."

"Do you ever download music?"

"A *lot* of music. I used to, I mean."

Piper gestured toward the Walkman clipped to her hip. "But you tape songs off the radio now, you said?"

"It's fun. You have to wait for the right songs you want on your playlist, then click Record before the first note. Otherwise it's incomplete when you listen back, and it's kind of annoying. You have to predict what the DJ is going to play before they play it." She twirled a strand of hair on her forehead. "I don't know, it makes it kind of exciting, I guess."

"What's on your tape?"

"Everything. Britney Spears, Matchbox Twenty, Christina. Whatever is on the radio. I don't really have a favorite. But yeah, it's better this way."

It's better this way.

It was a strange way of describing that activity, Piper thought.

"I just download everything," Piper admitted. "But your way sounds fun, too. My brother was the first person to show me Napster, and I got hooked on it."

"I used to use Napster and burn CDs for my dad before I started using the tapes."

Dad.

It was the first time Piper had heard it from her.

Avery looked off, and her eyes glistened. She seemed to be remembering something special. "He taught me a lot of computer stuff, a little bit about programming. I mean, it was really basic, the programming stuff. I didn't really know what I was doing. My dad bought me a book."

"That sounds cool," Piper said nonchalantly.

"Yeah. It was one of those super-thick yellow ones. What are those called? They kind of look like big manuals."

"Oh, the *For Dummies* books?"

"Yeah, those."

"We have a bunch of those here. We can look at them if you want."

Avery gently pulled at her dangling headphone cord. "Nah, that's okay."

"We probably have a bunch of books on programming. No one has ever asked me, but I'm sure they're on a shelf somewhere. Or my brother can send me some. He's a programmer. Did I tell you that already?"

"Really?"

"Oh, yeah. He's into super-nerdy stuff."

"Computers were, like, my favorite thing."

Again with the past tense.

Were.

Avery turned her head and looked wistfully at the bank of computers. Piper thought it odd, remembering how Avery had sat quietly next to the row of computers without using one while her mother had been searching online the previous week.

Then Piper noticed her expression start to change.

Avery's eyes narrowed.

Her body leaned forward, a small tilt.

It looked like she was biting down on her tongue.

"Do you have a computer at your cabin?" Piper asked.

A pause. Piper wasn't sure, but she thought the kid was shaking. Just a bit, some slight tremoring.

"I don't use computers anymore," Avery said, her voice growing lower, a hoarseness developing.

"Why not?"

"I just don't," the girl said sharply.

Her voice trembled, and Piper got the distinct impression that Avery was holding herself back from shouting. She turned away from Piper, and all at once, Susan appeared on the other side of the glass wall, opened the door, and reentered the room. She returned to her seat and picked up her novel, not noticing her daughter's changed demeanor. There was a fresh awkwardness in the air now, and Piper knew it was her fault, yet she wasn't sure why. Avery's lips were pursed, and Piper thought the kid might explode. Avery had her arms wrapped tightly around herself, her hands gripping and rubbing the backs of her upper arms so hard Piper feared she would leave marks. The girl's eyes blazed, and again she whispered to herself. This time it appeared she was counting—one of those defusing strategies people use to calm down.

What did I say to make her so mad? Piper thought.

All I did was ask her why she doesn't use computers anymore.

"Susan," Piper said, clearing her throat, "can you help us with this math stuff? I'm embarrassed to say I'm pretty lost here."

All at once, Avery's hands stopped kneading her arms, and they balled up into fists. She brought her arms up over her head and smacked the table, causing both Susan and Piper to gasp. Then the only sound in the room was the rattling of the table and Avery's labored breaths.

Susan looked a little shell-shocked. "Sweetie, what's the matter?"

Avery said nothing, merely letting her breath catch, her shoulders heaving. She looked up at her mother. "Can we go home now, please?"

Piper walked them to the exit, reeling a bit. Despite Avery's outburst, Susan shoved a $20 bill into Piper's hand, even though Piper had refused payment multiple times. As Piper watched them disappear into the night, she wasn't thinking about the odds of Mr. Brockway paying them a visit, or the fact that she'd seen that strange look of absolute terror return to Avery's face earlier in the night, a look that would make even the bravest person's blood run cold.

She was simply wondering what exactly she'd done to set the kid off.

CHAPTER 18

11:38 P.M.—Survey says . . .　　　　　MONDAY, OCTOBER 23, 2000

I'm officially an extremely paranoid person! Thanks to everyone for your kind comments and for putting yourselves in my shoes. Most of you think seeing that *black mist* a few nights ago has cranked up my anxiety and made me jumpy—and yeah, I can't argue with that. Tonight, it definitely got the better of me.

Going to try and get some sleep now. Fingers crossed I can actually do it.

10:11 P.M.—Update

Okay, I should've elaborated more. No, there isn't something in my apartment with me right now. It was just a jacket hanging off the door. My eyes were adjusting, and I'd forgotten I put it there. It kind of looked like something was behind me . . . so yeah, false alarm.

10:04 P.M.—I'm a Freak

Just had a weird moment. I was washing my face in the bathroom, and when I looked into the mirror, I thought I saw something behind me—I about jumped out of my skin. Has this ever happened to anyone else?

8:08 P.M.—Good Night, Landlady

I've got my landlady's routine down pat. At eight P.M.—seriously, nearly to the second—a small lamp flickers on upstairs next to her bed. She reads a book for no more than thirty minutes (usually romance novels, you know, the paperbacks you buy in line at the grocery store—I ran into her in the checkout line once and she was buying four of them) and then it's lights-out. It's weird, but the routine gives me comfort. She's going out of town tomorrow to visit her cousin in the Twin Cities, and I'm going to miss it while she's gone.

Back to IMs and emails. Just forwarded a chain email to ten people, because if I didn't, it said I would be dead in thirty days (before anyone comes after me in the comments, *yes*, I am aware of how ridiculous these things are, but if I'm going to be pestered with them, I'm taking others down with me!). On the plus side, since I passed it along, the email says I'll be blessed with good luck. So . . . yay.

Vibes: Nostalgic
Current Jam: "Merry Christmas, Happy Holidays" by *NSYNC

6:48 P.M.—Weird

Just got back from walking my dog, and I noticed something strange. I swear a stack of mail moved while I was gone. It was sitting on the end table next to my couch, and when I got back, it was on the kitchen counter. I'm almost positive it was by the couch because I was going through it right before putting on my shoes. Or maybe I moved it to the kitchen before I left? That's right—I had a glass of water right before leaving. Maybe I carried the stack with me? I don't know why I'm so paranoid about this. Moving on.

5:29 P.M.—Brotherly Love

Hey. Just got off the phone with my brother. He insisted, again, that I let my mom know that I saw a dead body, so I did. At least, I sent her an email. She hasn't emailed me back yet, but I suppose she could be trying to call me. But I'm literally online right now, so she would get a busy signal. Sorry, Mom:/

Going to take the dog for a nice long walk, and I think I'll leave my AOL running to download some songs. 37 of them, to be precise. And I'm currently seeding 189, so my modem is working up quite a sweat. Hope it holds up.

Vibes: Downshifting
Current Jam: "The End Is the Beginning Is the End" by Smashing Pumpkins

[comment on this | comments]

CHAPTER 19

With her shift not starting until the afternoon, Piper lazed around her apartment for most of the morning on Tuesday, watching old episodes of *Felicity* on VHS. She and her friends had taped every episode in college, doing their best to avoid recording the commercials. Despite their efforts, they often clicked Record too late, causing some scenes to start abruptly, cutting to Keri Russell speaking midsentence. They always blamed the VCR. Thinking back on their attempts reminded Piper of Avery talking about how tricky it was to tape songs off the radio, but she didn't want to think about Avery or anything else right now. She just wanted to switch off her brain and not feel anything for a while. Still, watching the show made Piper miss her friends, and she logged on to AOL about thirty minutes before her shift, hoping to catch any of them online.

You've got mail!

She sometimes ignored that announcement for a bit, because she'd been getting more and more spam lately. Piper wasn't sure how or why, but it seemed to be coming in droves. Still, there could have been an email from her mom responding to her message from the previous evening, so Piper clicked on the blue mailbox icon.

Not Mom.

It was an email from Susan Wallace.

It caught Piper by surprise. But then she remembered that she'd given Susan her email address the previous evening, and it all made sense. Nevertheless, she had not expected an email so soon. She double-clicked on the message.

Hi Piper,

Thank you again for sitting down with us the other night. It was helpful for Avery, and she is very appreciative. She wasn't feeling well today, so I kept her home from school. But she was inspired to write another story! She was anxious to share it with you, so we came to the library—she was well enough to do THAT, I suppose (kids!). You aren't here, so I typed it out below. She was hoping you would read it, because she knows how much you enjoyed her last one. No rush at all! She was just excited to pass it along.

We hope you have a lovely day, and maybe we'll see you at the library.

Best,
Susan

Flattered, Piper's eyes moved down the screen to Avery's story, and she began reading.

The Wall

Lungs burning. Feet pounding. You run. You run for your life, up the stairs, into the bedroom, and you slam the door.

Fear. Panic. Shaking. Wondering if this is it, if you aren't going to last any longer. Minutes, seconds. Not sure how much time is left. If you had woken up that morning knowing it was the last day, you might've done a few things differently. Kissed your mom and dad. Maybe you would've fixed your bicycle, which has been broken for a few weeks. One more ride could've been nice. One last ride.

You crawl under the bed. You reach your arm out and pull the blanket down, covering the gap. You put your hand over your mouth. You're breathing heavily, wondering if it can hear you. But you don't know where it is. You put your ear to the floor. You did this on train tracks once—the ones out past the quarry, right outside of town. A friend told you that you could hear a train coming even if it was miles away. You just had to listen for the vibrations. So you do that now. You listen for vibrations in your house, wondering where the thing is. Is it downstairs? Is it coming up the stairs, maybe right outside your door? Is it on your bed, and you don't know it?

You hear nothing. Maybe it's not your last day.

Your breathing slows. You can no longer hear your own heart pounding. The house is quiet. You wait some more. Your parents will be home soon, you know the sound of their car, and you can usually hear it from a few houses away. So you lift your head and listen for that sound, the comforting rumble of the engine. You will hear two doors open and shut, the front door squeak open, and you will know then that you are safe.

You wait. You know the car is close.

SMASH.

From behind you. It is here now, and it is angry. It grabs you by the ankles, and it pulls you away. It did not creep into your bedroom. It was not sneaky, like you thought it would be.

No.

It came from inside the wall.

Piper clicked out of the message. She clicked out of AOL. Then she completely powered down her computer, something she hadn't done in weeks. She just stared at the black, empty screen, before blurting out loud:

"Are they *fucking* with me right now?"

. . .

When Piper made it to the library, the Wallaces were already gone. The email must've been the last thing they did before leaving, because Piper arrived no more than twenty minutes after she'd read Avery's story at her apartment.

She was relieved, frankly.

She didn't know *what* she would even say to them at this point.

Do they know I visited their old house? Piper wondered.

Do they know I saw that wall?

Throughout her shift, Piper's thoughts swung back and forth. Sometimes she believed the "Wall" story was just a wild coincidence; other times, she was sure it was anything but. Yet she just couldn't shake the fact that, out of everything in the Wallace house in Grangeville, the *only* thing that had truly given her pause was a once busted-up wall.

And now the girl had seemingly written a story about it.

It was too much.

Piper was at a total loss, so she tried to focus on her work. Managing periodicals. Data entry. Arranging interlibrary loans. When her break came, Piper used an open computer to log in to her email. She printed Avery's story, hoping reading it on paper would help it all make sense. It didn't help. She read it three, four, five times. Nope.

Her head was hurting now. She dug a few Advil out of her purse, and she chased them with some extremely metallic-tasting water from the fountain near the restrooms. She made her way to the front-desk area, smacking her lips, walking past one of the computer banks. It was a little after four o'clock, and a handful of kids had come to the library after school's dismissal—two of the computers were being used by middle school boys. They looked to be playing some multiplayer game that Piper didn't recognize, and they were talking loudly. She was about to tell them to keep it down, but then she heard one of them mention the name Shane, so Piper lingered behind the pair, listening to their conversation.

"It's crazy, dude," one of them said. "I was online that night."

"You were?" the other boy said.

"Yeah. We were on IM."

"Was he acting weird?"

"Not really. But then he downloaded a weird file or something."

"He told you that?"

"No, Bryce told me. He said Shane got some weird file and he was nervous to open it. He thought it might be a virus or something. But then Bryce dared him to open it, and the virus killed him."

"No way."

"That's what Bryce said. He said after he told him to open the file, he didn't hear from him again. Like, he just logged off all of a sudden. And then he had that brain aneurysm, dude. It probably gave him a seizure or something."

"Dude, come on."

"Ask Bryce. He was talking to him."

"That's freaky, man."

"I know."

"Where did the file come from?"

"Bryce said the new girl sent it to him."

"The girl from the haunted house? With the weird mom?"

"Yeah, *her*."

Piper moved past the boys in a daze. In that moment, she forgot all about Avery's new story, forgot about the thing that came crashing from the wall. Shane's dead, twisted body assaulted her thoughts. He was lying there, stiff, motionless, and Piper could see him far too clearly. She could see his empty, lifeless eyes, and she wondered about the last thing the boy saw before he tumbled down the stairs.

She knew what *she* had seen: the dark mist, disappearing.

But what did Shane see?

Something on his computer, before the insides were all fried?

And the file came from Avery?

It was a wrinkle she was not expecting, and Piper's mind struggled to connect the dots. A virus didn't exactly scream "dark mist smothering a boy." Still, in Piper's apartment, Mr. Brockway had thought that Shane's broken computer might be connected to Avery in some way—and now the kids were saying *just that.*

But how is a computer file connected to what I saw over Shane's body?

It simply wasn't adding up. The more she thought about it, the more the "Avery sent a killer virus" thing felt off—like it was from an entirely different puzzle. The idea wasn't building on what she already knew; it was throwing a wrench into everything. She wondered, if she'd lingered around the computer stations a little longer, would the boys have tossed out five more wild accusations, and she just happened to catch that one? Bad timing then on her part, as all it did was throw her into more confusion. Still, Piper couldn't entirely dismiss it. She'd seen strange things before, and she still didn't have an answer. Maybe there was more to this than she could grasp right now.

I'll figure this out, she told herself.

That black mist exists for a reason. All of this is happening for a reason.

Her head throbbed again.

Piper needed answers, and she didn't know where to get them. Susan and Avery, maybe. Perhaps it was time to come clean with them. Her brother? No. Sam would tell her to back off, to stop, that this was stupid. She could hear his voice in her head. *Black mist doesn't exist, and a computer virus can't kill someone. Stop listening to nonsense.* Fisher, maybe? The gentle teacher's advice typically felt like a softer version of Sam's. Well-meaning, but not helpful.

There was only one place she could think to go.

. . .

She blogged.

Alone in her apartment that evening, Piper shared every new update she could think of. Avery talking to herself and spacing out, her little outburst, the official cause of Shane's death. She typed out the conversation she'd overheard in the library, then copied and pasted Avery's new short story into her entry—it was quite the lengthy post, and she wondered if people would stick with it until the end. Piper closed with a challenge to her readers:

What do you think this all means? Comment below.

And boy, did the comments come. Dozens and dozens, with commenters theorizing about every possible angle and then responding to their fellow commenters' theories. Piper was fascinated by the amount of activity she had seemingly summoned out of thin air. Some of them were pretty outlandish, but a few caught her attention.

I don't know how this connects with that black mist you saw, but a killer computer virus is actually possible. Have you heard of Pokémon Shock? It was this thing that happened a few years ago in Japan, where an episode of Pokémon *caused a bunch of kids to have seizures. I'm serious. Look it up.*

Piper had never heard of this, and she did a quick search on AskJeeves.com. The commenter wasn't making it up. In 1997, a sequence of red and blue flashing lights in a *Pokémon* episode on television resulted in 685 Japanese viewers being sent to the hospital. The children experienced headaches and blurred vision—some even had convulsions and seizures. A few viewers spent weeks in the hospital.

Is this what happened to Shane? Piper thought.

Maybe he downloaded something with flashing lights, had a seizure, and fell down the stairs.

But didn't the doctor say he had an aneurysm?

Another quick search on the Internet clarified the differences between seizures and aneurysms, and according to the medical articles she read, it was highly unlikely for visual stimuli to trigger an aneurysm. Still, maybe Mr. Brockway had misspoken and meant a seizure. None of that explained the black mist she had seen over Shane's body, though, and she *still* didn't know how any of this virus talk actually jibed with Avery—if it did at all.

She read on, returning to the more supernatural theories.

Okay, caterpillarguy mused, *I have a theory that ties everything together. What if the mom is a witch trying to spread a curse? Maybe she gets her daughter to write these cursed stories and then sends them around on the Internet. Like that second story you got in your email. What if she imbues the story with some kind of dark magic, so when you read it, you're cursed, too—and then a black mist comes to kill you. You know, like in* The Evil Dead *when they read from the* Necronomicon *book and it summons a Deadite creature. Maybe that's how the boy died—he read a cursed story on his computer that the girl or mom sent him online, and something supernatural and evil was "summoned" to kill him. That connects everything, right? Occult, computer, black mist. Honestly, I'd be careful if I were you. You might be cursed now, and maybe I am, too, just by reading the stories you posted. Who knows? If a black mist comes to kill me, I'll try to report back from the other side. Side note: I didn't read the story out loud, did you? I'm pretty sure that in* The Evil Dead, *you have to read the book out loud for the Deadite to come. Can't remember, though.*

Piper had never seen *The Evil Dead,* so the analogy didn't fully land with her. Curious, she returned to AskJeeves.com, and quickly found answers. The commenter was correct: In the movie, reading from the *Necronomicon*—the infamous *Book of the Dead*—unleashes a Deadite, an undead creature. Though it's never explicitly stated that the cursed passages must be read *out loud,* it's heavily implied in the film.

Could Shane have spoken a cursed story out loud, summoning the black mist?

Did I read any of Avery's stories aloud?

Piper was certain she hadn't—at least, she didn't think so. Could she have unconsciously mouthed the words? No, that didn't seem right, either. She squeezed her eyes shut, massaging her temples, her frustration growing.

Seriously? she thought.

I'm using horror movie logic now?

She didn't know the first thing about horror movies, so she wasn't prepared for talk of curses and all that. That world was very foreign to her—like a rule book she hadn't read. Still, she supposed the concept made sense: a cursed story, something emailed to you that could summon that black mist if you read it, bringing about your death. It was definitely a wild theory, but the logic tracked. That particular comment from caterpillarguy had sparked fifteen replies, the users going back and forth. Piper enjoyed the banter, even though she didn't really think the theory held water. It was too absurd for her—and this was coming from someone who had *seen* something unexplainable and supernatural.

She dismissed it and scrolled on.

Piper kept refreshing her page, lost in the excitement of it all, before looking at the time in the right corner of her computer's toolbar: 7:14 P.M. She wished she were sitting by the fire at a campsite, Ripley at her side, a freshly caught yellow perch sizzling on a frying pan. And she probably *would* have been doing those very things, if she hadn't covered her co-worker's shift that afternoon. She figured she'd be able to head into the wilderness the following day, after Shane's wake. She'd given it a lot of thought and decided she should probably go to the boy's memorial. It was the right thing to do, and it would show Mr. Brockway that she was sorry for his loss.

Best to stay on the man's good side, she thought.

She logged off, again somewhat amazed at the power she'd wielded from a small apartment on top of a garage in a nowhere town in Wisconsin. Piper took Ripley outside and walked him around Ms. Hermann's property—the woman's house was dark, the Buick gone. No romance novel routine that night. Piper wandered along the forest line, basking in the beauty of another crisp, clear northern night.

. . .

The funeral home was on the east end of town. For those entering Clover Creek from that direction, it was the first building they'd drive past, welcoming them to the city. On Wednesday afternoon, the funeral home was so crowded that people had parked along both gravelly shoulders of the highway.

Piper arrived about an hour after the wake began. Her camping gear was already in her car, and she planned on swinging back to pick up Ripley, then heading straight to the waterways she'd visited a few times in the past month. Overcast sky be damned, she was *going*. Her knees wobbled as she walked toward the front doors of Crump Funeral Home, and her overcoat fought against the harsh wind. Piper cinched the jacket closed and nodded at two morose-looking families who'd just exited. She wasn't sure if they knew who she was, but they returned her somber nod.

My God, they look absolutely ghastly, Piper thought.

She wasn't sure if she was mentally prepared, but she entered the double doors anyway. It was shoulder-to-shoulder inside the lobby, and low hums of murmured chatter filled the air. From Piper's vantage point, she couldn't see all the way into the viewing room. She wondered if it would be an open casket, and she was struck by the notion that she did not want to see Shane again—seeing the boy's dead body and being with him alone for five minutes before the authorities arrived had been more than enough for her—and Piper nearly turned around and left. But then she spotted Glen Fisher in line for the viewing—*Thank God you are here; thank the good Lord for you, Mr. Fisher*—and she made her way toward him, figuring no one would care if she cut in line.

They chatted softly as the assembly inched forward. Fisher was wearing a dark, wrinkled suit, and Piper learned that he'd come alone because his wife, Carol, was recovering from a real nasty cold. After exchanging the usual, subdued funeral home pleasantries, Fisher leaned a little closer to Piper, dropping his voice even more.

"Is it true that you were there?" he asked.

Piper raised her eyebrows in confusion, and Fisher nodded toward the viewing room ahead of them.

"That you found him?"

"I was there," Piper said quietly. "We haven't talked about this yet?"

Fisher shook his head. "I've only heard what others have told me. Real sad stuff. How are you holding up?"

Piper shrugged. "You know, holding."

The mourners shuffled forward, and Fisher and Piper followed.

"I'm sorry you had to see that," Fisher said. "That wasn't easy, I'm sure."

"You have *no idea*."

Inching closer, Piper smelled the aftershave of the man in front of her in a tan corduroy suit jacket. She thought he might be drenched in the stuff.

"What's the mood in the classroom?" Piper asked.

"It's been tough, that's for sure. The whole chemistry of my classroom changed, especially the class with . . . well, you know."

"How is she doing in your class? I know she missed a day."

Fisher knew who Piper meant.

"Still quiet, still a bit of a lone wolf, unless you count her mother, of course." Fisher looked around, appearing to check if anyone was eavesdropping. Satisfied, he leaned in closer. "There are even more rumors now. Uglier ones."

"I heard them, too. About Avery sending a computer virus?"

"That nonsense made its way to the library?"

Piper nodded.

Fisher looked off, frustrated. "I can't for the life of me understand why everyone keeps piling on this poor girl."

"How are you dealing with it?"

"I've personally taken three kids to the principal's office, had too many conversations to count out in the hallway. It just needs to stop. I've never seen anything like this, not in all my years. The kids usually change the target of their torments regularly, but she has *remained* the target, ever since she arrived."

Closer now. They were still about sixty, maybe seventy, people away, and most were taking their time talking to the family. Piper spotted Mr. Brockway, freshly shaven now, eyes puffy, his suit jacket too small for his body. She was worried the front button was going to pop as he shook hands and hugged the grievers shuffling through the line.

"There's no stopping these kids," Fisher continued, clearly agitated. "I just want to tell them he had a brain aneurysm. Simple as that."

"You're positive about that?"

"About what?"

"That it was a brain aneurysm. Not, like, a seizure or something?"

Fisher shook his head. "No, it was certainly an aneurysm. Carol is friends with one of the nurses at the hospital—they go to book club together. She told her about it, though I suppose she probably shouldn't have. You know, medical confidentiality and all that. Why do you ask, anyway?"

Piper considered explaining the Pokémon Shock incident to Fisher but didn't bother. "It doesn't matter," she said. Still, her conversation with Fisher had gotten her wheels spinning again.

A virus.

Is it actually possible?

"And about that virus baloney—" Fisher paused for a moment, collecting his thoughts. "Well, I'm certainly not at liberty to share this with students, but I want to tell them that the girl couldn't have downloaded him—"

"Sent him. He would've been the one to download it."

"Sorry. The girl couldn't have *sent* a file or virus or whatever it is they're going on about, because she isn't even allowed to use the computer. Her mother requested that, day one."

"You didn't tell me that."

"I'd forgotten about it. Probably because it's moot. We don't have any computers at school available to students. Only those teacher pilot laptops, and I broke mine the third time I used it." He stopped, looking troubled. "I just don't know what to make of any of this. I really don't."

Piper was thrown a bit. She recalled Avery telling her at the library that she didn't use computers anymore, so Fisher's comment certainly shouldn't have surprised her. And then there was Avery's outburst, of course. That was still fresh in Piper's mind. Computers were a touchy subject—*Perhaps her anger at the library was due to the mother's request of the school?* Nothing about this was adding up to her, and the familiar sting of a headache started creeping back.

"She wrote me another story," Piper interjected. "Another horror story. Just as dark as the first one. Maybe more so."

"Do you have it?"

"Not with me. It's in my email."

And on the Internet, she thought.

Even closer now. From her angle, Piper could see inside the casket, and she saw the boy's face. It was too much for her. She felt her pulse start to race, and she thought she might hyperventilate. She excused herself from Fisher's presence, and she got out of line, retreating to the lobby. A sliver of space on a sofa was available, and Piper crammed her body next to a man in a red tie whom she didn't know. She rested her elbows on her knees and put her head in her hands, gathering herself. As much as she wanted Mr. Brockway to know that she'd come, she couldn't go back in there.

Maybe he saw me.

Maybe I've done my part.

Piper sat on the sofa for fifteen or twenty minutes, and Fisher eventually emerged from the viewing room. His demeanor had changed. He was no longer his calm and composed self. His face was ashen, which Piper assumed was from his seeing the boy up close. Piper rose and followed Fisher out the doors and outside.

"Glen?" she called, catching up with him. She had to say his name a second time before he became aware of her presence. He stopped, looked toward the front double doors, then back at Piper. Still, he said nothing.

"Are you okay?" she asked. The wind picked up a bit, and Fisher's ponytail danced in the breeze. "What happened?"

"I tried to speak with Mr. Brockway," he told Piper. His voice was unsteady. "I was going to tell him how sorry I was, how broken I am for him. But I couldn't tell him that."

"Why not?"

"I didn't get the chance to. I was about to speak, and he grabbed my arm, pulling me close. He whispered something." Fisher looked toward the double doors, then gazed up and down the highway.

Piper saw his eyeballs twitch, noted the look of grave concern on his face.

"And his tone was . . . menacing. Sinister, even. Threatening. He dug his fingers into my arm, and—"

"Glen—"

"He *must* have been referring to the rumors, to what I told you the students were saying—"

"Glen, what did he tell you?"

Fisher swallowed, and he looked at Piper, troubled.

"All he said was, 'I know what she did.'"

. . .

She typed out an email to Sam when she got home. It read:

Hey,

I know you already think I'm crazy or whatever, and this next part will sound even crazier. I just have an honest question for you:

Can something on the computer kill you? Like a virus, or something? I read about this Pokémon Shock thing that happened a few years ago, how a bunch of kids got seizures from seeing flashing lights on TV. Wild, right? Are there other ways that something on a screen could affect your brain? Like, something in a computer file? This is your field, so you would know better than me.

Feel free to disregard if you haven't already. I mean, first I tell you I saw a black mist with a head and arms, and now I'm rambling about killer computer viruses. I'm really struggling here. How could those two things possibly be connected? Maybe they're not and I'm forcing it. Ugh.

I don't expect to hear back from you about this.

Love you, bro.
Piper

Her head pounded again. Her mouth was dry, too. And her chest was tightening. Piper was tired of thinking about this stuff; it wasn't healthy for her. If Sam emailed her back, great. If not, maybe it was for the best.

She clicked Send, then logged off.

The computerized AOL voice bid its farewell.

Goodbye.

CHAPTER 20

2:12 P.M.—Still Kicking   SATURDAY, OCTOBER 28, 2000

No, I'm not dead.

I'm assuming some of you thought a floating black mist appeared in my apartment and ended me. Nope. Still alive. Since everything reached a boiling point here, I've been trying to get back to me. Hiking. Canoeing. Time with the doggo. Keyword: *trying*.

I've been busy. A lot of working and then tutoring. Just the one kid. The scary-story girl. I've seen her every day this week (except Monday, I think?), and I'll be honest: She doesn't need tutoring. She's quite smart. A whiz at math, knows her American history. And she *really* loves to write—and not just freaky stories that may or may not contain elements of truth; she has a journal/diary she's constantly doodling in. The spiral kind. Not this type of online journal. No, I haven't asked to look at it. Actually, when we are together, I mainly just sit there. Mom is with us every time, and honestly, I think they just enjoy my company.

I'm happy to do it, to maybe make the girl's day (if that's what I'm doing?). The poor kid *really* needs positive things in her life because, look, her problems are not going away. The whispering, the zoning out, the *There is something in the room with us right now* looks—the greatest hits are constantly on repeat. If anything, they seem to be getting worse.

Something is up. And no, I haven't asked them about the rumors. No haunted house inquiries, no *So what really happened to your dad and sister?* icebreakers. And I certainly haven't asked if she or her mom sent a dead boy some kind of "killer computer virus." That would be weird, disrespectful. I emailed my brother (who is a computer whiz) to ask him about it, and he just blew me off. So maybe it is a ridiculous concept to entertain, even if there is some medical precedent for something on a screen messing with your brain. Call me crazy, but I'm not ruling it out. But this is also coming from the same person who saw a black mist monster or whatever it was—so take my opinion with a grain of salt.

But do you know who else is not ruling out the idea of a deadly computer virus? The father of the dead boy. Well, *maybe*. He said something cryptic about knowing the girl did something. I don't know his source—maybe he heard the same rumors I did, claiming she sent his son a life-ending virus. I can't be sure. He was obviously grieving, lashing out. I'm not the only one who knows what the father said. My teacher friend knows, too, and he said he would run it up the food chain, talk to administrators at the school. But it wasn't an explicit *threat* or anything like that, so it's not like anything would necessarily happen. I considered warning the girl and her mom, but I haven't told them. *Sigh* . . . I don't know. They've been through so much already. I don't want to add to any stress or fear they might be feeling, and I definitely don't want them thinking I'm part of the rumor mill.

If the guy is *actually* blaming the girl, I don't think he's confronted them about it. If he did, they didn't say. And I don't think he's around right now, anyway. His son's funeral was on Thursday, and since then, his house has been dark. I see it every day. Nothing has changed—no lights, no movement. I'm not sure if his car is in the garage. He might've left town, I guess.

Well, I'm out to pitch a tent and hopefully catch some yellow perch.

Vibes: Blah
Current Jam: "I Don't Wanna" by Aaliyah

[comment on this | comments]

CHAPTER 21

There were no yellow perch, which was a bit disappointing. No bites at all, actually. Still, freeze-dried lasagna boiled over a crackling fire managed to hit the spot, and Piper savored each forkful, wiggling her toes inside her wool socks and just enjoying the ambience. The rain had held off, and the clouds had parted. A wondrous, starry sky opened up above her, and Piper leaned back against a log, stretching out her legs, gazing into the night. Ripley snoozed at her side on a fleece blanket.

This, she thought.

This is why I live up here.

She and Ripley were all alone, she reasoned, as she'd passed four empty campsites on her Saturday afternoon paddle, not seeing another person on the entire flowage. The solitude was intoxicating. The gentle paddling had cleared her head, erasing all other thoughts and troubles of the past few weeks. It was the monotony of tasks, she'd always thought, the checklist of things to do, that put her mind at ease every time she set out into the wild. *Load canoe. Stroke, stroke, stroke. Locate area with solid footing to dock. Hop out, empty canoe. Set up tent. Cook food. Clean up. Raise pack.* There was never any confusion—the order of operations never changed—and everything was so eminently doable.

Relaxing by the fire, Piper found herself thinking of nothing else but the earthy aromas of the trees that engulfed her, the black smoke rising into the sky, the gentle lapping of the water against the rocks at the shore. She started to count the constellations, but there were too many. A shooting star flew across the sky, then another. She'd seen these many times before, but they never lost their luster. Piper pulled her knit cap lower against her ears and smiled. She didn't even have to bury thoughts about Avery or Mr. Brockway—those had buried themselves the moment her paddle had hit the water that afternoon. There was no hypothesizing, no theorizing. It was just her, the dog, and the wild, and she fell asleep that night moments after zipping up her tent, content to stay at that campsite forever.

. . .

Her newfound peace was short-lived. Hours after her heavy eyelids had shut, Piper heard noises from outside the tent. They were loud enough to startle her awake. She lay still, listening. She heard the noises again, identifying them this time. The rustling of leaves, the breaking of twigs. Something was nearby.

A moose, she considered. She'd have loved for her Wisconsin dream to be fulfilled, but not this way, not in the middle of the night when she was half asleep. *Maybe a bear?* Piper had raised her pack using a pulley system of ropes before heading into the tent, so her supplies should have been safe. She did this every time she camped, reasoning that the one time she *didn't* do it, her belongings would be ravaged, with perhaps something worse happening to her. Piper flipped onto her back, turning her head to look at Ripley. The dog hadn't stirred, which was a surprise.

Am I hearing things? she wondered.

Piper listened closely.

Crunch.

Snap.

Ripley didn't move. The dog was actually snoring. His awareness had dulled in his old age, but she'd have expected him to hear *that*.

My God, maybe I am hearing things.

The sounds stopped, and now Piper wondered if there really was something outside her tent. All at once, the grim and ghoulish things she'd experienced during her time in Clover Creek came roaring back into her mind. First, she was convinced the black mist was outside her tent, stalking her, waiting to strike. Despite her brother's attempts to convince her otherwise, and the common sense that screamed it wasn't possible, Piper remained confident that she'd seen a black mist with arms on that terrible night—a real, tangible thing—and now it had followed her here. Perhaps it would wait until morning, or perhaps it would just rip through the nylon right now, wrap her in a dark embrace, and cause the blood vessels in her brain to balloon like it had done to Shane a week earlier.

Piper couldn't fathom why the black mist would target *her*, but in the moment, the only possible reason she could think of was caterpillarguy's theory from her online journal: that by reading a cursed story on the Internet, she had inadvertently summoned it. As far-fetched as it seemed—and it was a doozy of a theory, all right—none of the other explanations made any sense to her.

Be reasonable, she told herself, pushing back.

You didn't believe it when you read it, and you shouldn't believe it now.

Piper pinched her eyes closed, listening. She heard nothing outside the tent. The silence should've made her feel better—but it only made her think that it wasn't the black mist but perhaps a person, keeping quiet, creeping around, waiting for the perfect moment to strike.

Maybe it was Mr. Brockway.

Yes, she decided, *he thinks I know more than I'm letting on about his son's death, and now he's here to settle the score.*

Piper imagined that he would enjoy it, take his time, really make her suffer. Maybe he had pliers or a blowtorch. Rural guys like him knew their way around a toolbox, had a wide array at their disposal. She would suffer now, and maybe she deserved it, for not telling him the truth.

Piper closed her eyes and listened.

Only the wind in the trees and the water sloshing near the—

Crunch.

Snap.

Softer this time, like someone testing their footing.

Definitely not the black mist, she decided, but she wasn't about to just sit around and wait to discover what it was. Piper finally rose, slipping on a fleece sweater. She grabbed the leash and attached it to Ripley's collar.

"Are you ready, boy?" she whispered.

The dog rose, alert. No matter the hour or the situation, the click of the leash always did the trick.

Piper unzipped the tent, and the two dashed toward the canoe. She quickly loaded the dog into the boat, and she shoved off with her paddle, not stopping until they were in the center of the lake. They floated there for some time, and Piper finally found silence. The light breeze ceased, and the lake was still. The water resembled a sheet of dark glass. Piper leaned back, face to the night sky. Her sweater was damp, but she didn't mind. Her thoughts were elsewhere. She was thinking about the sounds outside her tent, and she wondered if they were all in her head. She hadn't been chased, after all, and when she'd looked back at the campsite, she hadn't seen anything. Only the tent staked into the ground and the bag hanging from the tree.

Surely, Ripley would've heard the noises, she thought.

If someone was actually there, he would've reacted.

At that moment, Piper felt consumed by her own pathos—perhaps a bit like Avery, reacting to things around her that existed solely inside her own head. Piper wondered if she herself wasn't well, if maybe she was simply bending reality to fit a narrative that didn't exist. What if the black mist was a product of her imagination? She'd been jumpy in her own apartment a few nights prior—thinking something was behind her in the bathroom, when it was actually just a piece of clothing draped over a door—and what if now she was hearing sounds in the forest that weren't actually there? Piper had never truly considered that she might just be losing her marbles, but glancing again at her campsite—*There's no one creeping around out there*—and feeling the gentle sway of the water beneath her, Piper entertained that very option.

She sighed deeply.

How did I get into this mess?

It was many things. Her desire to help a bullied child, the fascinating rumors about the Wallace family, Avery's seemingly very personal scary stories, the undeniable thrill of having a captive audience of blog readers. Maybe all of those factors combined had distorted her perception. *Especially* the blog. There were rational explanations for everything that had occurred in Clover Creek and the Wallaces' old town, yet Piper kept pushing this other narrative—the *supernatural* narrative. She was no different than the middle school students, she decided, eagerly consuming gossip and spreading it far and wide on the World Wide Web. Piper had never been like this before, never engaged in rumormongering. Quite the opposite. She'd been a *victim* of that when she was young, so she knew firsthand the pain it caused.

My God, what is wrong with me?

Floating in the canoe, Piper looked up at the sky. Stargazing was one of her favorite activities—but right then, it brought her no solace. No joy. She felt her grip on reality slipping, unable to trust her own thoughts, her own judgments. It was the first time Piper had ever felt this way, and she desperately longed to wish the feeling away. She wondered if something was wrong with her brain, if it was misfiring in some way. Piper reached out for Ripley—the one constant in her life—and the dog responded by licking her hand. She savored the feeling, the familiarity, the love. She had to get herself right—for him, for her. The way she was living wasn't sustainable.

The dog nuzzled into her hand, and Piper continued to wish.

Wishing she'd never gone to Fisher's classroom, wishing she'd never been tasked with the scary story contest. That's how all this madness began. The girl's twisted stories, Piper's proximity to the family. It had all started with words on a page and Piper fixating on Avery's fearful gaze in the classroom.

All of that had done something to her brain, she decided.

It's like I'm infected.

CHAPTER 22

October 29, 2000

From the Diary of Avery Wallace

I don't dream much anymore, but last night, I did. I am back in Grangeville with other kids my age. They all look so familiar to me—I think they are my friends, but I can't place them. There are about five or six of us, and we are in a cornfield playing a version of hide-and-seek. Basically, everyone goes to the middle of the cornfield, and someone covers their eyes and counts to ten while everyone else runs and hides. When the counting is done, the people running away have to stop. In my dream, I am the one counting. I then have thirty seconds to find one of my friends in the corn, otherwise I lose.

I feel like I've played this before, and there's a name for it. Cornfield Countdown? Hide and Stalk? One of those? Was this even a game we played? I just doubt myself all the time now.

Anyway, in the dream, I start running, batting away stalks of corn, hearing them crack and rustle as I push through them. I hear my friends whispering and giggling from somewhere, one of them counting down from thirty, but I can't find anyone. The crops are just too dense. I leap to see over the corn, but it's too high. I know if the counter makes it to zero, I lose the game, so I run faster, charging through the field, and soon I am completely lost, engulfed. I'm panicking now, my chest tightening, my breath so short it feels like I'm about to suffocate. Everyone sounds so far away now, and I am almost out of time. I run faster, but I trip and fall, swallowing dirt and dust. I begin to gag, feeling like I'm choking. The counter reaches zero, and then I can't breathe at all.

I wake up coughing and spitting, with Mom right there to comfort me. I tell her everything. We don't know what it all means, what my brain is doing. According to Mom, it's probably just a representation of my fears. She asks who was in the cornfield with me, but I can't remember their names, so I describe them, and she says that one of them sounds like Olivia. I tell her that I can't remember who that is, but after a few seconds, I eventually place her.

I can barely remember Charlotte and Dad anymore, and now I've almost completely forgotten my old friends. I just hate all of this.

Seriously, what else more can go wrong with me?

CHAPTER 23

Piper burned a new playlist the morning after camping, something to keep her thoughts occupied, something to help her forget she'd actually run for her life the night before. She'd named it *Piper's Just Get Over It Mix* and had written the song titles and artists on the gray Maxell CD-R using a black marker. The track list included "Steal My Sunshine" by Len, "She's So High" by Tal Bachman, "Breathe" by Faith Hill, and "Country Grammar" by Nelly, as well as a handful of other songs released in the past year or two. Piper usually included songs from across all eras in her mixes, but not this time. She reasoned the current hits might be a good thing for her. She needed to move on, to stop dwelling on the past.

She was just done with it all.

One hundred percent *done*.

No more theorizing, no more horror movie logic.

Piper was officially out.

She listened to the CD straight through four times during her Sunday shift at the library, alone in the stacks, the low batteries in her yellow Discman hanging on for dear life. They survived the shift, and the downloaded songs were all without skips, pops, or abrupt cutouts—a rare Napster occurrence.

Piper wondered if her luck was about to change.

. . .

She returned to Fisher's class the next day, a Monday, the first time in a few weeks. Seated in the familiar cracked blue chair from her previous visit, she gazed at the students in the classroom. Two students shared a whispered conversation about what costumes they planned on wearing to school the next day—Piper had forgotten that Tuesday was Halloween. Her gaze moved past them, but not to Avery, who was in her usual spot next to her mother. Piper found herself staring at Shane's empty desk, a grave and ominous sensation spreading throughout her body, the hair prickling on the back of her neck.

It just felt so wrong, the boy being there one day but not the next.

A dark cloud seemed to loom over the entire classroom. Fisher taught, but it wasn't the same. His voice was softer, his mood less energetic. The students seemed subdued—it was like every single one of them had been drugged. Piper hated being there, but she couldn't leave. Not until she gave Avery the award for best scary story. Piper thought it still seemed too soon, but her boss just wanted to get it over with. So, she'd sent Piper to do the dirty work, even though Piper didn't want to think about Avery's story ever again—her first story *or* the second one.

She turned her attention back to the front of the classroom. Fisher was about to wrap up his lesson when a hand raised, a student asking him a detailed question.

Come on, Piper thought, her impatience growing. *Get me out of here.*

Her gaze shifted from Shane's desk to Avery's.

She was doing it again.

Talking to herself.

Only, it seemed worse this time. Usually, when Piper had seen her do this, Avery's words were barely a whisper, her eyes spaced out and glossed over. But now she seemed more focused, squinting behind her black spectacles. And whatever she was muttering had caught the attention of three other students. They turned their heads toward her, worried expressions crossing their faces. Avery's mother had noticed the behavior, as well. Susan straightened in her seat, sporting her own look of surprise and concern. Whatever Avery was doing right now, Piper didn't think Susan had ever seen it before.

One of the students near them, a boy, jumped out of his desk and backpedaled up the row toward the front of the classroom. Mr. Fisher stopped teaching, midsentence.

"Eddie, what's wrong?" Fisher said.

The boy raised a shaky finger toward Avery. "She's saying really weird things," he sputtered, continuing to backpedal. He made it all the way to the chalkboard and bumped directly into Fisher, who stopped him by placing both hands on the boy's shoulders.

All the students around Avery had stood and were clearing out of the area. Some of them looked absolutely terrified. One even darted out the classroom door. Every student in the room was now on their feet, mass commotion setting in. Piper jumped up to survey the madness, and she could hear Avery's voice rising amid the panicked chatter of the middle school students. She was growing louder, more agitated, but Piper couldn't make out the words. The students were now uncontrollable.

"*What is she saying?*"

"*Make her stop!*"

"*Why is she doing this?*"

"*Mr. Fisher, please help!*"

Fisher let go of Eddie and inched closer to the source of the chaos—the boy quickly got behind Fisher and nervously peered around him. The other students were retreating, pinballing into one another as they escaped Avery's general vicinity. Susan stooped low to meet Avery at eye level, and she began gently shaking her daughter. Piper stopped about fifteen feet from the pair, and now she could hear the words coming from Avery's mouth—they came steadily, continuously, with an undertone of menace.

"*Filth, disease, death . . . ,*" the girl snarled.

"*Filth, disease, death . . .*"

"Smelled . . ."

"Smelled . . ."

"Filth, disease, death . . ."

Avery appeared to be lost in a trance. Then she suddenly sprang from her seat, shaking off her mother's grip. The girl yelled out:

"It smelled of filth, it smelled of disease, and it smelled of death!"

Absolute chaos. Most of the students ran out of the room. There was tripping, falling, tears and cries and screams. The hideous chant kept pouring from Avery's mouth. Susan attempted to wrap her in an embrace, but the girl wiggled free. Her voice grew louder, until the phrase came out in absolute hysterics:

"It smelled of filth, it smelled of disease, and it smelled of death!"

The only ones left in the classroom were the adults and Avery. Fisher was frantically pressing the emergency call button near the doorway, but it didn't appear to be working. Piper couldn't help but notice the teacher's body language: He was slightly hunched over, his knees bent, his jaw quivering.

Piper swung back around to look at Avery.

The girl continued to rage, the words becoming more furious with each repetition. Avery's head suddenly snapped to the left, and she stared directly into Piper's eyes. She paused, holding her gaze, and Piper felt the child's absolute wrath. There was something behind her eyes, something Piper hadn't detected before.

Evil, Piper thought.

An eerie silence filled the room, before the girl howled once more.

"IT SMELLED OF FILTH IT SMELLED OF DISEASE AND IT SMELLED OF DEATH!"

Avery snatched a book off a desk and hurled it against the wall. Her chest was heaving, and Susan again attempted to subdue her. Avery lunged for another book, but Piper didn't stick around to see what she'd do with that one.

She finally ran.

CHAPTER 24

That evening, Piper walked Ripley for longer than she ever had before. They just kept going and going, exploring dirt roads and country highways, dipping in and out of the forest, Ripley practically bursting with excitement at all the fresh scents. Clover Creek was behind them now. They were two miles away from the apartment, then three miles. Piper finally realized what she was doing.

This is my swan song with him up here, she thought.

We're leaving.

She didn't have a reasonable choice in the matter anymore, she told herself. Her checklist of horror would only continue to grow. In the span of mere weeks, Piper had discovered a dead body, seen an unexplainable black mist hover *over* that dead body and then disappear, convinced herself she was being stalked by something in the forest in the dead of night, and, finally, witnessed something akin to a demonic outburst in a middle school classroom. She wondered how much more she could endure—what other grisly experiences awaited her on that checklist—before realizing it didn't have to be this way. *Any rational person would jump ship,* Piper told herself. She'd already had her moment of clarity floating in the middle of a lake after fleeing in terror from her campsite—*It's like I'm infected,* Piper had told herself then, feeling her grip on reality slipping—and now, perhaps it was time for action.

There was simply no reason to stay. Making her online readers happy was hardly an excuse, nor was sticking around to help Avery, being some shining example of how someone can overcome bullying.

What could I even do at this point?

She needs professional help.

Or some kind of help I have no way of providing.

Avery's haunting words replayed on a continuous loop in Piper's head, and she couldn't shake them. Piper never wanted to hear those words again, and she had no interest in discovering what Avery might say next—or why she was even saying them in the first place.

No, that's it.

I'm done.

For my own health, for my own sanity.

Packing wouldn't take long. A few hours at most. She still had her original moving boxes, folded up and stowed away in her bedroom closet. Clover Creek could be in her rearview mirror by ten P.M., Piper figured. She could make it to her mother's empty place in Kenosha well before sunrise—or, if she pushed it, to her brother's apartment in Des Moines by morning. Nothing was keeping her here. She was month-to-month with her apartment, and the wilderness certainly existed in places other than the Northwoods. She'd heard wonderful things about Idaho, on the west side of the Tetons. Or maybe she'd cross the border, settle in Banff, a place she'd always wanted to visit. There had to be work there. Work somewhere. It wasn't like she had health insurance and a 401(k) at the Clover Creek Public Library.

Leaving was the smart thing to do. Piper knew that. She would only find terror here. More mysteries, more pathos.

"Come on, Rip," she said, turning around on a lonesome gravel road tucked away in the forest. She felt swallowed up by the trees, which used to be a good thing. Now the sensation was foreboding. She pulled on the leash, and Ripley happily obliged. "I'm sorry, buddy. This is it."

. . .

She returned to the apartment to discover a blinking light on her answering machine. Her brother or mother, she guessed. No one else ever called her. Piper hit Play on the device and the tiny cassette tape began to spin, and a voice she didn't recognize greeted her:

This message is for Piper Lowery. This is Carol, Glen Fisher's wife. It's hard to explain over the phone, but we'd like you to come over to the house. Something's happened to Glen. We live at . . .

The woman went on to give the address, but Piper had stopped listening at that point. She was too struck by Carol's tone. Shaky, anxious. Piper listened to the message again and jotted down the address on a sticky note. Her packing would have to wait.

She didn't know what had happened to Fisher, but she could only draw two conclusions: Either it was something involving Dennis Brockway or it was something involving Avery.

Piper rushed out of her apartment, not sure which would be worse.

. . .

Fisher didn't appear well. The teacher had sunk into a recliner, his wife at his side, her hand on his knee. Piper studied his face. He looked frazzled, confused. His ponytail was undone, and his thin and stringy gray hair hung below his shoulders.

"Would you like some coffee?" Carol asked Piper. "You sit with him, and I'll get us some." The woman rose from her seat on the sofa, and Fisher's hand suddenly snatched her wrist.

"No," he said. "Stay."

Carol nodded, sitting back down. Her forehead wrinkled, and she bit her lip. Her face was flushed—she appeared shell-shocked. Something was terribly wrong, but Piper didn't know what it was. When she'd arrived a few minutes prior, she'd feared the worst. The fact that Fisher was physically uninjured and coherent was reassuring, but Piper could sense something was very off.

"Glen, what happened?" Piper asked from her position next to Carol.

The question settled in the air for a solid five seconds before Fisher began speaking.

"I was at the library," he said, his voice quiet and contemplative. "I was hoping you'd be there. After what happened in the classroom, and everything you've shared with me about Avery, I decided . . ." He trailed off, seemingly lost in thought.

Piper studied his eyes. It reminded her of the times Avery had spaced out in her presence, and her worry began to fester.

"Glen?" Carol implored, rubbing his knee. "Sweetie?" Her voice cracked, and Piper was worried she was about to start crying.

The teacher's awareness returned. "I decided to do a little bit of research. Those things, those terrible things Avery was saying in my classroom, they just sounded so familiar to me. Like I'd heard them before. It was the damnedest thing." He looked off, thinking, and then made eye contact with Piper. "Do you remember?" he whispered.

Piper did.

She didn't want to, but she did.

Fisher leaned forward. *"It smelled of filth, it smelled of disease, and it smelled of death."*

Piper was concerned that he'd keep going, that he'd keep repeating that awful phrase like Avery had in the classroom. Thankfully, he stopped, resting his head back on the recliner, the words themselves seeming to exhaust him.

"I *know* those words," he said with conviction. "They ring some kind of a bell, but I can't find the bell, you know? I went to the library to look through some books to see if I could locate where they came from, discover the source. Those *words*. They were eating away at me, like a nest of rats, nibbling at my brain. I could feel the familiarity. I can *still* feel it."

He rubbed his right temple in a circular motion with his thumb.

Piper gazed downward at Carol's hand—she was digging away at Fisher's knee, but the man seemed oblivious. Piper was worried her nails were about to rip through her husband's blue jeans.

"Glen," Piper said, "please tell me what happened. I want to help you."

"Can you?" he asked, his eyes pleading.

Piper said nothing. She'd wanted to help Avery, but she didn't have the first clue. How could she help *him* now?

"I can," she finally said, not believing her own words but saying them anyway. "We can. I promise."

Carol nodded.

Fisher sighed. "I paged through some resources. I didn't know what I was looking for. I started with history books, thinking those words may have been related to the plague in some way. The medieval plague, I mean. The Black Death."

Rats. Piper understood the analogy he'd made earlier. Even in his current state, Fisher couldn't help but be an intellectual.

"There was nothing helpful," the man continued. "My instincts were off. I was downstairs in the stacks, so I considered looking through the microfiche. I've explored the library's archive before—perhaps that's where I'd seen those words. But the more I considered it, the more I thought, no. I haven't *read* those words before, I've *heard* them. Heard them spoken out loud. Maybe from a television program, or a movie, or a news report. Heck, maybe it was a passing conversation. Someone in town."

Fisher paused.

"It was this *feeling*."

"I've heard them, too," Carol interjected, looking frustrated. "He's not crazy. I swear, he's not."

Piper thought that maybe Carol was placating her husband, but she sensed conviction in her words. No, they were familiar to her as well. Piper searched through her own thoughts, trying to find the source.

She came up empty.

"I needed other ways to research," Fisher continued. "The books, the microfiche, I wasn't going to find answers there. Not quickly. That's when I saw the computer, in the stacks. I'm no damn good at using them, and I wasn't even sure how to log in to the machine, but I assumed it might be of some help. I could cast a wider net. So I went upstairs and got the librarian to help me. What's her name? Ms. . . ."

He trailed off again.

"It doesn't matter, dear," Carol interjected. "What I need you to remember is what happened next. That's what's important. After the nice lady at the library helped you get on the computer."

Fisher's eyes twitched. He was thinking.

"I tried to search on the Internet," he said haltingly. "I remember clicking, and I went to a few different websites. Where did I go? Did I log in to . . ."

He looked away, frustrated and lost.

Carol turned her head toward Piper, her voice dropping to a whisper. "Someone heard shouting," she said. "They heard him from upstairs. They ran downstairs and Glen was—" Her voice was wavering now, and her eyes welled up with tears. "Glen was hiding under a table. He was hysterical. Screaming. Screaming that something was down there with him."

She paused and turned to look at her husband. Piper looked at Fisher, too. She recognized the look on his face.

It was *that* look.

Avery's look.

Fear.

"He was screaming that he was going to die," Carol choked out. The words were too much for her, and she covered her hand with her mouth, standing as she did so. She quickly walked across the family room toward the front window, and Piper followed.

"He doesn't remember that?" Piper asked her.

Carol took her hand from her mouth. She swallowed and sniffled.

"His memory is blank after he started using the computer. I had to come get him, pick him up. They called me. Told me my husband was raving, inconsolable. He was saying—" She stopped, looking back at Fisher.

He was distant, unfocused.

But then his entire body shuddered, as if something unseen had brushed past him. Fisher turned his head slightly, scanning the room. Piper followed his gaze, quickly examining their surroundings—everything appeared normal.

"He was saying," Carol continued, her voice again breaking, "'Don't leave me alone.'"

She gently clasped Piper's wrist, and Piper felt the old woman's leathery touch. The two locked eyes, their faces no more than ten inches apart.

"He was saying," Carol continued, "'If you leave me alone, it will kill me.'"

Piper didn't know what *it* was, but she could only think of one thing—something she had seen kill someone before.

The black mist.

CHAPTER 25

SAM'S WEB SCRAPING SESSION

2000-10-30 08:11:32.532 [main] samwise943@hobbitonstation:~$ ./
autoscraper.sh -s "killer computer virus" "death" "unknown source"
"downloaded"

2000-10-30 08:11:47.543 [main] INFO Project Virus Forum Scraper V57-
Starting web scraping session . . .

2000-10-30 08:12:02.425 [main] INFO Project Virus Forum Scraper V57-
Accessing URLS: http://dailytechbyte.net, http://techforumscape.com, http://
cpufederation.net, http://techtalk.net, http://narlyforums.net, http://
404errorchat.com

2000-10-30 08:13:39.794 [main] INFO Project Virus Forum Scraper V57-
Creating new accounts . . .

2000-10-30 08:16:34.452 [main] INFO Project Virus Forum Scraper V57-
Logging in . . .

2000-10-30 08:17:54.743 [main] INFO Project Virus Forum Scraper V57—
Extracting forum posts . . .

2000-10-30 09:05:45.124 [main] INFO Project Virus Forum Scraper V57- Web
scraping session completed successfully.

2000-10-30 09:06:12.903 [main] INFO Project Virus Forum Scraper V57- 0 Results Found

2000-10-30 09:08:40.487 [main] INFO Project Virus Forum Scraper V57- Terminating script after 57 unsuccessful attempts using 112 technology forum websites and 38 search parameter combinations.

2000-10-30 09:08:45.923 [main] samwise943@hobbitonstation:~$ # End of search. No further data to retrieve.

CHAPTER 26

Piper went directly to the library after visiting Fisher—she had to check out that computer.

Before she left, Fisher had insisted that something was in the living room with them, something that wanted to kill him. The same thing from the library, he'd said. But he couldn't see it; he just *sensed* that it was there. Carol and Piper neither saw nor felt anything. None of it made sense. But lately, nothing really did for Piper. It was like she'd become a detective working a crime tip line, fielding call after call, investigating every lead, no matter how absurd it seemed, always hoping to find the one piece that tied it all together. She still believed everything should connect somehow—she just hadn't figured out how yet.

Is it related to what Shane allegedly saw on his computer?

Some strange file?

Piper didn't know, but she was hoping to find out.

It was late, near closing time, so she beelined to the stacks. Piper was the only person down there—at least, she thought she was. It was quiet, except for the buzzing of a half-broken, flickering fluorescent light in the far corner. That, and the long, narrow rows of bookshelves, gave the stacks an ominous atmosphere, which Piper tried to ignore. She did a quick scan of her surroundings, but she didn't spot a black mist or anything out of the ordinary, so she felt safe. Momentarily, at least. Piper slowly approached the computer near the microfiche machine at the opposite end.

It was completely powered down.

Piper moved to turn it on but then hesitated, her index finger stopping inches from the power button on the gray tower.

Turning on the machine felt risky.

Will the same thing that happened to Fisher happen to me?

Piper desperately wanted to know what the teacher had seen on the monitor, and she'd promised to help him, after all. Investigating the cause of his terror was the obvious first step. Still, she couldn't bring herself to press the button.

Will I see something terrible?

Piper pulled her hand back.

Nope.

Not doing this.

She removed the power cable from the machine, then from the wall, and shoved it in her purse. Piper located a piece of scratch paper and a marker and wrote:

Out of Order.

She found some tape and stuck the paper to the monitor, figuring it would buy her some time.

But what if someone noticed the cord was missing and simply found another one to hook it back up?

What if something else terrible happened?

She grew nervous. Nervous that a fellow employee would discover what she was doing, unsure of the actions she should be taking. At that moment, she hastily decided two things: No one else could use the computer right now, and she needed to preserve whatever it was that Fisher had seen, in case it would help later on. She wasn't sure *how* it would help, but the thought struck her just the same.

Figuring that lugging a computer tower out of the library would be inherently suspicious, she had another idea. She spun the computer tower around on the table so that the back was facing her. Piper began unplugging everything. The blue VGA cable, the mouse and keyboard connections, the skinny phone line. Then she examined the tower more carefully, determining how to open it up completely. She saw screws but didn't think it was necessary to remove them. Instead, she ran her hand along the side of the tower, sensing a bit of wiggle. Piper pressed with her hand, and she slid off the side of the tower, exposing its inner workings. She didn't know what was what—Sam would, for sure—but it didn't really matter. Not for what she was about to do. She just needed to render the computer unusable, at least for the time being.

There were different chips and parts inside—Piper didn't know the terminology. She spotted a long, flat green piece—*The hard drive, I think?*—and slid it out rather easily, dropping it in her purse. Confident that the computer wouldn't function without it, Piper reattached the removed side of the tower and plugged everything back in. She turned the tower back around and decided that no one would suspect a thing.

No one here knows how these things work anyway, she thought.

There's no way they could fix it.

The Out of Order sign still affixed, and the hard drive and power cable safely stowed in her purse, Piper made her way toward the stairwell.

That was the easy part, she knew.

Where she was heading next might not go as smoothly.

. . .

The roof sagged slightly, some of the shingles rotting.

The walls were a hodgepodge of weathered, dark brown wooden planks.

In the front yard stood the creepy hand tree, the trunk splintering and rising as if five long fingers were reaching to snatch the moon from the sky.

Soft lights flickered in the windows.

Of course there are flickering lights in the windows, Piper thought. *Would there be any other types of light coming from this place?*

Piper had seen the cabin before, but she hadn't paid it much mind, save the tree. It was just a cabin, one of many she'd seen hiking the landscape. The structure certainly seemed different in the darkness, and she imagined the giant hand in the yard shifting and moving, bending at its wrist, reaching down to ensnare her. The idea caused her feet to move quickly, and she shuddered as she passed the tree, anxious to rap on the front door.

No more rumors, no more theorizing.

Only answers now.

Only the truth.

The tree did not enclose Piper in its wooden and rigid fist, but she looked back at it nervously one more time after she knocked on the door.

She waited.

Piper didn't know what to expect when the door opened. Avery could still have been raving, spouting terrible things, malevolence still dripping from her voice. Piper envisioned the child answering the door, her eyes mad, a wicked smile on her face as she unleashed:

"It smelled of filth, it smelled of disease, and it smelled of death!"

There was no answer.

The Wallaces were certainly home, Piper thought. A car was out front. And this *was* the cabin. It had to be.

Maybe they went for a walk.

Or maybe someone picked them up and they split town.

Piper knocked three times, harder.

She took a few steps backward, inspecting the cabin again.

A shadow in the window, only a blur.

There and then gone.

Piper felt terror run through her body, thinking of the dark mist in the Brockway foyer, and she wondered if it was inside the cabin right now, if it had just done something terrible to the Wallaces.

Or had been waiting for her to arrive.

She backed up into the tree, which gave her quite a jolt.

The door creaked open.

Susan was standing there.

"I didn't know who it was," she said, her voice heavy with worry. "It took me a second to recognize you through the window." Susan moved aside, and Piper took that as an invitation to enter.

She walked inside, slowly.

The door shut behind her, which startled Piper, but she kept her cool, inspecting the cabin. The interior was lit solely by candles—at least a half dozen of them, Piper estimated. The earthy smell was almost overwhelming. Susan noticed the expression on Piper's face.

"Sage candles," she said. "They're supposed to cleanse the air, carry away negative energy."

Piper nodded absently, but it wasn't just the candles that gave her pause. It was the *design* of the cabin—at least, the modified design. There was a bathroom, but it was totally exposed. It was in the back-right corner of the layout, but it looked as though its walls had been torn down. Remnants of the studs poked from the ceiling and floor, and they were jagged, sharp, the removal haphazardly done. Same with the bedroom. There used to be walls, but now they were gone. Only the studs remained.

The cabin had been turned into a studio apartment, but one that was in shambles.

What the hell?

She then spotted Avery asleep in the cabin's only bed. Piper immediately found the single bed for two people to be strange, but considering the relationship between Susan and Avery, and the weirdness of everything else, it didn't seem completely out of place. The girl had the covers up to her shoulders, and she was lying on one side. She looked to be resting peacefully, and Piper felt a wave of relief.

"Please, sit down," Susan said.

Piper noticed the gratitude in Susan's tone, and she removed her jacket and sat on the sofa, which was shoved up against the cabin's back wall. Susan took a seat next to her, and Piper looked her squarely in the eye.

"Mr. Fisher isn't well," Piper said. "I think you might know why."

Piper leaned closer.

"Susan, I need you to tell me everything."

The worried mother didn't hesitate. "It's quite the story," Susan said.

Piper responded, "I'm ready."

part three

CHECKING PASSWORD...

CHAPTER 27

The Wallaces

Susan Wallace would eventually refer to September 25, 1999, as "the last day," though when the day began, it was just a regular Saturday, filled with familiar weekend sounds and smells. Cupboards opening and closing, bottles gently clinking together in the refrigerator. The rummaging of hands in cereal bags, the aroma of freshly brewed coffee, the laughter of her children. Avery used a bottle of maple syrup as a microphone, dancing and singing around the kitchen, climbing on chairs and throwing her head back, hitting those rock star high notes. It was a weekend tradition—"Brunch and a Show," the Wallaces had dubbed it—and the kid never missed a performance. The garage door rumbled open, and Susan heard the growl of the lawn mower awakening. The scent of freshly mowed grass soon wafted in through the open windows. That particular smell would be the one to stick with her.

Now whenever Susan smelled newly cut grass, it took her right back.

She didn't see much of Charlotte that day. She had volleyball practice in the morning and then disappeared with her friends in the afternoon. *Going to the mall,* Charlotte had said, and Susan didn't lay eyes on her again until the early evening. Avery was mostly on the computer, Susan remembered, but couldn't be sure. It was likely true, because the kid was *always* on the computer. Playing games, chatting with friends. Susan never worried. The few times she really scrutinized what Avery was doing, there was never anything to worry about. Just games, chat boxes, blue download bars—*So many blue download bars;* Susan had no idea how there could be so many—and headphones. Always with the headphones, singing along loudly to pop songs that Susan couldn't hear. Avery sang new songs daily, and Susan hadn't seen any new CDs around the house in months, so she figured they were coming from the Internet. *Where* exactly on the Internet, she wasn't positive, but Avery sure knew where to go. And wherever that place was, the kid spent a lot of time there—so much time, in fact, that the phone stopped ringing over the weekend because Avery was always online. Susan couldn't complain. There were always things to do on the weekend, and she didn't have time for chitchat.

Especially on that particular Saturday, the last day. Susan had to crank through her to-do list faster than usual, because she and her husband had a date that night. She and Richard hadn't been on a date in years. On the few occasions they'd tried to make it happen, things always seemed to come up. Work, volleyball games, honors night at the middle school, get-togethers with the neighbors, movie nights at home with the kids. They never prioritized date night, and it was always easy to push back—there was no need to rekindle a spark. It was still there, they both agreed. And they would rather do things as a family, anyway.

The Wallaces were simply *happy*.

Still, when the opportunity for an actual date presented itself on that particular Saturday in September, Richard and Susan seized it. It was one of the few Saturday nights that autumn where Charlotte didn't have a volleyball game—one of two, actually, the other being a Saturday in late October, but Richard would be traveling to Philadelphia that weekend for a work conference. That left a single Saturday in September, and when Richard suggested that they give it a go—*Let's really do it this time*—Susan agreed. It *had* been a while.

Leaving the two girls at home, the Wallace parents visited their favorite sushi restaurant. They began their evening at a table in the dining room, and after miso soup, three different rolls, and a shared order of edamame, they moved to the bar for drinks. They each drank two Sapporo beers until about nine thirty P.M., and at that point almost decided to call it a night. But right before paying their tab, Susan mentioned how she'd heard wonderful things about a new movie called *American Beauty.*

We should see it tonight! she insisted, feeling a bit buzzed.

They found a newspaper resting on a chair near the host desk, and Susan thumbed through the pages, locating the movie times. The film was playing at their local theater, and if they hurried, they could catch the 9:50 P.M. showing. After paying, they hustled to the car. Richard called the girls from his cell phone—he owned a Nokia 3210 and a BlackBerry 850, the latter given to him by his work so he could stay frighteningly up-to-date on company emails—to let them know they wouldn't be home until after midnight, probably closer to one A.M. They were surprised when the call went through, expecting to receive a busy signal. *The kids will be on the Internet,* they'd thought. But the line was open, and every day afterward, Susan wondered what they would have done if it weren't. Surely, they would've had second thoughts about the movie, she decided. The kids were expecting them, and they couldn't just *change plans.* They would've gone home, and maybe their nightmare could've been avoided. Maybe it wouldn't have been the last day. But Charlotte answered the phone, and Richard told her they were going to see *American Beauty.* He asked what they were doing, and Charlotte said they were playing RollerCoaster Tycoon and watching movies.

Richard said, *Love you, kiddo.*

Charlotte replied, *Love you, too.*

He hung up the Nokia and rubbed his wife's knee, not realizing it was the last time he would ever speak to his daughter.

. . .

They were surprised to see Avery walking outside to greet them in the driveway at 12:40 A.M. She was wearing blue pajama pants and a gray hooded sweatshirt, her arms wrapped around herself as she shuffled barefoot toward the car. Richard had clicked the button to open the garage but stopped the car in the driveway when he spotted his daughter, shifting the station wagon into park and killing the engine. He and Susan were more confused than worried at this point. It was Susan who greeted Avery first on the passenger side, opening the door and stepping out of the car, asking what she was doing outside.

"I don't know," Avery replied. "I just feel funny."

Susan put her hands on her daughter's shoulders, looking down, examining her face. She thought it looked a little flushed, somewhat ashen. Her eyes were quivering.

"Honey, what's wrong?" Susan implored. "What happened?"

Richard walked around the car to join them. Avery attempted to formulate words and stuttered on a few before arriving at, "I just needed to be with someone. I was waiting for you guys at the window. I had a funny feeling, like something was . . . I just . . ." She trailed off.

Richard stooped down and took his daughter's wrists, looking up at her.

"Avery, what happened? Are you okay?"

"I don't know," she managed.

"Where is your sister?" he asked.

No response. Avery was now looking around in all directions, her eyes wide.

"Avery, is Charlotte inside?" His voice was firmer.

"I can feel it now," she said, her voice growing softer. "It was coming before and now it's . . . something's here with us—"

"Where is your sister?"

Avery snapped to attention, looking at her father. "She was sleeping, a little while ago. Then I—"

A scream filled the air.

It came from inside the house. A girl's scream—the scream of her eldest daughter, Susan immediately knew. Then that scream was immediately cut off, and an unnatural silence lingered in the air. It was as if something had muffled the girl's mouth, stopping the scream from reaching its natural conclusion.

Susan felt her heart leap into her throat, and she gasped.

Richard dashed toward the front door, and Susan moved to follow him, but she felt a heaviness on her left leg, which she realized was Avery pulling her back.

"Don't leave me alone!" Avery screamed, tears immediately forming.

Susan instinctively reached down to force Avery to let go, to push her away so she could run inside. But Avery wouldn't release her, and she howled into the night:

"It wants to kill me!"

. . .

The doctors ruled Charlotte's cause of death to be bacterial meningitis. Although uncommon, the affliction could develop over a period of hours, which is what happened to Charlotte, even though she had been vaccinated.

"An exceedingly rare tragedy," one of the doctors said.

Her scream had not been muffled by another person, which is what Richard Wallace had been thinking as he ran into the house and up the stairs. Instead, he found Charlotte alone and dead. The doctors speculated that the muffled scream was the result of a spasm, or perhaps inflammation that affected Charlotte's vocal cords.

"She was very likely in immense distress," a doctor said, and Susan hated the doctor when he said this, the way he described her daughter's dying moments with such clinical callousness.

She and Richard asked Avery if Charlotte had been experiencing any symptoms that night.

Did she complain of a headache?

Did Charlotte say anything about having a fever?

Was her neck stiff?

Avery couldn't seem to remember much but was adamant Charlotte hadn't mentioned any of those things.

"It wasn't meningitis," the girl insisted. "Charlotte wasn't sick."

"Then how did she die?" Richard asked.

"I don't know," Avery said. "Maybe she was killed by the same thing that's following me."

"Where is this thing?" Richard asked.

Avery shook her head. "I can't see it. But it's here."

. . .

The Wallace parents had two very emotional and pressing tasks to complete that week in late September: preparing for Charlotte's funeral and figuring out what was wrong with Avery. The child was an absolute wreck—devastated by the loss of her older sister and terrified that she, too, was about to die. Susan and Richard couldn't grasp it, how quickly Avery had gone from healthy, normal child to believing an invisible being was stalking her. They reassured Avery that they understood her fear, but privately they were deeply concerned. It was a delusion, the Wallace parents believed, something Avery had created to deal with Charlotte's death. Susan and Richard immediately sought help.

A family friend, Dr. David Perkins, was a child psychologist, and he shifted his schedule around to meet with Avery immediately. He sat down with her in his office. Susan sat on the couch next to her daughter, hands folded across her lap.

"What do you remember about that night?" Dr. Perkins asked. "Avery?"

"Yes," Avery replied.

"I understand this is very difficult. We can take it slow."

"Okay."

"Your parents told me you and your sister were very close."

"Yes."

"What kinds of things did you like to do together?"

Avery thought for a moment. "We liked to play games. On the computer." Her words were distant, her demeanor aloof.

"What kinds of games?" the doctor asked.

"RollerCoaster Tycoon."

"I haven't played that one. What do you do?"

"You make a theme park and build roller coasters."

"That sounds fun."

"Yeah. We liked to download music, too."

"For the theme park?"

"No. On Napster. You can download songs you like."

Dr. Perkins furrowed his brow. "I haven't heard of that."

"It's a program," Avery replied. "It has everything. Like, every song you've ever heard of."

"Were you using Napster that night? Or building theme parks?"

Avery didn't respond.

"Avery, honey, do you remember?" Susan interjected. "Charlotte told your dad on the phone that you guys were playing computer games."

"Maybe," Avery said, looking lost.

"Were you drinking Cherry Coke?" Dr. Perkins asked. "Avery?"

"Yes?"

"There were cans of Cherry Coke downstairs."

"By the TV?"

"Were you watching TV?"

"I'm trying to remember . . . but I can't."

"That's okay. And you and your sister made pizza rolls that night?"

"We did?"

"There were some leftovers on the stove. Sitting on tinfoil."

Avery grew irritated. "Why does that matter?"

"I'm trying to help you remember," Dr. Perkins said. "Can we try something, Avery? A little exercise?"

Avery looked at Susan, who nodded.

"Okay," Avery replied, turning back to the doctor.

"Imagine biting into a pizza roll," Dr. Perkins said. "It's piping hot, and the sauce burns your tongue. Has that ever happened to you before?"

"Yes."

"Imagine that feeling, like it's happening right now. The pizza roll is scalding, and you yelp a bit, and you rush to the refrigerator, swing open the door, and lunge for a Cherry Coke. It's a red-and-black can. Can you picture it?"

"Yes."

"You crack it open and gulp it down. The coldness is so refreshing, the most refreshing thing you've ever had. If you try hard enough, can you taste it right now?"

Avery smacked her lips together. "A little bit, I guess."

"Good," the doctor replied. "You take the soda and some pizza rolls to the family room. Then you and your sister watch a movie together, or a TV show, and then you go and build roller coasters on your computer."

"Okay."

"And then your sister tells you she has a headache and that she's worried she's coming down with a fever. She tells you she's tired and needs to lie down. Her throat hurts, too."

"That's a lie."

"I'm not lying, Avery. I'm merely suggesting a possible way that—"

"That's not what happened," the girl interrupted.

"Do you remember what happened?"

Again, Avery thought. She looked downward, eyes narrowing. "No," she insisted. "But she wasn't sick. Charlotte wasn't sick."

"Do you know that for certain?" Dr. Perkins asked.

"Yes."

"Then how did your sister die, if not from sickness?"

"I don't know. Maybe she was killed by the same thing that's in the room with us right now."

"And what is this *thing?*"

"I don't know what it is. But it wants to kill me. I can feel it. It hates me."

"And where is this thing right now?"

"It's over there."

"Where?"

"Right there."

"Can you see it?"

"No, I can't. I know you don't believe me, but I just *know* exactly where it is."

"Avery, I don't—"

"I can feel where it is. It's *right there.*"

Avery pointed over Dr. Perkins's shoulder, and he turned around. In the corner of the room where Avery was pointing, there were potted plants, a bookshelf, and a closed door. Besides that, nothing.

Susan put her head in her hands and began to weep.

.　.　.

Avery was extremely succinct and clear about her condition.

"There is something evil around me at all times," the girl explained. "I can't see it, but I know it's there. I can feel it in every room I'm in. Sometimes I can sense exactly where it is. It follows me wherever I go. And it's waiting for me to be alone. The second I'm alone, it will kill me."

She went on to describe it as the feeling you get when you're sitting in a chair, and someone is standing behind you. Even if you can't see them, you can sense their presence—you know exactly where they are. The thing with her was just like that, only heavier, somehow. Avery would often shiver involuntarily, and sometimes, she swore something had just brushed past her ear when her parents saw nothing—and neither did she. To Avery, the evil thing was always nearby, watching her, often just beyond the edge of her vision. She felt trapped, cornered wherever she went, like the walls were always closing in on her, and no matter how irrational it sounded, she was convinced that the invisible thing would strike if she were ever alone.

When did you first feel this presence? Avery was asked.

She wasn't exactly sure. She remembered waking up the night Charlotte died—even though she couldn't remember going to bed—with a strange feeling. Avery described it as "a shortness of breath, or a tickling in my chest," so she'd gotten out of bed. She'd walked down the hallway and pushed open her sister's bedroom door. Charlotte was sleeping soundly. Avery then went downstairs but still had that weird feeling—something was just *off*. It was a restlessness, an anxiety—like something terrible was about to happen, but she didn't know why. At that moment, she longed for someone to be with her, and she almost went back upstairs to climb into bed with Charlotte, but that was when she spotted the headlights coming down the street and into the driveway. Her parents were home. She immediately went out to meet them.

Minutes later, Charlotte was dead.

And it happened—Charlotte's horrifying scream happened—at *precisely* the same moment that Avery fully sensed the evil for the first time, hiding behind her parents' station wagon.

Where did this evil thing come from? Avery was asked repeatedly.

And if you don't remember much about that night, how can you say for certain that Charlotte wasn't sick?

Avery didn't have an answer for either of those questions.

Days passed, the wake and funeral came and went, and still, Avery couldn't remember the details of that night. She was also adamant that Dr. Perkins could not help her. At her request, Avery started sleeping in her parents' bed every night, and she demanded one of them be in the same room with her at all times. She even asked Susan to start escorting her to the bathroom, standing next to her while she did her business.

Can you feel that thing with us right now? her parents routinely asked.

Avery would nod. She couldn't see it, but she always knew it was there. It only ever took her a few seconds—no more than five—to figure out where it was. Sometimes, Avery could be *frighteningly* specific, especially when she felt it slinking across the floor past her feet. When that happened, she'd shudder violently, almost jumping out of her seat. Sometimes it was harder to pinpoint, but she could always sense where it was—whether it was perched near the ceiling, watching her, or hiding behind a curtain. Other times, it was right next to her, and if Avery focused hard enough, she swore she could feel its breath on her cheek, a disgusting scent she described as rotting garbage. At night, she often felt it hovering over her. With her eyes closed, it felt like a mass inches from her face, like someone leaning down to look at her.

Weeks passed. She made sure she was never alone, remaining at home, her parents withdrawing her from school. And her behavior changed. She was not the loud and goofy kid she had been before. Avery became withdrawn, not interested in her usual hobbies. She didn't touch the computer, wouldn't turn on a video game. Susan and Richard would routinely ask her—*Hey, do you want to play RollerCoaster Tycoon or talk to your friends online?*—and Avery just shook her head every time, not even willing to entertain the thought. Susan and Richard found it odd, but certainly no odder than everything else happening in her life.

Like the invisible thing supposedly trailing her every movement, biding its time until Avery was alone.

Avery worked up the courage to try out a few tests, at her parents' and Dr. Perkins's insistence. For the first test, Avery sat on a couch in the family room. Her parents moved to the other end of the space, near the entrance to the hallway, but remained in Avery's line of sight.

"How does that feel?" Susan asked.

"Okay," Avery responded with hesitation.

"Do you feel it?"

Avery nodded. "It's still here."

"Is it moving?"

She considered this for a moment. "No."

Susan and Richard backed up a step. They could all still see one another, but Avery looked concerned.

"Still okay?" Richard asked.

Avery nodded again, but more slowly.

The parents backed up again into the hallway, now completely out of Avery's sight.

The kid screamed bloody murder.

She jumped from the couch and sprinted toward her parents, her face already covered in tears, sobbing hysterically.

"It's going to kill me!" she screamed through the cries.

The second test was performed outside. Susan had the idea that the outdoors could be safer. Inside was so enclosed—there were so many places to hide. Plus, Charlotte had died inside. Maybe if they were outside, Avery's mindset would shift.

It was warm for October, midsixties, and the sun was shining. The perfect day for this experiment, Susan thought. The Wallaces still had their outdoor furniture on the patio in their fenced-in yard, and they all sat outside. Other houses were visible, but no one was watching them, they thought. Birds chirped from bushes in the backyard, and a squirrel darted across the fence and leaped into a tree.

"Are you ready?" Susan asked.

Avery tentatively replied that she was. Susan and Richard stood up, walked to the sliding patio door, opened it, and went inside. They turned and watched their daughter, who looked nervous but determined. Richard slid the glass door closed. They watched their daughter through the glass, and she fidgeted in her seat.

Ten seconds.

Thirty seconds.

One minute.

She was still fine. Richard pointed to his right, implying that he and his wife should move out of sight. Avery nodded, and her parents side-stepped into the kitchen.

The exact moment Avery could no longer see them, she lost it.

High-pitched, horrific shrieking.

The Wallace parents didn't know what to do. Dr. Perkins was of no help, so they went back to basics. Physical exams, blood tests, vision and hearing. The whole nine yards. Maybe there was something sensory going on that was triggering Avery's condition.

The tests came back normal.

They went to a different psychologist. Susan and Avery had many of the same conversations they'd had with Dr. Perkins, and, disappointingly, the results were the same. Avery still sensed an invisible figure following her. The new psychologist really dug into Avery's past, searching for any potential trauma that may have occurred before Charlotte passed. There was nothing, and Susan was relieved, in a way. Yes, they were no closer to answers, but at least Avery hadn't been keeping any dark secrets from her. It reaffirmed Susan's belief that she'd been raising Avery right, had protected her for her entire life—but it also laid her failures bare for all to see. Susan began to wonder if it was her fault, if she had done something wrong as a mother.

Why is this happening to my family, to my child?

No one had any answers.

More conversations with a psychologist. Cognitive behavioral therapy exercises, play therapy, art therapy, journaling.

The invisible presence remained, and Avery refused to ever be alone.

. . .

A potential breakthrough came four weeks after Charlotte's death.

On a Monday in October, Richard told his daughter he had some emails to write and asked if she would mind sitting with him in the den. She replied that she wouldn't mind and sat next to him as he typed away at the keyboard. But as he worked, he noticed something on Avery's face. She was thinking, turning white. Her lips began to tremble. She slowly backed away from the computer, and Richard didn't think she was aware she was doing it.

"Honey, are you okay?" Richard asked.

Avery shook her head. "The computer. I remember now. It came from the computer."

He knew what she meant.

The word *it* only meant one thing anymore in the Wallace household: That invisible, evil thing.

"It came from the *computer*," she said again.

The Wallaces hoped that Avery's realization would lead to an additional unlocking of memories from the night Charlotte died. But that was it. Avery's thoughts remained hazy, and while she didn't recall *what* the evil thing was or *how* it had come into existence, her gut was telling her it had originated from the computer.

Still, they didn't really know what that meant.

Had she seen something that frightened her?

A video or a file of some kind?

Richard explored every single part of the family machine. Every file, every download, every bookmarked website. He went through Documents and Settings, the program files, the C drive, the Windows directory, the temp directory, the system registry. The recycle bin hadn't been emptied in months, and he looked through those files, finding nothing strange. He bought numerous brands of virus detection software. He didn't know what he was looking for, but if he stumbled across anything that piqued his interest, he planned to ask Avery. But there was nothing that struck him as being out of the ordinary. He listened to every song that had been downloaded through Napster—hundreds of them over the past six weeks—headphones to his ears, eyes closed, locked in and focused. He was hoping he would hear something awful, some kind of spoken message overlaid onto a Backstreet Boys song that had spooked Avery, leading to her mental health crisis. But besides the usual pops and cracks often associated with downloads, there was nothing wrong with the songs.

He grew more and more frustrated. There wasn't much else he could do on the machine. His greatest lament was that he was a power user—and had trained his family to be extremely tech-savvy, too—so he regularly cleared his Internet cache and history, meaning there was no way of knowing what websites his two daughters might have accessed the night Charlotte died. At one point, he spent all night playing Roller-Coaster Tycoon, speculating perhaps that the version of the game they owned was corrupted, that a series of cryptic messages would appear on the screen, or a laughing skull would pop up and tell him he was going to die—a prank coded onto their disc by a programmer with a sick sense of humor.

The game played out as normal. No macabre messages, no skulls. Only a functioning and vibrant theme park, which made Richard all the more disappointed, because he knew how much Avery used to love to play.

She had to have been missing it.

Richard grew frustrated. He elected to try a new tactic, one not discussed with Avery's doctor. He brought Avery into the den, and while she stood by the doorway with her mother, Richard took a sledgehammer into his hands.

He began pummeling.

His targets were the monitor and the tower, the screen shattering and pieces of plastic and hardware flying through the air. Avery clutched her mother's side, turning her head away from the carnage. Richard had planned on performing only a couple of symbolic blows with the sledgehammer, just to break the computer, to perhaps show his daughter that the source of the evil could be destroyed. But as his grip on the handle tightened and his muscles tensed, he found himself grunting and then screaming as he smashed every piece of the machine to bits.

He *enjoyed* it.

He just kept going, not even noticing when Avery and Susan re-treated from the space. Richard began ripping cables from walls, shouting obscenities, and then he took the sledgehammer and began bashing the wall.

Three times, five times, ten.

The wall was in pieces. Bits of drywall dust floated in the air, and Richard cut his hand on a broken piece of wood, drawing blood. He dropped the sledgehammer to the floor and shoved his arms inside the open wall—this was never the plan, but he was really getting carried away now—locating cords and cables and yanking those, too, not sure what they were or where they came from, feeling them give, then pulling harder. If he got electrocuted or the family's phone line was permanently damaged, then so be it. Breath heaving and sweat dripping down his face, Richard finally collapsed to the floor, and he began to cry.

It was the first time he'd done so since Charlotte died.

. . .

Weeks stretched into months, and the year 2000 arrived. With the new millennium came renewed hope, Susan thought. Maybe Avery's fortunes would change. The Wallaces turned to a neurologist, and Avery underwent a series of exams. Every time she went into a tube, Susan held out hope that *that particular scan* would be the one to solve the problem. Every single one—MRI, EEG, CT, PET, SPECT—came back clean. There were no abnormalities in Avery's brain.

They turned to medication. One doctor wondered if it was epilepsy related, and even though the Wallaces saw this as a shot in the dark, Avery was prescribed antiseizure medication. No change, outside of side effects like blurred vision and fatigue. Seeing Avery struggle through the medication nearly broke Susan and Richard, but they made sure Avery followed through with the prescription, holding her hand and staying by her side as she swallowed the pills. Of course, they were always by her side—otherwise that *thing* would get her, Avery told them emphatically. She visited a sleep specialist—*How in the world can this be sleep related when she senses this horrible thing when she's awake?* Susan thought—but they tried it all the same, and Avery spent an entire night hooked up to blinking monitors in a sleep lab. There was nothing out of the ordinary.

Allergy tests found nothing. Then came more prescriptions. Anti-anxiety. Antipsychotic. Beta blockers. Herbal remedies like valerian root and chamomile, even acupuncture, aromatherapy, and nutritional therapy.

Nothing helped. Susan and Richard continued to validate Avery's fears and emotions—some variation of *We know you're scared, so let's figure this out together* was uttered too many times to count—while doing their best not to affirm what they thought was their daughter's delusion. Avery would come out of it eventually, they hoped. But as each day passed, the Wallaces feared they were losing their daughter, like the Avery they'd known and loved was collapsing into herself, never to emerge again—and it wasn't just Avery's insistence on a perpetual, evil presence that was the problem. She was losing weight, lacked energy, was prone to headaches. Some of that was due to the medications she was taking, but the Wallaces often felt like Avery had just *changed,* and it ate them up inside.

For six months, it was dead end after dead end. And the entire time, two things remained constant:

One, Avery still felt the invisible thing around her at all times, waiting for her to be alone.

And two, she was deathly afraid of computers. Even the *idea* of them. "That's where it came from," she insisted.

Avery begged her father to never replace the one he had destroyed, and he agreed.

In some weird way, it felt like progress.

. . .

Six months had passed since Charlotte's death. It was March 2000, Avery had not returned to school, and her spirit was waning. She was a shell of her former self. Susan couldn't quite articulate it, but it was like her light was going out. In a way, it reminded her of her own mother's final few years—there physically, and still sharp in some ways, but dulled.

The Wallaces mulled next steps.

Only, Susan thought, *what other steps are there?*

They'd tried everything, every doctor's recommendation, and Avery had reluctantly gone along with every single one. Every treatment, every pill.

"This won't help," was the kid's mantra.

And she'd been right.

Exhausted, and with nowhere left to turn, Susan met with a pastor at a local Baptist church. The Wallaces weren't members—they didn't attend any church—but she felt optimism bubbling once again when the pastor thought he might be able to help. The man wished to come to their home to bless both the physical premises and Avery. That method was new, different. *It's worth a shot,* Susan thought, although she was uncomfortable with the notion of turning to faith in God when she had none. That discomfort grew when *two* pastors arrived at their home, brandishing vials of holy water and healing oil. After flicking drops of water around every room and doorway, muttering prayers and incantations, they met the family in the living room and placed their hands on Avery's head, who was sitting on the couch next to her father. She immediately flashed her mother a distressed look, her eyes pleading:

Mom, make this stop, please.

To Susan, that moment was the culmination of a half year's worth of failures, all dictated by her and Richard, always with Avery's hesitant approval but never at her daughter's discretion. Standing next to the couch with her arms crossed, the pastors saying things like, "Any evil that is tethered to this child or in this household, understand that you are not welcome, and I send you back from whence you came," Susan watched her daughter closely. Avery looked uncomfortable, irritated, *pained* even—Susan felt positively awful, knowing this was her doing.

"That's enough!" she finally said.

The ceremony was over. Susan's voice was shaky and curt as she showed the men the door, hoping she wasn't being rude but knowing she absolutely was. She watched them leave, and when the car vanished down the street, she felt her entire body exhale. The release felt wonderful.

Susan's hand still trembled a bit as she stood on the front stoop, gripping the door handle, still recovering from the encounter. But she felt a sense of clarity wash over her.

She had a new idea.

. . .

"What do you want to do?" Susan asked Avery. They were sitting in the kitchen now, Richard fixing a pot of coffee.

It had struck Susan that she and her husband had called all the shots the last six months. Nothing was ever Avery's suggestion, only theirs. Susan's brainstorm was shockingly simple, and she couldn't believe she hadn't considered it sooner.

No more choking down pills, no more pastoral interventions.

Yes, she was the kid, and they were the parents.

But what does Avery think will really help?

The child thought for a moment. "Can we just leave?"

"Where do you want to go?" Susan asked.

Avery shrugged. "Anywhere, I guess. I just don't want to be here anymore. This is where Charlotte died."

"We can go anywhere you want," Susan replied. "Right?" She looked at Richard, who nodded, pouring coffee into a mug.

"We can explore every option," Richard said. "If you want to go to *Paris,* we could look into it."

"I don't care where we go," Avery said. "I just want to start somewhere fresh."

"You would be okay with a different school?" Susan asked. "New friends?"

"I don't want to go back to my old school," Avery said bluntly. "Like, ever. I know what the kids would say."

"What would they say?"

"There's the *haunted* girl. The girl with the monster following her around, or whatever."

"They wouldn't say that."

Avery flashed her mom a look. "Yes, they would, Mom. You know they would. Do you remember when Olivia visited me the first time? She was freaked out. It was so obvious. It happens when my other friends visit, too. They just know."

"How would they know?" Susan responded. "Did you tell them?"

Avery shrugged. "You're in the room with us the whole time. Do you remember me telling them?"

Susan did not. Avery's friends had visited her a handful of times over the previous couple of months, and when they did, they treated Avery with kindness, but also with a delicateness. It was clear they knew something was deeply wrong, and how couldn't they? She hadn't been back to school. But Susan couldn't recall Avery having a specific conversation with any of her friends about the invisible specter—Avery didn't want anyone to know, she'd told her parents. She was worried everyone would think she was crazy, isolating her even further from the other kids. So when her friends visited, the matter was left unspoken, and Susan and Richard had thus been tight-lipped about Avery's condition. Of course, this was after Susan had let slip to a few of her *own* friends in the days after Charlotte's death that Avery sensed a "presence" around her, and the women's wide-eyed, slightly alarmed expressions told Susan everything she needed to know. Susan had asked for discretion, but she knew how rumors could spread. It didn't take much to fan the flames—one friend mentioning it to her husband, who chatted about it during a round of golf with his buddies—and once it reached the ears of the kids, there was no stopping it. And yes, Susan had certainly noticed the reactions of Avery's friends when they came to the house. They were clearly looking for something. If they didn't think Avery herself was haunted, they might've thought the house was. Susan ultimately blamed herself for this, but she also knew that word about Avery's condition would leak out eventually. It was inevitable. But maybe in a new town, with different people . . .

"You really want to leave?" Susan asked.

Avery nodded.

"Then let's leave," Susan said. "Go somewhere where people don't know us. It will be like a new adventure."

Avery fell into her mother's arms and began to cry.

Susan was both happy and upset. She still didn't know how any of this was going to pan out, but she was going to work her hardest to see it through.

. . .

Susan, Richard, and Avery left less than a week after the two pastors visited their home. Word of that visit had snaked its way around the town, and the rumors about Avery's condition and the Wallace household had escalated. Richard had been at the grocery store and was approached by an acquaintance that he knew from his fantasy football league. The man had asked him, "Is it true you think your house is haunted?" Richard couldn't believe the gall.

My daughter recently passed, and this is what you ask me?

On another occasion, Richard was picking up coffee and donuts for his family, and he heard a woman whispering in line to her husband, *"That's him. Yes, him. They wanted to have an exorcism for their daughter, but his wife kicked the pastors out of the house. They didn't go through with it."*

That was a gross oversimplification—*And for the love of God, you actually thought we organized an exorcism?*—but he didn't bother to correct her. It wasn't worth making a scene, not when they were about to leave, anyway.

And leave they did. They took only what they needed—mainly clothes and toiletries—and hit the road, Susan and Avery in the family station wagon, Richard in the Chevy Malibu. The Wallace parents both obtained open-ended leaves of absence from work, not sure how long those would last for. They told their employers that they were leaving town for a while in the interest of their daughter's health—Richard received paid leave; Susan did not. They didn't say that they might not *ever* come back, even though they supposed it was true. Best to keep the paychecks coming, not mess with the health insurance. Not when they didn't have any concrete plans or new jobs lined up. And they still didn't know *where* they would settle—for now, they were heading about six hours northwest, close to the Minnesota border. Richard's brother owned a small townhome up there and was currently in Arizona, not due to return for another six weeks. The Wisconsin town wasn't Paris, but it would work for the time being.

The townhome was certainly smaller than their place in Grangeville, but no one seemed to mind. With Avery's condition, the lack of space made things easier—which provided some peace of mind for everyone. After only a few days in their temporary home, Susan noticed that Avery's spirits seemed to be lifting. She was chattier, less sullen. She spoke of missing her friends and wanting to reach out to them, which Susan took as a positive sign. The more Avery wished to embrace her old life and do the things that made her happy, the better. The invisible, evil thing was still always in the room with them, according to Avery, but Susan decided to take the win. Progress was progress.

One evening, a little more than a week after they'd arrived, the family was relaxing in the living room. Susan and Avery enjoyed a new episode of *Friends* on the television; Richard listened to music on his portable CD player. He took off his headphones and looked at his daughter.

"Kiddo, I love the playlist you made me," he told her.

It was the last playlist Avery had downloaded and burned before Charlotte died, before she stopped using computers altogether, before Richard had taken a sledgehammer to the family machine. Susan was concerned his comment might be triggering, but Avery just smiled warmly at her dad.

"Thanks," she said, turning back to the television to catch up on the developing romance between Chandler and Monica.

Susan thought it was another sign things were turning around.

We're going to get through this, together, as a family, she remembered thinking.

She was so, so wrong.

. . .

Susan wasn't sure of the time; she only knew it was very late.

She'd fallen asleep on the couch, and Avery had been at her side when she had. The TV was still on, some late-night talk show. Maybe Conan O'Brien. Richard had returned to Grangeville to take care of a few things and grab some items they'd needed. He'd said he'd be back very late that same night. Susan awoke to the clacking of computer keys, and she wondered what it actually was, because surely it couldn't be that.

Did Richard bring a computer back with him? Susan thought, still groggy.

Is he here right now?

She sat up, rubbing the sleep from her eyes, and looked toward the noise.

There was Avery, on the floor near the television. Susan noticed a pair of cables snaking across the room toward where she was sitting, cross-legged.

A laptop screen glowed in front of her.

Susan thought she might be dreaming, and she blurted, "Avery, what are you doing?"

Her daughter turned her head to look at her. "I don't know." There was genuine confusion in her voice. Susan reached and clicked on a lamp next to the couch, and she pinched her eyes together a few times, trying to adjust to the light.

This was no dream.

Avery stared at her mother, dumbfounded. Susan quickly marched over and stooped down, turning the screen toward her. A few windows were open, one of them being Avery's email.

"Honey, how did you . . . ," Susan stammered. "Where did you find this?"

She hadn't thought there was a computer in the house, and she wondered if it might belong to Richard's brother.

"I . . . ," Avery began. "I was looking for a pen, and I found this in a drawer, under some notebooks. And then, I don't know what happened. I just started *doing things*."

"What do you mean?"

"I . . . went online. I emailed Dad."

"What? Why?"

"I don't know. I just felt like I had to. I sent him something."

The girl's voice was hesitant, bewildered. Susan looked into her daughter's eyes. It was like she was coming out of a trance.

"What did you send him?" Susan asked.

Avery slowly clicked to the Sent area of her email account. She'd been telling the truth. There was an email sent to Richard two minutes ago, and the subject read:

Dad?

Susan noticed the tiny paper clip at the far right of the screen, indicating a file attached to that particular email. Her hand moved onto the trackpad, and she double-clicked on the email. There was a message inside, simply reading:

Can you tell me what this is?

Avery

And at the bottom of the email, Susan saw the file attachment. It was named:

COOLGAME.exe.

"I don't know why I sent it," Avery said, perplexed.

Susan moved windows around, exploring the screen. There were other windows open—each of them contained a long list of files, none of which Susan recognized. She scrolled through one of the windows. There were hundreds, if not thousands, of files listed. She felt like she could scroll forever.

"What is this?" Susan asked.

Avery looked at the screen. "I accessed some servers, while you were sleeping. I don't know why I was doing it. I don't even know what these servers are."

Susan had heard the term before. *Server.* She was good with computers, but she still didn't totally grasp the concept. Something about storing and accessing files, but you could get to them anywhere, from any computer, even if they weren't stored directly on the device you were using. You just had to know the web address and maybe type in a password. It was still a bit nebulous to her.

Avery accessed servers?

Why?

She looked again at the long list of files on the screen. "These weren't here, before? When you turned it on?"

Avery studied the screen, and then her eyes shifted upward, thinking. "No . . . I . . . installed an FTP client so I can get to them."

"A what?"

"It's how I find certain things on the Internet. Different servers. Remote ones. I just needed to go there again. I can't explain it. It's like something was making me do it."

Susan was baffled, and she moved the cursor to the email, hovering over the COOLGAME.exe file, preparing to double-click.

Slap.

Avery's hand shot toward the laptop, smacking her mother's wrist.

"Don't open it," Avery implored. Susan met her daughter's eyes. She saw fear, terror—but there was something else. Avery looked to be thinking, hard. Susan felt the girl's hand trembling.

"I remember," Avery whispered, her words dripping with recognition. Susan pulled her hand back.

"This is what Charlotte and I saw," Avery continued. She slumped against the wall, staring out past her mother, slack-jawed. "It's the file from that night. We opened it." She paused, and then said again, as if only speaking to herself:

"I remember."

Susan picked the laptop off the floor and rose to her feet. She yanked out the phone and power cables from the back of the machine.

"Richard!" she called out, still unsure if he was back and she just hadn't heard him come in.

Avery shook her head. "He's not here."

"I'm calling your father," Susan said shakily.

She moved swiftly to the kitchen, keeping Avery in her line of sight. The laptop under one arm, Susan grabbed the cordless phone and dialed Richard's cell phone. She heard the ringing before she even sat down on the living room couch. Avery remained in her spot against the wall, although she had brought her knees up to her chest, hugging her legs.

"Hey, what's up?" Richard answered. His voice was tinny, weak. Susan heard the radio playing in the background.

"Where are you?"

"Almost halfway home, why?"

"Did you get an email from Avery?"

"A little bit ago, yeah. I was going to call and ask you guys about it, but my reception is pretty bad out here."

"Did you open it?"

"Yeah, there was some file attached to it." He paused. "She sent that to me? Where did she find a computer?" His voice cut in and out.

"Richard, she said she sent you the *same* file that she and Charlotte opened."

"She said what? Say that again; I can barely hear you."

"She said it's *the file* that she and Charlotte saw. From *that night*."

"Honey, I can't hear you, I—"

Nothing more.

A lost connection.

"Shit," Susan muttered, immediately dialing the number again. It went straight to voicemail.

Susan wasn't sure how long she and Avery sat there, continuously trying to dial Richard. Twenty minutes, maybe? It was the same result every time. Straight to voicemail. Susan's heart was pounding, her throat tightening. She needed to tell her husband what had happened, how Avery had experienced a breakthrough.

But she was also stressed, worried for his safety.

She felt a little silly thinking that.

It's just a computer file.

The cordless phone ringing in her hand startled her so much that she nearly jumped off the couch. Susan clicked Talk and was greeted with Richard's panicked voice.

"Something's happening to me," he said.

Susan stood up, her heart racing. "Richard, honey, what's wrong?"

"I'm driving, but, *oh God,* it's like there's someone else in the car with me. I can't—help me, please."

She had never heard him so tense, so stricken with anxiety.

"Honey," Susan said, "pull the car over and—"

"I feel it."

"What do you feel, honey? What's—"

"I can't see it, but I can *feel* it. It's right next to me. *Oh God,* it's going to kill me! Wait—I *see* it. *Oh God,* Susan—"

"Ri—

"I *see it!*"

A bloodcurdling scream.

The roar of the engine.

A deafening smash.

The line went dead.

. . .

They were halfway to Grangeville when they saw the lights.

Flashing red and blue.

Susan knew immediately, and her heart sank into her stomach.

She spotted the police cars first, then the fire engine, then the ambulance. They were on the opposite side of the road. Flares were lit, and small orange safety triangles had been placed on the highway. Her eyes frantically scanned the scene as she veered off onto the shoulder, slamming the brakes, fiercely grabbing Avery's thigh with one hand.

She saw it then.

Their Chevy Malibu.

Crumpled into a tree just off the ditch.

It looked like an accordion.

Susan burst from the car, flying across the road, brushing past police officers and heading straight for her husband's car. She covered her hand with her mouth when she got there, not realizing that an officer was holding her by the shoulders. The vehicle was destroyed, the windshield shattered, and Richard was not inside.

Everything else was a blur.

She didn't remember seeing her husband's body in the ambulance, couldn't recall any of the words the officer said to her, did not remember her hysterical screaming or collapsing onto the gravel near the ditch. Nor did Susan hear the screams of her own daughter after she'd sprinted from the car, Avery chasing her in a fit of panic, the child terrified of being left alone.

One thing was not a blur, though.

Richard's BlackBerry, which an officer handed to her.

The screen was shattered.

But something on the screen was still visible.

Still there, frozen.

A collection of numbers, letters, and symbols. They weren't in any discernible order. Total gibberish. Though, at the very top of the screen, Susan could make out one thing. It read:

COOLGAME.exe.

The phone dropped from her hands, and Susan fell to her knees.

A thought blared inside her head.

He opened it.

\part four\

CONNECTED

W e think it's a virus," Susan told Piper. "A computer virus. Not the medical kind. But it's more than just a computer thing. It's supernatural. There's no doubt in my mind. There's a lot to this, but that file, the *virus* . . . that's how it starts. And that's how it spreads."

Susan had been speaking for nearly ninety minutes—it was now after ten P.M. Although she hadn't moved once from the sofa in the Wallace cabin, Piper felt transported; by the end of the tale, she was completely thrown off her axis. She had to gather herself, regain her bearings. Avery's outburst in the classroom, Fisher's sickness—those felt like days ago now. But no. Those things had happened earlier that same day. So much had happened in the span of about ten hours, culminating in Susan pouring her heart out while her daughter slept. Avery hadn't stirred, which Piper thought was a good thing. The kid needed to rest. A couple of times during Susan's story, Piper was convinced Avery would awaken. Despite the fact that she was outlining all the horrible events that had afflicted her family, there was a giddiness in Susan's voice. The woman was animated, even excited at times. Susan had been carrying this weight for so long—Piper imagined it felt good to finally *unload*. She was happy to bear some of the burden.

And what a burden it was.

At least five times during the story, Susan paused to ask Piper, "Are you believing me right now?"

The story should've been impossible to believe, but Piper *did* find herself believing it, and told Susan so. It was a combination of things, Piper thought. Susan's conviction, primarily. If any of this was made up, she was doing a darn good job of getting her details straight. Granted, there was no way of proving any of this, outside of actually leaving Avery alone and seeing what happened. But that would be an extremely hellish thing to do to Avery—even if it was all in her head, it would be akin to torture. But Susan definitely believed that her daughter and husband were killed by a computer virus, and she believed in Avery's condition. The woman believed her daughter was afflicted with something supernatural.

And, somewhat remarkably, sitting in the cold and dark cabin lit by softly wavering candles, so did Piper.

She was certainly primed to believe the tale. If anyone heard this story coming in fresh, they might laugh Susan out of the room.

But Piper believed. She was all in.

Still, she had questions.

So many questions.

"But," Piper began, "what happened today? Why did she . . . lash out like that at school?" She gestured over at the sleeping Avery. The covers were up past her ears, and Piper spotted tufts of the kid's red hair poking out.

Susan shook her head. "I don't know. This particular symptom is very new. After Charlotte died, there was the obvious change in Avery's behavior. Being despondent. Withdrawn. And there was the memory loss, of course, from that night. Her ability to remember things—even people—has slowly degraded over the past year, as well. And lately, ever since we moved up here, she's been more—I don't know, what's the word—spacey? She spaces out. A lot. I'm sure you've noticed."

"I have."

"And the talking to herself—that's new, too. Within the last couple of weeks. And then there was that outburst in the classroom earlier today." Susan rubbed her forehead with her hand, frustrated. "I don't know what that was."

Earlier today.

It still felt like so long ago.

"What happened this afternoon?" Piper asked. "Did she say anything else strange?"

"Thankfully, there hasn't been another episode. I got her in the car, and we came back here. She began talking normally, complaining of being tired. She's just been sleeping." Susan paused, turning her head to look at her daughter, then back at Piper. "I feel like we've been managing this thing for over a year, and now I don't know what to do."

Susan's eyes were pleading, desperate. She was looking to Piper for answers, but Piper had none. Only more questions.

"Why did she send the file to Richard?" Piper asked.

Susan shook her head. "She still doesn't know. Just that she felt compelled to do it. She emailed her dad more than anyone else before she was infected, so maybe typing in his address was old hat or something, I don't know. But it was like a switch was activated inside her head."

"So, she went from being terrified of computers to—"

"Feeling the urge to use them."

"Out of the blue?"

"In a way, yes."

"Like, she can't stop herself?"

"That's what she says. As long as she's not looking at computers, she's fine. But if she *sees* one . . ." Susan thought for a moment. "She says it's like a tingling. A tightening in her chest. She desperately wants to log on and share the file."

Piper thought back to being at the library, to Avery sitting behind Susan and not looking at the machines, her head down.

It made sense.

Susan's story was tracking.

"She sent Richard the virus, what, seven months ago, now?" Susan continued. "Has it been that long?" She looked off. "What happened to my daughter, this *virus*. It's almost like it's come in stages. There's the *can't be alone* problem, then there's the urge to spread it, then the spacing out, and now . . ."

Those monstrous things she said in the classroom, Piper knew.

Susan didn't need to say it.

Susan looked over at her sleeping child.

"It's taking everything," Susan said, distressed. "It's consuming her."

A silence filled the space. Piper could hear the wind blowing in the trees outside, Avery softly breathing in the bed. The wavering candles cast a ghostly glow on Susan's face.

"How can a computer virus do this to someone?" Piper asked. "Do any of this?"

There was no judgment in Piper's voice. She wasn't accusing Susan of lying or telling an extremely tall tale.

She just wanted to know.

"There's no logical answer for how a computer virus could do this," Susan said. "I'm fully aware of that. But the facts have just stacked up for so long, and I've given this so much thought, you have no idea. Every single day, mulling it over, for more than a year. And honestly, the best that I could come up with is that on the night Charlotte died, she and Avery were on the computer. They downloaded that file, the COOLGAME.exe file, and they looked at it together. And it somehow *infected* both of them, I suppose, for lack of a better word. Something that takes about twenty minutes to activate, I guess, after you view it. And when it kicks in, you can't be alone. If you are alone, you will die. Which is what happened to Charlotte. She was alone in that bedroom, and it got her. That evil thing got her."

"Why that amount of time?"

"The twenty minutes?"

"Yeah, the activation."

Susan shook her head. "I don't know. But that's about how long it took for Richard to *feel* the thing after he clicked the file on his Black-Berry. I do have a theory."

"Go ahead."

"When you think about installing a program on a computer, it takes time. Depending on the size, it might take quite a while. Maybe it's the same principle. Maybe that's how long it takes for the virus to *install* inside of a person, you know?" She paused, collecting herself. "But what I do know is that Charlotte screamed at the *precise* moment Avery sensed an evil presence outside with her. It was like it was synchronized, for God's sake. Which tells me that they viewed the file together, and that they eventually went to their own bedrooms. Charlotte was sleeping, so she didn't know it was coming for her, and when she did wake up, she was alone. Avery was lucky it didn't get her that night. If she hadn't woken up, I think it would've taken her, too."

"What about the meningitis thing?"

Susan shook her head. "I know that's what the doctors found. They weren't *lying* to me. I believed that's how Charlotte died, for the longest time. When we were trying to get help for Avery, I believed her crisis was all in her head. The *being followed by an invisible monster* thing—how could you believe something like that? Sure, you can believe *Avery thinks that,* without believing it's actually occurring. But after being with my child nonstop for over a year, after what happened the night Richard died . . . eventually you start believing other things. *Supernatural* things. You start to think, maybe a computer virus *can* do this to someone. Maybe it leaves behind an honest-to-God medical reason for why someone dies, but it's actually something else. Something more sinister. Something otherworldly. Metaphysical." She paused before adding:

"Something that comes for you when you're alone."

Her words made Piper shiver. "How long do you have to be alone before it comes?" She remembered Avery screaming from inside the custodian's closet, that brief time she was separated from everyone in the hall.

"About thirty seconds," Susan answered. "That's my best estimation, based on my phone call with Richard and what he experienced, when he sensed the thing forming next to him in the car."

"Why thirty seconds?"

"Why any of this?" Susan responded, stifling laughter, as if the situation was too incredible to believe. "Do you think there's reason behind what this thing does?"

"I mean, there has to be something, right? Someone must have made this virus. There must be a reason, no?"

Susan shrugged. "Maybe so, maybe not. I tried to come up with reasons long ago, but when I couldn't find any, I just focused on enduring. Now, could there be something? Sure. Avery had a dream the other night, something about playing a game in a cornfield with her friends, having to find someone in a field in thirty seconds or you lose. That was oddly specific, wouldn't you say? Now, does the virus have something to do with that game? I don't know. Was the dream just a representation of what would happen if Avery was alone? Simply a nightmare? That seems the more likely scenario, but who am I to say? In the end, it doesn't matter. Avery opened the file, and it imprinted this *thirty-second countdown* virus inside her. It happened to both my girls, and it happened to my husband."

"You're positive that's what happened to Richard?" Piper asked. She felt bad digging in like this, but she needed the clarification, for her own sake. Susan had had a year since this all started; Piper had learned the mechanics in the past hour or so.

"He was alone in the car, so yes."

"And that was—"

"About twenty minutes after he clicked the file on his BlackBerry. Just like what happened to Charlotte and Avery. The timing is the same. And the way he described what was happening to him in that car: feeling something next to him, only being able to sense it. Then, when that countdown ended, he *saw it*. That's what he said—'*I see it.*' Then he crashed." She looked off. "There's only one possibility. It makes *sense*, right?" Susan stared intensely into Piper's eyes, looking for validation.

Piper acknowledged it with a nod, still coming to terms with everything.

"I didn't tell the police that, of course," Susan continued. "About what I really believe happened to Richard."

"Why not?"

"I thought about it. But I knew they wouldn't believe me, of course. I would've sounded like a loon. And I didn't want to drag Avery into any of this. If I explained myself to them, explained what I thought was happening, my child would become a target. Someone to investigate. Or maybe they would've taken her away from me." She shook her head. "In the end it was just a simple single-car accident. Distracted by his phone, the police suggested. That's one way of putting it."

It was a lot to take in. With each moment that passed, there was more information to process, more inquiries.

"Do you still have the file?" Piper asked.

Susan furrowed her brow. "What do you mean?"

"The one from the night Richard died. On the laptop. You said it was his brother's laptop?"

She nodded. "I never opened it again. I destroyed it."

"The laptop?"

"It was too risky. I didn't want it anywhere near me, near us."

"But that doesn't really destroy it, right? The virus, I mean. Because Avery knows where it is, online."

"She does. Well, not consciously. She still doesn't remember exactly where she found it the night she and Charlotte first viewed it. It's on some server, somewhere, and I know that because I saw it with my own two eyes. I have no idea who it belongs to, how Avery even got access to the server. But she was a tech kid, remember? She was always downloading stuff. Who knows how she got there? *She* doesn't even know. But she obviously *remembered* how to log back in. It was like muscle memory to her once she was back behind the keyboard. Or like something was guiding her. I don't really know."

"So it's still out there," Piper said. "The file."

"Yes," Susan said. "As of last March, yes."

Piper shuddered. She imagined a deadly virus just sitting on someone's server, waiting to be discovered, waiting to wreak havoc.

Only . . .

Piper followed the breadcrumbs in her head.

It's not just on that server.

She emailed that virus to her father.

Which means the file is currently sitting in . . .

"It's still in Avery's sent items," Piper said. "In her email account."

"Probably, yes."

"You haven't trashed it? Deleted it from outgoing messages?"

"We haven't logged back in to Avery's account since the night Richard died. It's too risky. I refuse to do it."

Piper had been listening for so long, simply trying to keep up with the discussion of supernatural viruses and paranormal murders, asking clarifying questions, that she'd somehow lost sight of other pressing matters. More specifically, a recent death in the community—one with remarkable similarities to the deaths of Charlotte and Richard.

"Do you know what happened to Shane?" Piper asked Susan.

Susan offered a confused look. "What do you mean?"

"The boy from Avery's class. Is that how he died? He received the virus somehow? Got infected?"

Susan appeared genuinely baffled. "It was an aneurysm, right? I heard the rumors, though, of course."

"Are you saying it wasn't . . ." Piper nodded toward Avery.

"She hasn't touched a computer since the night her father died."

Piper almost told Susan about seeing the black mist over Shane's body—his death certainly shared parallels with Charlotte's and Richard's. He was alone; the rumors said that he opened a weird computer file. That black mist that Piper saw could've been the same thing that was tethered to Avery, the same type of being that Richard sensed in his car when he was alone, which then presumably materialized after thirty seconds, killing him.

Could it be the same black mist that killed Shane?

Or some variation of it?

Maybe . . .

"What does it look like?" Piper asked.

"What does what look like?"

"The thing following Avery."

"I don't know. No one can see it. Not even Avery. She just senses it, all the time. It moves, and it creeps. She can always pinpoint its location. Can you imagine living like that? Feeling something in the room with you, something radiating with hatred, wanting to kill you?" Susan exhaled. "We don't *want* to know what it looks like. Avery sensed it forming in the custodian's closet at school when she was alone. But she didn't see it. Richard did, but by then it was too late."

"You're sure?"

"I remember every word he said on that phone call. It was all about what he was feeling, *sensing.* If he had seen it, he would've said something. Described it. Quite frankly, I feel like if you *do* see it, it's the last thing you ever see. And that's exactly what happened—Richard saw it, and then the timer was up."

A soft whimper from the bed.

Avery.

"One second," Susan said, rising and moving toward the bed.

The break in the action allowed Piper a few moments to reassess. Shane's death flashed in her mind, along with the memory of what she had seen attached to him before it vanished—a black, swirling mist in the vague shape of a person. Susan claimed that they didn't know what the thing stalking Avery looked like, but Piper assumed that she had seen it floating above Shane—if the boy had been infected, that is. That *had* to have been what happened, right? Both things must be connected.

But why was I able to see it?

It was only for a few seconds, sure, but I saw it.

It didn't make sense to her. She thought about Charlotte's death, how Richard had sprinted inside, reaching his daughter's bedroom probably no more than ten seconds after she'd screamed. He hadn't seen a black mist—surely, Susan would've mentioned that detail.

So, what happened?

Piper reconsidered everything Susan had just told her: the infection, the invisible menace, the thirty-second timer.

Something clicked.

It vanishes after killing, she thought.

Piper played out a potential scenario in her mind, picturing Shane's death as a series of morbid countdowns, applying all the logic that Susan had just laid out for her.

Shane views the virus on his computer, and twenty minutes later, the virus activates inside of him.

He is alone.

The thirty-second countdown starts.

He panics—kicking out the computer cables and knocking over a bottle of soda on the computer tower—runs for help, and falls down the stairs, injuring himself.

The thirty-second countdown ends, and the evil entity forms, killing him.

At that precise moment, I open the Brockway front door, catching the shortest glimpse of the black mist before it disappears. If I'd walked in at twenty-nine seconds, Shane might've survived, because he wouldn't have been alone. If I'd walked in at thirty-three or thirty-four seconds, I might not have seen the black mist at all, because it would've already vanished.

Piper sighed deeply.

Did I really walk in on Shane at that precise thirty-second moment?

Good God, what are the odds?

She closed her eyes, rubbed them with her fingers, put her head down.

This was all too much.

"Are you okay?" Susan asked. Piper didn't realize that she'd returned to the sofa.

"I'm sorry, I'm just . . . thinking." She thought about sharing what she'd seen hovering over Shane's body, checking her new theory with Susan, but held back. She figured it would only make Susan worry more, wouldn't help her with the new problems Avery was currently experiencing.

"She's still sleeping," Susan said. "Just a false alarm."

"What about Mr. Fisher?" Piper rerouted, lifting her head back up.

Susan straightened up in her seat. "You mentioned he was sick. Are you saying he viewed the file?"

"It sounds like he did. I was at his house right before I came over here. He says he can't be alone. Just like Avery. He'd been using a computer in the stacks at the library, and then he just *lost it*. He thinks something is in the room with him."

"Are you positive?"

"Yes."

Susan appeared perplexed. "Did someone send it to him? The virus, I mean."

"I don't know," Piper responded. "Maybe Shane emailed it to him before he died, and Fisher just checked his inbox today. I guess that's possible."

"That's *if* the boy was infected. We don't know that. Does Mr. Fisher remember what he was doing when he—"

"He doesn't remember. He has that memory-loss thing, also like Avery. But this can't be a coincidence, right?" It was all Piper could think to say about it. If there was more to it than that right now, Piper wasn't capable of putting two and two together. She felt bludgeoned with information, her body on the ropes, reeling.

Fisher used a computer, and now he can't be alone.

That's all she really had.

Susan took stock of the Fisher development. "I don't think . . . well,

I'm trying to . . . I really don't know how this is possible. Avery couldn't have, she *wouldn't* have . . . I would've seen her do it. She's never alone."

Those words echoed in Piper's head.

Never alone.

All of this talk of computer viruses and email attachments had distracted Piper from the real horror, the true terror that Susan had laid out at the very beginning of her story:

Being perpetually stalked by an invisible presence.

Something truly evil.

All it wanted to do was kill you, and if you were ever alone—for thirty seconds, according to Susan—it would.

Is there really any way to fully protect yourself from that?

It was then that Piper looked around the cabin. The jagged leftover remains of wall studs, the exposed bathroom. It was next to impossible for Avery to be out of her mother's sight. That made sense now. And there was no computer in the cabin, which also made sense.

"You're wondering about my *redecorating,*" Susan said, noticing Piper's gaze.

Piper smiled sheepishly. "No, I get it. With everything you told me, I'd probably do the same thing."

"I know it seems extreme. I'm willing to try anything, take any precaution necessary. Hence the sage candles. Who knows if they'll do anything at all? It's a daily struggle, it really is. Finding the balance, determining what's right and what's wrong, still letting Avery have some semblance of a childhood. Again, I have my theories about the virus, but it's not like I'm an expert. Anything could happen." She gestured to the corner of the room, where a boom box sat. "I make compromises where I can. She can't download music anymore, so I let her tape songs off the radio. That seems basic enough, right? It's just a radio signal and a cassette tape. But I just don't know. What if this virus can be transmitted by radio signals?"

"Do you think it can?"

She shrugged. "I doubt it, but you never know, right? I didn't expect

Avery to start saying those *awful,* horrific words today. There are so many things we don't know about this. I'm still holding out hope for a way to cure her somehow, if that's even possible. God knows I would try anything. I've read books, done research online. Searching for any possible way to remove this thing that is *haunting* my daughter. In the end, that's what it comes down to. She's haunted."

The term Susan had searched for on the library computer flashed through Piper's mind:

Haunted.

It all made sense.

Piper gazed past Susan at Avery. Still sleeping.

"Do you think her stories help her process everything?" Piper asked. As Susan considered this, Piper let out a nervous laugh. "Actually, do you want to hear something weird? The other day I had this random thought that maybe Avery's stories were cursed or something. Like, they summon a creature if you read it aloud. Have you seen *The Evil Dead?*"

Susan stared at Piper, confused.

"Forget it," Piper said. "I haven't, either."

"There's only one way this thing spreads that we *know* of right now, and it's not by writing stories," Susan replied. "That's not how someone gets infected."

Infected.

Piper remembered the incident at the campsite—the event was still far too vivid in her mind. The noises outside of the tent, the running. She'd wondered if Avery's words had somehow infected her, if she herself had been drawn into the madness somehow.

But knowing what she knew now, the mechanics of everything . . .

Piper still wasn't sure what had been outside her tent, but after listening to Susan explain the history of her family and the virus, Piper was confident that, at the very least, she hadn't *actually* been infected and wasn't being stalked by the black mist, if that's what came from the file. It had simply been her own anxiety getting the better of her.

At least I have that going for me, she thought.

"But you didn't think her stories might raise suspicions?" Piper continued. "About your situation?"

Susan laughed. "As if people needed more ammunition. Kids would have targeted Avery regardless of whether she ever picked up a pencil in her life. And those stories certainly aren't retellings of what happened to her, what happened to us."

"Some of it is. Looking back on them now, I guess."

"You're right. Something coming after her and her sister, the wall being destroyed. She took some creative license, that's for sure. Avery just likes to express herself, and she likes you. You're one of the few people who has treated her—*us,* I suppose—with kindness, since everything happened. I wish I could say the same of her teachers. They see me in the classroom, always by her side—I see the looks on their faces every day."

"What are they?"

"Contempt? No, that's too strong. Irritation, maybe? Irritation that they have to deal with this, that they have to deal with *us,* like it shouldn't be part of their jobs. These teachers think, *She's the disturbed child with the mother for a learning aide, and the system shouldn't support a kid like that*—like they should just be able to ship Avery off and let someone else deal with her. But that's not what we want. That's not what Avery wants. Avery wants to be a kid, and Avery wants to go to school. That's why we moved here, found this cabin on the cheap using Richard's life insurance payout and the money from selling the house in Grangeville. We wanted a fresh start, where nobody knew us at all. Grangeville wasn't for us. Richard's brother's place wasn't for us. People *knew* us up there, too, for God's sake. Knew our story, knew we went there to get away after a tragedy, only to experience *another* tragedy right after. We stayed there for about six months, but it wasn't working. I—we—decided that the only thing that might help was a new beginning. In a totally different place. Normalcy. Well, relative normalcy. School, other kids. Avery was excited about coming here. She even spoke of how fun it would be to enjoy Halloween in a new place. When we first got here, she was looking forward to it, and now she hasn't mentioned it in weeks."

"I can see Avery really liking Halloween," Piper said.

Piper had always looked forward to the day as a kid, too—trick-or-treating, gorging on candy, staying up late, all that fun stuff. Sure, she was a bit of a baby when it came to horror, but that didn't mean she didn't enjoy Halloween growing up. Now it was just another thing taken away from Avery.

Susan glanced over at Avery, shaking her head. "I've just watched my daughter change so much—retreat into herself. And I don't know what to do. Do you understand?"

Piper nodded.

"And I have to keep it secret," Susan continued. "Now, it's certainly an unbelievable thing for most people to believe anyway, but if we were open about it, we would be treated like lepers. Crazy people. We might even be institutionalized. No, secrecy is the only way to maybe obtain *any* sense of normalcy, to give my daughter the faintest chance at a regular life." She ran her hand through her hair, edgy. "That's not even mentioning the dangers inherent in all of this, in our story getting out, if people actually believed us—believed in what happened to my family. We can't have people digging into our history. The email attachment, the virus. Can you imagine what might happen, if it got out?"

"I believe you," Piper simply said. "And we'll fix her. I promise. I don't know how yet, but we will."

Susan smiled. "I appreciate your confidence." She paused, glancing at her sleeping daughter again, her brow furrowed with concern. Piper knew that her promise was empty, and she suspected Susan sensed it, too.

How can we possibly fix this?

I haven't the first clue.

"You know, she won," Piper said, shifting the conversation to a piece of good news.

Susan looked at her with confusion.

"The library contest," Piper clarified.

"She didn't tell me that!" Susan's face lit up.

"She doesn't know yet. Don't you think you would've been next to her when she found out?"

"Right," Susan said, somewhat embarrassed. "I guess I forgot for a second. I suppose I'll never fully get used to this arrangement."

"We can tell her when she wakes up, if that's okay."

"Oh, she'll be so thrilled." Susan's eyes sparkled, and Piper allowed her the time to relish the moment. "Of course, I wanted her to win. I thought it would do wonders for her confidence. But also—I wouldn't tell her this—I was secretly hoping that Avery's stories would somehow expel the evil that surrounds her. That it would be some kind of *creative writing expulsion therapy,* like what she does with her diary. That's one of the only things that carried over from the psychologist. But that's not why she wrote those stories, of course. She just wrote them because she wanted to. But I was hoping it would be another chance for us to fix this thing, another arrow in the quiver. You know what I mean?"

Piper did, and the utter hopelessness of Avery's condition began to settle in.

What hadn't they already tried to cure her?

Piper imagined that they were running out of options. Doctors, pastors, expulsion therapy.

Yet Avery was worse than ever.

The child was still sleeping, but Piper feared what might happen when she woke up. Those words, those horrific words that had spilled out of her mouth, that phrase Fisher thought he recognized, causing him to go down the rabbit hole and eventually become infected himself.

What could possibly stop all this madness?

Then she remembered.

Piper reached down and pulled out the piece of computer hardware she'd snagged from the library. She held it out toward Susan.

"This is from the computer in the library," Piper said. "From the computer that Mr. Fisher was using. I think it's a hard drive. I think . . ."

She stopped, choosing her words.

"I think that the virus might be on here. Or a copy of it, I guess. Maybe. If Mr. Fisher downloaded the file and got infected, the file could still be on here."

Susan glared at the device, and Piper noticed the dread in her eyes.

"What are you doing with that?" Susan asked.

"I don't know," Piper said. "But isn't it worth looking at? Couldn't the answer be in the virus itself?"

Susan opened her mouth to speak but said nothing.

"You've tried everything under the sun," Piper continued, "and Avery isn't getting better. And judging from what I saw in Mr. Fisher's home today, I don't think he's far behind. I think the only thing left to do is examine the file, if it's even on here."

"Don't you think I've thought of that?" Susan snapped. "We already *talked* about this. Weren't you listening?"

"Yes, but—"

"I already destroyed one laptop—the one with Avery's *FTP server access* or whatever it's called—so that no one could get to it from that machine. I made darn sure of that. And that file, that *virus,* is sitting in my daughter's email account. It's in Richard's account, too. I know his password. I could've logged in to either account at any time, but I haven't. Nothing good can come from doing that. It can only spread. Looking at that file in *any form* can only make things worse."

"How do you know that?"

Frustration marked Susan's face. "Don't you get it? This *thing* killed my daughter and my husband. And I have lived beside this evil for nearly every waking moment of an entire year. I don't wish it upon anyone."

"I think it's already too late," Piper replied.

Susan sighed. "If you're right, then God help us all. But I refuse to entertain the idea of plugging in that hard drive, or whatever it is you're thinking about doing. This virus somehow *made* my daughter send a copy of itself to her father, and now he's dead. That's a power, a darkness, I'll never be able to understand. Quite frankly, I'm not sure I want to."

Piper sat in silence.

She had no reply.

"Please, put that away," Susan said. "One evil thing in this cabin is enough."

Piper meekly returned the hard drive to her purse, and as she did, she heard Susan's words echo in her head.

This virus somehow made my daughter send a copy of itself to her father . . .

"Oh my God," Piper sputtered.

"What?"

"Fisher. I'm so stupid. I just realized."

It finally clicked.

Within the dizzying cascade of information from Susan, a very obvious problem had slipped through the cracks, and Piper grew more and more anxious as the realization crystallized in her mind.

"If Fisher is infected," she said, "wouldn't he feel compelled to send the virus to someone else, too? What if he has access to it? If he does, and he sees a computer, then—"

Piper couldn't finish her thought. A groan from the bed caught Susan's and Piper's attention.

It was a hideous, guttural sound.

It was Avery.

She'd woken up.

CHAPTER 29

Piper felt a wave of fear wash over her.

The child groaned again, and Susan locked eyes with Piper, silently pleading with her for help, for suggestions, for *anything*, but Piper had nothing to offer. Susan peered down and examined the items on the coffee table. Piper followed her gaze.

Candles, notebooks, Avery's Walkman.

Susan moved to grab something, but her trembling hand paused, hovering.

Another moan from the bed.

Just as throaty and gravelly as before.

Susan pulled her hand back, grabbing nothing.

She doesn't think anything will help, Piper thought.

Susan rose to her feet instead.

"Honey?" Susan called out. "How are you feeling?" The shakiness in her voice was impossible to miss.

Another moan.

Then Piper heard murmuring, whispering, from the bed. Susan again locked eyes with Piper, and the two women just stared at each other, listening.

More muttering.

It was soft but deep.

The hair on Piper's arms prickled. She felt like running, but she was glued to the sofa. Her hand instinctively moved to pet Ripley, but of course, he wasn't there.

Avery was speaking again.

Piper tried to home in on the words, the cadences, curious if they matched up with the words Avery had shouted in the classroom.

It was a challenge to make them out, but she didn't think they were the same.

They sounded like gibberish.

They were . . .

No.

Not gibberish.

She could hear the words more clearly now.

They were another language, she realized.

But Piper still couldn't make anything out.

Her terror began to build. Piper thought of Susan's story, the part where the two pastors visited the home.

What would they think of this right now?

The evil had always been outside of Avery, but now it seemed to be inside of her. That seemed to change the equation. Piper thought of demons, of unknown creatures crawling up from the depths of hell. Perhaps one of them had wormed its way inside of Avery, and now it was calling the shots. And then a single word flashed in Piper's head, blinking quickly, impossible to miss.

Exorcism.

She knew next to nothing about the practice, had only a loose idea of what it meant—mainly from pop culture. Speaking in tongues seemed to be the giveaway of a possessed person, and Piper thought that might be what Avery was doing right now.

She listened more closely, trying to determine what the kid was saying.

Finally, Piper deciphered a few words.

"*. . . cabeza . . .*"

". . . cabeza hermosa . . ."

Piper finally got it.

It was Spanish.

It had been years since Piper had studied the language—she'd taken four years in high school and hadn't gone any further. Yet, rather remarkably, she knew what those two words meant.

Cabeza hermosa.

Beautiful head.

"She's speaking in Spanish," Piper blurted, and Susan snapped her head toward her. "Something about a 'beautiful head.' What is she talking about?"

Susan hesitated, lost. The woman's face was tortured and broken, and Piper could see her eyes welling up. She thought she might be sick.

"Susan," Piper implored, "why is she saying that? What does it mean?"

Susan looked back toward Avery and moved to go to her daughter.

But she suddenly stopped.

Avery had sat up in bed.

The covers had fallen off her shoulders, and the girl sat, frozen, staring blankly ahead. The candles cast flickering shadows across her yellow, baggy T-shirt. Avery wasn't wearing her glasses, and Piper got a good look at her eyes from across the room.

Even from a distance, Piper noticed how glassy they were.

How *distant* they seemed.

Vacant.

The silence in the cabin was now deafening. Piper didn't know what to do, and neither did Susan, it seemed. She still stood in the same position, gaping at her daughter.

"Baby?" The mother finally spoke. "Are you all right?"

Avery cast the covers aside, spun her body, and put her feet on the floor. She began walking toward Susan, very deliberately. The girl's arms hung limply at her sides as she shuffled toward her mother. Piper instinctively scooted farther down the couch, again thinking of Ripley, wishing she were lying with her head on the dog's chest, listening to the comforting and rhythmic beating of his heart.

Avery continued to move closer. The kid was whispering now, muttering to herself, an instant replay of what she'd been doing in the classroom. She reached Susan and stopped.

The words stopped, as well.

Now she just gazed numbly ahead.

Susan stooped to Avery's eye level, taking her child by the hands.

"Sweetie," Susan said. "What's wrong? How can I help you?"

Nothing.

"Avery, sweetie?"

Susan let go of one hand and waved her own hand in front of Avery's face.

Still nothing.

The child didn't even blink.

Susan jerked her head toward Piper, looking for answers. Piper simply shook her head quickly from side to side, mouth agape.

Susan looked back toward her daughter.

"You've been sleeping for some time," Susan told Avery, her voice steadying. There was tenderness there, compassion. "Why don't we get you washed up a bit? See if that doesn't wake you up?"

Susan rose and gently led Avery by the hand toward the exposed bathroom. The girl mindlessly followed, her feet shuffling, the blank expression not leaving her face.

They walked through the empty doorframe, in between the jagged-edged remains of the two-by-fours that jutted from the floor. In a way, it looked like they were walking into an open mouth, between rows of sharp teeth. Piper remained on the couch, and she watched as Susan dampened a rag in the sink, wrung it out, and then shut off the faucet. Susan again stooped to Avery's level and wiped her daughter's face with the rag.

Piper was struck by Susan's gentleness. This was an impossible situation, and Susan was no doubt flustered—Piper wondered if she had the urge to run like Piper did, if she was also dripping with uneasiness. But Susan's parental instincts had won the day. She was caring for her daughter, doing whatever she could to help.

Not fleeing, not showing fear.

Only love.

Susan lightly dabbed at the corners of Avery's lips with the rag, and then those lips began to move.

The words.

The words were coming *again*.

Piper stood, shaking off her own fear, consumed now by morbid curiosity. She inched closer to the bathroom.

What is she saying? Closer now. Susan was still stooped low, her hands on Avery's waist.

"... *cabeza hermosa* ..."

Piper heard it again. And then she heard more, the whole phrase. Avery was repeating it ad nauseam.

"*Quédate quieta, cariño. Tu cabeza hermosa será enviada a tu padre.*"

Piper's Spanish failed her.

She could make out *your beautiful head* and *your father*.

Not the rest.

But the principles of the language hadn't left her. Although she didn't know the translations, she knew the spellings, knew the accent marks, even knew the location of the tilde.

Closer.

Five feet, now, peering through the teeth, about to enter the mouth herself. Piper imagined her head as a tape recorder, and she mentally clicked the red circular button.

"*Quédate quieta, cariño. Tu cabeza hermosa será enviada a tu padre.*"

She would remember this.

She had to.

She *needed* to.

Piper stopped when she reached the broken two-by-fours. Avery's voice grew in volume, then it grew some more, and now the girl was *shouting*, screaming, and Susan's grip on her daughter's waist tightened.

"*¡QUÉDATE QUIETA CARIÑO TU CABEZA HERMOSA SERÁ EN-VIADA A TU PADRE QUÉDATE QUIETA CARIÑO TU CABEZA HER-MOSA SERÁ ENVIADA A TU PADRE QUÉDATE QUIETA CARIÑO TU CABEZA HERMOSA SERÁ ENVIADA A TU PADRE!*"

Avery's arms began thrashing, and Susan grabbed them, attempting to pin them to Avery's sides. The child's arms thrust upward, knocking Susan off balance and sending her spinning toward Piper—then everything happened so fast that Piper couldn't react.

Susan's body spun around.

For a split second, her eyes locked with Piper's.

But as her body careened toward the floor, the sickly realization of what was about to happen struck Susan, because she looked downward and tried to scream.

She didn't have time.

Her neck collided with the serrated edge of a two-by-four.

One of the *teeth*.

Avery stopped shouting.

All Piper heard then was a sickly, thick gargling.

She gawked, horrified at the pool of blood that was gathering near her feet.

CHAPTER 30

12:32 A.M.—Help me   TUESDAY, OCTOBER 31, 2000

Hey. I shouldn't be writing about this stuff anymore. But I honestly don't know what to do.

The kid is with me right now. Her mom had an accident, I'll call it. It's a little more complicated than that. Without getting too much into the details, the girl "loses" control sometimes. She spaces out or trances out, and then she gets weird and violent, saying these horrid, *god-awful* things. The mom tried to help and . . . she fell onto a jagged piece of wood. It was gruesome. I've never seen so much blood before in my life. But somehow, she's alive. She's in the ICU. Significant internal damage, emergency surgery . . . just terrible stuff. She might not make it. The doctor I spoke with seemed kind of hopeful? I honestly don't know.

The girl doesn't remember it. After the *accident,* she went kind of numb. I've seen her behave like this before, but now it's much, much worse. For a few hours, it was like she was sleepwalking. She eventually came out of it, and I explained to her what happened. She had no memory of it. Not the thrashing, not the things she was saying. None of it. The kid is just kind of broken from it all, knowing she put her mother in the hospital. I can't even imagine.

They let me take her back to my place. She had nowhere to go. They have no other family in the area; I think the closest is an uncle in Arizona. I don't know. I'm supposed to call the hospital in the morning for updates, and then I'm assuming bring her back there. After that, I'm not sure. If the mom dies, I have no idea what they'll do with her.

There's another big problem here that I haven't mentioned yet: She can't be alone. And I mean that in the literal sense. All the overbearing parenting, the girl's edgy and fearful behavior—it's because she's being stalked by something people can't see. *She* can't see it, either, but she knows it's there. And it will kill her if she's ever alone.

That's why the mom was always by her side. To protect her. And she's not the only one in town like this right now: This teacher friend of mine was messing around with a computer, and he's unwell, too. Paranoid, anxious. *He* can't be alone, either.

That's where I'm at. It's late, and she's on my couch watching TV. She's pretty lucid right now, but at any moment something could happen. She might have another outburst. Also, if I leave the room . . . she could die. I positioned my computer and chair so I could see her as I type. I'm honestly afraid to turn my back on her. My brother is on his way, so that's good. He should be here by dawn.

I should probably log off now. There are other things that I want to research, but maybe I'll wait until she's asleep. I feel like I should be with her right now. To keep her safe.

[comment on this | comments]

CHAPTER 31

P iper clicked Post and immediately logged off. Avery was on the couch, Ripley lying at her feet. The kid hadn't glanced in Piper's direction the entire time she typed, and Piper remembered what Susan had told her about Avery's condition.

As long as she doesn't look at a computer, she can control the urge.

Or something like that.

Piper picked up the phone and dialed Fisher's number.

Answering machine.

She left the same message as before, wondering if Fisher's wife had taken him to a hospital—the woman had mentioned the idea when Piper visited. Piper considered going over to their house with Avery but decided that would be too dangerous. Plus, her car was still at the Wallaces'—she and Avery had taken a cab back from the hospital, after riding with Susan in the ambulance.

No, they needed to stay inside the apartment.

What if we were outside and she ran off?

What if she had an episode at Fisher's house?

The weight of this responsibility bore down on Piper. Outburst or no, Avery could never be alone, ever again. There was so much that could go wrong at any given moment, and Piper wondered how Avery and Susan had made it through an entire year of this.

Avery slowly turned her head toward Piper, and Piper was afraid to look in her eyes. She thought this might be it, that this might be the moment she started chanting more terrible words, in English or Spanish or an ancient and forgotten language she had no business knowing.

"Ms. Lowery . . . ," Avery started.

Piper exhaled, the tension easing. The measured way Avery spoke her name was a good sign.

"Can I have something to drink?"

Piper crossed into the kitchen and filled up a glass with water from the sink, dropping in a few ice cubes, as well, never letting Avery out of her sight. She also grabbed the girl's knapsack from the counter. Piper had taken it with her from the cabin, almost as an afterthought, thinking it might come in handy at the hospital. She'd shoved Avery's notebooks and Walkman inside, as well as a few cassettes she'd spotted by the boom box. Ripley hopped off the couch, and Piper plopped down next to Avery, handing her the glass. Avery took a long drink, wiping her lips with her sleeve when she finished.

"How are you holding up?" Piper asked.

Avery shrugged, reaching down to pet Ripley, who had settled on the floor.

"We'll call the hospital first thing in the morning," Piper said. "But I wouldn't be surprised if they called us before then."

"With good news, do you think?"

Piper crossed her fingers and held them up in the air. "I don't know your mom very well, but she seems tough. A fighter."

"Really?"

"She's been fighting for you for so long, right? Making sure you're safe?"

Avery smiled softly and glanced downward. "I guess." She paused for a second, then looked back up at Piper. "She told you about us? What happened to me?"

Piper nodded.

Avery didn't respond to this, merely gesturing at the knapsack on Piper's lap. "Thanks for bringing my stuff."

"Oh, yeah. No problem." Piper placed the bag in between them. "Maybe you can play me some of your mixtapes. Can I see them?"

Avery reached into the knapsack, pulling out a few tapes. Words were scribbled on each white label. "I only get, like, three stations on my boom box." She held up one tape. "This one is all country, and I'm not the *biggest* fan, but I'm kind of coming around to it. Sometimes they play Shania Twain, and she's cool. I like LeAnn Rimes and the Dixie Chicks, too, so I always tape them if they come on." She put down the tape and grabbed another, fiddling with it in her hands. "This is just classic rock stuff. My dad always played it in the car growing up, so I know, like, every popular rock song from the seventies. What's that song they sing from *Wayne's World*? When they're driving and, like, head-banging?"

"Oh, 'Bohemian Rhapsody'?"

"Yeah, that's on here. There are a bunch of Pink Floyd songs, too. Those were his favorites." Avery held up a third tape. "This is all newer stuff. Pop, mainly. I tape these songs the most. I have a bunch of cassettes from that station. The reception is pretty good, which helps."

Their completely normal conversation struck Piper as the oddest thing, knowing what she knew now. Knowing there was *something* evil in the room with them, perhaps hovering over Avery as she spoke; knowing she could spiral into madness or a catatonic state at any time.

Avery slipped her hand into the knapsack, and she pulled out another object. Not a tape. She studied it curiously in her hands.

"What is it?" Piper asked.

"It's a BlackBerry." She said the words haltingly, like she'd never seen it before.

"Let me see it." Avery handed the device to Piper. She first thought it was Richard's, but then she remembered what Susan had told her about the screen. Shattered, unusable. This phone looked pretty new. Piper jabbed at the buttons. It was completely dead.

"I . . . ," Avery started. "I'm remembering something."

Piper just listened.

"I remember taking it. It was . . . on a desk, I think? And then, did I use it? It seems like a dream. But . . . I was in bed. My mom was next to me, asleep." She stopped, continuing to think. "I can picture myself using it, but I don't know if it actually happened."

It didn't take long for Piper to connect the dots. She wasn't certain about her conclusion, but she found it pretty likely.

Avery had sent the virus to Shane using the BlackBerry.

Maybe Mr. Fisher, too.

And the black mist must have been the *thing* that formed just before the thirty-second countdown ran out.

She knew both of their email addresses, after all. Piper remembered the first day she met Avery in Fisher's classroom. Fisher had mentioned that he put his email address on the syllabus, and she clearly recalled Shane loudly sharing his AOL username with everyone within earshot. That's how Avery knew—and when she had access to a connected device, it was those two email addresses that floated to the top of her thoughts. It likely wasn't intentional. It probably could've been anyone, Piper thought, but those were recent. Fresh. Something her brain had not yet erased.

Susan was adamant that Avery hadn't used a computer, and Piper believed her. Susan was just unaware. Avery had probably sent the virus using the BlackBerry, right next to her sleeping mother in bed. Then the battery likely died, which explained the phone's current state. Avery probably had no way of charging it—otherwise she might've done just that, blasting off the virus to more recipients. Those two emails were likely all she could send.

Avery gently took the phone from Piper's hands. She stared at it uneasily, rubbing the screen with her thumb. "Whose is this?" she asked.

"I honestly don't know."

Piper thought back. Shane died the same day he shoved Avery into the custodian's closet, the same day Piper was called to the principal's office . . .

Principal Christian's BlackBerry.

It was right there, on the edge of his desk.

Avery must have snatched it.

She was even more certain about her conclusion now, and was about to share her thoughts with Avery, but then she held back. There was no need.

Why make the kid suffer?

If she didn't remember, she didn't remember. Knowing whose it was didn't help anything.

"I've never seen it before," Piper lied, taking the BlackBerry from Avery. "Do you want some more water?"

Avery nodded, and Piper took Avery's glass to the kitchen, along with the BlackBerry. She walked backward slowly, never losing sight of Avery. When she grabbed a few fresh ice cubes from the freezer, she shoved the BlackBerry inside, hoping the freezing temperature would destroy the device for good.

. . .

They watched TV for another hour and a half, Ripley joining them on the couch. Avery had rummaged through Piper's VHS collection, finding a tape that contained episodes of *Dawson's Creek,* and she slid that into the VCR. Piper wondered exactly when Avery would get sleepy, before remembering that her sleep schedule was all screwed up—she had slept all afternoon the day before when Susan took her home from school after the "it smells like death" incident.

It was close to two forty-five A.M., and Piper thought they might just stay up all night. Then Avery took off her glasses—Piper had grabbed these from the cabin, as well—and rubbed her eyes, yawning. Piper figured it might be time, before realizing that she didn't know how sleeping would work. Susan had certainly outlined their situation—Piper grasped the basics, she believed—but she wasn't sure she knew *all* the rules to keep Avery safe.

Piper clicked the remote, and the TV went dark, taking James Van Der Beek and Katie Holmes with it.

"Hey, before you fall asleep, can we talk about something?" Piper asked.

"Yeah, sure," Avery said through another deep yawn. Ripley's head was in Avery's lap now, and Avery scratched behind the dog's ear.

"This might sound really dumb, but what do we do when we sleep?"

"What do you mean?"

"Like, do I have to be facing you? Do I have to be next to you? *Can* I sleep?"

Avery continued to pet the dog's head, then moved her hands to the back of Ripley's neck. "No, you can sleep. You just have to be in *my* potential line of sight. That's what my mom always says."

"But what if your head is facing the opposite direction?"

Avery stopped scratching Ripley and looked confused.

"You know," Piper continued, "line of sight. If you're lying next to me, but your head is facing away from me, I'm not in your potential line of sight." Piper looked away from Avery as she said this, then looked back at her. "If you're not facing me, could that *thing* come and get you?"

Avery chuckled. "Don't overthink it."

"I kind of have to right now."

"I just can't be alone. So when I say *line of sight,* it doesn't matter what direction my head is in. Just as long as I could spin around and see you. Does that make sense?"

"Kind of."

Avery thought for a moment. "We tried a bunch of things. My mom, Dad, and me. Then me and my mom. Imagine I was going to be murdered. By a person. Like, if it *actually* happened right now, you would see who did it. But if I was in the bathroom and someone killed me, and you were out here, watching TV or whatever, you wouldn't see it. You wouldn't know who did it or what they looked like. They might get away with it."

Piper was blown away at the breeziness of Avery's words, at how casually she could talk about being murdered.

"So, what you're saying is," Piper said, "as long as we're in the same room together, you're fine."

"Sort of."

"What do you mean?"

Avery gestured behind her with her head. "Let's say you were sleeping on the floor behind the couch, and I was sleeping on the couch."

Piper looked behind her. Her couch was in the middle of the room, unlike the Wallaces' couch in the cabin, which had been shoved up against the wall.

"If I was back there," Piper said, speaking slowly, putting it all together, "then you wouldn't be able to see me."

"And I could die."

"Do you know that for certain?"

"I think so. We tried that before, at my old house. Just to see what would happen. It didn't go well."

"You felt it forming?"

Avery nodded. "Don't sleep behind the couch. Trust me."

Piper envisioned that potential scenario in her head. The two of them asleep in her apartment, Avery on the couch, Piper on the floor behind the couch. And she imagined the culprit as a person, not a mysterious black mist with arms and a head. If someone crept inside and stabbed Avery, even if Piper had her eyes open, she wouldn't be able to see who did it.

But if she was next to her . . .

She was starting to get it.

Still, the rules seemed vague, even if Susan and Avery had refined them over the course of a year.

Piper wasn't about to take any chances.

"Why don't we just sleep in the same bed tonight," Piper offered. "Just to be safe."

"Can Ripley be there, too?"

Avery had recommenced with the scratching, and Ripley was now softly snoring, his big, droopy brown eyes closed.

"Believe me," Piper said, "he would like nothing more."

Avery smiled, but then she jolted, her entire body trembling for a moment.

"Was that . . . ?" Piper asked.

Avery nodded, relaxing. "It just moved past me. Right past my head."

"And you felt it do that?"

"Yeah."

"But you've never seen it? Not once?"

Avery shook her head.

"I hope you never do," Piper said, stating the obvious. As Susan had said, if Avery ever saw it, it would likely be the last thing she saw.

. . .

Avery was asleep, Ripley curled up at her feet in Piper's bed. The child had drifted off moments after her head hit the pillow. Piper kept trying to imagine what was going on in her head, but she hadn't the first clue. She was simply thankful that Avery had *come back* for the time being, at least long enough to have a conversation about how to keep her alive. Piper knew at any moment Avery's mind could be gone again, and she was dreading what she would do when that moment came. For now, though, she had a respite. And she needed to use her time wisely.

Piper slowly climbed out of bed and walked the six or seven paces over to her computer. She sat down, immediately glancing back at Avery. Ripley stayed on the bed, and Piper wondered whether the dog's presence could perhaps save Avery's life.

Is she technically not alone because Ripley is with her?

She dismissed the idea as quickly as it came. It didn't jibe. Avery had explained the infection to her as if a person had to be an eyewitness to a murder to keep her safe, and Ripley wasn't a person. Besides, if beating this thing was as simple as having a dog around 24/7, they'd have just opened a kennel. Surely, Susan would have thought of that.

Piper turned to the computer and wiggled the mouse. The monitor woke up. Piper double-clicked on the AOL icon, and the modem did its thing.

She looked over at Avery.

Unmoving, still asleep.

Piper fired up the Internet browser. She impatiently watched it load.

She checked on Avery again.

Still sleeping.

The browser loaded, and Piper navigated to a site called BabelFish. She remembered her housemates using it in college—it was the go-to language translation website. Piper clicked the drop-down, selected "Spanish to English," and began typing, doing her best to get the spelling just right.

Quédate quieta, cariño. Tu cabeza hermosa será enviada a tu padre.

She clicked the blue "Translate" button and waited.

The translation arrived quickly.

Stay still, darling. Your beautiful head will be sent to your father.

Piper stared at the screen, tapping her thumb on the desk. She didn't know what it meant. She had not the first clue. She copied the English translation, opened a new tab, and searched the two lines.

Nothing.

She then copied the original Spanish and searched for that instead.

Again, nothing.

She checked on Avery.

Asleep.

Piper turned back to the computer, frustrated. The words were dark, no doubt. But besides being macabre, they didn't hold a deeper meaning for Piper. She'd thought that maybe searching for them would unlock something about Avery's condition, but that wasn't happening.

But what about . . .

The other phrase, the one from the classroom. Those words were still branded on Piper's brain. She typed them into the search bar.

It smelled of filth, it smelled of disease, and it smelled of death.

Loading bar, slowly moving.

Avery check—still snoozing.

And then . . .

Search results.

There it is.

That phrase was apparently infamous, although Piper had never heard it before. She was too young; it was before her time. But it explained why the words had triggered something in Carol's and Glen's minds.

Piper clicked on a link and began to read.

The words had been uttered by Geraldo Rivera when he was a young reporter for ABC. In 1972, he recorded an exposé on Willowbrook, an institution for children with intellectual disabilities located in Staten Island, New York. Details of the facility turned Piper's stomach. Naked children lying on the floor, screaming and wailing, covered in their own filth. Piper tried to read on, to see if something might tie directly back to Avery or the Wallace family, but she couldn't. The suffering of these children—the abuse, the neglect, the squalor they lived in—was simply too much. The screen grabs of the television report were difficult to look at, the details too horrid. Piper was on a hunt for information, but she immediately wished she'd never learned about Willowbrook's existence. She knew she'd never be able to forget what she had seen, would always remember Geraldo's words describing the heartbreaking institution.

It smelled of filth, it smelled of disease, and it smelled of death.

Piper closed out of the page, then signed out of AOL.

Goodbye, the friendly computerized voice told her.

Piper reached underneath the desk and yanked the computer plug from the wall—partially because she'd had enough Internet for the night, but also because she couldn't risk Avery waking up and logging on. The monitor zapped to black, and Piper was satisfied. She gathered herself, glancing over at Avery again, wondering how long she'd been staring at the computer screen. Thankfully, Avery was still asleep, and Piper wondered what the kid knew about the facility, if anything. She'd have to ask her in the morning, she decided, even though she never wanted to think about Willowbrook again.

Her more immediate set of problems then came roaring back into her mind, mainly revolving around the sleeping arrangements. There were too many variables.

What if I sleep like a stone and the kid wanders off?

What if she goes to the bathroom, alone?

What if she plugs the computer back in and goes online?

What if . . .

Piper stood and walked to her small closet, looking back at Avery every couple of steps. She opened the closet doors and rifled around in a plastic bin until she found a handkerchief, a leftover from a college team-building exercise. It had been used as a blindfold in a trust walk activity through a forest but would now serve a very different purpose. Piper returned to the bed and, without waking Avery, tied the handkerchief around the child's wrist and then around her own, cinching it tight. There was no way Avery could try to get up and walk around without Piper knowing, she thought. The makeshift handcuffs seemed a little dramatic, but it was the best solution Piper could think of.

With that, Piper lay down next to Avery, and within seconds, she was out, too.

. . .

Piper dreamed she was in Willowbrook, wailing on the floor along with the other children, an orderly with a grim face and fire in his eyes

attempting to drag her away. He tugged at her arm, screaming obscenities, promising he'd beat her unless she listened. Piper couldn't stand
up, and the howling around her reached a fever pitch—the orderly kept
yanking and pulling, swearing on his mother's life that he would make
her and the other children pay.

The dream fuzzed a bit, and reality crept in.

But she still felt the *tugging*.

And then she realized—what was happening, where she was. Piper
was on the floor of her apartment, and Avery was walking, their wrists
still bound together. She must've fallen out of the bed, crawling without
realizing it, following the girl's lead. Avery was mumbling, shuffling
along, and Piper, not knowing what to do, crawled along beside her.

Her mind became clearer, like adjusting the rabbit ears on a television. She thought back to Avery's other episodes, not sure if she was
about to have another or if this was just good old-fashioned sleepwalking. Piper remembered the cabin, right before her outburst, Susan attempting to calm the girl down, speaking to her, washing her face. It
hadn't worked. Avery had thrashed about, and Susan had been gravely
injured—Piper couldn't let the same thing happen to her. So there, in her
dark apartment in the middle of the night, she made the snap judgment
to do the opposite of what Susan had done. She would just let Avery
mumble and wander, thinking that might not trigger an episode.

Piper rose to her feet, walking beside Avery. The child continued to
murmur to herself, and Piper still couldn't make out what she was saying. For this, she was thankful—she imagined the words would not be
pleasant. Avery shambled past the couch, past the island counter, and
onto the cold linoleum floor in the kitchen. She lifted her free arm and
brushed the drawers with her fingertips as she walked past, still whispering, walking as if she were floating. Avery rounded the kitchen and
then returned to the living room, Piper hoping she would just take a lap
and go back to bed.

Avery stopped at an end table next to the couch, and Piper waited
with bated breath beside her. She realized she hadn't looked at the girl's

face, so she hesitantly did so now, noting Avery's half-opened eyes and blank expression. Her lips moved, but no words were spoken—Piper didn't know if this was good or bad, but a chill ran through her just the same.

Avery then started groping at the lamp with her free hand, running her fingers from the shade to the base, then finding the handle of the drawer and pulling it open. She dug around inside, and her hand emerged holding an object.

A pair of shears.

They'd been there since Piper moved in, but she hadn't used them. She also hadn't thought to clear her apartment of weapons when she returned with Avery, and her heart sank. Piper hadn't imagined this scenario happening—*For the love of God, how could I?*—and now she had to decide what to do.

Avery's lips trembled, and the kid shifted her grip on the scissors, grasping the handle like one would a butcher's knife, about to carve a jack-o'-lantern. Piper felt her own hand shaking. She considered trying to slip out of the handkerchief, but it felt tight, and she didn't want to disturb Avery. Piper gazed back at the bed, and through the darkness could see Ripley lying on top of the covers, curled up. She couldn't tell if the dog was watching them or not, and she hoped he was fast asleep, that he wouldn't come over to investigate.

Piper wiggled her hand, testing the tightness of the knot. There was no way to get out of it without undoing the knot completely, and she reached over to do just that. Her free hand touched the loose end of the fabric, and this sparked something in Avery, the girl's head twitching in that direction, the scissors moving toward their bound wrists.

Piper froze.

Avery ran the shears from the handkerchief up Piper's arm, and Piper felt the cool tip of the blades tickle her skin. The blades continued to ascend Piper's body, until they reached her neck, where they stayed.

The shears shifted in Avery's hand, the girl rotating the blades left and right and back again. They weren't particularly sharp, and Piper didn't feel pain—but she was well aware that a sudden jab to her jugular could be the end. Piper shifted her gaze from the scissors below her chin to Avery's face, and she studied the girl's eyes. It was dark in the apartment, yes, but Piper was still able to judge Avery's coherence.

There didn't seem to be any.

The child was looking through Piper, past her, at something unseen, or maybe nothing at all.

Totally and completely lost.

A movement near Piper's feet caught her attention, and her heart sank. It was Ripley. The dog sniffed at Avery's feet, and he then raised his head near Avery's and Piper's wrists. Avery noticed, and her head jerked that way. Ripley began licking their hands, and Piper held back a scream, afraid it might startle Avery, causing her to lash out. She still feared breaking the girl's trance and instead tried to communicate with the animal telepathically.

Oh, Rip, she thought.

Please go away, please please please please.

She considered kneeing the dog, or even softly nudging him with her foot toward safety. Piper did neither and the dog continued to lap at their bound wrists. Avery watched him, keeping the shears trained on Piper's throat. The child then lowered the blade, bringing it toward Ripley.

Piper knew that she had to act. She moved her free hand ever so slowly toward the sharp edge, her entire arm moving as if underwater.

Eight inches.

Four inches.

The blade was pointed at Ripley's face, and Piper knew all it would take was a short stab. The dog seemed oblivious. He lapped away with his tongue, and Avery stared at him with her empty eyes.

Piper's hand was close now. Her fingers grazed the tip of the shears, then the center, then the handle. She touched Avery's hand, ever so slightly, and it made the girl's hand dip in the air—a few centimeters, maybe, but she did not thrust her hand forward, which was what Piper feared the most. Feeling confident, Piper gently coiled her fingers around Avery's hand and began to lower it to her waist. For the first time, sounds emerged from Piper's throat. No words, only shushing and cooing sounds.

Avery's lips quivered, and she blinked rapidly, her eyes gradually widening. Even in the darkness, Piper saw them glisten with recognition.

"Ms. Lowery?" she said.

"It's me, it's me," Piper responded. She felt Avery's grip on the shears loosening.

"You . . . you . . ."

Loosening still. Then she released the blade completely, the scissors dropping harmlessly to the carpet near Ripley with a soft thud. Piper quickly undid the knot of the handkerchief, pulling her hand free and tossing the makeshift handcuffs aside. She picked up the scissors and placed them on the end table before putting her arms around Avery.

"You . . . ," Avery said.

Piper gently shushed her, running her hand from the crown of Avery's head to the back of her neck, over and over again. "Yes, sweetie? What is it?"

Piper relaxed her grip on Avery and leaned back, looking into the girl's eyes.

She immediately regretted this.

The kid was gone again, replaced by something else. Whatever it was, there was no humanity. Avery smiled wickedly at Piper, her voice turning low and throaty.

"You shouldn't be here!"

The child lunged for the shears, her right hand falling upon them. Piper reacted instinctively, grabbing Avery's left wrist and pulling her back, attempting to wrestle away the weapon with her other hand. Ripley began bouncing and barking, circling the pair, adding to the chaos in the tiny apartment. Piper felt the sharpness of the blade as she yanked the scissors free from Avery's grip, flinging them across the room to the kitchen, where they clanged and skidded on the tile. Piper bear-hugged the girl from behind, taking her to the ground. The child squirmed and yelped, repeating the phrase:

"You shouldn't be here!"

"You shouldn't be here!"

"You shouldn't be here!"

Gradually, Avery's struggles lessened, and her words ceased. She went limp in Piper's arms, returning to the catatonic state Piper had seen before.

Ripley stopped barking and lay down next to them, whimpering softly. Piper felt a stinging on the inside of her hand, no doubt where the blade had sliced her.

Her own ragged breath slowed, and then there was silence.

They stayed like that for a few minutes. Eventually, Piper rose to her feet and carried Avery to the bed, positioning her on the mattress next to the wall. She lifted her head and slid a pillow underneath, pulling the quilt up to her shoulders. The kid was out cold, potentially unconscious—or maybe worse, Piper worried. She placed two fingers on Avery's neck, searching for a pulse. The throbbing was immediately evident, but it was faster than it should've been, Avery's heart beating a mile a minute.

Piper now felt a different throbbing, one coming from her own head. The situation had never seemed more dire, Avery's health never in greater doubt. Piper was no doctor, no authority on evil viruses that originated from the Internet—but in her heart, she felt like Avery didn't have much longer. Not as herself, anyway. Something was taking over, and soon Avery wouldn't be Avery anymore.

She would be something else.

Perhaps for good.

Piper felt a mixture of terror and sadness bubble inside of her, and she wanted to cry. She held back her tears, instead applying a bandage to her hand, then retrieving the handkerchief and binding their wrists together again, pulling the knot tighter than before. At the very least, she could make sure the child didn't wander off to die. That was something she could control.

Ripley jumped up on the bed and positioned himself against Piper's legs, sprawling out toward her, and Piper reached out and scratched the top of his neck. She had never been more grateful to feel his soft fur between her fingers.

Piper lay back, resting her own head on a pillow, hearing Avery's rapid and shallow breaths inches away.

She knew she wouldn't be getting any more sleep that night.

CHAPTER 32

T his is the craziest shit I've ever heard," Sam said, taking another long sip of coffee.

Her brother had arrived, as Piper had hoped, near dawn. Her bed was next to the window that faced the road, giving her the perfect vantage point to watch for Sam's arrival. She thought she'd recognized the rumble of his red Toyota Camry getting closer, and she undid the handkerchief around her and Avery's wrists, popping out of bed, pinching the blinds open to see. Piper had nearly burst into tears when she saw that it *was* his car, feeling a renewed sense of hope. She'd raised the blinds so Sam could see her, knocking on the window, motioning for him to come up the stairs. It was a gloomy morning, drizzling rain—Sam quickly ascended the staircase, dumping his canvas bag on the floor when he walked inside, immediately complaining about the inefficiency of the MapQuest directions he'd used while driving. The mere sound of his voice made Piper feel like everything might be okay.

Avery was still sleeping, and her heart rate had finally slowed. Piper was confident enough to leave her in the bed as she and Sam drank a freshly brewed pot of coffee at the kitchen table, Piper positioning herself so she was facing Avery on the other side of the apartment.

This is my life now, she thought, *at least for a while.*

Piper had, however, received a piece of good news, just after her brother arrived. She'd called the hospital, and Susan was currently in a stable condition. Responding well to the surgery, but still sedated. Her vital signs were being monitored closely. The next twenty-four to forty-eight hours would be crucial, the nurse told her. Piper detected a cautious optimism in the nurse's voice, but it sounded like she wasn't out of the woods yet.

It buoyed Piper's spirits to know that Susan had survived the night, and it gave her the energy to recount the Wallace family saga—well, an abbreviated version—to Sam. Her brother had a dubious look on his face for the entirety, often scratching his unshaven cheeks with his right hand. It seemed like he was only partially listening, instead paging through Avery's journals, which Piper had placed on the table. She would sometimes pause to see what he was looking at—they read entries about Avery's fascination with *The Blair Witch Project* lore, her Computer Club friend visiting and looking for evidence of a ghost, Avery's recounting of her "hide-and-seek in the cornfield" dream—and Piper thought that Avery's distressed and intriguing words might lend some authority.

Here is confirmation, Piper had thought. *By the kid's own hand.*

But they didn't seem to convince her brother.

Nothing did.

The skepticism never leaving his face, Sam ran his fingers through his short brown hair. His head appeared a bit flattened, a thin indent across his forehead—he'd taken off his backward blue Chicago Cubs baseball hat when he'd arrived, and Piper imagined he'd been wearing it all night. "Okay, do you mind if I recap all of this out loud?" he asked.

"If you think it'd help, sure," Piper responded.

"So, this virus thing causes three big problems if you're infected. Number one, if you are alone for thirty seconds, something materializes and kills you."

Piper nodded.

"Two, if you look at a computer or BlackBerry, you feel some really intense, compulsive urge to send the virus to other people."

Another nod.

"And three, it eventually eats you up from the inside. Memory loss, saying weird things. Is that all accurate?"

"Yeah, that's basically it."

"Geez, you made it sound *way* more complicated than that." He stood and walked to the counter, refilling his mug. "I am so not the right person to help you with this, by the way."

"You are literally the only person who can help me," Piper replied.

He took another sip of coffee, smacking his lips together before sitting back down across from Piper. "These are good beans. Where are they from?"

"I don't know. The store? Does it really matter?"

"I'm just curious."

"I know you don't believe me. About any of this stuff. But you really should."

Sam leaned back in his chair, sighing. "I'm here, aren't I? I listened."

"That's not good enough right now. We need to do something for this kid before something really bad happens to her."

"No, a *doctor* needs to do something for this kid before something really bad happens to her. We should take her to an *actual doctor,* right now."

Piper shook her head. "They can't help. You should've seen her last night. It was terrifying."

"All the more reason to take her. You aren't qualified for this."

"I'm the only one who is. I'm the only one who knows what's actually wrong with her. With her mom in the ICU . . . there's no one else." She paused. "I promised her, Sam. I promised Susan I'd help fix her daughter, and then she was *speared* by one of those—" Piper stopped there.

Sam furrowed his brow and craned his head, looking at Avery. Ripley was still sleeping at the foot of the bed. He drummed his fingers on the white coffee mug. "I'm sorry you saw that, by the way. I imagine that's not easy."

Piper just nodded at Sam, lips at her mug.

"It's just—" Sam started.

"What?" Piper interrupted, not liking his tone. "It's just what?"

"Piper . . ." He didn't finish his thought, merely making an exasperated sound. Piper knew he was tired; he'd been driving all night. She hadn't slept, either, and it comforted her in a strange way to know they were on the same level in that regard.

"I know you want to poke holes in this," Piper said. "So get it out of your system now. Before we really start trying to figure this out. Because I don't know how much time we have with her."

"What do you mean?"

"I have to bring her back to the hospital. I'm surprised they let me take her here to begin with. I'm not a relative."

"Does she have any?"

"Yeah, an uncle. And I don't know what he knows about her. He might not even know anything about her condition. Definitely not the acting-possessed stuff. I think there's a decent chance that, outside of Susan, I know the most. And Susan is out of commission now, for God knows how long."

"So that makes you Linda Blair's super nanny, right?"

"Who's Linda Blair?"

"The actress. She played the possessed girl in *The Exorcist*. You know, the kid with the spinning head, puking up pea soup and—"

Piper flashed him a look.

"I'm sorry," he sighed. "I'm not trying to be a jerk about this."

"I know. Just go ahead. Be a jerk. Start poking holes."

Sam smiled to himself, and Piper noticed a bit of cunning in his hazel eyes, bringing her back to their childhood, when he would play pranks on her. Popping out from under her bed, covering the toilet bowl with Saran Wrap. Always out of love, he'd said.

"Well, for starters," he began. "The virus. The COOLGAME.exe."

"What about it?"

"You can't install an EXE file on a BlackBerry. It's for a completely different operating system."

"I mean, if it's supernatural, I think it's allowed to bend the rules a bit. You probably just need to try to open it for something bad to happen to you. You know, *click*."

Sam rolled his eyes. "Okay, fine. If you believe it's supernatural, then sure. *Maybe* file compatibility logic would not apply in that scenario. I'll give you that. But still, with what happened to the father—"

"What about him?"

"The way he died. I mean, a single-car accident—it could've been anything. It doesn't mean that he was alone and attacked by something."

"But Susan heard him freaking out, saying he *felt* something in the car—and then, in his last moments, he *saw it*. That's what he said. *I see it*. Susan saw the email; she saw the BlackBerry. She *literally* saw the name of the virus, that COOLGAME.exe or whatever it was—"

"*Piper . . .*"

His condescending tone made her want to explode.

"Yes?" she said through gritted teeth.

"Let me show you something." Sam got up from the table, and he retrieved his laptop from his canvas bag. He returned to the kitchen, opening the computer, quickly jabbing at a few keys, then turning the laptop toward Piper. She looked at it, seeing what resembled a command log of sorts, like something that would show up on a hacker's computer in a TV show.

"What am I looking at?" she said.

"You emailed me like a week ago, remember? Asking me to research killer computer viruses?"

"I didn't think you would take it seriously."

"I didn't, at first. But then a few days ago I was bored, so I wrote some scripts, searched some forums. I tried a bunch of different websites, so many different keywords. I thought I would only search a little bit, but you know me. I guess I got motivated, and I kept modifying the scripts, trying different keyword combinations, different forums, to see if I could actually find something for you. And you see this number?"

Sam pointed at the screen, and Piper read aloud the number he was pointing at:

"Fifty-seven," she said.

"And that one?"

He pointed at another line.

0 Results Found.

"I ran *fifty-seven* different and extremely thorough website scraping sessions," Sam explained, "searching for anything at all about a killer computer virus, and I came up with nothing. Tech websites, paranormal websites. No one is talking about this stuff. No one. It just confirms that this doesn't exist. This type of virus, as much as the mother insists on it—it's not out there. Don't you think someone would've mentioned it? Like, someone would've died before this, or someone else would've gotten infected, and we'd all have heard about it?"

"Unless . . ."

"Unless what?"

Something clicked for Piper, a thought she hadn't yet considered.

"What if Avery herself made it?"

Sam closed the laptop, saying nothing.

"Think about it," Piper continued. "It's only affected her family and people in her orbit. She was in Computer Club, into programming. And her diary entries—she's into spooky things, movies and books. She was into *witchcraft lore* and all that stuff."

"What are you saying? That she wrote a code for a killer computer virus?"

Piper shrugged. "Maybe."

"She didn't mention that?"

"Her memory is really bad, remember? Because of the virus."

He sighed. "First off, how does anyone write a code that does the stuff you're describing? I'll say it again, it's not possible."

"Sam—"

"And *who cares* if she made it or not? If she doesn't remember doing it, how would that even help us?"

"I know that, I was just saying—"

"And I wouldn't put too much stock into those diary entries. Yes, it seems like the kid was into horror. And sure, maybe she did do a deep dive into witchcraft, and it messed her up reading about it. Actually—" He stopped for a moment, gathering his thoughts. "Maybe that's the cause of all this. You know, she went too far online, convincing herself that all of this supernatural and occult stuff is real. Had a mental break-down."

Piper felt like she might explode. "How would *reading about some-thing online* make someone act possessed, make them think there's an evil entity in the room with them at all times? One that they can't even see?"

"I don't know, okay? I told you before. Let an *actual doctor* make that call."

"Yeah, I know. You said that."

Piper felt like smacking him across the face. She'd done it before, of course. Not in probably fifteen years. But there was precedent. She re-sisted the urge, merely shooting up from her chair, wanting to pace around the kitchen but remembering she had to keep an eye on Avery. So she sat back down, dramatically, for good measure.

"I know you're pissed," Sam said.

You think? Piper thought.

"You're pissed because you want me to believe you," Sam continued, "and here I am, saying, *Oh, the dad was just distracted and drove his car off the road.* And, *Well yeah, if the doctors say the sister died of menin-gitis, then that's what it was.* I'm really sorry, sis, but there's just no way to prove any of this. Outside of . . ." He trailed off, thinking.

"Outside of what?"

Sam shifted his body and nodded toward Avery. Piper knew what he was thinking, and it made her stomach turn.

"We *cannot* leave her alone," she retorted, a hint of anger in her voice.

"Why not?"

"You know why not."

"Let's just try it. It sounds like her parents never did."

"Yes, they did."

Sam shrugged. "Not while she was sleeping. Wouldn't we know then, for sure?"

As difficult as he was being, Piper still wanted his help, so she considered his suggestion. She pictured them walking out of the door onto the landing, or even just going into the bathroom and shutting the door. That would break the rules. They could stand there for twenty seconds or so . . .

No, Piper thought.

It could kill her.

Piper shook her head decisively. "We're not doing that, Sam. And trust me, this is real. Once she wakes up, you'll see. The things she's saying—I can't even wrap my head around them."

"You don't think she's making them up?"

"One of them is definitely real. The Willowbrook thing."

"I know. I didn't mean that she's *making it up* like it didn't happen, just that she's saying it to get a rise out of you. Like she's faking it."

"Oh, *come on.* She literally held a blade at my throat, at my dog's face."

"Okay, okay. Maybe she's just sick. It sounds like she's sick, Piper."

"She is definitely sick."

"So why aren't we getting her help?"

Piper banged her fists on the kitchen table, and the mugs shook, spilling coffee over the rims. "Goddamn it, Sammy, you know why!" She wanted to turn away from him, not look at her disbelieving brother's face. But no, she was resolved to keep the sleeping Avery in her peripheral vision. "I have experienced the weirdest and worst week of my entire life. I have seen things I didn't think were possible, but now I know that they are. And thank you, yes, I'm grateful you're here. You didn't need to do that. You didn't need to call in to work. You could've stayed home. And you are coming into this pretty fresh, so I understand why you don't believe me. But you *have to believe me.* And, you know what, I think you *want* to believe me."

Sam just stared at her.

"That *web scraping* thing," Piper continued. "Why'd you spend all that time, running *fifty-seven* versions, if you didn't think it mattered? Why did you even create that searching script in the first place? I think your curiosity is piqued. I think there's a tiny part of you that *does* believe."

Still, no response.

"Sam, her mother did everything imaginable for her over the past year, and Avery's only getting worse. I don't know how much time she has. I'm sorry that I dragged you into this, but it won't be for very long. I promise. I just want to try something with her. I want to see if we can fix her, and if we can't, we can take her somewhere. To the hospital, whatever. But I need your *help.*"

Sam said nothing. He just listened, never breaking eye contact. Piper had to give him credit for that.

Finally, he spoke.

"What do you want to try?" he asked, his tone soft and contrite.

Piper thought for a moment, and then placed her mug on the counter and walked into the living room. She dug around her purse and returned to the kitchen—keeping one eye on Avery, *always* one eye on the kid—holding an object out to Sam.

"What do you want to do with that?" Sam asked.

"It's from the library where I work," Piper said. "I think it might have the email attachment on it. The one Avery sent to Fisher."

"It doesn't," Sam said definitively.

"Why do you have to be such a naysayer all the time? We haven't even looked at it yet."

Sam tried to retort, but Piper cut him off.

"Sam, her mom tried everything," Piper said. "The one thing that Susan was afraid of was the virus itself. She never wanted to see it again. When I showed her this, she flipped out. She wanted it out of her sight. I really believe the only thing she didn't try to fix Avery was going to the source. And this *could* be the source."

Again, Sam tried to cut Piper off, but she wouldn't let him.

"The only way to find a solution for something is to understand the problem, right?" she continued. "Now, I don't know exactly what we can do with this, but maybe just seeing the file icon could trigger something in her memory. It could unlock something, something that helps. Maybe the answer to fixing her is right here on this hard drive."

She shook the computer component in Sam's face, and he took it from her hands.

"Piper," he said slowly, "I know you think I am being the ultimate wet blanket right now, but I assure you, this is not going to help."

Piper felt the rage boiling underneath her skin, but she held it inside, taking a few deep breaths before speaking.

"How do you know that?" she asked very slowly, resisting the urge to completely freak out on her brother.

"Because this doesn't store files," he said. "This is a RAM module. Did you happen to grab the hard drive, too?"

Piper felt despair wash over her.

"Piper?" Sam asked.

She'd grabbed the wrong component. The hard drive was still in the computer in the library stacks, waiting to be discovered.

Piper collapsed into a kitchen chair.

She was officially out of ideas.

Sam placed the green RAM module on the table and reached to grab Piper's hand.

"I'm sorry, sis."

Her mind raced. She could go back to the library and snatch the hard drive from the computer, she thought. That was at most a twenty- or thirty-minute detour. But who knew if it was even there? Maybe a fellow coworker had discovered the Out of Order sign and moved the computer after she'd left last night. She just didn't know. And she didn't want to go to the library alone—what if Sam tried the experiment he was talking about before, leaving Avery alone, just to see what would happen? He seemed like he wanted to help, but she didn't trust him not to do that. Or they could simply *all* go to the library.

But what if Avery has an episode there?

No, she needed the kid to stay in the apartment, and she needed to be with her. It was Avery's best chance to stay safe—this was a controlled environment, away from other people. She supposed she could send Sam to the library to grab the hard drive, but that would be extremely suspicious. And again, the file might not even be on there. The entire scenario was a reach; she knew that.

"It's in her email, right?" Sam said.

"What?"

"If she's sending the virus around town, it's probably still in her sent items."

Piper perked up. "Oh my God. You're right. I completely forgot."

"Can't you just log in and get it?"

Piper glanced at Avery.

Still sleeping like the dead.

"Just ask her for the password," Sam continued. "Shouldn't be too hard, right? Then I could look at the file, see what's inside of it. I have software that lets me examine the code within programs. I could do that without actually launching the virus, maybe see when it was made and who made it."

Logging in to Avery's email account was a simple solution, one Piper hadn't thought of. It made her thankful for Sam's presence. Despite his contrarian opinions on basically everything, he was able to think more logically than she was right now.

"You know," Sam continued, "for what you're saying is a deadly computer virus, you really want us messing around with it?"

"Well, not necessarily *messing around with it* . . ." Piper admittedly hadn't thought it through, and she was already doubting her idea. She just thought that having the virus file might give *some* answers. Piper honestly didn't know exactly what they would do with it—just that it might help. It was something, at least.

Sam thought for a moment. "I mean, it should be fine. Like I said, I could examine the code without *launching* the file. See what's in there. See how it's written."

"And that's not the same as opening it, right?"

He shook his head. "Think about it. If I looked at the code for the Microsoft Word install package, do you think it would look like a blank white screen that you could type on, with formatting buttons and all that? You know, how it looks when you actually open Word?"

"No?" Piper was growing more confused.

"It's like—how do I put this—imagine you're making pancakes. You know, you need flour, sugar, salt, baking powder, whatever—"

"Eggs, milk."

"Right, eggs and milk. If you had all of those ingredients sitting out in front of you, and you tasted each one individually, or even one right after another, it would taste nothing like pancakes, you follow?"

Piper nodded.

"All I would be doing is looking at the ingredients." He paused, smiling. "But then again, you said it is supernatural and it opened on a BlackBerry, so I don't know that looking at the code would actually be safe."

She wondered if he was humoring her, if he actually believed it could be supernatural. Piper didn't ask.

"We don't even have the file, so this is a moot point," she said, glancing over at Avery. "And I don't want to wake her, talking about log-ins and passwords and stuff. I just don't think that's a good idea. Disturbing her could make her . . . you know."

Still, she considered it. She could softly rub her shoulder, whisper Avery's name, make the waking process as gentle as possible.

No.

You know what might happen when she wakes up.

You've seen it happen, twice.

Piper wasn't even sure the kid *would* wake up, at all. She was breathing, thank God, but she hadn't stirred in hours. Besides, Sam was right. Even with the virus file, looking at the code could be dangerous.

"I could probably make some calls," Sam spitballed. "Wasn't there a paranormal club or something in our high school? I know my web scraping came up empty, but maybe they know something about *supernatural viruses* or something. Oh man, what was that guy's name? Robbie? He was a member, I think, and I played football with—"

"Wait," Piper said, straightening up in her chair.

Sam's comment had sparked something in her.

"I've got a better idea," she said. "What's better than one paranormal club member?"

Sam looked confused. "*Two* members?"

Piper shook her head.

"A whole lot more than that."

CHAPTER 33

Piper plugged the computer back in, booted it up, and typed faster than she ever had in her life.

"You've been blogging about this stuff?" Sam asked incredulously.

"It helps me."

"You said the mom wanted to keep it private."

"It's anonymous."

Sam rolled his eyes. Nothing more needed to be said on his end.

The words came pouring out of Piper. She'd given readers a taste of her situation when she'd gotten home from the hospital, but now she would get into the nitty-gritty. The most important details were made plain—Avery's condition, the rules of her existence, where her parents thought the virus emerged from, the likelihood that Avery had sent the virus to two people. That the mist was likely the creature that formed at the end of the countdown to kill you. Piper shared the terrible things Avery had been saying, a recap of the previous night, when she feared for her own life and Ripley's. She requested that readers supply suggestions in the comments—*What should I do?*—and asked that people give their thoughts quickly. Time was of the essence.

Piper glanced over at Avery, still sleeping soundly—it was eight thirty A.M., and sunlight was streaming through cracks in the closed blinds. The light rain had stopped. Piper imagined how exhausted the kid was, and she thought she might sleep well into the afternoon. Sam had checked on her, too, because Piper didn't trust herself. He'd confirmed it: alive and zonked.

Piper clicked the Post button.

Then, they waited.

It didn't take long for the comments to start filtering in.

Clearly, these anonymous people had been waiting for Piper to post again, and wow, were they eager to share their opinions.

The suggestions were all over the map, and Piper and Sam struggled to keep up. A common suggestion was to take Avery immediately to a priest. *Those two pastors were not priests,* a user named mypetfish wrote. *She needs an actual Catholic priest to perform an actual exorcism. Bring her to the man in the black robe with the white collar, and then things will get real.* Piper put some thought into that one but quickly decided against it. That wasn't what Susan wanted. Other blog readers encouraged Piper to transport Avery to the Willowbrook grounds, confident that the solution lay there. The institution had closed in 1987, but the buildings were still standing, maintained by the City University of New York—a user called livvylife provided those nuggets of information. At the very least, many commenters urged, Piper should research any potential Wallace connections with Willowbrook, guessing that Avery might be haunted by a previous resident, that a ghost might have some unfinished business. *Why else would she be saying those things?* asked bluegnomegarden. It wasn't a bad idea, Piper thought, but she didn't have time for that. Willowbrook was halfway across the country, and that research could take days or weeks. Other commenters suggested spells, burning incense, some form of a witch's brew—but Piper wasn't too enthused. Susan had already tried burning sage candles, and they didn't have time to spin the wheel with random spells or concoctions. *And where would I find these anyway? I don't have a spell book lying around.* There was that *Blair Witch* book at the library, but that was just a movie tie-in. Fiction. And really, what were the odds that some random incantation—from a book, or maybe the Internet—would actually work? Did she believe in spells now, too? Sam was particularly intrigued by a comment that Piper thought veered a little too close to ghostbusting. One of Piper's mainstay commenters, candlecatnip, wrote, *Why don't you try putting her in a room alone for a little bit? Then when you hear her screaming, run in and douse the thing with holy water? If you think it should appear at exactly thirty seconds, and you time it right, it might work.* For starters, they didn't have holy water. And there was no guarantee that course of action would do anything besides potentially kill Avery if they were too late. Still, Sam was intrigued by the suggestion, probably because he was desperate to summon the black mist, to see if this was all baloney or not. Piper shut down the idea rather quickly. No chance, she told him. Mooncorpse floated a similar strategy, only using fire instead. *It's the ultimate purifier,* they wrote. *Get the evil thing in a room and burn it.* They even sourced biblical backup, dropping a quote from the Old Testament that read, "God is a consuming fire," as well as providing examples from the Bible of God's wrath involving the use of fire. A few commenters actually agreed with the suggestion. Piper couldn't scroll the comments away fast enough.

Fire, really? she thought.

Do they actually want me to kill her?

She read on, refreshing the page, and more comments came—the majority replying to the exorcism comments, discussing the merits, often agreeing it was worth a shot; others practically begged Piper and Sam to somehow let them access and view the virus themselves, just to see what would happen. Piper grew more and more disheartened, but then a new comment appeared, one that caused Piper to stop hitting the refresh button. It was from a user named Jackflash72, and they wrote:

She's infected with a computer virus, no? Treat her like a computer. What would you do if a computer got a virus? You would run some antivirus software and clean it out. That makes sense to me. Giant caveat, though: I don't know how you do that with a person. But I think that's what she needs.

Piper stared at the screen, thinking.

"Are you reading this one?" she asked Sam, pointing at the comment.

"Yes."

"What do you think?"

"I don't know. What do *you* think?"

"I think it's *something*. This is a computer thing. So why wouldn't it have a computer solution?"

"Okay, but what do we do?"

"You're the computer guy. I don't know anything about antivirus software."

"But this is a person, Piper. I can't install software in a human."

Piper grimaced, and she refreshed the page a few more times. The commenters were still going off. She couldn't believe how many people had been waiting for her to post. People were now responding to the Jackflash72 comment, agreeing it was a solid idea. One person even wrote, *Yes, it's like a technology exorcism! A tech-orcism!* The idea was well-liked, but no one knew how to actually do it. Someone suggested wrapping an Internet cable tightly around Avery before cutting the power to the apartment, and then making Avery wiggle out of the cables— symbolizing her breaking free of the Internet. *Creative,* Piper thought, *but silly*. A suggestion from mrsoundwolf involved them inserting a phone line down Avery's throat, and Piper stopped reading there, finding the idea appalling. A different commenter suggested having the kid hug the computer tower while Piper launched an antivirus program, which caused Sam to laugh out loud.

"These people are idiots," he said.

Still, Piper couldn't shake the idea of wiping out the virus using technology. Maybe it would heal her, destroy the evil thing tethered to her.

The principles of it were sound.

She checked on Avery. Still not moving. She looked at the clock: a little after nine A.M. They'd been reading and debating her journal com-ments for more than thirty minutes. Piper refreshed her blog a few more times, growing antsy, wanting to free up the phone line.

What if Glen or Carol is trying to call me right now? she thought.

She still had no resolution on that front. Fisher could have been home, he could have been on the road, he could have been at a hospital. Piper had no idea. But it was a loose end she still needed to tie up, after they finished here.

And she still didn't know what *finishing here* actually entailed.

Frustrated, Piper quickly scrolled to the bottom of the page, glanc-ing at a new comment that simply read, *im coming for you,* but she didn't give it a second thought, and it blended in with the hundreds of other comments on the page. She hit refresh a few more times, scrolled some more. A new comment appeared from billyboy that read, *Hey! You might remember me. I'm the guy who lives in the family's old house. Bill. I went looking for your blog, and I found it. This is pretty wild stuff. Good luck with everything. Anxious to see what happens!* It gave Piper pause. She didn't like that this guy knew who she was, and it broke the illusion of separation between her online journal and her real life. Piper put it out of her mind, swallowed hard, continuing to scroll. There weren't many *new* suggestions. Most were simply giving Jackflash72 props for their out-of-the-box thinking.

"We're doing this, aren't we?" Sam asked. "A tech-orcism?"

It was outlandish, no doubt.

But it was worth a shot.

Piper logged out of AOL, and seemingly right on cue, Piper heard a soft moan come from the bed. She and Sam jerked their heads in that direction.

Avery was beginning to stir.

CHAPTER 34

The sunlight crept in through the window blinds on Avery's shifting body. Ripley jumped off the bed, stretched out on the floor, then joined Piper and Sam at the computer, lying at Piper's feet underneath the desk. She and Sam gaped at Avery—Piper had wrongly figured the kid would sleep all morning. This wasn't a mid-snooze adjustment; she was waking up. Piper looked at Sam with pleading eyes.

"How do you get rid of a computer virus?" she asked.

Sam didn't respond. He just stared at Avery, and Piper saw the fear gathering in his eyes.

Avery moaned and shifted.

Sam shook his head, like he couldn't believe what he'd gotten himself into. He paced in circles behind Piper's chair, his hands on his head.

"I have no idea what to do," he said.

"Come on, you're the expert. This is your job."

"Piper, she's a person. Not a computer."

"Pretend she's a computer. What would you do?"

Another moan. Piper knew she should go check on her, but she was worried about what she would find.

"Come on, Sammy," she implored. "What would you do?"

Sam dramatically exhaled and stopped pacing, bringing his hands together and twiddling his fingers. Piper could tell he was nervous. "Okay, okay, okay," he said. "Let's think about this rationally. She's infected with a virus. We obviously can't run software on her, we'd have to do the human equivalent—"

His words stopped cold. Avery had sat up in bed, saying nothing, the covers on her lap. She stared straight ahead. Piper only saw the child in profile, but she recognized the look in her eye just the same.

Gone. Lost.

Piper felt her stomach drop. She feared what was coming.

Avery's head slowly swiveled until she was looking in Piper and Sam's direction. A heavy silence hung over the room.

"Piper," Sam said haltingly, "what is she doing?"

"I don't know."

"Piper . . ."

"I said *I don't know.*"

Avery's lips moved now—slowly, assuredly. There were words there, soft and hushed. Piper didn't want to hear them, but she knew it was only a matter of time. She turned her head to look at Sam, who was fixated on Avery, dread in his eyes. She wondered about the bombardment of emotions that was hitting him. He'd heard the child's entire story, knew what she was capable of. But the highlights were one thing—it was another to catch the live performance.

"How do we stop this?" he asked, his eyes not leaving Avery.

Piper didn't know. If she did, she would've stopped it before. All she could think to do was consider how Susan might react, picture the mother's potential actions. Susan would've tried to console Avery, cure her with love. But that seemed like a nonstarter right now.

Did anything else help? Piper thought, flailing blindly in her mind for something, *anything,* that Susan had mentioned that could possibly help this kid.

Then she remembered.

The stories.

"Okay," Piper said quickly, pushing the chair back and rising to her feet. "Avery likes writing stories. They were dark stories about her condition. Scary stories. Susan thought they might be therapeutic."

"What am I supposed to do with that?" Sam responded dumbly.

Piper stuck her arm out and snapped her fingers a few times in front of Sam's face. "Hey, hey, come back to me. I need you right now."

That did the trick, and Sam jerked his head to look at Piper. "Sorry, sorry. Yeah, the stories. You told me about those."

"Right. Susan thought they were helping."

Sam considered this, and his eyes twitched quickly from side to side. It was a welcome sight to Piper—she'd seen her brother do this many times before, when he was really thinking hard about something. She hoped he was close to an answer.

"Okay, okay, how about this," he said, his voice gaining confidence. "If there's a virus inside of her, maybe writing those stories was like purging pieces of the code. But those pieces came back, obviously, because . . . well, look at her. Are you with me?"

"Kind of."

"Maybe if she writes out everything that happened to her, we could destroy vital parts of the virus. And if we destroy enough of it, the code might stop working."

"That's . . ." Piper trailed off, thinking.

It made sense.

She wanted to hug her brother at that moment, but there wasn't time for that. Instead, she rushed to the end table by the couch, yanking open the drawer and pulling out a pad of paper and a pen. She returned to Sam's side, but neither of them approached Avery.

"Well, go ahead," Sam said, motioning toward Avery. "You know her better than I do."

Avery's whispering was growing in volume, and Piper wondered what awful phrase she was going to repeat ad nauseam this time. She could already make out a few words.

"*Revelator . . .*"

"Monsters . . ."

"Him . . ."

Piper had no clue what the words meant, but they made her stomach turn anyway. She slowly approached the child. Avery had spun around now, facing Piper and Sam, her legs dangling off the bed, toes scraping the floor.

"Revelator . . ."

"Monsters . . ."

"Him . . ."

Avery was just a few feet away now. Piper squatted to meet her at eye level.

"Avery, what do you think about writing another story?" Piper asked gently, holding out the pad of paper toward her. "Wouldn't that be fun?"

Avery's lips trembled. They were slightly chapped, and Piper caught a whiff of her morning breath. Avery did not reach for the yellow notepad; her arms stayed at her sides. Her eyes were still impossibly vacant.

The words ceased.

Piper wondered if maybe this might work.

Something changed. Avery's eyes slowly returned from the abyss, and her focus shifted to Piper. The two were extremely close now—Avery could easily strike Piper with a simple thrash of her arm. But she didn't move. Avery's hard stare made Piper feel more and more uncomfortable, and she considered springing to her feet and retreating to Sam's side, before choosing to stay the course.

Avery smiled devilishly, and she leaned forward, now nose-to-nose with Piper, who was gripped with terror.

The child spoke.

"Only the Revelator does not fear the monsters in the dark, and I am HIM."

The sheer intensity with which Avery spoke the word *him* made Piper fall to her backside, and she quickly crab-walked away from the child in fear. Piper felt something on her back, and then hands gripping her underneath her armpits. They were Sam's hands, pulling her to her feet.

"What is she saying?" he asked. "Are those Willowbrook things?"

Piper shook her head quickly. "I don't know. She just *says things*. And they're different, every time she has an outburst."

Sam's face had gone white. "I didn't know anyone could act like this. She's straight-up possessed."

"You thought I was lying?"

"Not *lying*, but—"

Avery hooted in laughter, which stopped Sam's words in their tracks. They both just stared at her now, and she started repeating the "Revelator" expression again, words that held no meaning to Piper outside making her blood run cold. It was the only common denominator she had between all of her outbursts. That, and all the expressions were sinister, creepy. But that was it.

"What happens next?" Sam asked.

"What do you mean?"

"What does she typically do next?"

"She might start flailing everywhere. Freaking out. Then, if we're lucky, she'll calm down."

"And if we're not lucky?"

Piper didn't answer. Avery had nearly killed her and Ripley the previous night. Every outburst so far had been worse than the last, and Piper feared the current episode might never stop.

"We have to keep going," she said. "We have to try something else."

Avery was *screaming* now, repeating the "Revelator" phrase, but her voice grew raspy and harsh, and the words came out in a menacing growl. She seemed to have spooked the dog, who had curled up in a ball against the far wall under the desk, almost out of sight. Piper hoped he'd stay there.

"How do you remove a computer virus?" Piper asked Sam.

"I don't know."

"Yes, you do!"

"I'm sorry! It's kind of hard to think right now with . . ." He motioned over at Avery.

He was right. Avery's snarling recitals of *monsters in the dark* were echoing around the apartment.

"What if . . ." Piper was thinking out loud. "What if she mentally removed it?"

"I don't get it."

"You know, talk her through it, like you're a hypnotist or something. She's a tech kid. She knows the lingo. Maybe she can dig down inside and find the corrupted file. And, you know, destroy it?"

Sam looked to be forming words, but his mouth merely opened and closed a few times.

"Sam, just do something!"

"I've never been to a hypnotist before!"

"Yeah, but you know what they do, right? Have you seen one on TV?"

"I guess, but—"

"That's gonna have to be good enough."

Sam sighed deeply, rocking back and forth on his heels. He was biting his lower lip. "Okay, okay. But you're coming with me."

They slowly approached Avery, and as they did, her outburst ceased, like a stereo suddenly unplugged. She watched them come closer, and Piper felt her anxiety heavy in her chest. They stopped a few feet away, keeping their distance, and stooped down in front of her. Piper waited for Sam to speak, and when he didn't, she elbowed him in the ribs. That did the trick.

"Hey, Avery?" he said delicately. "I want to try something, okay?"

Her head twitched a couple of inches, so she could stare directly at Sam. Piper saw him swallow hard.

"I want to play a little game, if that's okay?"

No response from Avery.

Only staring.

Piper gazed at the girl's hands, and they were quivering a bit. She decided to use that as her gauge. Once those hands started shaking really badly, they would back away.

"Well," Sam continued, clearing his throat, "we think there's a computer virus inside of your body. And we need to work together to get rid of it. So I want you to close your eyes and picture it there. In your chest. It's something you downloaded. Then you launched the file, and it spread everywhere. To your head, your arms, to your legs and feet." He paused and side-eyed Piper, who nodded at him to keep going.

He's good, she thought.

How is he doing this so well?

Avery's eyes seemed to soften.

It appeared she was *listening*.

"There are a lot of things going wrong with you. You're saying things you've never said before. You crash, unexpectedly, just like a bad computer. Act up out of nowhere, like a pop-up appearing when you don't want it to. And these symptoms won't stop. And it's all because of the virus. It's corrupted your system, your memory, and you need to quarantine. You need to remove the virus. Can we try to do that?"

Piper couldn't believe it. Avery's trembling hands slowed; they were nearly still. And Piper saw it in her eyes—she was hearing him.

"Imagine you purchase antivirus software. You insert the disk into your CD-ROM drive, and the software is installed in your body. You launch the program, and it starts to search. It scans all over, finding the infected files. They're inside your brain, here and there, everywhere. The number keeps going up. Thirty, fifty, one hundred, two hundred. So many of them. You see them on a screen inside your head, the counter ticking, and then the program stops. It found them. Every single one. All of the infected files, and you're about to click the button that says Quarantine. This will remove all the infected files from your body. Are you ready to do that, Avery? Are you ready to click that button?"

Piper's jaw was nearly on the floor. Sam glanced subtly her way again, and Piper mouthed, *Holy crap, Sam,* trying not to disturb the process, not wanting to spike the ball in the end zone too soon.

Avery slowly nodded—*she was ready to click the button*—and Sam couldn't help but crack a smile.

"All right," he said, "click it."

Avery closed her eyes, and she went limp. Her chin dropped to her chest, and Piper carefully reached out her hand to touch her, to see how she would react. She placed her fingers under Avery's chin, and she slowly lifted the child's head. In her peripheral vision, Piper caught a blur of movement.

Avery's hand.

It was trembling again.

Faster.

Piper dropped her right hand from Avery's chin, and her left arm shot across Sam's body, forcing him backward and onto the floor.

Avery's clawed hand missed his face by mere inches.

She'd gone for a striking blow and came up empty but seemed to enjoy it anyway, because she was laughing now, maniacally. Piper and Sam quickly jumped to their feet and backed up all the way to the island separating the kitchen from the living room.

Avery continued to roar with laughter.

"We were so close," Piper said defeatedly. "I feel like that should've worked. It was *working,* wasn't it?"

"Is she that good of a faker?"

"I don't know."

"I thought it was working, too."

Avery flopped onto her back, the hysterical laughter not stopping. Ripley stayed under the desk, petrified. Piper thought for a moment.

"What happens if an infection is so bad that antivirus software doesn't work?" she asked Sam.

"Usually, you throw out the computer."

Piper formed a quick analogy in her head.

"Like, *kill* her?" she responded.

"What? God, no. I don't mean throw *her* out. I'm just saying."

"Is there anything else to do? Besides getting rid of the computer?"

Sam thought for a moment. "I mean, you can reboot the system from scratch. That sometimes works."

"How do you do that?"

Avery's howls persisted from across the apartment.

"Typically, you would use a recovery disk," Sam said. "New computers usually come with one. It basically deletes everything and restores the machine to its factory settings." He paused. "You want to do that with her?"

Piper nodded, thinking.

"What's the human equivalent of a boot disk?" Sam asked.

She had an idea. Potentially a terrible one—she knew, undoubtedly, that Susan would not approve—but it had to be done. Piper looked at Avery, who was smashing the bed with her fists, then back at Sam.

"I know we talked about this before, but do you think there's any way she'd give up her email password?"

CHAPTER 35

Piper locked the door to her apartment, unsure exactly why she was doing it. Nerves, probably. Sam guided Avery to the chair in front of the computer. Ripley was still curled up in a ball underneath the desk against the wall, which he vacated quickly when the trio approached, hightailing it to the kitchen and cowering underneath the small, circular table.

The kid had really freaked the poor dog out.

For now, Avery's hysterics had ceased, and she was giggling intermittently and mumbling things, seemingly at random. Piper recognized at least four different languages—English, Spanish, French, and Arabic—and others she didn't. She couldn't help but wonder where these words were coming from, how everything was connected. Willowbrook, the Revelator (whatever this was—Piper had *no idea*), everything else she couldn't make heads or tails of at the moment. With a clearer mind she might have been able to solve the puzzle, but her lack of sleep was catching up with her. Piper felt a dull throbbing in her forehead, and she was running solely on medium-roast coffee and adrenaline. She wondered what was going on in Avery's head. Her thoughts returned to something Sam had said in the failed hypnosis routine, about Avery having "pop-ups" she couldn't control.

That's what's happening inside of her, Piper thought.

It's like going to a website and having pop-ups appear out of nowhere.

She hoped what they were about to do would fix everything.

Or it could be a disaster.

Sam pushed down softly on Avery's shoulders, and she was now sitting in the computer chair. Piper was holding the keyboard and mouse off to the side, and she shook the mouse to wake up the monitor.

Avery flinched.

The giggling stopped, and she stared at Piper's desktop background. It was a photo of the Grand Tetons, the mountain peaks reflecting in the crystal-blue waters at their base.

The child said nothing.

"Hey, Avery?" Sam probed. "Do you remember the name of your email account?"

Another flinch.

Piper leaned forward, studying Avery's eyes. The kid was intrigued by what they were doing, why they had put her there. The plan was to show Avery her email account. *Really* show it. Spend some time scrolling around, clicking and exploring. It was a window into her past, Piper thought. The messages, the jokes among friends, the memories—her life before the virus upended her very existence. Maybe those reminders were what she needed, her version of a "system restore."

It was a long shot; Piper knew that. But it was the best she and Sam had, and now they were going to see it through.

"Avery?" Sam repeated. "I'm going to log in to AOL, okay? You just think a bit. See if you can remember your email account." He nodded at Piper, and she double-clicked the America Online icon on her screen, and they were off to the races. With each sound that emitted from the computer, Avery's attention returned more and more. The dialing, the beeps, the whirs and squeals, the crackling static. Piper continued to study Avery's eyes. She saw more intrigue, and then recognition—to Avery, it appeared that the sounds of the modem were like the comforting words of an old friend.

Welcome! the computer intoned.

You've got mail!

"Should you just give her the keyboard?" Sam asked.

"You think she can type right now?"

"Maybe. It's worth a go. And it'd be easier."

"But what if she sends the virus off somehow?"

"We'd stop it in time," Sam said. "Just grab the mouse from her."

That made Piper nervous. Again, she thought she knew the rules, but these were uncharted waters. Yes, it certainly seemed like Avery had previously sent the virus along the old-fashioned way: in an email attachment. It was what Susan had said, after all. But Piper figured there was so much she didn't know about this. And what if Avery was too quick for them? Or she thrashed around again, knocking them both aside, and quickly sent the virus to someone else?

"Let her have it," Sam insisted.

Piper hesitated but took Sam's suggestion, slowly sliding the keyboard and mouse in front of Avery.

"Here you go," she said gently. "Avery, can you go to your email for us?"

Avery gaped at the keyboard before placing her hands on it. She stayed like that for a few seconds, then moved her right hand to the mouse. It wasn't a clean grab, more like a drunk lunging toward a beer bottle at last call. The cursor moved to the top of the screen, then the bottom right-hand corner. Avery placed both hands on the keyboard again, repeatedly smacking the keys with all ten fingers.

"She's not doing anything," Sam said.

"What did you expect?" Piper replied. "She's out of it. We're lucky she's even semiconscious."

"Do you think she'd give us her email address? Her password?"

"Sammy, I don't think she could tell us her own *name* right now."

Her brother thought for a moment. "Let me try something." He slid the keyboard and mouse to his side of the desk and began opening tabs in the Internet browser.

"What are you doing?" Piper asked.

"Giving her options."

He opened email website after email website—Lycos, Yahoo!, Hotmail, EarthLink, a half dozen more that Piper herself hadn't even heard of—and waited for them to display. Once they'd loaded, Sam clicked between them, and they both watched Avery closely for a reaction.

Nothing.

"Avery, are any of these your email accounts?" Piper asked.

Sam kept clicking, opening Piper's AOL inbox. "How about this one? Did you have an AOL account?"

No response.

In fact, the kid was getting worse.

Droopy eyelids, slack jaw. Her tongue was partially hanging out of her mouth.

"Why is she acting like this?" Sam asked.

"What do you mean?" Piper said. "You know what's wrong with her. You explained it better than I ever could with that virus removal analogy."

"I know that, but I mean—shouldn't she be freaking out right now? Screaming or speaking in tongues or something." Sam began clicking through the tabs again, trying to instigate a response from Avery.

Click, click, click, click, click . . .

"I don't know, Piper, she doesn't look too good."

She couldn't disagree.

Avery's behavior *did* seem different, something Piper hadn't seen before.

"Do computers ever just . . ." She didn't finish her thought.

"Ever just what?"

Click, click, click, click, click . . .

"Not come back?" she said.

Sam stopped clicking, and he just looked at his sister with sympathy on his face.

Piper knew the answer.

"I think we should take her to a doctor," Sam said gently. "We tried our best, and it didn't work. Let's take her, before she gets any worse."

Piper desperately wanted Sam to be wrong, but she thought he might be right. At least at a hospital, doctors could hook her up to machines, give her fluids if she needed them, shock her back into existence if it came to that. This was different from what Susan had encountered. Sure, they'd had no success with doctors in the past, but she'd never seen her daughter like *this* before.

"*Shit*," Piper blurted, rising from her chair and pacing around the room. Her chest was tight with stress.

"This was always a long shot," Sam said. "Or maybe we should wrap the phone cable around her like that one weirdo on your blog suggested."

Piper assumed he was joking, but she didn't respond.

This was working.

Avery immediately responded to the computer.

When we sat her down and she heard the beeps and squeals and sounds . . .

The thought echoed in her head.

Sounds.

"I have an idea," she said, reaching across the desk and grabbing the keyboard and mouse from her brother. Piper immediately started minimizing windows.

"What are you doing?"

Piper launched Napster.

"She loves music," she said, waiting for the program to load. "She used to download songs all the time. Susan told me that she liked to burn CDs for her dad. Maybe this will reboot her. Maybe it will bring her back, I don't know."

Sam looked to the door, then back at the screen.

He was anxious. Piper could tell.

"One last shot," she said. "Then we take her."

The Napster window was open now. Piper began scrolling through her downloads, looking back at Avery every few seconds, looking for a response.

Eyes cast downward.

Blank stare.

Shallow breathing.

Wait . . .

There's something there, Piper thought. A twinkle of recognition. Avery's gaze rose, and she looked at the monitor. Piper double-clicked a song, opening it in the Winamp media player.

"Save Tonight" by Eagle-Eye Cherry.

Avery was still watching the screen.

And listening, Piper hoped.

Please, God, just listen.

More scrolling. Thousands of songs, a variety of artists. Santana, Pink, Macy Gray, Vertical Horizon, Brandy, Train, Goo Goo Dolls. Piper clicked on different song downloads, listening for twenty or thirty seconds, then moving on to another. She thought the samples might work—what if she landed on one of Avery's favorites? Would that help? She remembered the kid saying she liked LeAnn Rimes, and she located "How Do I Live." Piper found the song title morbidly fitting for the moment, and the tune crackled through the small computer speakers, complete with a pop or two. Piper looked at Avery.

Still looking at the screen.

Not fading.

Is she coming back? Piper hoped.

She looked at Avery's hands. They were twitching.

Voluntary or involuntary?

Piper wasn't sure, but she pictured them rising, moving to the keyboard and mouse, taking control of Napster, something the kid had to have done countless times before she was infected by this terrible, evil thing.

Again, more scrolling. Clicking on different downloads, Piper playing the role of apartment DJ. Usher, Ben Folds Five, No Doubt, Blues Traveler, Ricky Martin.

Then, movement.

Avery's lips quivered, like she was trying to say something.

Even Sam looked surprised.

Piper stopped scrolling, and she reached over and softly raised Avery's chin.

"Avery? Are you trying to say something? What is it?"

The girl's mouth trembled.

She was saying . . .

Wait.

No.

Her eyes narrowed, and her lips curled into a smile—reminiscent of the wicked smile Piper had seen before. The girl's eyes started to burn with rage. With whatever strength remained inside her, she was using it to stare malevolently at Piper.

"You shouldn't be here," Avery whispered, the words oozing with menace.

It was the same thing Avery had told her the previous night, before trying to fillet her with a sharp object. It made Piper jump back, fearing what might be coming next. Sam backed away from the computer, too.

"It didn't work," Piper said, her voice breaking.

She kept repeating it over and over again.

It was all she could think to say.

Avery leaned her head back until it was nearly over the back of the chair, looking at the room upside down, her glasses slipping off her face and falling to the carpet.

The girl simply giggled.

Weakly.

Piper was worried she'd topple over.

"We need to take her," Sam sputtered. "Now."

Piper just nodded dumbly, and the two cautiously approached Avery, wary of an attack—if the kid could even muster one. Piper wasn't sure. They were within arm's reach of Avery, and Piper's lips parted to give directions to her brother.

CRASH!

The sound of something *smashing* behind them stopped them cold. Piper and Sam jumped, their heads simultaneously jerking toward the doorway.

CRASH!

CRASH!

At the third *crash,* an object broke through the cracking and splintering wood, and Piper could see what it was.

The metal blade of an ax.

Piper's heart sank. She knew without a doubt who was clutching its wooden handle.

CHAPTER 36

Dennis Brockway burst into Piper's apartment wearing orange bib overalls, kicking away splintered pieces of the doorway with his boots. Besides the ax that Piper remembered being buried in a log in the man's backyard, he also had a rifle strapped to his back, and he was carrying a red gas can. She remembered the can, too. The rifle appeared bigger and heavier than the one Shane had fired a few weeks back, and Piper immediately decided it was a different one. Something used for hunting, she guessed. Still, it looked smaller than it should have in the gigantic man's hands. It made her legs tremble, and she had the sinking, terrible feeling that her own death was imminent.

Mr. Brockway's cheeks were beet red, and he stumbled a bit as he stepped through the destroyed doorway. His eyes were glassy and bloodshot. The gas can slipped from his hand and fell to the floor, and he dropped the ax as well, fumbling with the rifle as he slipped it off his back. Piper knew he was piss-drunk. He pointed the rifle at the trio, who hadn't moved from their spots near the computer—Piper had her hand on Avery's shoulder, holding her up. The kid hadn't even turned around. The weapon wobbled in Mr. Brockway's hands, but Piper was convinced he wouldn't miss his target if he pulled the trigger.

"You know why I'm here," the man announced, his words slurred, and Piper remembered so clearly now the comment that had appeared on her blog post probably no more than an hour ago, the one that read *im coming for you,* the one she'd scrolled right past. She felt an intense pang of guilt, wondering if it was Mr. Brockway who wrote it. Piper also assumed he'd read the comments that recommended destroying the evil thing with fire, which was why he'd brought the gas can. She glanced over at Sam, and the two shared a look of dread. Avery said nothing, and Piper snuck a look at the girl.

Eyes open, spacing out.

Mr. Brockway kept the rifle trained on them, moving it from person to person, his movements erratic and unsteady.

"I know what happened to my boy, and I know why it happened," he said, staying near the doorway. Piper could already feel the cold morning air drifting inside. "People been talking, and I've been listening. And I did some reading this morning on that Internet blog of yours. Sealed the deal for me."

There it was.

The confirmation Piper feared.

She exchanged looks with Sam, and despite being gripped with fear, she also saw his disappointment. He'd rolled his eyes about the "anonymity" aspect of her posting about this stuff online, and he'd been right. Brockway had found out. Somehow, he'd discovered Piper's journal. She wondered where he'd been the last few days—if he'd traveled to his brother's place in Grangeville, or maybe he'd been holed up in his own home on one hell of an all-time bender, surfing the Internet for alternative theories about what could have happened to his son. Didn't matter, Piper decided. She simply could not believe that something as simple and stupid as posting something online would lead to their deaths, but here they were.

"Are you going to kill us?" Piper asked, her voice shaky.

Mr. Brockway considered this. "What gave it away?" He grinned, and Piper's heart sank. "Not sure in which order, though. Haven't thought that far ahead yet. But she's the first one, for sure." He turned the gun on Avery. Even though he couldn't see Avery's face, he knew it was her. It was the red hair, probably. And the fact that Piper had written about her being there in her journal. "She don't look too good," he added.

"She needs help," Sam chimed in nervously. "We need to take her to a doctor."

Brockway chuckled. "Little too late for that, wouldn't you say?"

"You can walk away," Piper told him. "You haven't done anything yet. Nothing has happened."

"Nothing has *happened?*" Brockway hooted. "Well, considering my boy is dead because of *her,* it sure as hell seems like something *happened*. Naw, I ain't gonna walk away. I'm gonna take care of business, right now. Make things right. Kill her and that *thing* you wrote is attached to her. The same thing that killed my boy, I imagine."

"She didn't do anything," Piper said. It was a bald-faced lie—everyone in the room knew it, and the man with the rifle burst out laughing.

"Are you trying to tell me that she didn't send my boy a virus? After what people in town told me, after what you yourself wrote on the computer? That's rich. I'm offended you'd lie to me so blatantly right now, missy, considering what I'm holding." He turned the rifle on her. "Consider yourself lucky if I use this, and not that." He motioned toward the ax on the floor. "This will be far less painful."

"How did you find out about the blog?" Piper asked.

Keep him talking, she thought.

The longer he talks, the more he sobers up.

The greater the chance someone shows up to help us.

Mr. Brockway snickered. "My brother was at the funeral; he knows what's what. He visited the child's old house down in Grangeville. New owner was out of town for a few days, but when he came back, he told my brother you paid him a visit."

He swung the rifle toward Piper, his finger on the trigger, and Piper was concerned he might pull it accidentally.

"Fella told me you were writing on the Internet," Mr. Brockway continued, "about the dark things going on with the Wallace family and what had happened at that house. Took me some time, but I found it. Found your blog. Read what was there this morning. Figured it was meant to be, confirmed what I always thought—that you're a no-good liar, not telling me the truth about what happened to my boy. Protecting this girl over here. I've been thinking about doing this—taking care of you, taking care of her—for the better part of a week now, but I haven't had the gall. That blog of yours gave me the push I needed, is what it did. Thank you for that."

Piper couldn't help but feel betrayed, even though it certainly wasn't Bill's fault. She'd never told him to keep it a secret, and she was the one actively *publishing* the information online.

"You don't have to do this," Sam told him. His voice was shaky, uncertain.

But at least he's talking, like me, Piper thought.

Just keep the man talking.

Mr. Brockway turned toward Sam, leveling the gun at his chest. "You see, that's where you're wrong, boy. I do have to do this. It's just unlucky for you that I didn't do it sooner, because you wouldn't have found yourself in this situation. I had my chances earlier to take care of business, but like I said before, I didn't have the gall. Well, half of my business." He glared menacingly at Piper.

She knew he meant her.

Half of his business.

"You've really been thinking about killing me?" Piper asked, almost incredulous that premeditated murder was actually a thing.

"Almost did the deed a few times," Mr. Brockway responded, a little too nonchalantly.

"When?"

"Oh, I can't really remember. I was outside your place one night, seeing what you were up to. Even knocked on your door. When you didn't answer, I wiggled the doorknob, and it opened right up. You weren't there, but I took a look around, searching for some kind of proof that you were lying about how my boy died." He shrugged. "Didn't think I'd find anything, but I looked anyway."

Piper thought back, immediately pinpointing what she thought was the night in question.

The stack of mail.

It had moved from the end table to the kitchen.

I wasn't just being paranoid—Brockway had been inside, and he'd moved it.

The thought terrified her, knowing he'd been inside her apartment without her realizing it, that he could've stuck around and killed her that night.

Like he was about to do right now.

"You're a monster," Piper said, her words coming out as a whisper.

Brockway sneered. "Oh, I'm the monster? I haven't been *protecting* a killer, like you have. Didn't *lie* to the face of a father looking for answers. I poured my heart out to you, right here in this apartment." He paused, exhaling deeply, looking like he was holding back tears. "Like I said, I should've taken care of my business earlier. Out in the woods is when I shoulda done it. No witnesses out there."

"The woods?" Piper asked.

"A few nights back I followed you out of town in my truck. Kept my distance, then put my own canoe in the water and found your campsite. Had my buck knife. Came pretty close that night. Wasn't feeling up to it then, I s'pose. Couple more shots of bourbon, and I might've gone through with it."

Piper was horrified.

She recalled the sounds outside of her tent, she and Ripley fleeing into the night. Like the stack-of-mail incident, Piper had chalked it up to paranoia, to her mind being *infected* in its own way.

She was wrong.

There had been something outside the tent.

A *human* monster.

Brockway reached up and scratched his unkempt beard, smacking his lips together when he was through. The crazy hadn't left his eyes.

"Don't y'all get it?" he asked, his voice rising. "My boy is dead because of this girl right here. And you've been enabling her all this time. I'm here to do what's right. I'm here to take care of what killed my son."

Piper glanced at Avery.

Still unmoved, but eyes open, breathing.

She looked at Sam.

Lips trembling, pale faced.

Piper knew she had to think fast. She'd certainly kept him talking, but Brockway's explanations for his intended actions were about through, she figured. All that was left was the actions themselves.

She peered back at Brockway, who had picked up the gas can, twisting the lid while holding the rifle pinched against his side, tucked under his armpit.

Piper needed to say something, to stop him.

She froze up.

Brockway continued to spin the lid.

Piper tried to come up with words.

There were none.

The lid was nearly off.

"Killing Avery won't destroy what killed your son," Sam interjected.

Brockway stopped, the lid still attached. He leered at Sam. "What did you say, boy?"

Sam swallowed hard, perhaps knowing that his next words could be his last. "We still don't know everything about this. We know that there's something attached to Avery, yes. We think we know the rules—the thirty-second countdown. That's undoubtedly what happened to Shane. The clock ran out, and then something came for him. What we don't know is what *exactly* killed your son."

Brockway stiffened, intrigued, removing his hand from the lid. "You better be getting to your point, and fast."

"My sister saw that black mist over Shane's body—that's what kills you when the timer runs out."

"I read all about that," Brockway responded, staring daggers at Piper.

Sam continued. "And that mist, that thing, was probably attached to Shane the moment he got infected. It's invisible, it stays with you, and it waits for you to be alone—and if you are alone, at the end of that timer, it materializes. Then it comes for you." He glanced downward. "And right now, one of those things is attached to Avery. It's waiting."

"Why are you telling me stuff that I already know?" Brockway barked. "I know what killed my son, and I know what's attached to her."

"Now, wait a second," Sam replied. "That thing attached to Avery— is it the *same* one that killed your son? Or did Shane have a different thing attached to him? That's what we don't know."

Brockway took a moment to take it all in.

Piper couldn't believe a few things: First, that Sam's stall was actually working. Brockway was listening, communicating, hadn't killed them. The other was how well Sam seemed to process everything. He had listened to her, really put it all together. And there was conviction in his voice.

He sounded like he believed.

"So . . . ," Brockway stammered, "you're saying that there might be more than one of these things? Is that what you're saying?"

Sam nodded. "If the virus was sent to Shane, then he downloaded a copy of the file. So why wouldn't there be a copy of the invisible creature? That black mist. It probably was a different one that killed Shane, and my sister saw it disappear." He paused. "If you somehow manage to kill whatever is attached to Avery—and we honestly have no clue how to do that—you're taking your vengeance out on the wrong thing."

Piper hadn't considered this part of the equation yet—just how many black mist creatures there actually were. The one that had hovered over Shane had vanished, and she didn't know where it had gone. She had never *assumed* it was simply the same thing attached to Avery, but she hadn't really thought about it.

A copy, she thought.

Every time someone is infected, a new tethered creature is created.

If the virus behaves like a downloaded program, it makes sense.

Still, did any of this really matter? It seemed like Sam was splitting hairs, but then again, maybe splitting hairs *was* the point of what he was doing. To get Brockway thinking, to get him to question everything. More time to survive.

It was then that Brockway smiled, devilishly. Piper didn't like it.

"I know what you're doing," Brockway said. "Trying to confuse me. Trying to stop me on account of a technicality. So I should just let y'all go, is that right? No punishment for the girl? No punishment for her?" He gestured at Piper.

"Sam's right," she said suddenly, not even meaning to say it. But off she went, even taking a baby step forward, her hand leaving Avery's shoulder. "If you really want to kill the thing that killed your son, you can't. Because it's gone. I saw it disappear. It just vanished, probably for good." She wasn't sure about that last part, but she said it anyway. Actually, Piper wasn't sure about any of this. She was simply looking to pick up where Sam had left off. "So you can kill me, and you can kill her. But that's not everything. That's not what you really came for, right? And if you can't do that, what's the point of any of this? You read my journal. Avery can't even remember sending the virus. This *child* is not the enemy, Dennis. It's the virus."

Mr. Brockway's entire body seemed to tremble. He bit down on his lower lip, and Piper could see his yellow and crooked teeth. His fingers danced along the rifle, and Piper saw him put his finger on the trigger. He steadied the rifle in his hands, and he aimed it at Piper's chest, before moving it a few inches so it was pointing at Avery.

Piper heard his breathing, heavy.

"Please, put down the gun," Piper said, raising one hand to shoulder height, the other holding on to Avery. "We can figure this out."

She took another small step toward Mr. Brockway, which caused the man to flinch and raise the rifle back toward Piper.

"Piper . . . ," she heard Sam say from behind her.

She brushed it off, moving another step closer.

Sam said his sister's name again—Piper noticed the worry and concern in his voice—but again, she ignored it. She thought that she could do it—she could really talk Brockway down, appeal to his humanity. Her left hand slowly reached out, planning on lowering his gun, which was a few feet away. Piper was staring at Brockway intently, and she noticed that his eyes had changed. They were more focused, as if the drunkenness had left them. He was looking past her now, squinting. Watching something behind her.

"Piper, don't look at it!" she heard Sam say loudly from behind her, and she didn't know what that meant, but her head instinctively swung around.

The next few moments were a blur.

Avery was at the keyboard, and there was something on the computer screen. She had *done something,* brought something up for them to see—Piper didn't know what it was, but she certainly had one guess:

The virus.

She wasn't certain, but her gut told her it was.

She avoided the screen, and her hand shot up, covering her eyes.

Still, Piper caught the tiniest of glimpses.

A quarter second, maybe.

She saw *flashing* on the screen.

Couldn't make out the colors, if there were any images, words.

Just flashing.

And then she heard a *crashing* sound—this made her look up. Avery was still at the keyboard, and Sam was next to her. It appeared he had shoved the computer monitor off the desk, and it lay on the floor, a few cables detached, nothing on the screen. Sam looked at Piper, chest heaving, apparently still filled with adrenaline after his sudden burst of action.

"She—she went to her email and pulled it up," he stammered. "I didn't stop her from doing it . . . I thought—" He paused. "Did you look at it? Tell me you didn't look at it."

Piper shook her head.

I didn't look at it, right? she thought.

It was only out of the corner of my eye.

"I didn't see it," Piper told him.

A look of relief filled Sam's face. But that look quickly turned to fear, and Piper turned around, understanding why. The gun was pointed directly at her.

"What the hell was on that screen?" Brockway asked.

CHAPTER 37

It had been fifteen minutes since Avery had pulled up the virus, and now the four of them were just *waiting*.

Piper was surprised that Brockway hadn't simply killed all of them after what just occurred. Sam had explained it the best he could. While Piper had been attempting to talk down Brockway, Avery had come to, grabbing the mouse and navigating to an email website. He didn't stop her because he was afraid that Brockway would shoot him, Sam claimed, if he suddenly lunged at the computer to stop her.

He'd watched Avery log in to her email, go to her sent items, and open the file called COOLGAME.exe. That's when he stopped looking at the screen, because he knew what was about to happen. But Brockway saw it. He'd been transfixed, almost hypnotized. That's when Sam—eyes closed, he said—sprang toward the monitor, swiping it off the desk. The power cable detached, and Brockway jolted back to reality.

But he'd seen it.

Oh, he'd *seen it* all right.

Brockway couldn't articulate what he had seen—he described his memory as "foggy," which made sense to Piper, given everything she knew about the virus.

And now they were just waiting.

Piper, Sam, and Avery were on the couch now. Brockway was slowly pacing the apartment, rifle in hand. No one had said anything for the previous ten minutes, after Sam had explained what had happened. Brockway didn't push Sam to justify his actions, why he had let Avery pull up the virus—yes, Sam claimed he was afraid he was going to be shot, but Piper thought she knew the real reason.

Sam saw an opportunity, Piper thought.

When he knew what Avery was doing, he just let her do it, hoping Brockway would get infected, thinking that might throw a wrench in his plans, perhaps even save us.

He tried to warn me, after all, but not him.

Piper looked at Brockway. He was anxious. Sweating buckets. He had seen the virus, and now his twenty-minute "installation activation" period was almost up. She knew the man was scared, but he wouldn't admit it.

He wants us around, she thought.

He needs us for what's about to happen.

Brockway had admitted as much. "We wait," he'd said after seeing the virus. "And don't think about moving from that couch."

They were still in danger, she knew, even if they didn't move. He had a rifle, a gas can, and an ax. There was still plenty that could go wrong for them. Brockway could very well still kill them. Piper had hoped in the last fifteen minutes that someone would show up, that a neighbor had heard Brockway break down the door, or perhaps heard the commotion. But Ms. Hermann was out of town visiting her cousin, Piper's house was the last on a dead-end street, and the neighbors weren't particularly close by. Even if someone had heard the ax, they might've thought it was someone chopping wood.

Piper glanced at her watch.

It had been about eighteen minutes.

Brockway's infection seemed pretty certain, but Piper still didn't know what would happen to her. She had seen the flashing—barely, but she'd seen it—and she didn't know if that counted, if the infection was also taking root inside of her. Brockway had been mesmerized; she had

not. Her countdown would be similar to his, just a few seconds behind—
he had seen it first, after all, before she'd turned around.

I could still have it.

But perhaps the strangest thing of all about their situation was the
person who seemed to *not* have it anymore.

Avery.

Since she had pulled up the virus on the computer, she'd been getting gradually better. With each minute that passed, Avery's attention
was returning more and more. The confusion was gone from her eyes,
and Piper didn't think she would sink into another comatose state or
start spouting terrible things.

My God, Piper thought, *she just seems normal.*

Edgy, sure—there was a behemoth with a rifle stalking around the
room—but if Piper hadn't known any better, she would have sworn that
Avery was cured.

And it made no sense to her at all.

None.

She didn't know *how* or *why* Avery had woken up in the computer
chair, if she had consciously or unconsciously pulled up her email and
launched the virus file, and why now, thirteen months after being infected, Avery seemed to have miraculously recovered. She didn't think
it was a coincidence, though. She remembered the previous night, when
Susan told her the story of their family's tragic and hellish history—
Piper had used the word *reason*. There had to be a *reason* for everything
that was happening, perhaps something within the virus that would
give them answers. She still thought that. Avery was better for a *reason*
now, and they just didn't know what it was yet. Piper longed to ask Avery what she was feeling, but she didn't dare. She worried that if Avery
said she was better, it would set Brockway off, knowing his son was
dead and the girl who had sent him the virus was now cured. Best to
keep quiet for now; those questions could be asked later.

Hopefully.

If we get out of this.

Piper gripped Avery's hand, and the girl smiled. A nervous smile, of course, but she flashed it just the same. Piper looked deeper into her eyes. There was a coherence, an awareness, she'd never seen before.

I think she's all the way back, Piper thought.

She looked at her watch again.

It had been about twenty minutes.

Piper swallowed hard.

Time's up.

Brockway stopped in his tracks. He was across the apartment, standing near the bed. The rifle pointed toward the floor, and his gaze darted around the room. He appeared weak, vulnerable. "There's something here with us," he said. "I can feel it. It's . . . watching me. I can *feel it.*" He waved the gun around wildly. Toward the ceiling, the TV, toward *them.*

Sam instinctively slid farther down on the couch, and Piper wrapped one arm tightly around Avery.

"Why can't I see it?" Mr. Brockway yelled at the group, spit flying from his mouth. Piper was a bit surprised at his confusion—he *knew* what was going to happen to him, knew he wouldn't be able to see it, but she imagined the sensation was still frightening and bewildering all the same.

Then she felt it.

A tickling, in her chest.

Something happening inside of her.

No.

And then, something *outside* of her.

A presence in the room. She couldn't pinpoint it yet, but she was beginning to feel a bit like Brockway.

Something was watching her.

Piper knew that didn't matter right now. As far as her problems went, surprisingly, the feeling was lower on the list—the unstable and panicking man waving a gun was currently at the top. Brockway moved from the bed to the shattered doorway. He was behind them now, pointing his gun at the ceiling, tracking something no one could see. Not even him. He spun around, turning his back to them, pointing the gun above the doorframe.

"It's up there!" he shouted. "I feel it up there!"

Piper locked eyes with Sam, and she knew he was thinking the same thing as her.

This is our chance.

Piper yanked Avery off the couch, and the three dashed toward the bathroom, Sam in the lead. The three tumbled inside, and Piper slammed the door shut, locking it.

"Thirty seconds," she huffed. "If he's alone for thirty seconds, we might get out of this."

"Piper—"

"Just hold the door closed with me, in case he tries to get in!"

She heard the man's boots quickly stomping around the apartment, and then splashes of something hitting the floor.

Piper knew it was the gas. She was a little surprised he hadn't gone after them. In his panic, he must've decided one thing:

Destroy the evil thing with fire.

And it will be here in about twenty seconds, as long as he remains alone.

"He's gonna burn this place down!" Sam blurted.

He lunged toward the handle, but Piper grabbed his hand.

"He might shoot us!" Piper said, not sure if Brockway actually would, but she wasn't about to take the chance.

"We have to do something!"

Her gaze darted madly around the bathroom. Avery was one step ahead of her, standing on the toilet trying to open a small window.

She grunted as she fiddled with the lock.

"It won't open!" she cried.

Piper had never before opened that window—*Does it open?* Maybe she could help Avery and they could all squeeze through the small opening, but it was a pretty far drop to the ground.

Better than being burned alive.

Ten seconds.

We run out there, we stop the evil thing from coming . . .

Five seconds.

But then he could unload the shotgun on us.

Piper heard the sound of a flame igniting.

Then a bone-rattling scream.

A shotgun blast.

BOOM.

A portion of the door seemed to *explode,* throwing Piper backward, the aroma of splintered wood filling the air. Sam collapsed to the ground.

Piper knew immediately that he'd been shot.

He grabbed his left shoulder, crying out in pain, and Piper saw the blood oozing from between his fingers where he held the wound, his white T-shirt turning dark red. There was no more screaming, no more gunshots, no more stomping of boots.

And Piper knew why.

The thirty-second countdown had expired.

Dennis Brockway was dead.

Avery hopped down from the toilet and rushed to Sam's side. Despite the urgency of the moment, Piper couldn't help but think how incredible it was that the girl was *back,* no longer a passenger to whatever dark thing had been controlling her, no longer tethered to an evil creature. The child pressed her hand on Sam's wound, and he grimaced.

"It's okay, it's okay," Avery told him.

No spaciness, no dullness.

Maybe the Avery of old.

The Avery she'd never met.

Piper didn't stop to smell the roses. She jumped to her feet, pulling Sam up with her, Avery doing her best to help him staunch the bleeding in his shoulder.

Piper's nostrils flared.

She smelled the smoke.

They had to go.

Piper threw open the bathroom door, and the three ran back into the living room. The couch and end table were ablaze, the flames growing quickly, nearly kissing the ceiling. Mr. Brockway was lying flat on his back, his open eyes projecting a look of abject fear, the rifle lying uselessly at his side.

He'd tried to burn the dark thing, and he'd tried to shoot it.

And it had cost him his life.

The trio darted toward the smashed-up entryway, Sam in between Piper and Avery, one arm around them both. They climbed through the wreckage, dashing down the stairs to safety, the brisk October air a respite from the inferno inside.

The second Piper's bare feet hit the grass at the bottom of the stairs, she realized her grave mistake.

"*Ripley,*" she cried out. "Oh my God. He's still up there."

She wasn't sure if Sam or Avery protested, as complete and utter tunnel vision seized her. Piper bounded up the stairs, charging through the wrecked doorway, her eyes searching maniacally around the apartment. It was difficult to see. The fire had spread fast, and black smoke was beginning to billow.

Piper knew she didn't have much time.

She went with her gut, which was to check under the kitchen table, the last place he'd been—and Ripley was still there, curled up in a ball, his eyes wide and fearful. Piper dove under the table and scooped him up, rising to her feet, and then she felt something hit her.

It wasn't an object.

It was an awareness, a *heaviness.*

I'm infected and I'm alone, she thought.

And that thing is forming.

Piper began running with the dog in her arms, her feet moving faster than she thought possible, and she flew through the debris of the doorway onto the landing, grateful for the fresh air, and more than grateful to see Avery and Sam at the bottom of the stairs, her brother sitting on the cold ground with his hand still at his shoulder, a pained expression on his face. The moment she saw them, she felt the heaviness diminish—she was no longer alone; she was safe—but she still felt the presence behind her, trailing her, nipping at her heels as she descended each step.

She knew no one could see it—not even her, even if she turned her head—but she still felt it.

Piper was nearly there now, the most important thing in her life quivering at her chest, and she wondered how surprised the people at the hospital would be when she returned with her brother, who was currently bleeding onto Ms. Hermann's lawn.

She imagined she'd have some explaining to do.

\part five\

SIGNING OUT

CHAPTER 38

It was pure luck," Sam said. "A miracle, maybe."

They were debriefing, just the three of them. Discussing the nearly impossible odds of Avery being cured just a few hours ago. None of them could wrap their head around it.

"I think there is a reason," Piper said. "We just don't know what it is yet."

"Who cares, right?" Sam responded. "She's better."

It was the afternoon, close to twelve thirty P.M. Sam lay in a hospital bed, and Piper sat in a chair next to her brother. Avery was sprawled out on a couch. Sam's injury was relatively minor, and it'd been cleaned, stitched up. X-rays had been taken, and he was in a recovery room. Susan was nearby, still in the ICU. She couldn't have any visitors yet, but her condition was still stable. Avery was anxious to see her.

But not yet, the doctor said. Maybe not until that night or the next day.

If all continued to go well.

"Do you remember pulling up your email and opening the virus?" Piper asked Avery. She thought that maybe it was a conscious decision, that Avery had been *trying* to infect Brockway, thinking it might get them out of their situation.

"I don't remember doing it," Avery responded.

"Did you feel it leave you?" Piper asked Avery. "The invisible thing."

Avery shook her head. "It was like . . . waking up from a dream. Like, I was sitting in a chair, and I couldn't feel it anymore. I knew immediately. You live with something for a year, and you just know. It was just gone." She hesitated. "It killed him, right?"

Piper nodded. She'd seen Mr. Brockway's eyes—the same as Shane's. Dead.

Avery thought for a moment. "I can't believe it's not here anymore." She paused. "It's just nice knowing there's not an evil thing in the room, you know?"

That wasn't entirely true.

Something was with them right now.

Avery just couldn't sense it, because it wasn't attached to her.

It was Piper who felt it.

Now an evil thing belonged to *her*—all she'd done was look at the screen for a quarter second, and she'd gotten it.

But she hadn't told Avery or Sam.

It was in the room with them, behind a curtain—at least, that's where Piper *thought* it was, based on the feeling she got when she looked that way. It had followed her all the way from her burning apartment, in the ambulance, all the way to the hospital. Piper had even sensed it in the lobby as she spoke with Clover Creek police officers—*We hid from the crazy man with a gun; he fired his rifle at us and started a fire, and I'm not sure how he died*—and now it was in Sam's recovery room.

It was the strangest sensation.

Avery had been right.

Piper couldn't see it, but she could *feel* where it was located. Sometimes it seemed to hide, other times it seemed to float above her. It had moved past her a few times, causing Piper to flinch.

Her new evil companion.

She didn't feel like telling Sam and Avery yet, didn't want to sully the moment. Piper was still coming to grips with it herself, honestly. And Avery's victory deserved to be savored. Piper would confess later.

But not yet.

"I just don't get why Avery is cured," Piper said, not letting it go. "I'm like, baffled, to be honest. Happy, don't get me wrong, but baffled."

The word still stuck in her head.

Reason.

There had to be a *reason*.

"Ms. Lowery is right," Avery said, sitting up. "My evil thing was with me for *so long*. Why then? Why all of a sudden?"

"Maybe it was because you showed the virus to someone?" Sam wondered aloud from the bed. "Like, you have to infect someone else? Then you're cured? You know, like those stupid chain emails I'm always getting."

"But she'd already done that," Piper responded. "She's passed it along before."

Avery nodded from the couch.

"Maybe it was different this time?" Sam offered. "Like, *actually* pulling it up versus sending it?"

"That just doesn't make sense," Piper said.

"I'm just thinking out loud here," Sam said. "Okay, I got another one. What if those nerds on the Internet were right? And the tech-orcism worked?"

"It *definitely* didn't work," Piper said. "She was worse by the end of it. You saw it. She—" Piper looked at Avery. "*You* were in rough shape. I swear you were a few minutes away from dying, you seemed so lifeless."

Avery smiled. "Well, I'm happy to be here. Dying would have sucked, I bet."

Interacting with a completely lucid, normal Avery was still a bit of a shock to Piper. Gone was her somewhat slower way of speaking, the hesitations, the timidness. Piper was witnessing the pre-infected Avery emerge from the darkness, and it pleased her to no end.

"Why was I—" Avery started. "*Acting* the way I was?"

Piper had explained the episodes to Avery earlier—the outbursts, the things she was saying—and the kid had looked absolutely flabbergasted. She had no memory of any of it.

"I don't know," Piper said. "I think there's a lot we still don't know about this virus. What it does, and why it does it. *When* it does it."

Sam made a pained noise, and Piper turned toward him.

"Does it hurt?" she asked.

"I've been shot. What do you think?"

"Yes?"

"Eh, it's not so bad."

Piper smiled, looking off. Sam was hooked up to an IV pump and a heart monitor, which beeped intermittently.

All things considered, he looked pretty good.

"Did they say when you would get out of here?" Piper asked.

"Tonight, I think. As long as there aren't any complications."

Piper nodded. It was then that she sensed the evil presence in the room, creeping closer, as if it were lurking just behind her. Piper shifted in her seat, but Sam didn't seem to notice her edginess.

It's the painkillers, Piper thought. *He's probably doped up pretty good.*

"Oh man," Sam suddenly said.

"What? What is it?"

"Do you think my computer is all burned up? It was in your apartment."

"I don't know. I haven't been back there yet."

Piper sensed the invisible thing *directly* behind her now. She could feel its breath on her neck.

Avery never mentioned that sensation, Piper thought.

"I *liked* that computer," Sam said.

"Do you have another one?"

"Yeah, two more. But I *really* liked that one. Aw, well." He attempted to shrug, and his face contorted in pain.

"One of the police officers said he would go back to the apartment today," Piper said. "I asked him if he wouldn't mind grabbing a few things, you know, if they aren't charcoal."

"My Walkman?" Avery asked hopefully.

Piper nodded. "I told him about that. I figured you'd want it, and your tapes and journals, if they survived. I can call over to the station, see if they wouldn't mind grabbing your computer, too, Sam. I should probably see how Ripley is doing, anyway."

The hospital hadn't been too keen on the dog staying there, so the police officer who interviewed Piper had offered to take him to the station for the day. He said everyone would like having him around.

Small-town hospitality, Piper thought.

Sam yawned. "And what about Fisher? Any luck with him?"

Piper shook her head. She'd called his home multiple times throughout the morning, leaving more messages, imploring him or Carol to call her at the hospital.

She still had no idea where he was.

Sam adjusted in the bed. Avery stretched out again, moving a pillow underneath her head. They were both exhausted. Her brother closed his eyes, and Piper saw Avery's eyes flutter as well. Piper wondered how good Avery must have felt—she was still worried about her mother, no doubt, but there had to be a renewed sense of freedom, knowing she could walk down the hall alone without fear. Avery had already tested being alone after they first entered Sam's recovery room. She had gone into the bathroom, closed the door, and emerged minutes later with a broad smile on her face, tears welling in her eyes.

Those eyes were now firmly closed.

It looked like she was already asleep.

Sam, too.

Piper didn't know what to do.

She should try to take care of the Fisher problem—she knew that much. But her body was shutting down. She was just so *tired*.

Just a short snooze, she thought.

It'll clear my head.

Then I'll figure this out.

Piper considered lying down on the floor, but she thought she might be out of a *potential line of sight*.

Piper instead grabbed a pillow from near Avery's feet, returning to the chair next to the bed, adjusting her position, and wedging the pillow against the wall and Sam's bed. She was about eye level with him.

This is my life now, Piper thought.

She closed her eyes.

. . .

Her body craved sleep. She dozed in the chair for hours, the events in the hospital room merging with her dreams. Nurses walked in and out, and a doctor appeared at one point, but they were mostly blurs in Piper's mind. She never fully awoke to engage with them; they were there and then not there, examining the machines next to Sam's bed, scribbling notes onto clipboards. A police officer entered the room at one point, then vanished. Piper wasn't sure if that even happened at all. Avery was still sprawled out on the couch, her back to Piper—her red hair was always the last thing Piper saw before slipping back into sleep.

Her body ached; every muscle felt weak and heavy. Piper's position next to Sam was uncomfortable, but it didn't matter. Her body had shut down all the same, and when she finally woke, straightening up in the chair and shaking off the grogginess, the first thing she noticed was that sunlight was no longer streaming through the curtains.

It was dark.

Piper looked at her watch:

Six forty-six P.M.

Sam was still asleep; Avery, too. Piper rose and stretched, examining the rest of the room. An item sat on the floor next to the couch, and Piper didn't remember it being there before.

Avery's knapsack.

The cop, Piper thought.

He's been here.

She had never called to ask to look for Sam's laptop—she felt a little bad about that. Piper walked to the couch and bent down, exploring the contents of the bag. The journals had survived, although she could tell that they'd been doused with water. The Walkman was also inside, as well as a collection of Avery's cassettes. Then Piper grabbed something else—the piece of the computer from the library. She was surprised to find it here and she assumed the officer must've tossed it into the bag along with the journals and tapes she'd asked him to grab. It was on the kitchen table, after all, next to Avery's stuff.

What did Sam call this thing?

A ROM or RAM or something?

She couldn't remember, and then a terrible thought struck her, something she should have considered earlier but had slipped through the cracks.

That hard drive is still at the library.

The virus might be on there.

If Fisher downloaded and installed it, then it's there.

Piper pictured a patron logging in to the computer and horrible things happening to them, but then she relaxed. That computer didn't work. She had taken a presumably vital part from inside the tower. The technology know-how of the library staff was basically nonexistent—there was no way they would be able to fix it.

Still, maybe they would call in a professional to look at it or send it away.

Piper stood, contemplating next steps. The hard drive needed to be retrieved. She also needed to check on Fisher and confirm if he really had been infected.

RING!

The noise startled her. It caused Avery to stir. It was the ringing of the phone next to Sam's bed, and Piper walked to it, picking up the receiver and saying hello.

A pause on the other end.

"Is this . . . Piper Lowery?" an older woman's voice finally said, sounding a bit unsure.

"Oh my God," Piper responded. "Mrs. Fisher—Carol—is that you?"

It was her, and Piper bombarded her with questions. The woman's voice was heavy with concern—and Piper sensed that she seemed in a hurry to get off the phone—but she answered all of Piper's inquiries.

I took Glen to a friend's house last night—she's a doctor. We're going to stay there for a while, until we figure out what to do.

Glen's not well. He talks to himself, and he thinks something is in the room with him. And his zoning out is getting worse.

He hasn't used a computer.

I came back to the house to grab a few things, and then I'm going back to be with him.

Fisher's condition was certainly worrisome. He was deteriorating much more rapidly than Avery—the child didn't start speaking to herself until a year after her infection, according to Susan.

Why are their progressions so different? Piper wondered.

"Has Glen said anything . . . strange?" Piper asked tentatively.

"What do you mean?"

"Similar to what happened in the classroom."

"No, dear. He hasn't. Just the mumbling, and I can't make out the words."

That was a minor relief. Still, Piper's stomach was in knots. She wanted to go to Fisher, to provide comfort, at the very least. But without a car, and still on the line with Carol, Piper saw an opportunity to kill two birds with one stone.

I can both see Fisher and get that hard drive, right now.

Piper begged the woman to drive to the hospital and pick her up, not wanting to explain over the phone, promising that it would be worth her efforts, that it would help other people not suffer from the same sickness that had seized her husband.

Carol hesitated, but she agreed.

Piper hung up the phone, and she realized she was shaking a bit.

"Ms. Lowery?" a voice said from behind her.

It was Avery.

"Can I come with you?" she asked.

"You want to see Mr. Fisher?"

Avery nodded solemnly. Piper hadn't told her that her teacher was infected—Avery must have gleaned that from listening to the conversation.

"You can come," Piper told her. "He'd like to see you, I bet."

And I need you, she thought, *to be my escort to make sure I'm never alone.*

Piper sensed the invisible thing floating directly above her head, and she felt its malicious energy.

Its pure *hatred.*

It wanted to swallow her whole.

She shuddered, wondering how Avery had lived so close to this evil for so very long.

. . .

They passed numerous trick-or-treaters en route to the library, Carol driving slow and careful once they reached the streets of Clover Creek. Piper watched Avery's reaction as she looked out the window—Halloween was one of her favorite days, after all. Would she be wistful or sad? Maybe even joyful, happy for the other kids, hamming it up in their costumes? But Avery gave no response, merely staring out the back-seat window. Piper wondered if she'd retained that part of herself—the joy of Halloween—or if the virus had taken it away.

Even though she's back now, is it possible she's lost some things forever?

They arrived at the library a little after eight P.M. There was one car in the library parking lot, which Piper found strange, since the library was closed.

Cleaning crew? she thought.

My boss working late?

Carol parked, and she, Piper, and Avery walked to the entrance.

They were about fifty feet away when Piper noticed the large window next to the front door.

Shattered.

Piper checked the door.

Locked.

She wondered if the broken window was an accident, or an act of vandalism, perhaps. If it had occurred during working hours, the area would have been cleaned up, the gaping hole in the building tarped off.

No, it must've occurred after they'd locked up for the night.

Piper swallowed hard.

She didn't like this.

The three slowly and carefully stepped through the empty window frame, shards of glass crackling beneath their feet. Carol held on to Piper's arm, and Avery took the lead, glancing around as she moved. Piper didn't hear any noises as they walked toward the front desk. She was wary of someone popping out—of disturbing a potential break-in— and she carefully examined her surroundings, looking for movement. But it was just so dark. She could barely make anything out.

Her next thought was to turn on the lights, which were controlled by a panel near the main office behind the checkout station. She imagined that once that happened, if someone else *was* in there with them, they might hightail it for the exit. Piper braced herself for that scenario as she put her hand on the light switch panel.

She hit the switches, and the dozens of lights around the library flickered to life, a gentle buzzing filling the space.

But there were no other sounds.

No movement.

And then Piper saw him, and she *gasped* so hard she backed up into the wall.

There was a man, hunched over one of the computers. He was in a chair, and he was slumped over the workstation, his head resting on the keyboard. His arms hung loosely at his sides.

Piper spotted the tie-dye shirt and the man's long, gray hair.

She knew it was him.

Fisher.

Carol immediately recognized that fact as well, and she ran to her husband, not screaming but merely sputtering Glen's name over and over, her voice desperate and panicked. Piper and Avery followed, and when they arrived at the workstation, Carol grabbed her husband with two hands and lifted his upper body, so he was sitting upright.

His body was limp.

His jaw, slack.

Piper couldn't get over Glen's eyes.

Bulging, fearful.

She'd seen that look before.

On Shane Brockway, on Dennis Brockway.

She knew what had gotten Fisher.

The dark mist.

He'd been alone, and it had gotten him—his thirty-second timer had expired.

But who was with him before that timer started, and where are they now?

Carol shook him a few times, gently slapping his cheeks, tearfully repeating his name, trying to get him to wake up. Piper knew it was in vain. What she *didn't* know was why Fisher was there. The computer terminal he sat at was powered down, the screen black. Her thoughts raced as she tried to determine how he'd gotten into the library—surely, he hadn't been alone; someone had been here with him at some point—but her thoughts didn't go any further.

"HELP ME!"

It was a man's voice.

Fear-stricken.

Screaming.

"WHERE ARE YOU? OH GOD, WHERE ARE YOU?"

Piper's hand instinctively shot to the side, grabbing Avery by the girl's sweatshirt. Fisher slipped from Carol's hands, and his lifeless head smacked the keyboard.

"PLEASE, COME OUT! OH GOD, OH GOD, OH GOD!"

It was coming from the stacks, Piper thought.

The three didn't move.

A gut-wrenching shriek filled the library—a tortured, anguished wail that echoed off the walls—and then it abruptly ceased.

Snuffed out, Piper thought.

Silence.

Piper wasn't sure what to do, so she simply stood there, waiting, still gripping Avery by the sweatshirt. Carol just collapsed onto her husband's body, weeping.

Avery looked up at Piper. "Should we go down there?"

There still hadn't been another sound from the stacks.

Piper released her grip, nodding.

The two walked across the library toward the stairs, leaving Carol behind. She didn't protest. As they approached the staircase, Piper suddenly stopped.

"I need you to stay with me, okay?" she told Avery.

Avery gave her a knowing look. "It's latched on to you, hasn't it?"

"How did you—"

"I can tell. The way you're always looking around. Shivering randomly. If anyone would know, it would be me."

Piper didn't know what to say.

"You didn't see the virus, did you?" Avery asked.

"Barely. But I saw it."

"In your apartment? When I showed it to Mr. Brockway?"

Piper slowly nodded.

"I'm sorry," she muttered, dropping her head. "All I do is hurt people."

Piper put her hand under Avery's chin, gently raising it. "Hey, it's not your fault. None of this is. You hear me? None of it."

There were tears in Avery's eyes, and she wiped them away.

"Say it," Piper said. *"It's not my fault."*

"It's not my fault," Avery repeated.

She didn't know if Avery meant the words or not but felt it was important that she say them. The poor girl had been *supernaturally infected,* for God's sake; her actions weren't her own. She hoped Avery understood this—if not now, in time, at some point.

But they had bigger fish to fry at present.

Piper peered down the staircase. The lights were on downstairs, too. Still, it brought Piper little comfort. "We have to go down there. Just don't leave me alone, okay?"

Avery nodded and took Piper by the hand. The two descended slowly, peeking around the corner at the landing before heading down the remaining steps. From the entryway, they could see across the stacks. Bookshelves stretched from floor to ceiling along the sides, forming a maze. Tables and study carrels were scattered around the center, with more along the far wall of the basement where the shelving stopped. Piper could see the computer station against the far wall across from the stacks, the Out of Order sign still affixed to the monitor. On a nearby table sat a laptop, the screen facing away from her and Avery, with a few other devices next to it. Piper didn't recognize them. It was a little darker in that area of the library—bad lights, in desperate need of replacement—and whatever was on the laptop screen was casting a flickering glow against the wall.

She didn't know for certain what was on the screen, obviously, but her stomach dropped when she saw the flicker. It was a *little* too similar to the flicker she'd seen that morning in her apartment.

"Hey," Piper told Avery, "whatever is on that screen, don't look at it."

Avery put two and two together, and she nodded.

It was still eerily quiet. Avery tugged on Piper's hand, and she pointed with the other.

"Look," she whispered shakily. "There, on the floor."

Piper looked that way. It was hard to spot, but she made it out. Maybe ten feet from the laptop, an arm was splayed out on the floor between two of the last rows of books. She couldn't see the rest of the body.

"Hello?" Piper hollered.

Nothing.

Piper repeated herself.

Still nothing.

She looked down at Avery, then motioned in the direction of the body.

Avery just nodded nervously, and Piper began slowly moving across the stacks, her hand still gripping Avery's, her fingernails digging into the child's wrist. They continued to call out, not sure if someone else was down there, perhaps hiding between rows of books. They passed tables, a collection of encyclopedias, the atlases.

Inching closer now.

Forty, thirty feet away.

The arm on the ground didn't move, and Piper spotted dark hair on it, a *man's* arm, she decided. She still couldn't see the body. The laptop screen continued to flicker, almost like a strobe effect on the far wall.

They began to move again, inching closer, now fifteen feet away. Piper and Avery angled around an empty table so they could potentially see the entire figure on the floor. The laptop screen was not in their line of sight, and Piper was determined to keep it that way.

"Hello?" Piper said.

No movement, but now she could see most of the body.

It was a man, his face turned away from them. He had dark hair, thinning around the crown. He wore a short-sleeve, plaid button-down shirt that had ridden up, exposing his lower back and the green band of his underwear.

"I'll check him, okay?" Piper said to Avery.

"I'll stay with you."

Their hands were still clasped tightly, now slick with sweat. Just as Piper was about to approach the body, a strong hand grabbed her from behind.

"Please . . . ," a voice said.

Piper nearly jumped out of her socks, spinning around and screaming, pulling Avery with her, the child yanked to the floor.

A man stood before them.

His face was pale, his pupils dilated.

Piper recognized him.

"Oh my God," she said. *"Bill?"*

The man from the Wallaces' old house.

She'd met him once before; he'd even commented on her online journal. Billyboy, she remembered. Piper had never expected to see him at the library.

"What are you doing here?" Piper continued.

His breath was rapid, and he collapsed into a chair, putting his arms on the table and dropping his head, weeping. Bill finally raised his head, and he ran his arm across his face, wiping away snot and tears.

"He's *dead,*" Bill said, his voice trembling. "I heard it all. It was awful. I . . . never want to hear anything like that ever again. Oh *God.*"

Avery had risen to her feet, and she sat in the chair next to Bill.

"Bill, what happened here?" Piper asked slowly.

He appeared shell-shocked, but he managed words. "I drove up here. Your blog, it was just so interesting, so real. I needed to see it for myself, to see what was happening. I just drove into town—"

"I never mentioned my town on the blog," Piper interrupted.

"People figured it out in the comments sometime this morning."

"How did people know where—"

"The stuff about the Northwoods, a boy dying. Someone found an obit, did some cross-checking. I think you had mentioned something about the number of churches in town . . . people just figured it out.

There was this huge discussion. I drove up this afternoon. So did a bunch of other people."

Piper hadn't checked her online journal since very early in the morning, since before the failed "tech-orcism." She wondered how many comments there were now.

Hundreds more?

Thousands?

"What do you mean, 'a bunch of other people'?" Piper asked. "How many people drove up here?"

"I don't know, like fifteen or twenty? That's how many people on your blog said they—"

"You have a blog?" Avery said, looking at Piper. "About all of this stuff?"

Piper was at a loss for words.

She met Avery's gaze, reading a mixture of surprise and disappointment.

Piper felt absolutely awful.

She looked back at Bill.

"Bill," she said, motioning toward the laptop. "Is that what I think it is?"

Bill nodded.

"Did you look at it?"

He shook his head.

"You *need* to tell me what happened."

He wiped away more snot. "I met this guy, Frank. He was at a gas station, right out of town. He was coming up here to check things out, like I was. He said he had a lead on your teacher friend."

"People figured out who he was?" Piper asked, shocked.

"Frank knew, somehow. Pieced it together—figured out he was the boy's teacher, and the age matched up with the way you described him, the class he taught."

"Is that Frank?" Piper gestured toward the dead man on the floor.

Bill nodded. "He really wanted to find your teacher friend, to see if he was actually infected, to see if this was real. Frank convinced me to go with him, and I did. God, I don't know why I did that. It was just, the *adrenaline,* the mystery. I . . . we looked up his address, went to his house. The teacher. He wasn't there, but we talked to some neighbors, and we figured out where he went. So we went there, instead. This was about an hour ago, I think?"

About an hour ago, Piper thought.

Carol was probably on the road then, driving to the hospital to pick her up.

She wouldn't have known any of this was happening.

Bill paused, looking distressed. "I didn't plan on doing any of this. It was just so *exciting,* like a real-life ghost adventure. We found him, and Frank convinced him to come with us, to show us where the virus came from. I felt weird about that. That felt wrong. But Frank really wanted to see if the virus was real, and he asked your friend to show us. And we didn't *kidnap* him or anything. He came with us willingly. He seemed almost manic about it. The mere mention of him using a computer is what did it. He wanted to use one, he said. And then he saw Frank's BlackBerry—it was like leading a dog with a treat. The person he was with—this woman—was confused, and she tried to get him to stay, but your friend wouldn't have it."

There it is, Piper thought.

The compulsion to use a computer.

Fisher's symptoms progressed much, much faster than Avery's.

Shockingly fast.

Like everything that had happened with Avery, Piper assumed there was a *reason* but she just didn't know it yet.

"She *let* you take him?" Piper said. She still wasn't over that part.

"Your teacher friend wanted to go with us. Insisted on it. Got in the car himself."

"She didn't know where you were going?"

"It all happened so fast. I don't think the word *library* was even mentioned. It was all, 'Show us the virus; you can use a computer.'" He shook his head, disbelieving. "My God, how did this happen?"

"But you took him here," Piper said.

Bill sniffled. "We did. Broke a window to get in. I should've stopped before that happened, but I kept going. Meeting your friend, it just seemed so real. Like he had an honest-to-God supernatural infection. And Frank kept *pushing,* and I kept following his lead, and then we were here in the basement, your friend showing us the computer, and he was upset that it was broken. He was desperate to use it. It was the strangest thing. He asked about Frank's BlackBerry, but at that point Frank and I had already started taking apart the computer tower. I looked up, and your friend was gone. I'm not sure when he left us."

Piper pictured it.

Fisher, frustrated after they ignored his request to use the Black-Berry, still feeling the urge. He knew there were more computers on the main level. He went upstairs, sat at a station.

Thirty seconds after he was completely alone, it got him.

Piper wondered if Bill had heard Fisher scream, if the man *did* scream.

She didn't ask. She didn't want to picture it.

"You didn't go after him?" Piper asked, appalled. "Even *knowing* that he couldn't be alone?"

Bill's gaze dropped toward the table. "I don't know what I was thinking. Maybe, deep down, I didn't believe any of this was real, because stuff like this shouldn't exist. So, it didn't matter if he was alone. Or maybe I was too excited to take apart the computer, I don't know. But he was there, and then the next moment, he was gone. And I didn't think to look for him."

"He's dead now," Piper said. "You should know that he's dead."

Bill swallowed and nodded, saying nothing.

"How did Frank see the virus?" Avery chimed in. "That library computer is broken, right? Out of order? Did you take out the hard drive?"

"We did," Bill replied, gathering himself. "Frank had a bunch of tech gear with him. His laptop, adapters, a docking station. We hooked the hard drive up to his laptop, and we found it. COOLGAME.exe. It was in the downloads folder, but it had been installed before. Frank was just so curious, wanted to look. He wanted to see it. To see if it was real, to see actual evidence of something supernatural."

"Even if it could *kill* you?"

"Maybe he didn't do it on purpose. I don't know. There was a part of me that wanted to see it, too. And even though I *still* didn't quite believe it was possible to be killed by a computer file—*this is like a movie, for God's sake*—my gut told me not to look at it. So I didn't. Once I saw the little file icon on the screen, I walked away. But Frank opened it. He watched it. Maybe by accident, I don't know. I watched him from across the library. He was just *staring* at it." Bill looked off. "And I didn't know what to do. Everything felt wrong. He just kept staring, and I sat down over there, out of sight." He pointed across the library. "I sat there for a while."

"Twenty minutes?" Piper asked.

"Could have been. I just didn't know what to do, wanted to be alone. I felt like a terrible, god-awful person, just—wondering how it all got carried away so fast. I grabbed a book, and I was mindlessly going through it—and then Frank started *screaming*."

That's when we were upstairs, Piper thought.

We heard it.

The three of them looked over toward the laptop simultaneously.

The virus was still running.

Something was flickering and casting shadows on the wall—rhythmically, hypnotically. Piper wondered what was actually on the screen, as she had only really seen it out of the corner of her eye before. She tried to put the thought out of her mind.

She didn't *want* to know.

"Why didn't you help him?" Avery asked. She looked appalled.

Bill shook his head. "I was scared. The *screaming,* oh God, the screaming. Something was coming after him. I read your blog—I knew the rules. If I was with him, the thing wouldn't kill him. But I was just *so damn scared*. I've never heard a man scream like that. I thought I might piss myself." He exhaled, and Piper noticed he was trembling. "So, I stayed hidden, on the other side of the library, behind a bookshelf. Crouched down, knees to my chest. I stayed like that for some time, even after the screaming stopped. Even after I heard you come down here."

He paused.

"It was *here*," he said. "That evil thing was here. I still can't believe it's real."

He dropped his head again and began to weep.

Piper just turned, looking at the laptop. She wasn't sure if the virus had transferred to Frank's laptop or if it was still just on the hard drive in the adapter. It could be in both places, she reasoned. Either way, it had to be stopped. It had to be destroyed. She didn't have a clear plan yet, but she moved toward it—until a hand pulled her back.

"I'll do it," Avery said.

Avery walked that way, but not cautiously—there was a defiant strut to her steps. When she reached the table, she crouched down, so she was eye-level with the back of the laptop. Avery reached out one hand and gently closed the laptop lid, her face turned away from the machine.

The flickering ceased.

Then she unplugged the hard drive adapter, picked up the laptop, and hurled it to the ground. A few pieces broke off, and she retrieved the laptop, slamming it against the floor once more.

Pieces flew in every direction.

CRUNCH!

SMASH!

Avery did this again and again.

She then removed the hard drive from the adapter, placed it on the floor, and stomped it with her shoe.

And she just kept *stomping*.

By the end, the hard drive was in dozens of pieces. Bill was still weeping, and Piper just watched.

Avery looked over at her. "We'll burn everything later," she said.

Piper thought it was a fine idea.

CHAPTER 39

They went back to the hospital that night.

At around ten P.M., Piper was standing in the doorway of Susan's ICU room. Susan was hooked up to a variety of machines, tubes sticking out of her. Her neck was wrapped with large, thick bandages, layered with gauze. Above the bandages, Piper could see swelling and bruising on Susan's skin. But as Avery gently spoke to her, caressing her mother's hand, Piper didn't see pain or worry on Susan's face.

Only relief.

And love.

Endless love.

Piper and Avery had just spoken to the police. *Again.* Explained what they could about people thinking there was a killer computer virus. The cops certainly had dubious looks on their faces. Every word they'd said was impossible to believe. One of the officers was the man who had walked through her burned apartment, grabbing a few things for her, earlier in the day. Piper asked about her computer tower on the desk, if he happened to notice its condition—she was curious if it had survived. Avery had launched the virus on it—the machine was compromised, she thought. Sure, the odds were exceptionally small that anyone would hook up a working monitor to the tower, if it was even functional *at all.* She wondered if the virus would be sitting there, installed, waiting to be launched again. Still, she'd come this far. The thing *was* supernatural, after all, and it was best to destroy any machine that came into contact with the virus, just to be safe. She was starting to feel a bit like Susan.

The officer thought for a moment and said, "Yeah, I remember the monitor was on the floor. Looked like it caught fire. All scorched up. The tower, too, on the desk." He paused, reading the expression on her face. "You look kind of pleased about that."

She didn't disagree.

Piper wondered what Bill was telling the officers about the situation, if anything would happen to him, legally. Probably not. The autopsies of Fisher and Frank would reveal something natural. Heart attack, stroke. Piper knew the game by now. Everything else would be chalked up to ghost-hunting hysteria from a group of online wackos, a Halloween prank gone wrong, perhaps. Piper had seen *more* of those Internet commenters milling around the hospital lobby when she arrived—she could just tell they didn't belong there—and had ducked away, avoiding them in case they recognized her. One of the men had an electronic device in his hands, like something out of *Ghostbusters.* Piper hoped the cops would kick them out.

Ghosts and evil things aren't real, fellas.

But Piper knew the truth.

So did Susan and her daughter.

Avery scribbled something on a sheet of paper and walked over to Piper, handing it to her. Piper looked at it.

It was an email username and password.

"Can you delete what's left of the virus?" Avery asked. Her eyes were still red from tears after her reunion with Susan. "I think I'm done with this stuff. My mom, too."

Piper gazed at Susan, and the two women shared a smile.

There wasn't any more to be said. Besides, Piper wasn't sure Susan could talk due to the extent of her injury.

The smile was enough.

Piper promised Avery that she would delete the virus from her email account, and she hugged Avery close. "I'm sorry about the blog. About everything that happened."

"I know," Avery said.

Piper released Avery, and the girl looked up at her.

"Who would believe this stuff anyway, right?" Avery said.

She walked back to her mother, and Piper almost turned away then, almost started down the hallway, before remembering her own predicament.

I can't be alone, she thought.

She'd have to wait for a nurse or doctor to come by, keep them close while making her way to her brother's room. Sam would be discharged soon. She was planning on attaching herself to his side and picking up Ripley at the police station.

Then, one more thing.

Getting the hell out of Clover Creek.

CHAPTER 40

The next day, they were in Sam's apartment, nestled in the heart of Des Moines. To Piper, no city had ever felt bigger. She hadn't grabbed much from her scorched apartment, just her purse, a few of Ripley's chew toys, and Sam's laptop, of course. The laptop, surprisingly, had escaped fire damage, but it had been doused with plenty of water. Sam didn't think it would ever function again. Before leaving, she destroyed the remains of her computer and the BlackBerry from the freezer.

Then, Piper and Sam were gone.

It was late evening, and Piper had just woken from a nap on Sam's couch—she had driven Sam's car the entire way to Iowa, insisting that her brother not drive with only one good arm. Piper had finally told him about her *predicament,* and the two discussed it for much of the car ride. How it made Piper feel, especially when she sensed it behind her, looming over her. She had wondered if her brother would believe her, if he'd revert to his old self, poking holes in everything.

He didn't.

The things he'd witnessed since arriving in Clover Creek had changed him, Piper thought. He seemed upset, spooked. Many times during the car ride, Sam had muttered, "We will fix this."

Not "A doctor will fix this."

We.

Lying back on Sam's couch, Piper yawned, and she felt Ripley at her feet. The familiar clacking of a keyboard caught her attention, and she glanced that way. Sam was busy on the computer—a common sight—though the activity looked awkward with his arm in a sling. Watching her brother type, she remembered one of the rules of the virus: the compulsion to use a machine.

She didn't feel it, and she wondered why.

Has it just not set in yet?

Piper was thankful, obviously, but still, she wondered.

"You shouldn't be doing that," Piper said, sitting up. "That can't be good for your shoulder."

"It's fine. These pain meds are superb."

Piper rose and shuffled over to Sam's workstation. As she did, she felt the invisible presence in the room. She sensed it loitering behind her, and it almost made her jump. Piper had momentarily forgotten all about it.

"What are you up to?" she asked through another yawn. There was an impossible array of letters, numbers, and symbols on one of Sam's monitors. He had two of them, both oversized.

"You aren't going to like it," he responded, before quickly spinning in his chair to completely face her. "Hey, are you—I mean, you're looking at my computers right now. Do you feel—"

"I don't feel it," she said. "The urge to spread the virus, if that's what you're asking."

He looked relieved, spinning back toward his workstation. Piper looked at the monitors again, noticing Avery's email inbox open on one of them.

"Did you delete everything?" she asked.

"Well . . ."

Piper did not care for his hesitant tone. She looked again at the monitor with the numbers and symbols.

"Is that—" she started, looking again at the monitor. "Tell me that's not what I think it is." She instinctively backed away from the screen.

"It's not," Sam replied. "Well, *technically* not."

"*Technically* not?"

"It is the virus, yes, but—"

Piper spun around so she wasn't facing the monitors.

"*Sam!*" she blurted. "Are you kidding me right now? Just—get it off the screen. Unplug it or something. Are you, oh my God, are you—"

"You didn't let me finish! I was saying, but—*but*—you're not looking at the virus as if you double-clicked and opened it. It's not that. I downloaded it from Avery's email, and I used a different program to view the code of the virus. It's like being on the inside. Piper, it's crazy stuff. You won't believe this."

Piper slowly turned around. She had covered her eyes with her hand, but she was peeking at the screen between her fingers.

"I couldn't help myself," he added. "And I'm fine, by the way. I've been doing this for hours. I don't feel any different; I don't feel anything weird in the room with us, like you do. Not infected."

Piper removed her hand from her face and plopped down on the floor. Ripley joined her. "You're crazy, you know that?"

"I know."

"Will you explain to me what it is you're doing, exactly? How you're not going to get infected doing this?" Piper still wouldn't look directly at the screen.

"Don't you remember what I told you yesterday? It's like looking at the ingredients of pancakes."

Piper remembered. She'd understood the analogy then, and she understood it now.

Still, it seemed incredibly reckless.

But she had to admit that she was intrigued.

"All I'm doing is looking at the ingredients," Sam continued, paging through the code on the screen. "And I tell you, it's insane, Piper. This code. It's so incredibly complex, and—I don't think it's entirely man-made." He paused, thinking. "It shouldn't exist."

"That's an understatement," Piper sighed. As she said this, she felt her invisible thing creep past her from behind, slinking in Sam's direction. It astonished her that he couldn't feel it.

"But you should know," Sam said, "I figured out some of it. The man-made part. That part I understand." He turned and looked at his sister. "Piper, I know who made this. I know why it does the things it does: the thirty-second countdown, the urge to spread the virus. It's all here."

Piper hesitated, caught off guard. She was not expecting this. "You know?"

Sam nodded. "The man-made part is buried in the code, and it paints a picture. It tells a story."

Piper swallowed.

"Tell me," she said.

CHAPTER 41

September 25, 1999

Avery leans forward in her chair, eyes glued to the screen of her school laptop. Her parents are out—date night, their first in ages. It's just her and Charlotte. Her sister is watching a movie and eating pizza rolls.

Avery stays focused on her computer. She's never coded anything this sophisticated before—she is, admittedly, a bit of a novice, but she's desperate to get this program right. If she succeeds, the prank will be *legendary*.

An email attachment to freak out her friends.

Something that will really give them nightmares. It's a simple idea. An executable program—filename COOLGAME.exe—that, when installed on a user's computer, will do a handful of unnerving things.

When the program is launched, the user's screen will turn green. Then, a ghost appears in the center. The spirit resembles a black mist— arms, head, torso—with no legs. Its form ends at its waist; the rest seems to melt away. Avery had stumbled across the image on some paranormal website and found it creepy. At first, she wasn't quite sure why it gave her goose bumps. She eventually decided it must have been the feature-less face, because she kept thinking there *should* be something there; her imagination filled in the horrifying possibilities.

Hopefully, Avery thinks, *people who install COOLGAME.exe will think the same.*

According to her program code, the black mist ghost stays on a user's screen for three seconds before vanishing.

Then a countdown appears over the green background—large white numbers, in a Halloween-style font. It starts at thirty and immediately begins ticking down. A message appears on the screen below the numbers:

You have 30 seconds to find another person, or you will die!

Avery got the idea for this while playing hide-and-stalk with her friends in a cornfield. She had thought how creepy it would be if the game's elements were translated to a virus—*Instead of having thirty seconds to find someone in the corn or you lose, what if you had thirty seconds to find someone or you die?* That's where the idea for her prank started, and this countdown is at its core.

The numbers tick down.

When that timer hits zero, a button appears on the screen.

It reads:

If you survived, click here!

When clicked, a new message pops up:

Oh no! The ghost is still with you! On Halloween, the curse will be broken—but ONLY after a year of fear!

Avery particularly enjoyed that part—the idea of the curse lingering for a full year, at minimum, before the viewer could be released on Halloween. But it *always* ended on Halloween. That was the rule. It was something of a fun twist, she thought, that mixture of hope and dread. Even when people realized it was just a silly prank, she hoped they might wonder—as the next Halloween approached—if something had *been* with them and just hadn't revealed itself yet.

It's the planting of that seed that puts this over the top.

In the end, two final things appear: a message—*Make sure to pass this along :)*—and Avery's calling card:

An image file of a white and fluffy cartoon bunny wearing black glasses.

My friends will know it was me who made this, she thinks. *Then they'll pass it along, and everyone will know.*

Send, send, send.

Avery absolutely loves it. If she gets it working, she will be the queen of pranks in her group of friends and beyond.

Only, she can't get it working.

She is a coding novice, after all.

Avery tries everything she can think of, using lessons from the coding book her dad bought her, looking things up online—but her program fails every time.

It doesn't work.

She's frustrated.

Maybe it's the countdown?

Is that the problem?

Or is it the button?

She thinks having only text appear might be easier. No videos, no images, no clicking to advance. Maybe just some weird text on the screen, and that's it. That might be enough to freak people out, especially if they think they're about to launch a game. Avery clicks Enter, starting a fresh line in her code. She decides to leave her failed attempts intact, thinking she might return to them later.

She has a new idea.

Avery opens her Internet browser and accesses her bookmarks. She's looking for a website she stumbled upon the previous spring when she and Charlotte learned about the upcoming movie *The Blair Witch Project.* It was a strange website—a catch-all for all sorts of scary and ghoulish things, laced with paranormal photos and tales of urban legends and folklore. A large chunk of the website was dedicated to the occult—primarily dozens upon dozens of spells and incantations in languages that Avery didn't recognize. Some were written solely in symbols.

The website was certainly not related to *The Blair Witch Project* at all—
or any film, for that matter—but somehow the girls had discovered it
while scouring the Internet for sites related to witchcraft. It felt like
they shouldn't have found it—like it was hidden in a dark corner of the
web for a reason. The website was foreboding, wrong. There was no
fanfare, no welcoming interface. Zero logos or copyrights—it wasn't
clear who had made it. Certainly not a company. The website didn't
even have a name, just a plain, white interface divided into different
sections—including a portion at the bottom devoted entirely to videos,
of which Avery counted hundreds. The first couple of videos were on
brand with the rest of the site: a woman chanting in Latin, a thirty-
minute MOV file of a man carving unrecognizable symbols into a table,
grainy footage of a séance in a forest. Then the videos got worse—
torture videos, animal cruelty videos, other things that made the girls'
stomachs turn. They clicked away quickly from those.

Still, Avery bookmarked the website. The videos were disturbing,
yes, but she was more interested in the spells. Maybe it was the fact that
the site simply felt like a repository—like someone was simply storing
information, with limited descriptors—and it just seemed so *real*. So
non-flashy, so wonderfully creepy that she and Charlotte had passed it
along to a few friends the previous spring, hoping to spook them. It
hadn't gained any traction among their friend groups—maybe they'd
ignored it, or they weren't interested—and Avery hadn't been back to it
since.

Now she's ready to return.

Avery navigates to the site, searching for text to copy and paste into
her code—something sure to inspire goose bumps. *The occult stuff is
perfect,* she immediately thinks. Avery scrolls toward the dark-arts section and decides on a portion called "Summoning Shadows." She copies
a bunch of text and pastes it into her code, planning on having it appear
on the screen once the COOLGAME.exe file is launched. Avery has no
idea what the text says—again, it's written in different languages and
symbols—but she hopes people will think they're looking at *actual*

spells. It looks pretty legit to her, not that she would know. Avery moves on to two other occult sections: "Mind Decay" and "Malevolent Propagation."

Copy, paste.

Finally, she accesses the website's source code, thinking that if her prank contained random HTML coding and scripts, it might be even creepier to a user, as if something were just going *wrong* on their screen. Avery envisions the spells and the HTML text simply rolling down the screen, perhaps one symbol or line at a time, endlessly scrolling, with the helpless user unable to stop it.

Avery highlights a large chunk of text, including some strange-looking scripts that she doesn't understand.

Copy, paste.

It's after she pastes in the scripts from the source code that something strange happens.

Her code-writing software program begins to glitch.

The screen flickers once, then again.

Suddenly, new lines of code appear on the screen, as if the program is writing itself. It continues, on and on, and Avery can't make sense of it. She struggles to read the fresh code flooding the screen.

It's all coming so quickly, fast and furious.

Thousands of new lines of code.

She knows the program is not supposed to do this—Avery has never seen the program *create* code before, and she is intrigued.

More code.

Tens of thousands of new lines.

The intrigue turns to unease.

Hundreds of thousands of new lines.

Panic creeps in. A ridiculous thought emerges, one that she immediately recognizes is silly:

Did those witchcraft spells do this?

Sanity returns.

No, that stuff isn't real.

The code keeps coming. Avery can barely make out anything as the new text flies by, her eyes catching glimpses of strange symbols, making her heart pound faster and harder. She thinks now that she's done something wrong, that she's done something terrible.

Resolve takes over.

Stop this.

Avery reaches a shaky hand toward the power button, prepared to simply turn the entire machine off, hoping it will stop the torrent of new code.

Her finger is inches away.

Then, all at once, the code stops.

The program closes.

Avery pulls her hand back.

On her desktop, a newly created file appears:

COOLGAME.exe.

The stillness calms her, and Avery's fear begins to fade.

She's simply looking at a file.

Just a *file*.

Suddenly, Avery is worried about losing it, about something going wrong with her computer. She immediately makes a copy of the file to a private, password-protected remote server.

Then, curiosity gnaws at her.

She wants to open it.

But first Avery goes to get her sister.

CHAPTER 42

I can't believe Avery made this," Piper muttered for the third time.

"*Kind of* made this," Sam clarified. "But she started it, that's for sure. And her attempts at coding are still here."

Sam had just finished laying out his theory, and Piper was still taking it all in. It took him close to forty minutes to get through it all, sitting in front of his workstation in his Des Moines apartment, and throughout his explanation, Sam had clicked on different links and files in the virus code to show Piper. She was still blown away by everything, especially the reason for Avery's recovery.

Piper had been right all along.

Avery's getting better wasn't just some wild coincidence.

There was a *reason*.

"The cure was inside the virus the whole time," Piper said, her voice still laced with disbelief. "The Halloween part of her original prank—she wrote that portion. She experienced her 'year of fear,' and then it left her." Piper paused, then started babbling again, unable to stop the rush of words. "I mean, she had no idea. She couldn't remember making it, couldn't remember the original prank at all. The virus messed with her head."

She remembered something else then: a specific part of her long conversation with Susan at the cabin. Susan had mentioned how much Avery had been looking forward to Halloween, but Piper now realized it wasn't just excitement. Deep down, Avery knew—she had *specifically* written it into the code: *On Halloween, the curse will be broken.* Perhaps fragments of that memory had been trying to surface in Avery's head, but they never fully did.

Piper was a bit stunned, and Sam noticed the look on her face.

"This is crazy, right?" he said.

Piper blankly nodded. Avery's cure wasn't the only thing that was crazy to her, although that was at the top of her list. There were other things as well—mainly images Sam showed her after clicking on links embedded in the code.

The picture of the black mist—intended for Avery's original prank—which Piper immediately confirmed as being identical to the thing she had seen hovering over Shane's body.

The image of the bunny in black glasses—Avery's digital calling card, Sam remembered, from reading about it in one of her diary entries.

"It proves she had a hand in creating this," Sam insisted. "She probably saved the file to some remote server somewhere, and that's how she got back to it. Remember, in her diary entry? Her friend was asking her for server passwords, and she couldn't remember. Her memory was all screwed up at that point. But that's probably where she stored it, and that's where she accessed it again before sending it to her dad."

Piper agreed.

Other elements pointed to Avery's involvement in the creation of the virus, as well. It made sense that an occult website was used—Avery had mentioned visiting one in another diary entry, along with how she enjoyed pranking her friends. The cornfield hide-and-seek game seemed like more than a coincidence. And the *novice* code—the original code, Sam said, before it looked to have been abandoned—outlined the virus symptoms to a T.

Not being alone for more than thirty seconds: *You have 30 seconds to find another person, or you will die!*

Avery's playful parting message—*Make sure to pass this along :)*—that triggered the compulsion to spread the file.

These were the two main symptoms of the infection.

And, of course, there was the cure: making it to Halloween, but only after suffering for at least a year. Avery had certainly served her time.

Sam scrolled back to the top of the screen.

"Avery's code would never have worked. It wasn't written correctly, but she never deleted it. And then right after that"—he pointed at another section—"is all this weird witchcraft stuff that I traced back to that occult website. A bunch of text is pasted in, copied from those different sections I showed you. 'Summoning Shadows,' 'Propagation,' 'Mind Decay.' After *that,* the code really takes off, making her prank come alive."

Piper nodded.

Come alive.

That was one way of putting it.

"The rest is *really* sophisticated," Sam continued, "and some of it I can't make heads or tails of. And it seems to go on forever. Like, so much code. It's crazy. That's why I think the code self-created, in a way." Sam exhaled, leaning back in his chair.

"You figured all this out while I was sleeping?" Piper asked, still on the floor with Ripley, scratching the back of his neck. The dog was snoozing.

"Well, you were sleeping for a really long time."

Piper was still thrown, taking it all in. Avery was adamant she couldn't remember where the evil came from, just that it originated from a computer. Piper believed her. There was no reason not to. But Sam's idea made sense—it was all right there in the code. Avery *had* created it, at least some version of it, before the supernatural portions from that website took over. She wondered what Avery would think if she was presented with this information—the guilt she would feel, the additional pain. Avery was already aware that she'd passed the virus around, but if she knew she'd *created* it, as well?

That type of regret could very well do her in completely.

Piper decided right then and there:

Avery must never know.

"Just so we're clear about this," Piper said, "why does the code work?"

"It must be the occult stuff," Sam said, shrugging. "That's my only guess. I think that whatever text Avery pasted in from that website is actually real. Like, they are *actual* spells. I dug around and figured out some of the languages. There's Elder Futhark, Celtic, some Latin. Real ancient stuff. Maybe whatever specific combination of things Avery pasted in set something in motion—a perfect storm of occultism. Like, one symbol off and none of this works. Who knows? It just *works*. Avery's original prank is at the core. You can't be alone for thirty seconds, or you'll die. You're *haunted,* followed by that black mist, the one from the image file. You feel compelled to spread the virus, like she tells you to do. It's all the stuff from her prank *literalized* by the ancient spells and incantations she pasted in."

"The mind decay," Piper added. "That's why Avery was breaking down. It was one of the occult spells. That's literally the name of that section of the website. It was affecting her mind."

"Bingo."

"But what about Fisher?"

"What do you mean?"

"I mean, he seemed to decay way faster than Avery. It took her a long time to start breaking down, and he started breaking down almost immediately."

"I can't be sure, but—this is still a computer virus. Supernatural, yes, but still a virus. Think about Avery and Fisher as computers. Avery is young, a newer operating system. She's more equipped to handle a virus. Fisher was older, more prone to his system being corrupted. Maybe their bodies deteriorated at different rates, like computers with actual viruses." He paused. "I'm sorry, I know he was a friend of yours. I don't mean to talk about him like this."

Piper nodded, and they sat in silence for a few moments.

"Piper," Sam finally said, "I haven't even gotten to the craziest stuff yet."

"You've got to be kidding me," she groaned, lying back and closing her eyes. "Sammy, this is all extremely illuminating, yes—but also, like, super exhausting. How can there possibly be more?"

"Don't you want to know why Avery was saying those weird things when she was acting all possessed?" he asked. "What they mean?"

This made Piper sit right back up.

"Yes," she said, climbing to her feet and joining Sam at the computer. It still felt wrong to be looking at the code, even if Sam insisted it was harmless. She felt like it could jump through the screen and strangle them at any moment.

"It's wild stuff," he said. "The prank was easy to decipher. That was basic, not written correctly. Child's play. And the occult text was easy to track down. But *after* all that—now I'm talking about the supernatural, self-written stuff—there are links and URLs embedded in the code. Some of them are direct links, and others are all jumbled. There are patterns, algorithms. I haven't figured it all out. But there are massive chunks of data, some of them encrypted. . . ."

Piper nodded along, not quite getting it. "Speak English, Sam."

He thought for a moment. "It's like the virus contains tens of thousands of videos inside of it. Maybe hundreds of thousands."

"Videos? You mean, Internet videos?"

"Yes. They're inside the code, everywhere. And that's why the virus *looks* the way it does."

"You didn't see it."

Piper had barely seen it herself.

To her, it was nothing but flashing.

"Well, no, I didn't *see* it," Sam said, "but the code explains what it looks like on the screen."

"And what does it look like, exactly?"

"On the screen, it appears as a mosaic of videos. Like, you'd be viewing thousands and thousands of videos at the same time, all of them ridiculously small. So, it wouldn't really *look* like a traditional video. Just flashing—like you said. Colorful. But it's the videos themselves that I think you'll find interesting. It helps to explain the infection."

Infection.

Piper's gaze traveled around the room, and after a moment, she sensed where it was—her invisible friend hovering above, perched on the ceiling.

She tried to block it out.

Sam clicked a few buttons on the keyboard, and the code on the screen changed. It looked like he'd executed a search of some kind. Among the seemingly infinite number of figures on the monitor, one word was highlighted, and Sam pointed to it. It read:

Willowbrook.

Piper gasped.

"I know," Sam said. He moved his cursor to the desktop, pulling up a video. It sat there among a few other MOV files, and he opened it. "There was a direct link to this video in the code. Again, not all of them were direct links. Only some. But this one was easy to find, so I downloaded it for you. I figured you'd want to see."

The video launched on his screen, and Sam dragged the playhead to a specific part. Piper watched as a young, feather-haired Geraldo Rivera appeared, holding an ABC 7 microphone. His voice carried through Sam's speakers:

"It smelled of filth, it smelled of disease, and it smelled of death."

Piper just shook her head.

"I can't believe this," she said. "And those other videos you downloaded?"

Sam didn't say anything, merely clicked on another MOV file. The video was grainy—recorded with a home camcorder, no doubt. Very *Silence of the Lambs* vibes. A bald, bespectacled, middle-aged man sat behind a card table in what looked to be a basement. His button-down shirt was missing several buttons, and a dark smear stained the front— Piper guessed it was blood. The only thing behind him was a crumbling brick wall. The man leaned forward, saying into the camera:

"Only the Revelator does not fear the monsters in the dark, and I am him."

His tone was soft, calm—unnervingly so.

Piper was creeped out.

Sam clicked another file.

This video was simply a black screen, but there was audio.

"It's a recording of a phone call, but it was uploaded as a video," Sam said. "Listen."

Piper heard a female voice.

"Kevin?" the woman said desperately.

A man on the other line responded, *"Beth? Is that you?"*

Then, commotion from the woman's end of the line. What sounded like a door banging open, feet stomping. Then, an angry man's voice:

"You shouldn't be here!"

The line went dead.

"I found more info about this one online," Sam said. "About ten years ago, a woman named Beth Paisley disappeared. At the time, no one knew what happened to her. Her husband, Kevin, thought she'd been kidnapped, so he started recording all of his incoming phone calls, in case the kidnapper contacted him or something. A year after doing that, he got *this* phone call."

"Oh my God," Piper said. "Was that Beth?"

"Her husband was positive it was her, and he was certain she was going to tell him where she was. And all those sounds in the background, that pissed-off guy shouting 'You shouldn't be here'—"

"It sounds like Beth made a phone call she wasn't supposed to make.

Like, she was somewhere she wasn't supposed to be. Then someone barged in and got *really* pissed."

Sam nodded. "And that was the last time her husband ever heard from her. Her body was found a few years later—in the attic of an old, abandoned house, miles away from where she was last seen. No one knows how she got there or who the man on the other end of the line was. The police never found any suspects, and the case went cold."

Piper got goose bumps.

Sam moved his cursor to another video file, but he hesitated, not clicking on it. "This is the *cabeza* video. The Spanish 'your beautiful head' one. It's a cartel video of a beheading. You don't need to watch that, trust me."

Piper had heard about cartel videos. Some friends in college had dug up some terrible videos online once. One of them included a cartel execution. They'd regretted it immediately.

"Do you want to take a guess as to where all of these videos came from?" Sam asked.

Piper didn't need to think for very long.

"The website that Avery was using," Piper replied. "The one with all the spells and witchcraft."

Sam nodded. "Yep. It seems like whoever made this site just dumped every dark thing they could find on it. And those specific videos—the ones that include the weird things Avery was saying when she was act-ing all possessed—are linked at the bottom of the site."

Piper could only shake her head. "But what about the other videos? You said the code has like thousands—"

"Maybe hundreds of thousands—"

"Fine, maybe *hundreds* of thousands of videos. Are there that many on the website?"

Sam shook his head. "No. The website has a lot, though. Maybe close to a thousand, I guess. But here's the kicker. When Avery copied a bunch of the source code from the website into her program, she brought something else with her. Not spells, not just video URLs and stuff like that. She brought a piece of code that was embedded into the website. A programming script. It was hidden, and she just grabbed it, maybe by mistake."

"Show me," Piper said.

Sam clicked a few times, and he highlighted text on his screen. It was a series of commands and symbols not familiar to Piper. "You shouldn't know what this is, but I do. Do you remember how I scraped websites for you?"

"Yeah, you said you were scraping those paranormal and technology websites, looking for things for me."

"Right. That's what this part is that Avery copied in—it's a scraping code. It's designed to pull in content from specific websites. And this particular script was set to search for videos using different search terms. *Deadly, scary, creepy, grotesque.* A bunch more. When the code became supernaturally enhanced, this scraping tool got supercharged. Pumped up. That's how it pulled in hundreds of thousands of videos. It's like it was scouring the entire Internet all at once." He paused, a look of disbelief crossing his face. "Honestly, this is some of the most messed-up stuff I've ever seen. Part of me wants to show the guys at work, but there's no way I'm doing that. Still, it's just so wild—I can't get over it."

Piper couldn't, either.

A mosaic of the worst videos on earth.

No wonder your mind eventually turns to mush after viewing the virus, she thought. *Who could view all that at once and stay sane?*

"But you get it, right?" Sam continued. "Why Avery was saying all those things?"

She got it. In her apartment in Clover Creek, Sam had described Avery's condition as an infected computer with unwanted pop-ups. These pop-ups were snippets of the videos—Avery was saying things that were embedded in the code, inside of her infected mind. But it was more than just the girl parroting words from the videos, Piper thought. These videos were some of the worst of the worst on the Internet, brimming with murder, hatred, malevolence. Consuming hundreds of thousands of these in a matter of seconds, the essence of them entering your body and coursing through your veins—that had to really affect you, Piper assumed. Change you. Overwhelm you. She recalled Avery's violent outbursts—hurling the book across the classroom, pressing scissors to her own throat, lashing out at her brother—as if her very DNA had been wiped clean, replaced by the evil drawn from the videos. In a way, she had become a minion of that virus—a virus with only three goals:

Haunt, kill, spread.

But Avery's fine *now,* Piper thought.

She escaped its clutches—Avery shed the code.

Piper couldn't have predicted any of this, but overall, she had been right: There was a *reason* for all of this.

It was all right here.

She felt the thing in the room with them move past her, radiating pure loathing.

A shiver ran through her.

"Don't go anywhere, okay?" she implored Sam.

He looked at her, furrowing his brow. "Do you honestly think I would leave you alone?"

"I'd hope not. Because if I'm alone for thirty seconds—"

"Thirty seconds!" Sam blurted, making Piper jump a bit in surprise. He brought his voice down. "Sorry, I got excited. I want to show you one last thing. I know I've shown you so much, and you probably need a break, but this one is just so cool. Well, not *cool,* but you know what I mean."

"I've about reached my limit for today," Piper said, sighing.

"Last thing, I swear." Without waiting for an answer, Sam executed a search on his screen, highlighting a piece of code:

```
function witnessMist() {

displayMist(true); // Show the Mist

setTimeout(() => {

removeMist(); // Hide the Mist after a short delay

}, 3000); // Adjust the delay (in milliseconds) as needed

}
```

"Do you remember when you saw the black mist?" Sam asked.

"I will *never* forget that."

"You walked into that house *precisely* thirty seconds after Shane's infection kicked in. And look here, this part right here." He pointed at the screen, his finger hovering over the code. "The three thousand part."

Piper leaned in, her eyes narrowing as she examined the numbers. "Those are milliseconds?"

"That's right. The code literally dictates that the mist only shows up for three seconds. Just a moment while it's . . . doing its thing. Killing. Then it vanishes. It's so *precise*. Is that how long you saw it for?"

She thought back. It was in the foyer, smothering Shane, and then it rose and looked at her before vanishing.

One one thousand, two one thousand, three one thousand.

"I'd say three seconds is about right."

Sam grinned—Piper could tell he was impressed.

She thought the killing precision was interesting as well but was also running on fumes at this point. It was a lot of information—still, it explained why she was the only person who had seen the dark mist and lived to tell the tale.

If I'd walked in thirty-four seconds after Shane was alone, I wouldn't have seen the mist at all—only the boy's body.

And maybe I wouldn't have kept going with my blog, would have let it all go, wouldn't have gotten so involved and gotten infected and—

She stopped herself.

The what-ifs didn't matter.

"No more, okay?" she told Sam. "You can impress me more after we watch a little TV or something."

She plopped back down on the floor. The two remained there in silence for a few seconds, but Sam didn't make a move for the TV remote like she hoped he would. He simply remained in his computer chair, thinking for a bit, before starting up again.

"Piper," Sam said, "don't you want to talk about your condition?"

"What about it?"

"I mean, you're infected. You've got it. We have to figure out what to do."

"Can't we deal with that later? We know what to do."

"What's that?"

"Wait it out. A 'year of fear,' right? I got infected on Halloween morning, so I should be cured next Halloween. That's officially a whole year. I just have to make it until then. Just never be alone."

"Well, *yeah,* but what if you start . . ." Sam trailed off, and Piper knew what he was thinking.

I could eventually start saying terrible things, acting all possessed.

Maybe put a pair of scissors to someone's throat.

Haunt, kill, spread.

Or maybe not . . .

Something occurred to her.

"Sammy, I barely saw the virus," she said. "It was out of the corner of my eye. And I remember, *vividly,* what happened. Avery, Fisher—they couldn't remember seeing it. I do. Their memory was immediately damaged, but mine isn't. That suggests that I'm different, right?"

Sam ran his fingers through his hair, thinking.

Piper continued. "We've been wondering why my other symptoms haven't set in yet, why I don't feel a compulsion to send the virus. I can look at your computer just fine. I'm not afraid of it, like Avery was at the beginning." She stopped, thinking. "Maybe I didn't absorb all the code.

I don't know. What if that part of the code—the stuff with the videos, the mind decay, the impulse to share the virus—isn't inside me?"

"I don't know. It's possible, I guess. But if that's true, that might mean—"

Piper put her hand up, stopping him.

She knew what he was going to say—the terrible thought had dawned on her, too.

"Maybe I didn't absorb the cure," she said, her voice trembling with worry. "Maybe the Halloween part, the 'year of fear,' isn't inside me, either."

Sam recognized her distress. "We barely know anything about you yet, only that you can't be alone," he offered gently. "It's been, like, twenty-four hours." He immediately started paging through the code, as if the answer would magically pop out at him, then and there.

Ripley flipped over onto his back, and Piper scratched his belly.

The dog whined happily.

"I'll find something in the code that can help you," Sam continued. "There has to be something here—more answers. Something about not seeing all of the virus."

Piper exhaled deeply. She didn't know what the road ahead would look like for her. Could be short, could be long. There was still so much to learn, so much to uncover.

She sensed the invisible thing move closer, floating above her like a canopy, and for a moment, she thought it might smother her. Piper felt like she could almost reach out and touch it, and she raised her hand a few inches before bringing it back down. Her hand found Ripley instead. It brought her solace to know that the dog didn't seem to sense the hostile presence.

She looked at Sam, ready to face the future head-on.

"Show me that code some more," she told her brother. "But can we delete the virus from Avery's email first?"

"Shoot, I forgot to do that. Sorry."

Sam clicked on Avery's sent items, and Piper saw them.

The three deadly emails and their recipients.

Richard Wallace.

Shane Brockway.

Glen Fisher.

Seeing the evidence laid out like that made her shudder.

"I still can't believe this is real," Piper muttered.

Sam selected the emails, clicked Delete. Then he went into the trash and emptied it.

Everything was gone.

EPILOGUE

September 2024

I t's still with you, isn't it?" Anders asked.

He'd noticed the signs during Piper's interview.

The constant shifting in her chair.

Her twitching eyes.

The involuntary shudders.

Piper nodded, and Anders looked around the family room of the farmhouse. He didn't sense anything at all. According to Piper and the rules, he shouldn't have been able to, but he looked all the same.

It felt like just the two of them.

They'd been speaking for hours, breaking for dinner halfway through. Robbie had grilled the best steak Anders had ever tasted, and the buttery corn on the cob and garlic toast weren't too bad, either. It was dark, and the nighttime brought the insects to life outside.

"So, the next Halloween came," Anders said. "And it didn't leave you?"

Piper shook her head. "You know, for the first couple of Halloweens after I was infected, I would think, *Maybe this is the one*. But it never was."

"And you were never alone?"

"Nope."

"You haven't been alone *once* in, like, twenty-five years?"

"If you're thinking about running out of the room right now, please don't."

Anders smiled. "And the rest of the code didn't help? Sam didn't find an answer?"

"The code only made things more complicated."

"What do you mean?"

"The more Sam dug around, the more the code would change, right before his eyes. The letters would move, the symbols and numbers would shift on the screen. New lines of code would appear out of nowhere, things that weren't there the previous day. Sam said it was *evolving*. It just proves beyond a shadow of a doubt that this thing is supernatural."

Anders scribbled a few things on a notepad.

"So, what did you do with the file?" Anders asked.

"Sam trashed it, decades ago. We gave up, essentially. It was just too dangerous to keep around. The way it was changing. He was worried it would *leak itself* out somehow, that someone wouldn't need to manually pass it along at some point. I mean, it was supernatural, right? If it could *write* itself, at what point would it be able to *send* itself?" She paused. "We did the right thing. It never went further than me, not that I know of. I feel like we stopped it."

Anders jotted down a few more things—he was still processing everything, but he couldn't help but empathize with Piper, especially after seeing the relief on her face when she said, *I feel like we stopped it.* He'd been wondering about what happened with the virus, and he was anxious to start searching on his phone later—corroborating this could push his thesis over the top. He was curious if any of her blog readers had ever written about it more, had searched for it themselves. Perhaps there was more to be found online.

"What about your blog?" he asked.

"Oh, we deleted that, too. The first day we got back to Des Moines. Sorry, I forgot to mention that."

More scribbles. He was hoping he might be able to find it somewhere—

it would give her story more credence. If it truly had been deleted, maybe he could access it through the Wayback Machine, a website that archived snapshots of web pages, even those long gone. He made a note to check.

"You look disappointed," Piper continued.

"Do I?" Anders looked up at her. "I'm sorry. I guess I'm just bummed that nothing worked for you."

"Don't be," Piper said. "I've had a great life. I somehow managed to find an amazing partner, despite my condition. And, you know, I'm lucky. I really am. It could've been so much worse for me. I never got the virus sickness, either—the memory decay, the outbursts, the compulsion to send. Another consequence of not absorbing all the code. And, in a way, I feel like I deserve this terrible burden. I never should've written that blog. It got a man killed, and it could've been far, far worse. This is my penance, and I've accepted it."

"But you still don't use computers or cell phones?"

"Robbie does, but I don't."

"But you're not at risk of passing the virus along, right? You don't even have *access* to the virus file."

"That's *true,* but you never know. We never figured this thing out completely—why the code was evolving, what was actually in those occult spells. What if I stumbled across the file online somehow? Like, something guided me there? I know that sounds unlikely, but you never know. I won't risk it, even if it doesn't jibe with how we *think* the virus affected me, specifically. Besides, my life is just fine without computers or cell phones. I think it's better, actually, without all that stuff."

"I was going to ask you about that," Anders said.

"What's that?"

"About technology."

"What do you mean?"

"About *why* you decided to tell me all of this now. I thought that maybe with the rise of artificial intelligence, media literacy issues—you know, everyone just mindlessly sharing things online with the click of a button, whether they're true or not. Maybe you thought your story was more relevant in today's world, that it was worth telling. That we could all learn something."

It had struck him somewhere near the end of Piper's tale, especially the comparison to artificial intelligence. The way Sam had described Avery creating the code for the virus—doing a bit of work and then watching as it essentially wrote itself—sounded eerily similar to how AI operated. Doing things for you, finishing the job—sometimes with dubious results. At times, it seemed downright sketchy to him, even dangerous. And now here was this kid, dabbling in what could be considered "AI" at the turn of the millennium. If he could pull this all together, he thought, he might have a hell of a thesis.

Piper thought for a few moments, and she smiled. "You should put that in your paper. AI, media literacy. That was good—write all of that down."

He did, then looked around the room.

"Where is it right now?"

Piper knew what he meant. Her gaze swept the room.

"It's behind you," she said. "On the wall."

Anders looked over his shoulder. He saw nothing, of course. "This is just so *weird*."

"That's one way of putting it," Piper said. "So, what else do you want to know? It feels like we're wrapping up."

"I guess, how is Avery? Please tell me she's okay."

Piper smiled. "She's fine. Great, actually. We still talk often. She's out in California, has two adorable kids. And her mother lives down the road from them. 'Grandma Susan' now. I couldn't be happier for them."

"And the sickness never came back for her?"

She leaned down to pet one golden retriever, then the other. Their tails slapped the floor. "No," Piper responded, whispering something to the dogs, which made their tails wag faster.

Anders reached for the tape recorder on the coffee table. He thought he was about finished, his questions answered, his head reeling with information. His mind was still racing, trying to make sense of it all. Anders was about to hit the Stop button, but he pulled his hand back, thinking of one more question he needed to ask, perhaps the entire reason for his interview.

"So why didn't this go more viral?" he asked.

"What do you mean?"

"Not the virus itself, but your story. I couldn't find much about it online, which, don't get me wrong, is a great thing for you. I guess I'm just surprised that this isn't some massive thing in the online paranormal community. I kind of figured it would be all over the place online. Why isn't it?"

Piper took some time thinking about this one.

"This is ancient Internet stuff now," she said. "Twenty-five years is almost a lifetime by today's standards. You know, with information moving so quickly, technology evolving. It *was* a thing when it happened, don't get me wrong. A bunch of people came to that town. They visited the hospital, harassed the sheriff for information. Ms. Hermann was pestered for weeks. Someone even stole the *Clover Creek* sign off the side of the road. But they eventually moved on. And I think because I kind of went into hiding, and so did Avery, in a way, it just kind of petered out. Again, I deleted my online journal. And, obviously, the virus never spread. In *theory,* there weren't many copies of the virus left. There was the one in Avery's remote server—the one she pulled up at her uncle's house and sent to Richard."

"She definitely had a private server?"

"We never found out for sure, but we think so. If the virus never leaked out, then it was probably something only she had access to. I mean, if the virus was on a public server, it would've leaked out like *that*." Piper snapped her fingers for effect. "And Avery never could consciously remember the password to that server, so it's probably safe there, if it's even there at all. That server could've been taken offline decades ago."

"Right."

Anders jotted down a few notes.

"Let's see," Piper continued, "it was also in Shane's email account and Avery's father's account. Oh, and Fisher's. But those accounts have to be long gone by now . . . I told Glen's wife to get rid of his, specifically, but I mean, it was so long ago. If anything were going to happen, I feel like it would've happened by now." She paused, then added, "Does that answer your question?"

"I think so, yeah." Anders reached for the tape recorder again, and this time he hit the Stop button. He suddenly had the dreadful feeling that maybe none of this had recorded, even though he had run a test before they started.

"Hey," Piper said, "can I ask *you* a question?"

"Sure."

"Do you believe me?"

Anders sensed mischief in her eyes, and he half expected Robbie to pop out from the kitchen, the two of them saying *"Gotcha!"* in unison.

"Why wouldn't I?" Anders responded. "I mean, it's so detailed. This would be the craziest lie of all time."

"It would be, wouldn't it? And this paper you're going to write—"

"Yeah?"

"I know I said I didn't want this published widely—and I still don't want my name on it—but you can share it."

"Really? I don't have to."

"No, it's just that—telling it all now, with so much time passed, I feel like it might be a good thing for people to know. Like what you said earlier. It's *relevant*. That . . . something like this virus is possible. Maybe this would help the world in some way. Prepare it, if this happens again. Does that make sense?"

Anders nodded. "You can change your mind—just let me know. I haven't written a word of this thing yet, obviously. I won't have a first draft for months."

He took the tape recorder off the coffee table and slipped it into his bag, rising to his feet. He yawned and stretched, and as he did so, he noticed the clock above the mantel. It was nearly eight thirty P.M.

"You should stay the night," Piper said, noticing his gaze. "It's a long drive."

"That's okay," he said. "I don't mind driving at night. I do it all the time. No one on the road, it's kinda nice."

"You won't fall asleep?"

"Nah, I'm good."

"Ah, to be young."

Anders thanked her—many times, profusely—as she led him to the door. He realized then he had more questions, but they were unimportant ones. He wanted to know how she and Robbie had met and fallen in love, if she had any *I was almost alone* close calls over the last twenty-five years. Anders imagined he could circle back with her to have those questions answered. For now, he obviously had enough to get started.

"You know," he told Piper, stepping outside, "the whole time you told me that story, I was worried about one thing in particular."

"What's that?"

"That something was going to happen to Ripley."

Piper grinned. "He lived another four years. He was a really, *really* good boy."

With that, Robbie appeared by her side, almost like magic. Anders had nearly forgotten—she couldn't be alone, and he'd almost walked away. He imagined he wasn't the first person to have nearly done that to her. It had been decades, after all. Anders made his way to his car, and he opened the door, looking back to see Robbie and Piper still standing in the doorway. He thought of one final question, and he shouted it to her.

"Hey, did you ever see a moose?"

Anders heard Piper's laugh echo across the farmland.

"Sam and I saw one leaving the hospital!" she called out. "No joke!"

Anders drove off, thinking one specific thing, something he wouldn't have dared to tell Piper when she asked the question.

He didn't believe her.

. . .

Despite his robust night-driving résumé, Anders found himself becoming sleepy. He blamed it on mental exhaustion—the interview had been long, and he was still thinking about it as he crossed the border into Minnesota, a steaming cup of gas station coffee in his hand. The story was simply too fantastic, and he didn't believe in ghosts, in the supernatural, in evil, in invisible things that could leash themselves to your body.

Still, he couldn't stop thinking about it, but it was more like reading a captivating book or seeing a good movie and wanting to know more. Anders's head was still spinning with questions about the "virus" as he drove, something to keep him awake. One question in particular wouldn't stop niggling him:

How come Richard couldn't locate the original file on the family computer?

It was a fair question, he thought, one that was left hanging in Piper's story.

If Avery made it, where was it?

Where was the code-writing software?

Everyone just assumed that Avery made it on the family machine, but what if she didn't?

Maybe Piper had mentioned it, but Anders couldn't remember. He'd text or email Robbie, at some point. Check the tape. Maybe it was on there.

Anders turned his car east and made it to Wisconsin before realizing he wouldn't make it all the way home in his condition. He felt his eyes closing, his brain shutting down. Any more time on the highway and he might end up like Richard Wallace. He exited, stopping at the first hotel he found. It was a popular chain—decent enough, he suspected, but he didn't really care. All he wanted was a soft mattress. He opted for the cheapest rate, despite the fact that the history department would foot the bill. Anders practically sleepwalked to his room, dumped his overnight bag on the floor, and fell asleep in seconds. He never even bothered to pull down the covers.

. . .

In the morning, he realized he was ten miles away from Grangeville when he pulled up Google Maps on his phone to search for coffee joints in the area and happened to spot Avery's hometown.

He figured it was meant to be.

Anders still didn't believe Piper's story, but perhaps certain elements of it were true. The deaths, the people involved. Maybe certain individuals actually *believed* in a killer computer virus, even though it wasn't possible. But maybe it didn't matter if it was true, Anders thought. All that mattered was that people showed up to Clover Creek. Piper's blog was *active viral content,* an expression he was debating using as the foundation for his thesis.

Still, more would help. More than just Piper's words. Anders thought he could supplement his paper with additional research, even some photos of the Wallaces' old place, if they'd *actually* lived in Grangeville, if they were real people—not just fictional characters in Piper's story. It didn't take long for Anders to figure out that, yes, Richard and Susan Wallace were real, and he found their address from 1999. He only had to search for ten minutes—forking over his credit card info to some sketchy-looking website to access old residence records, but again, he would be reimbursed. The Wallaces' previous address appeared on his phone screen.

After a shower and a short drive, he was outside their old house. It had tan siding with black trim, and the roof looked recently redone.

Anders parked, snapped a few pictures with his phone, and walked to the front door, experiencing a sense of déjà vu that didn't belong to him. He felt like Piper all those years ago, showing up out of the blue, about to ring the doorbell without having figured out what to say. Lying crossed his mind—*My family lived here a long time ago, and I wanted to check it out*—but in the end, Anders went with Piper's method, which was the truth. He explained to the man who answered the door that he was working on a college thesis project, and he'd learned the house was allegedly haunted. He wasn't Bill from Piper's story—this man was much younger, and he had a wife and three kids—and it turned out he'd attended a college in the same athletic conference as Anders. A happy coincidence. He was friendly and interested in Anders's story and invited him inside.

They looked at the den first, Anders expecting the wall that Richard Wallace had pummeled with a sledgehammer to still look recently fixed up. Of course, that had been twenty-five years ago, and he wasn't sure which wall had been destroyed. He couldn't tell—each wall looked exactly the same, painted a light green. They walked through the downstairs, Anders sheepishly saying hello to the three children, two playing video games, the other on a tablet. Their mother was fixing coffee, looking slightly irritated that her husband had rolled out the red carpet for a complete stranger, but she allowed it just the same. Anders didn't take any pictures, realizing it might be rude, and there was nothing interesting to take pictures of, anyway.

They went upstairs, and again, Anders felt just like Piper, wondering exactly where she'd stepped, what she was feeling as she'd explored the home. The man showed Anders one of the kids' rooms, and that's when it finally hit him. A jolt of understanding, a feeling that caused Anders's entire body to stiffen. It was an idea, a theory—something that Piper had missed, something everyone had missed.

Avery's second story.

The evil that came from the wall.

In that story, the child had been dragged away by something from the wall while hiding under her bed. It was never the den. Granted, Avery's stories weren't fact—merely echoes of what had happened to her. The kid never did remember that night, after all, but according to Piper's story, Avery's pieces were more than just fiction. There was truth to be found in her words, and Anders, despite his disbelief, was interested in playing this scenario out. At the moment, he was particularly interested in the white baseboard that ran along the edges of the floor. Anders started on one end of the room and stooped down, running his hand along the baseboard, searching for wiggle.

It was just a theory he had—a daft one, in all likelihood. But there was another piece he felt added to his theory. Piper had mentioned one of Avery's diary entries, composed a few weeks after Richard had passed. Avery had been blaming herself for her father going back to the house, and she ended the entry with:

Something is still there.

What if that something was . . .

Anders felt something stirring inside of him.

He needed to check.

Maybe it's here.

Again, everyone had just assumed that Avery made the virus on the family machine, but what if she didn't? What if the virus was never created on the family computer, the one Richard examined so thoroughly? Avery could have created it anywhere—at school, on a friend's computer; she likely had access to a variety of machines.

Again, he thought of Avery's words.

It came from inside the wall.

One wall of the room down, three to go. His hand moved slowly, gently testing inch by inch, rounding the corner near the closet and approaching the bed.

He found a wiggle.

It was minor, but it was there.

Anders got down on both knees, gripping the section of the baseboard with two hands, and he pulled. It popped right off, a sprinkling of dust billowing into the air. He looked back at the man, who said nothing. He simply sported a confused expression, perhaps wondering why this stranger was taking apart his wall, or maybe baffled that he'd never noticed the slightly loose baseboard himself.

Anders reached into the wall, felt around for what he hoped he might find, and his hands discovered an object. It was bulky, and his fingers slipped on the thick layer of dust that had accumulated—but he found his grip, sliding the object into the bedroom.

It was an old laptop.

. . .

He stopped at his parents' house outside Madison, laptop in tow. The family had allowed him to keep it, as well as the charger that was also hidden behind the wall. He hadn't powered it on yet—obviously, it was long dead, in desperate need of an extended charge. If it even worked at all. Anders was also nervous, bouncing between believing and disbelieving during the drive, but never losing his sense of excitement.

His parents weren't home, and Anders considered joining them at his sister's basketball game. But he elected to stay home with the laptop, which was charging. He had laundry, too, which was spinning in the basement. Anders played around on his phone, receiving a text from his mother—a short video of his sister soaring for a breakaway layup. He was part of a group text, and his mother had shared the clip with him and ten other people, including his sister, with the message *"We won!"* Anders began to respond, but then he gazed over at the laptop, seeing that the light along the bottom had turned from red to green.

It was *functional*.

Anders put down his phone and cautiously opened the lid. He held down the power button, and the Windows machine slowly booted up. Anders didn't know what he would find, if he'd be able to log in at all— he wondered why Charlotte and Avery even had a secret computer. There once had been a sticker on the outside of the laptop, long peeled off—but a few faded numbers still remained near the torn edge, perhaps an inventory number from their old school. Anders assumed they'd swiped it from there. It was just a guess. Avery was a gifted tech kid, and maybe there were things she wanted to do that she didn't want discovered on the family machine. Something with downloading or servers, maybe, that she wanted to keep private. It made sense—she was a kid, after all, and Anders remembered doing things on his family computer growing up that he didn't want his parents to see.

The desktop appeared. There was no log-in required, and Anders grew edgier when he saw the icons slowly appear. Internet Explorer. Napster. Network Neighborhood. Outlook Express. WordPad. Windows Media Player. Winamp. Paint. Microsoft Visual Basic 6.0.

The last one gave him pause.

Microsoft Visual Basic 6.0.

Anders quickly searched on his phone, and he learned that the program was, indeed, code-writing software.

Is this it? he thought.

There were folders now, emerging. *Stuff. New music. FTP stuff. Hey this one. More files. Stories.*

And then, he spotted it. Right there on the desktop.

The file.

COOLGAME.exe.

He sat, frozen. At first, Anders couldn't believe he was looking at it, that the virus was actually real. He still hadn't totally come around to Piper's story, but finding the laptop and seeing the file . . .

Anders began to believe.

He pictured Avery and Charlotte then—together in Avery's bedroom— on "the last day," as Susan had put it. They weren't using the family computer. Instead, they were hunched over this laptop. Avery was showing Charlotte this strange file that her coding software seemed to have created on its own. Nervous, they launched the file and watched the mosaic of videos, unaware that they were being infected. Avery then powered down the computer and put it back in its hiding place inside the wall—it was very late; their parents would be home from their date soon. Charlotte returned to her own bedroom, and unbeknownst to the sisters, the infection was already taking root inside them.

It all started on this machine, he thought.

And Avery didn't remember having this laptop at all.

Anders knew he should leave it alone, that he should probably burn the damn thing.

Fire is the great purifier, he thought, remembering Piper's story.

But curiosity nagged him.

He just wanted to know.

Anders moved his finger on the trackpad, and the cursor hovered over the file. He knew it was a terrible idea. After hearing Piper's tale, he couldn't help but think of what he'd see—the mosaic of videos, perhaps colorful and flashing, a deadly panorama that would transfix his gaze to the screen. Could something like that actually exist?

His positioned his index finger.

"Hey, loser!"

The voice startled him.

It was his sister, Grace, standing in the doorway of his bedroom. She was still in her mesh basketball jersey and shorts, her ponytail sweaty.

"You scared the *crap* out of me," Anders said, rising and embracing Grace in a hug. "Where are Mom and Dad?"

"They went to dinner with the Larsons; they just dropped me off." She looked over at the laptop. "Is that an antique?"

Anders told her the story—the heavily truncated version.

Grace was wide-eyed, her eyes sparkling with curiosity. "That was sitting inside a wall for twenty-five years?"

"Looks like it."

"And the file is on there? The one the kid saw?"

"I was just about to launch it when you walked in."

"Oh my God, we *have* to open it!"

"Grace—"

"Oh, come on, what are you afraid of? Don't you want to know what she saw that messed her up so bad? I bet it's pretty freaky."

"I mean, I *do* want to see it, but—"

"Nothing is going to happen, you big baby." She took a seat at the computer chair.

"I'm feeling a little weird about this."

"Why? You don't actually think she was infected, do you?"

"I mean . . . no. It was probably all in her head, I guess."

"Exactly. Let's just see what it was that spooked her. Wait, hold on."

Grace took a photo of the screen with her phone, and she shared it online with the words: *About to open a deadly Internet file! Wish me luck! RIP Me.*

Her excitement and skepticism began to rub off on him. Anders temporarily cast aside his growing belief in Piper's story, forgot about the mixture of adrenaline and dread when he'd actually found the computer in the Wallaces' old home. Grace hadn't sat with Piper for hours on end, hadn't heard the conviction in her voice. To her, this was just a silly urban legend. And, at that moment, he saw things from her side.

So, they opened it.

Nothing happened at first, and Anders wondered if it would stay that way, if the laptop would just finally die.

But then something filled the screen.

A flashing mosaic of colors, just like Sam had predicted. They seemed to blend together into one rippling substance, reminding Anders of what Piper had said about the dark mist over Shane's dead body, how it seemed to swirl with life. The screen pulsed and moved, and Anders tried to home in on each pixel, looking for the individual videos that Sam said existed within. For a moment, he thought he could see them—decapitations and murder and cartel men and *worse*—but then everything would merge together again, and he found himself simply transfixed by it all.

The walls of his bedroom seemed to cave in around him, crumbling and then fading into the background, until nothing else existed but the laptop. His eyes adjusted. The laptop screen no longer seemed flat to him—it seemed as deep as the ocean, and he pictured himself crawling into it, sinking forever, never finding the bottom.

He wanted to gauge Grace's reaction, but he also couldn't look away from the screen. It was beautiful and terrible at the same time, and then he felt a coldness. He wondered if he had made himself feel the sensation because that's what *should* happen when you view a deadly Internet file. Considering that idea made him snap out of the trance he was in, and he reached out and slammed the laptop lid shut.

Anders was breathing heavily. He finally looked over at his sister.

"Grace?" he asked.

A pause.

"That was *it?*" she exclaimed, not hiding her disappointment. "That was so lame." She got up and moved to the doorway. "I'm going to shower. *Byeeeeeeee.*"

Anders sat down on his bed and looked around the room.

No evil things present.

But doesn't it take twenty minutes to activate?

He got up and walked around the house. Moved his laundry to the dryer. Grabbed a soda. Went back upstairs, lay on his bed, and scrolled through his phone.

And then, something.

A tingling in his spine.

A shiver.

An awareness.

His breath turned short, and he sat up.

Is that . . .

Footsteps moving quickly down the hall, faster now. Someone was sprinting. Grace barged into the bedroom. Her hair was still wet, and she was dressed in shorts and a long-sleeve T-shirt.

"Something was . . . ," she sputtered. "It was like I could feel eyes watching me, and . . ." She didn't finish. Tears were forming, and she sat down next to her brother.

"I felt it, too," he said.

They sat there together, no longer alone.

No evil things materializing.

But it's here, Anders thought.

It's in the room.

I can feel it.

He felt the urge to call Robbie on the phone, to beg to speak with Piper. Confess. Maybe track down Sam, see if he could help in some way. No one knew the virus better than him.

Anders looked at his phone.

As soon as he did—the instant his eyes landed on the device—a different urge struck him.

Send it.

Send it to everyone.

Anders realized that this urge seemed to go against some of the established rules of the virus, that it shouldn't have happened so quickly. But he had *stared* at the virus on the screen, so very intently—maybe he had absorbed every single line of code. And, after twenty-five years of just sitting on that machine, maybe the virus had changed.

Grown stronger.

Perhaps it was as Piper had told him.

It had *evolved*.

He looked at Grace, who was staring at her phone, which was still sitting by the old laptop. Anders knew she was thinking the same thing.

Let's send it.

He plugged a USB stick into Avery's laptop and copied the file onto it. That took longer than he would've liked—it was a *very* old computer, after all—but the file transferred successfully. Anders then fired up his own laptop, plugged in the stick, and dragged the file to his desktop.

The computer made a *whoosh* sound.

It was ready to go.

He started with emails first. Friends, family. Then Anders realized he could email every student in his history thesis cohort at once, so he did. It was efficient. Then he AirDropped the file to his phone and Grace's, and the two began texting it to all their group chats. They moved to social media, posting it to their pages and feeds. They ignored the messages coming back their way—*What is this? What did you just send me?*—and kept going. Grace was able to email every single student at her high school through a group email address. The faculty group email address worked for her, too, so she sent it there as well. Sometimes Anders and Grace included little messages, sometimes they didn't. If they did, they were short:

Check this out!

This is so much fun!

Can you take a look at this for me?

Anders wasn't sure how long they'd been doing it. Time meant nothing to him. If anything, the urge was getting stronger, and he didn't think it would ever stop. He returned to his text messages and scrolled through, seeing who he hadn't sent it to yet.

He found the text thread between him and Robbie. Anders first changed the name of the file, simply calling it *Interview* without an extension. He attached the file to a new message and wrote:

Here's a transcript of my interview with Piper. Would you mind taking a look at it?

He hit Send.

Anders continued blasting the file to other people, not waiting for a reply from Robbie, but eventually it came.

Is this what I think it is?

ACKNOWLEDGMENTS

Thank you, first and foremost, to my family. Sheryl, this book would not exist without you. Isla, thank you for being an endearingly joyful and inspiring presence every day. I love you both to the moon and back! And Nutty, too, of course.

My literary agent, Liz Parker, and my manager, Josh Dove, were instrumental in getting this project off the ground. Thank you both!

Everyone at Dutton has been amazing. Thank you to my editors, Lindsey Rose and Rachael Kelly, for their invaluable guidance and support. Your insights elevated every page! Many thanks also to Charlotte Peters, Jamie Knapp, Nicole Jarvis, Melissa Solis, LeeAnn Pemberton, Laura Corless, Aja Pollock, Alicia Hyman, and Erica Ferguson.

Alex Robbins, your cover design is a doozy! Thank you.

Thank you to Michael Swanson for your help with coding.

Finally, thank you to the horror community, especially the readers and contributors of Nosleep on Reddit, and the creative team and listeners of *The NoSleep Podcast*. Your support means the world to me. Special shout-out to David Cummings: Thank you for believing in me and my twisted stories.

ABOUT THE AUTHOR

Jimmy Juliano is a writer and high school educator. Several of his stories have gone viral on the Reddit "NoSleep" forum, and his debut novel,
Dead Eleven, is currently in development at A+E Studios. He lives outside Chicago with his wife, daughter, and miniature goldendoodle.